Romantic Times praises bestselling author
Bobbi Smith

"*Arizona Caress* is a sensitive, fast-paced, satisfying love story. Chalk up another winner for Bobbi Smith!"

"*Sweet Silken Bondage* is a double-barrel romance that captures your imagination and your heart!"

Bayou Bride
"Ms. Smith's wonderful characterization and sparkling dialogue are what make her such a fine storyteller!"

A KISS OF DECEIT

Luke could see all the questions in the depths of Cody's green eyes, and he muttered under his breath, "Just kiss me."

"But..." she started to argue.

"Please," he whispered, and his lips sought hers.

His mouth moved over hers in a persuasive assault, and suddenly Cody wasn't thinking about fighting him anymore. She told herself it was because Juana was watching that she had to make the embrace look good. She told herself it was to convince the other woman that she was Luke's. She told herself to act like she was enjoying his kiss, but, in truth, there was no acting involved. Luke's kiss was the most magnificent one she'd ever had in her life.

BOBBI SMITH

Lady Deception

LEISURE BOOKS **NEW YORK CITY**

This book is dedicated to the wonderful Jim Gee, for his invaluable help with research, and to Constance O'Banyon, Leann Shoaf and Gina Stratman for their friendship. It's also for Dr. Kansteiner, Dr. O'Donnell, and Dr. Santos. Without their incredible talents, I wouldn't be seeing quite so well right now.

I'd like to thank Bill Black and Alicia Condon of *Leisure Books* and Evan Marshall, my agent, for believing in my work.

There are many wonderful booksellers out there, and Amy Templer of B. Dalton, Mid Rivers Mall, St. Peters, Missouri, is a perfect example. Not only is she a fantastic store manager and successful 90's business woman, but she's also a big fan of romance. She along with her terrific staff—Janet Ryan, Jason Elliott, Alecia Hoyt, Tanya Badgley, Christy Shultman, Shelly Hoffmeister, Terry Sanders, Beth Smith, Jeanne Smith, Ann Toawaradom, and Lisa DeClue—have been truly supportive of my career (even hosting a champagne party for me when I changed publishers and came over to *Leisure Books* last year). I thank them all for their kindness and support.

A special note of thanks to John Ferguson of the West Texas Collection of Angelo State University in San Angelo, Texas. His help with research was greatly appreciated.

Lady Deception

Chapter One

The raucous, slightly off-key strains of the piano player's tune set a boisterous mood in the crowded, smoke-filled Last Chance Saloon. Cowboys eager for a good time drank heavily and gambled freely. Several scantily clad saloon girls hovered near the big spenders, tempting them with occasional glimpses of shapely legs and burgeoning breasts.

As Joe, the bartender, kept the liquor flowing, he glanced around, wondering where Delilah, the new girl, had gone. When he'd watched her coming down the stairs earlier, he'd been struck again by her beauty. Clad in a tight green gown, with her flame-colored hair pinned up high in a mass of curls, and wearing just enough rouge and lipstick to emphasize her perfect features, she'd been gorgeous. He'd done well when he'd hired her a few weeks before.

For a minute, Joe considered that maybe some lucky cowboy might have taken the lovely Delilah upstairs, but he doubted it. Delilah was picky, and her good-natured elusiveness added to her attraction. The men swarmed around her, wanting what they couldn't have.

Human nature . . .

Well, wherever she'd disappeared to, Joe hoped she'd show up soon. It was payday for the cowboys, and the Last Chance's busiest night of the month.

Delilah was closer than Joe suspected. She was sitting alone at a partially secluded table at the far back corner of the saloon. Her gaze was fixed on the saloon's main doors.

"Delilah!" Candy, a buxom blonde, saw her and called out from across the room where she sat with two drunken cowboys, trying to keep them both happy. "Come join us, honey!"

"Not right now," Delilah answered, her gaze never wavering from the entrance.

"There's plenty to go around!" Candy urged as she playfully slapped away one of the cowboys' groping hands.

"Yeah, sugar, c'mon. . . ."

"Can't tonight. I'm expecting someone."

The cowboys with Candy looked a little disappointed at Delilah's refusal.

Not wanting to lose their favor, Candy quickly

promised, "Don't worry, fellas. I can show you both a good time." She boldly ran a hand down each of their chests and then let her fingers linger knowingly at their belt buckles.

Immediately distracted, the two forgot all about Delilah's rejection and turned their full attention back to the hot-blooded woman who wanted them.

Delilah breathed a sigh of relief at getting off so easily. She was in no mood to play with the boys tonight. If Joe found out what she was doing, he wouldn't be happy, but right now she didn't care. Word had it that this was the night. Tonight, at long last, he was going to show up at the Last Chance. Tonight he would be here.

Delilah wasn't normally one for drinking. She liked to keep her wits about her while she worked, but this was different. She needed one. Lifting the tumbler of bourbon before her, she took a healthy sip. The liquor burned all the way down. Suppressing a shudder, she wondered why her father had always said bourbon was the best drink. She lifted her gaze to the swinging doors again and continued her vigil.

If there is a God, she silently prayed, Hank Andrews will show up here soon.

Her nerves stretched taut, Delilah started to take another drink, but she stopped herself. One drink would steady her hands and temper her excitement; two might relax her too much. If Andrews came, she had to be ready for him—in all ways.

It was then that it happened. The saloon doors swung open, and the man she wanted, the man she'd been waiting for, strode into the room.

Delilah would have recognized Andrews anywhere. He was tall, his shoulders broad and powerful. His hair was dark brown, and he wore a full, flowing mustache that gave him an almost sinister look. His gun rode low on his hip, and he moved with a confidence that bordered on a swagger. She watched, almost transfixed, as he shouldered his way through the crowd to the bar.

A hunger rose within Delilah and, along with it, her excitement surged. It seemed she'd been waiting an eternity for this moment. Hank Andrews had come to the Last Chance just as she'd hoped he would! Now, finally, he would be hers!

Delilah rose slowly, provocatively, from the table. Her prey was in sight. She straightened her shoulders and glanced down at the decolletage of her gown to make sure the neckline revealed just the right amount of cleavage. She wanted Andrews's full and undivided attention upon her. Whenever she went after a man, she got him.

Picking up her drink, she walked toward Hank Andrews—the man of her dreams. Her movements were deliberately sensuous and designed to draw male attention. She knew what she wanted, what she was after, and she intended to get it.

Her movements did not go unnoticed. Most of the men in the room found themselves distracted by her sensuous assault. Many stopped in midsentence to watch her progress.

Andrews stood at the bar, unaware that he was being stalked. He ordered a beer from Joe, and when the drink was set before him, he casually tossed the man a coin. Lifting the mug, he took a deep, thirsty drink, then stopped suddenly after the first swallow. His expression turned ugly, and he slammed the mug back down on the bar, sloshing beer everywhere.

"This is warm!" He glared at the bartender.

"Most everything is this time of year," Joe countered, dismissing his complaint.

"I like my beer cold!"

"That's the coldest you're going to get in this town."

"Maybe you didn't hear me right," he said threateningly.

"I heard ya, but this ain't January, you know. I can't help ya, *friend*. So drink it or leave. Makes no difference to me." Joe shrugged off his complaints. He heard too many of them in his line of work.

Andrews didn't like being ignored. His hand was sliding toward his sidearm when a very feminine voice purred from behind him, "You may like your beer cold, mister, but how do you like your women? Cold . . ." There was a definite pause. "Or hot?"

The last was said softly yet seductively, and at the sound of the invitation in the woman's voice, Andrews turned. He had always been partial to redheads, and the woman standing before him was without a doubt the most beautiful female he'd ever seen. From the challenging look in her knowing green eyes and the delicious sight of her breasts so alluringly displayed, he knew bedding this one would be a treat for any man.

Andrews forgot his argument with the barkeep. A slow, leering smile spread across his face.

"I like my women hot," he replied, and an answering heat settled in his loins as he imagined taking her upstairs.

"I was hoping you'd say that." Delilah paused breathlessly as she met his gaze straight on and deliberately ran the tip of her tongue across her full bottom lip. "Because I am on fire."

He gave a low chuckle. Snaking an arm about her slender waist, he drew her to him. "I think you might be just what I need tonight, darlin'."

"I know I am," she breathed, moving suggestively against him.

Andrews didn't know why fortune had chosen to smile on him, but he wasn't going to question his good luck. The best-looking girl in the place was his for the taking, and he was going to do just that. It had been a long time since he'd been able to relax and really enjoy a woman.

"Let's go." He was ready.

Delilah gave him a smile that hinted at much pleasure to come. "Don't you want to finish your beer before we go upstairs?"

"The only thing hot I want tonight is you. What's your name, honey?"

"Call me Delilah."

"Name fits you. The first Delilah was a temptress who could make a man forget himself."

"Am I making you forget yourself?" She leaned into his chest and looked up at him, almost innocently.

"You'd better believe it." His voice was a husky

growl as he ran his hands over her.

Delilah allowed him that freedom for a moment, then coyly moved away just out of reach. "What's your name, mister?"

"My name's Hank, and you and me are going to have one good time tonight." He grabbed her and pulled her back to him, kissing her hungrily. "Let's go have ourselves a private party." He started toward the steps, keeping his arm around her.

"When I first saw you, I knew you were the man I'd been waiting for . . . the man I wanted."

"You're damned right I am."

Delilah led him upstairs and down the hall to her room at the far end. She tried to ignore the sounds coming from behind the other closed doors they passed on the way.

"This is it," she said, opening the door and holding it wide for him to enter.

Hank was so eager to have her that he paid little attention to anything as he stepped inside. The minute she closed and locked the door, he was there, taking her in his arms, kissing and caressing her.

Delilah was thrilled. All of her plans had worked. Hank Andrews was here! With her! He would be hers.

Kissing him back, she let him know how much she wanted him. Her fingers worked eagerly at the buttons of his shirt. She wanted him undressed and on that bed as quickly as she could get him there. She had been waiting a long time for this! Too long!

"You are a hot little thing, aren't you?" Hank

muttered as she helped him strip off his shirt.

"I want you. It seems I've been waiting for you forever." She tossed his shirt aside and ran her hands over his bare chest. "You want me, don't you?"

"You bet I do, darlin'. Come here. . . ."

He reached for her again, but Delilah backed away toward the bed.

"No. Not yet," she said with a small smile. "You come here. This is right where I want you." She sat down and patted the mattress beside her in invitation.

Hank was ready. He crossed the room, unbuckling his gunbelt and laying it on the bureau as he went. He then worked his belt buckle, fumbling in his haste to be rid of his pants.

Delilah watched his efforts and smiled as he shucked them.

He came toward her clad only in his underwear and pushed her down on the bed.

"Yeah," he said, his need sounding in his voice.

He was rough in his eagerness. His hands were upon her, squeezing, fondling. When he tried to unfasten her dress and push it from her shoulders, she managed to slip from beneath him and stand back up, covering herself.

"What're you doing?" he demanded, annoyed. He didn't want to play any damned games. He had been a long time without a woman, and he wanted her beneath him now.

"Nothing, honey," she said, still smiling. "I want to undress for you. I want you to watch me. I want to make this night special—for both of us. . . . I want it to be something we'll both remember . . ."

Hank's eyes lit up as she moved sensuously before him. She took off her shoes first, then paused at the end of the bed to lift her foot and brace it against the mattress. Slowly, provocatively, she slipped her stocking down her leg and tossed it aside before repeating the move on her other leg.

Hank was about ready to come straight up off the bed. He wanted to run his hands up those shapely legs . . . to explore all the heat he knew lay beneath the secrets of her skirts. He started to get up on one elbow, but she stopped him.

"Oh, no, Hank . . . We're going to take this slow and easy."

"But—"

"Do you have somewhere else to go? Someone else you want more than you want me?" She sounded irritated, as if she might leave him.

"No, darlin'." He immediately settled down. "I don't want nobody more than I want you."

Delilah gave a soft, triumphant laugh. "I feel the same way."

As she spoke, she reached behind herself to unfasten her dress. That done, she shrugged her shoulders and the dress fell away. When it caught at her hips, she wiggled a little and it dropped all the way to the floor. She stood before him clad only in a fancy corset.

Hank's body, already aflame, burned even hotter at this teasing ploy. His gaze was hungry upon her, devouring the sight of her. Desire pounded through him. He started to come up off the bed again just to get to her.

"No, no. Stay right where you are. I'm not done yet. . . ."

"You're torturing me."

She laughed again. "We haven't even begun." Delilah turned to the bureau and opened a drawer to take something out. She looked over her shoulder at Hank, a wicked gleam of dominance showing in her expression. "I thought it would be fun if we were tied up for a while. After all, you are all mine for the whole night."

Hank stared in disbelief as she came toward him dangling two pairs of handcuffs from around one finger.

"You are a wild one," he muttered.

She laughed, low and soft. "You have no idea. By the time this night is over, you'll have had the ride of your life."

The illicitness of her actions and her words excited him as no other whore ever had.

Delilah climbed up on the bed and straddled him high, taking care not to touch that most intimate part of him. When he tried to pull her down to him and hurry things along, she stilled his hands.

"Don't rush. I want to make this memorable for you," she said. She kissed him this time, murmuring, "The longer you wait, the greater your pleasure."

"You're crazy," Hank growled between kisses as she took his left arm and pressed it up toward the metal bedstead.

"Ah, but crazy can be exciting, don't you think? How will you feel when I have you at my mercy?

When I can do anything I want to do to you and you can't resist me?"

Her words were hypnotic. The heat and weight of her body upon him, along with the mental images she was creating—of her hands and mouth upon him, left him ready to explode with excitement. "I can't resist you now, darlin'. What other little surprises do you have for me?"

"More than you ever dreamed." She lifted one pair of the handcuffs and snapped one end around his wrist, then the other to the bedstead in a way that could not be freed.

Hank tugged at the restraint. He did not like feeling restricted, but Delilah moved quickly to distract him. She kissed him, and after a moment, he forgot about everything but the thrilling, half-naked woman in bed with him.

Delilah lifted his other arm and put the second set of handcuffs on that wrist, then linked it to the bedstead on the other side, successfully spread-eagling him. He was hers, nearly naked, helpless, and she was free to do with him as she pleased. She smiled at what she'd accomplished.

"I like your smile, woman," Hank said in a desire-slurred voice, awaiting the pleasure she'd promised. It was a different kind of arousal for him. He was caught up in her game. He wasn't worried. The worst she could do to him was rob him, and since they were in the saloon, he felt certain there was no danger of that. People were nearby, and all he had to do was call out if he needed help.

Delilah moved from the bed, and Hank fully expected her to undress completely. When she went to the window and opened it, he frowned. "What are you doing now?"

"I don't want it to get too hot in here." Her tone was sweet as she leaned slightly out and called in a hushed voice, "Stalking Ghost!"

For the first time, it dawned on Hank that something strange was going on. He watched helplessly as she skirted around the bed, grabbed her dress, and slipped it back on.

"Wait a minute! I came up here for a good time."

"So did I," she agreed.

"What are you doing, calling out the window like that? What the hell are you up to?" His passion of moments before faded. Tension was etched in every line of his body, and his expression was turning ugly. "Look, you little whore—"

"I'm no whore, Mr. Andrews. I'm Cody Jameson."

"Cody Jameson?" Hank's eyes widened with fear, and a chill went down his spine. He'd heard of the bounty hunter of that name, but he'd always thought Jameson was a man.

"That's right, and you're going for a ride, all right, but not the one you expected. You're wanted for murder in Texas. I'm taking you in."

Chapter Two

It had been a long and dusty trip from Galveston to Austin, and Luke Majors was more than ready for a hot bath, a hot meal, and some good whiskey as he checked into the hotel. He registered using just his first name of Lucas, for he didn't want to draw attention to himself. His reputation as a fast gun was well known, and the last thing he wanted right now was trouble.

After cleaning up, Luke deliberately left his gun in the room when he went down to dinner. He wanted to enjoy a quiet evening without any incidents. He ate in the small hotel restaurant and then headed across the street to the Lone Star Saloon for a drink.

It was a weeknight, yet the saloon was reasonably busy. Luke entered and stopped just inside the door to take a quick look around. The customers were absorbed in their own business of gambling and drinking, and paid little attention to him. He was glad. It wasn't always that way.

"Whiskey," he ordered as he came to stand at the bar.

"You're new in town, aren't you?" the barkeep asked as he set a glass before him and sloshed a good portion of the amber liquid into it.

"Just passing through."

"Where you from?"

"Around." Luke kept his answer short and curt as he slid some coins across the counter.

"Enjoy your drink." The barkeep had sense enough to know when a man wanted to be left alone, and something about this stranger didn't invite questions. He moved away.

Alone and enjoying it, Luke took a deep drink. It wasn't the best whiskey, but it would do. He idly studied the painting hanging in the place of honor over the bar: a half-nude woman reclining on a settee. A few girls were circulating the room, trying to stir up extra business, but he ignored them. There were a few poker games going on, too, but he wasn't about to gamble tonight. His luck had held in Galveston when he'd won big, and he was smart enough to quit while he was ahead. Same went for his gunfighting. The night in Galveston when he'd won the ranch was the night he'd quit. He was a rancher now, not a gunman.

Luke finished off his first drink, and the barkeep immediately appeared to refill his glass. Halfway through his second whiskey, he began to feel more relaxed than he had in a long time. Maybe life could be good again.

Across the room at one of the poker tables, Texas Ranger Jack Logan looked up from his game. He noticed the man at the bar and frowned. There was something familiar about him, and Jack wondered if possibly . . .

"Jack," one of his Ranger friends prodded, reminding him that it was his turn.

Jack glanced down at his pitiful hand and tossed the cards on the table in disgust. "I'm out."

He stood and started toward the bar and the man he thought he recognized. He studied the way the stranger stood, the set of his shoulders, and he knew this had to be Luke Majors. Jack didn't know what the chances were of both of them showing up in the same saloon in Austin on the same night, but he was glad. He'd been waiting a long time for this moment.

"I think I know you, friend." Jack stopped several paces behind the stranger.

At the sound of the man's deep voice, Luke tensed. It wasn't the first time he'd been greeted by those words, and Luke knew there could be a subtle threat in them. Something about the voice sounded vaguely familiar to him, and that worried him more. This was someone from his past. Suddenly he was sorry he was unarmed.

"I'm new in town," Luke offered. He set his glass down with infinite care and kept his hands away from his body, making no quick moves as he turned very slowly. He didn't want the man to mistake his actions for an attempt to go for a gun.

"I figured as much."

Out of the corner of his eye, Luke caught a glimpse of the man. He was tall, lean, and dark-haired. There was an aura of power and authority about him, and he was wearing his gun as if he were born to it. His dark-eyed gaze was riveted on Luke with piercing, challenging intensity. Then Luke faced him fully, and their gazes met and locked.

Suddenly the stranger—the man Luke thought was out to fight him—smiled. "What the hell are you doing in Austin, Luke?"

"Jack?" All the tension, all the fear that had filled Luke, drained from him as he stared at the friend he hadn't seen since the war. "I can't believe it!"

"Neither can I!"

They shook hands, clapping each other enthusiastically on the back.

Around them, the other men in the saloon let out a collective sigh of relief. For a moment, everyone had feared something ugly was about to happen.

Jack got a drink from the bartender and settled in with Luke at a table in a quiet corner, to talk and catch up on their years apart. They had been friends in their youth back in Georgia, Jack having grown up on Riverwood, a plantation near the Majors family's own Belgrove. They'd lost contact during the war, and by the time Luke had returned home, the Logans had already moved on.

"The last I heard about you, the neighbors said you'd gone to Texas," Luke said, still smiling over the unexpected pleasure of his company.

"Here I am." Jack nodded. "There was nothing left at Riverwood. Sherman's men burned it. Then I got word that Father was dead." He was silent for a moment as he touched on those long-suppressed memories. "Of all our kin, there was only my mother, my sister, Ellie, and her husband, Charles, left. We packed up what little we had and moved on. We settled just outside of Galveston. Ellie's still there with her family, but my mother died a few years back."

"I'm sorry." Luke meant it. He'd always loved and respected Mrs. Logan.

"So am I. I call Charles and Ellie's place home whenever I'm around, but that isn't too often these days. I'm a Ranger now. What about you? What happened to you after the war? We checked on Belgrove and saw that it was still standing. I spoke with Clarissa and was sorry to hear about your mother."

Memories of that time flooded back. Luke took a stiff drink. His gaze was hard as he looked up at his friend. "My brother Dan and my father never made it back."

They shared a look of understanding. Each had seen the horror of the battlefields and knew first-hand the death and destruction that had been wrought. "What about Belgrove and Clarissa?"

"By the time I got back, it had already been sold and Clarissa had married the man who'd bought it. She'd told me once that her dream was to be the mistress of Belgrove, and, by God, she made her dream come true."

Jack was surprised. He'd thought Clarissa loved Luke and was going to wait for him. They'd been engaged before he'd gone off to war and had seemed so happy. "What did she say?"

"What could she say?" Luke countered bitterly. "It was over." Her betrayal had been the final blow that had severed all his ties with the land that had been his home. He'd left Georgia then and had never gone back.

"So what have you been doing since?" Jack asked, forcing Luke from his dark thoughts. "Is what I heard about you true?"

"Depends on what you heard." Luke was evasive.

"Word around is that you're fast with a gun—real fast."

"I'm not wanted anywhere, if that's what you're asking."

"It wasn't, but I'm glad. I'd hate to think that I might have to come after you one day." Jack grinned, relieved by the news, and took another drink.

"It'd be interesting." Luke smiled, too. As youths, they'd often taken target practice together, and each had taken pride in his own accurate shooting ability. "But you don't have to worry about my reputation anymore. Those days are over," Luke told him.

"You're sure?" Jack knew how hard it was for a man who lived by the gun to give it up.

"I won a ranch in a poker game in Galveston, and I'm heading there now to settle down." He went on to tell his friend everything he knew about the property, which wasn't a lot—just that it was located near Del Fuego and had some cattle and a few head of horses on it. "It may not prove to be much, but at least it's mine."

Jack lifted his glass of whiskey in salute. "I'm glad your luck is changing. Here's to the future. What's the name of the place?"

"I'm calling it the Trinity, after my poker hand. I won it with three threes."

Jack gave him an incredulous look. "That must have been one helluva poker game."

"It was, but it was worth it. The Trinity is home now. It's where I'm going to stay."

"But you haven't even seen it yet."

"It doesn't matter. It's mine, and nothing is ever going to take it from me."

Jack heard the fierceness in his tone and knew Luke meant every word. He admired his friend's courage. Sometimes it could be difficult to escape the past, but if anyone could do it, Luke could.

They talked long into the night, reminiscing about a gentler, more elegant time. They had been different men then, and they knew things would never be that way again.

It was very late when they finally parted. Jack had to ride out early. He and his other Ranger friends were due in Waco for a meeting. Before the two men separated, they promised to stay in touch. They hoped they would.

Luke slept for only a few hours before rising and setting out once more for Del Fuego. With each passing mile, his affinity for the Texas heartland grew. There was something about this wide-open place that touched a chord within him and made him want to stay, to put down roots. A man could prosper and build a good life here.

Luke's feelings of anticipation grew as his days of travel passed. He tried to deny his excitement, for he had suffered too many disappointments in the past. But when he came upon the low-running creek that marked the eastern boundary of his newly acquired range, a thrill shot through him.

Reining in, he turned in the saddle to survey the land around him. To the west and north, the countryside stretched in an endless sea of low, rolling hills and mesquite trees, and it was all his for as far as the eye could see.

More than ready to reach his journey's end, he spurred his horse on, watching for the road that would lead to the ranch house. To his surprise, he found the beaten track easily and turned down it. He had ridden for better than a mile when he finally topped a low rise, and there spread out before him was the prize he'd sought—what had been the Jackson ranch and was now the Trinity.

The ranch was much as George Jackson, the losing gambler, had described it when he'd turned over the deed. There was a main house, a few outbuildings, corrals, and some stock. Jackson had told him about the hired hand named Jessy who helped run the place for him, but Luke could see no sign of him.

Urging his mount down the slope, Luke stopped before the house and swung slowly down from the saddle. He looped the reins over the hitching rail and stood, hands on his hips, staring at his new home. The house was small, not more than four or five rooms, and had a porch across the front. It was run-down and in need of repair. He was just starting up the walk when he heard a deep, threatening voice call out to him.

"Hold it right there, mister."

Luke stopped in his tracks as a tall, serious-looking, gray-haired man appeared from around back. He was carrying a shotgun, and it was pointed straight at his chest.

"Afternoon," Luke greeted him cordially.

"Maybe it is and maybe it ain't. What are you doing here? What do you want?"

"Are you Jessy?"

"I am."

"George Jackson told me about you. I'm Luke Majors, the new owner of the ranch. I won it from Jackson in a poker game in Galveston. I have the deed in my saddlebag, if you'd like to see it." He nodded toward his horse, but made no move to retrieve it. He knew what a blast from a shotgun could do to a man, and he didn't want to find himself on the receiving end.

"Get it." Jessy waved him toward his horse with the weapon.

Luke retrieved the document and handed it over. Jessy read it and then slowly lowered the gun.

"That man always was a damned fool." He looked up at Luke with new respect. "Sorry about the shotgun, but a man can't be too careful around these parts." He finally smiled and offered his hand in friendship. "I'm Jessy Hardy. Been working here since Mr. Jackson hired me in seventy-three."

"Good to meet you, Jessy." Luke found his handshake firm and steady, and the look in his eyes honest and forthright. He liked him immediately.

"I guess this means you're the new boss. Come on in, I'll show you around the house."

"Thanks."

Half an hour later, Luke stood with Jessy at the corral watching the few head of horses that had come with the property. Jessy had shown him the extent of his holdings—he now owned 20 horses and about 200 head of cattle.

"Will you stay on and work for me?" Luke asked.

"I'd like that." Jessy was relieved at the offer. Certainly, his life couldn't be much worse with this new owner. Luke Majors seemed like a smart man. He had to be better at ranching than Jackson had been.

"Good. There is one other thing." At Jessy's curious look, Luke went on, "I'm changing the name of the place. I want to name it after the winning hand I had in the poker game."

"What's it gonna be? The Ranch Royale? The Full House?" Jessy asked with interest, thinking the hand must have been a great one to have won such a prize.

Luke's smile was wry. "No. I'm going to call it the Trinity."

"The Trinity?" The other man glanced over at him in disbelief. "Jackson lost this place to three of a kind?"

"Three threes, to be exact. Jackson had two pair, and the way things had been going all night, that probably seemed like enough to win to him. I was lucky." Luke gazed out over the land that was his, and for the first time in years he was filled with a sense of well-being and peace. "Very lucky."

Two strangers who looked like they'd been traveling a long way entered the Lone Star Saloon and came to stand at the bar. There was a hardness about them, a single-mindedness of purpose that made the bartender instantly cautious of them.

"We're looking for a man," the younger of the two men announced.

"There's a lot of men come in here."

"This man's name is Majors, Luke Majors, the gunfighter. You know him?"

"I've heard the name."

"We know Majors was in Galveston a while back, and we heard that he might be heading this way. We need to find him. Has he been here?"

"Maybe he has been and maybe he hasn't. What's it to you?" the barkeep asked. Majors had tipped him handsomely the night he was there, and the man wasn't about to betray him.

"It's personal. We're just trying to locate him."

The bartender studied the two for a minute, and then said, "It's been a while since I last saw him. Sorry, I can't help you any more than that."

The man who had done all the talking nodded and slid a coin across the bar to him for his trouble.

The bartender pocketed it and watched as the

two left the saloon. There was something troubling about them, but he couldn't put his finger on it. A desperation of some sort, but God knows what. The good news was, he hadn't given anything away about Majors and he wasn't going to. If they found him, they were going to have to do it without any help from him.

Chapter Three

"You mean you're not going to loan me the money?" Luke's jaw was set in a hard line and his eyes flared with sudden anger as he stared at the banker.

Coming here had been one of the most difficult things Luke had ever done, but he'd done it for the ranch. In the six months since he'd taken over the Trinity, he'd kept a low profile, working hard and only going into town when he needed supplies. He'd wanted to live a quiet, dignified life again, and he'd been working day and night toward that goal. Just when he'd thought he was going to make it, the bill for back taxes had come—to the tune of some 250 dollars. What money Luke had had to begin with had all been spent fixing up the ranch. There was no way he had that kind of cash, and so he'd come to Jonathan Harris as a businessman wanting to get an honest loan. It enraged Luke, now, to discover that humbling himself before this pompous ass had been for nothing.

"The decision is nothing personal," Harris went on quickly, growing even more nervous now that he'd seen the look in Majors's eyes. The man was a killer! He'd heard of Majors's reputation. "It wouldn't be a sound investment for the bank to make. You're new to the area. You have no money on deposit with us. You haven't proven the ranch to be profitable, and certainly Jackson never made any money off that land. That, plus what we know of your background . . . you, er, seem to have little ranching expertise." He cleared his throat and glanced away, wishing the man he knew was a gunfighter would just leave. He didn't want Luke Majors anywhere around his bank. Why, he'd even come in here today wearing his gun! Harris was hard-pressed not to shudder openly.

"But I only need two hundred fifty dollars to pay the back taxes that Jackson didn't pay. I've made improvements on the structures, I've fenced, and I've added to the herd. You won't lose your money. I give you my word that it will be repaid within a year." Luke repeated his story, wanting the man to understand his resolve to make the Trinity pay off. He planned to make it a showplace. He planned to invest in some new horseflesh and start breeding horses, too, as soon as he could afford it. His family had had a fine stable at Belgrove.

"I'm sorry, Mr. Majors," Harris replied coldly.

"You're sorry?" Luke ground out, feeling cornered and angry and frustrated. He snatched his hat up from where he'd laid it on the banker's highly polished mahogany desk and rose from his chair. There was an ominous tone to his voice as he spoke. "Not nearly as sorry as—"

"This is a holdup! Give me all the money!" At the teller's window a man of nondescript dress was drawing his gun.

The clerk started to scream.

"Shut up! We're the El Diablo gang. Another sound and I'll shoot everybody in here!"

Luke saw what was happening, anticipated the robber's move, and automatically went for his own weapon.

"No!" Harris shouted, terrified that the infamous gang of killers was in his bank. He fumbled at his desk drawer in an effort to get the small derringer he kept there, certain Luke was one of the gang.

The robber saw both Luke and Harris going for guns and fired in their direction. Harris let out a shriek of pain as he collapsed to the floor.

The robber saw that Luke was still armed, and he fired again. Luke returned his fire, his shot splintering wood on the counter near the other man.

A cry of alarm was already sounding in the streets, and people were running for the sheriff. Two more robbers had been standing guard outside, and they charged inside, shouting at their partner to hurry.

The teller was still stuffing money in the bag when the robber impatiently snatched it away from him. He ran for the door with Luke chasing him. Luke would have fired at the men and taken some of them down, but there were too many people around. He didn't have a clear shot.

The three robbers emerged from the bank, guns drawn and ready for trouble. The one with the money vaulted onto his horse and galloped away, leaving the other two to follow.

The sheriff appeared out of nowhere with two deputies, their guns blazing. When one robber was wounded, the two gang members backed toward the bank, seeking protection inside as the sheriff closed in. Another deputy had forced his way into the back entrance of the bank. He'd seen Harris lying wounded and bleeding on the floor and was coming up behind Luke, gun drawn, ready to kill.

"Drop your gun, Majors!" the deputy ordered.

Luke was shocked. He'd been concentrating on getting the second outlaw, who was retreating toward them, as the sheriff closed in on him from the front.

"There's the man you want, Deputy." Luke tried to explain as he turned slowly toward the lawman. "I was only trying to help."

The deputy's gun was pointed unerringly at the center of Luke's chest. "Save your lies, Majors. We know all about you. We've been watching you for weeks now, expecting you to pull something like this."

"You're wrong. I was only here trying to get a loan. . . ."

"Shut up and put your gun down. Now!"

"Jonathan's been shot!" the teller shouted as he rushed over to where Harris was lying on the floor beside his desk. "Majors was the one who did it! He's one of them!"

Luke couldn't believe what was happening. He had never considered robbing a bank, even in his wildest days. He had only drawn his gun to help, and now they were accusing him of being a part of the gang.

"Deputy, I didn't shoot Harris. I can explain," Luke said, trying again to reason with the lawman as he lowered his gun.

"Shut up! You're going to jail for a real long time, if they don't hang you first. Now drop that gun real easy like and step away from it!"

Luke did as he was told, hoping to get a chance to tell someone who would listen what had really happened.

The two robbers, realizing they were trapped between the sheriff in the street and the deputy behind them in the bank, laid down their own guns and put their hands up.

As the deputy forced Luke to move outside, Sheriff Sam Gregory smiled thinly. "Well, well, well, if it isn't Luke Majors. We've been aching to get our hands on you. Looks like keeping an eye on you was a smart thing to do. Thought you could just come in here and steal from us, did you?"

"Sheriff, Jonathan Harris has been shot," the deputy advised him.

"Is he dead?"

"No, he's still breathing."

"Then somebody send for the doc, quick, and let

me know how he is right away." He turned back toward the prisoners. "Now, you three, keep your hands up. Let's go. I got a nice jail cell just waiting for you."

Luke attempted to tell him what had happened in the bank. "Sheriff, I was trying to explain to your deputy that I only drew my gun because I was trying to—"

"Tell it to the judge and jury, Majors. Right now you're going to jail."

"But, Sheriff, I was only there to get a loan!" Luke was furious.

The sheriff found humor in his statement. "So were these other two, Majors. We'll have the trial just as soon as we can put it together, and you can explain all you want to then. For now, you're all under arrest for bank robbery!"

"Dear God! What happened?" a beautiful woman cried out to the sheriff as she came running down the street, her face white with terror.

"Elizabeth . . ." The sheriff looked worried.

"I thought I heard gunfire, Sam. What happened? Where's my Jonathan? Is everyone all right?"

"Jonathan's inside. They've already sent for the doctor," he told her.

"Oh my God!" Elizabeth Harris ran inside the bank, not waiting to hear more.

Luke was filled with rage as he was marched off to jail. He had come to town only to take out a loan! Not to rob the damned bank! Now no one would listen to him. They had him all but convicted, not only of bank robbing, but shooting the bank officer as well. He only hoped that when Harris recovered, he would tell them all the truth. Until then he was going to be forced to bide his time—under arrest and in jail for a crime he didn't commit.

When the deputy had locked them up and gone, and they were alone, the two outlaws stared at Luke with open interest.

"So, you're the famous Luke Majors," the outlaw named Carson said matter-of-factly. "I heard a lot about you."

Luke shot him a look of disgust.

"So you were at the bank trying to get a loan, eh?" Jones, the robber who'd been wounded, said, grinning wickedly at Luke's folly.

"Hell, you shoulda taken out a loan our way. If you had, we'd be far away from here right now countin' our money, instead of sitting here." Carson's expression was ugly. If Majors hadn't been in the bank, they would have been out of there free and clear.

"I may be many things, but I am not a thief."

Carson shrugged indifferently at the news. "It don't matter that you weren't with us to start. All that matters is that they thought you were."

Luke hated what Carson was saying because he knew it was true. He'd seen the banker's reaction to him. And the people around town had shunned him once they'd learned about his reputation. With little money and only Jessy to vouch for him, things did not look good. Silently, Luke wondered what perverse twist of fate had led him to this end. Somehow he had to get word to Jessy to wire Jack in Waco. Jack was probably the only one who could get him out of this one.

Jack was in Waco the day after the robbery when his captain, Steve Laughlin, called him in for a meeting.

"I've just gotten word from Del Fuego that three members of the El Diablo gang were caught during a bank robbery there. The banker was shot and almost killed. The sheriff's worried about possible trouble, and he wants extra help. I'm sending you down to give him a hand."

"The El Diablo gang." Jack was surprised that any of the gang had been arrested. "They're fast and mean and deadly. Something must have gone wrong for them to have been caught. I wonder what happened?"

"You can find that out when you get there. I want you to give the sheriff whatever help he needs, but I also want you to see what you can find out about El Diablo himself. See what these men have to say; see what you can get out of them. The gang's been terrorizing that area for some time, and I have orders from the top to stop them by any means possible—as fast as possible. Use your discretion."

"Yes, sir."

Jack made the trip to Del Fuego in record time. He was trail-weary, dirty, and hot when he arrived, but he didn't bother to stop at the hotel. He went straight to the jail.

"What can I do for you?" Sam Gregory asked

cautiously from where he was sitting behind his desk as Jack entered the office. His instincts were telling him this tall stranger was dangerous. His hand hovered near the gun he kept in his top desk drawer.

"I'm Ranger Jack Logan. Capt. Laughlin sent me."

At his words, Sam's mood immediately brightened. He quickly rose to shake hands with Jack. "Thanks for coming. It's been tense around here since we arrested the three of them, I can tell you that."

"Everything's been quiet so far?"

"So far, but you know how the El Diablo gang works. That bunch is bloodthirsty. They'd just as soon kill you as look at you. I've got extra deputies on duty, keeping watch."

"I've heard a lot about this gang, and I've seen the aftermath of their handiwork. It isn't pretty. Capt. Laughlin told me that a banker was shot. Is the man dead?"

"No. He's still hanging on, but the doctor doesn't know if he's going to recover or not. He's still unconscious."

Jack nodded. "What about the three you arrested? Are they talking yet?"

"No. They're as closemouthed as they come, except for the one man. He's a notorious gunfighter, and we knew he was going to be trouble the minute he came to town."

Jack went suddenly quiet. "What gunfighter?"

"Majors. Surely you've heard of him—Luke Majors."

Jack's smile was tight as he stared at the sheriff, his gaze hard and cold. "I've heard of him."

"Majors keeps trying to tell us that he had nothing to do with it, but he's the one who shot Harris."

Jack couldn't believe what he was hearing. Luke involved in a bank robbery? It didn't make sense. "Majors shot Harris? Are you sure?" he asked, revealing nothing of his friendship with Luke.

"There's a witness who says he did it. It doesn't get much more sure than that."

"I see." Jack spoke tersely. "I want to talk to all three of the men, but I want to do it individually. You got a place around here I can do that?"

"Sure. There's a sleeping room in back." He nodded in the direction of a small room off the opposite side of the office.

"Thanks. I'll use it."

Sam was relieved to have him there. "Which one do you want to see first? I got Majors, one named Carson, and another one who was winged in the arm, named Jones. The doc took a look at him, and he's gonna be fine."

"Bring me Majors first." Jack disappeared into the small room that contained only a cot, one small table, and a straight-backed chair.

The sheriff hurried to get the dangerous and deadly Majors. He carried his gun at the ready. He would not be caught unprepared. If these three tried anything, he was going to shoot first and ask questions later.

"Let's go, Majors," he ordered.

Luke was stretched out on one of the bunks, his eyes closed. At the sound of the lawman's voice, he was instantly concerned. "Where are we going?"

"That's none of your damned business. Now just come on out of there, nice and easy." The sheriff stepped back a little to give him room to leave the cell. He kept the gun trained on Luke and an eye on the other two.

Luke had no more love for his companions than did the sheriff, and he kept an eye on them, too, as he passed through the cell door. He waited as the sheriff slammed and locked it behind him.

"All right, let's go." Sam gestured him on again, and Luke moved forward into the main office.

"Where to now, Sheriff?"

"Back there, in that room. There's someone there needing to talk to you. The Rangers have been sent in to bring down the El Diablo gang, and they're starting with you."

Luke did not for one minute allow himself to hope that Jack would be there. He prayed only that the Ranger might know Jack and be able to relay a message to him. Jessy had sent a wire to Jack shortly after the robbery, when he'd come into town to see Luke, but there was no telling if it had even reached Jack. Luke took a deep breath, ready to plead his case to someone who might not be as closed-minded as the townspeople. He stepped through the door and Sam shut it behind him.

"I'm Luke Majors," he said to the man standing with his back to him.

"What the hell are you doing in here?" Jack demanded in a low voice as he turned on him.

"Jack! Thank God it's you!" Luke could not believe his good fortune. "Did you get the wire I had Jessy send you?"

"No. What wire? I'm here because my captain sent me. I didn't even know you were involved until a few minutes ago. What the hell is going on? They're damn well ready to hang you around here."

"It's all a terrible misunderstanding, but no one will listen to me. Until Harris recovers enough to talk, no one's gonna believe a word I say."

"Tell me what happened. I want the truth."

Luke glared at him. "I don't lie."

Jack met his steady regard. Neither man flinched as they acknowledged that truth about each other.

"What happened, Luke?"

For the first time since the robbery, Luke knew he had someone who would believe his version of what had happened in the bank that day. He began with the unexpected news that he had owed back taxes on the Trinity and then went on to tell Jack all of what happened at the bank. "When the man drew his gun and started shooting, I drew mine. I wanted to help the bank, not rob it. Harris went down with Carson's first shot. I got off one round and was chasing them from the bank with my gun drawn. I couldn't fire because there were too many people around. I guess it must have looked to the tellers like I was running with them, instead of going after them. When the deputy came in the back door, all he knew was that I was standing there with my gun in hand, and one of the tellers was yelling that I had shot Harris."

Jack muttered a curse under his breath as he wondered how to get Luke out of this one. "So Harris is the only one who can corroborate your story."

Luke nodded. "And he hasn't regained consciousness yet. Of course, as scared as he was of me before the robbery, he just might go along with their version to get rid of me. The man was positively terrified sitting across the desk from me, not to mention the fact that he had just turned down my request for a loan."

An idea began to form in Jack's mind. "What about the other two in back? Have they said anything or done anything that might help us track down El Diablo?"

"They haven't said much. They keep telling me I ought to join up with them since the law already thinks I'm one of them." He sounded disgusted. "They're convinced that I'm going to hang right along with them, and the way things are going, I'm beginning to believe they're right."

Jack smiled. "How much do you owe in taxes?"

"Two hundred fifty dollars. Why?"

"How would you like a job? Working for me? I have orders to bring down El Diablo any way I can. You're my in. I want you to stay in the cell with them. Listen to what they have to say, act interested in joining up with them. See what you can find out about the leader, El Diablo. We know next to nothing about him personally. Anything you can find out will help. This gang is one of the most bloodthirsty riding the range. This town should be thanking you, instead of threatening you. If you hadn't been there to interrupt things, everyone in the bank probably would have been killed. These men are wild and deadly, and I want them. . . . I want El Diablo." Jack's eyes were ablaze with fierce emotion.

"I came to Del Fuego to get away from killing."

"All I want you to do is get as much information out of them as you can while you're locked up with them. Will you do it? I'll pay your taxes plus a hundred dollars for your time. Do we have a deal?"

Luke was trapped. "If I don't?"

"I'll still get you out of here, but you won't have the money."

Luke tried to rationalize what Jack wanted him to do. He told himself that he'd be helping the law, and the townspeople would appreciate him for it later. But he hated being in jail. He hated the loss of his freedom. He hated most of all the company of men like Carson and Jones.

"Well? Will you do it?" Jack pressed. "I need you to find out as much as you can about the location of their hideouts. They must have more than one. And find out about El Diablo himself. Who is he? If we learn that, we can shut them down. Three hundred fifty dollars, Luke."

Luke wanted to refuse, to walk out of the jail that minute and never look back. But he still wouldn't have the money. "All right. I'll do my best."

They shook hands.

"Are you going to tell the sheriff the truth?" Luke asked.

"I'll tell him everything, so he'll know what we're doing. There's talk that there might be trouble, so take care. There are extra men on guard, but you can't be too careful."

Luke nodded. "How do I get in touch with you if I learn something?"

"I'll be working with the sheriff here in town. You'll be seeing me."

Luke was returned to the cell, and the sheriff took Jones away for Jack to question.

"What's going on?" Carson asked.

"They've brought in the Rangers. That's who's talking to Jones now."

Carson frowned. "What did he want to know?"

"He kept questioning me about El Diablo. I told him I didn't know anything, but like everyone else, he wouldn't believe me."

The outlaw's smile was tight. "He won't get anything out of me or Jones either. We ain't fools. You don't tell what you know about El Diablo and live."

"El Diablo must be one helluva leader."

"Let's just put it this way: as long as you do what is asked of you and mind your own business, El Diablo takes care of you. You don't ever want to cross the boss, though. Two men thought they could get away with it once."

"What happened?"

"They tried to run off with some money from a robbery. We found their bodies about a week later," Carson told him. "Once you join with El Diablo, you stay."

Sam came for Carson then, bringing back Jones.

Jack questioned the second outlaw at length,

too, but with no success. When they were locked up again, Jack took the sheriff into the back room with him so they could speak privately, without being interrupted or overheard. He quickly told him the truth about Luke.

"You're wrong! Everybody knows Majors was one of them!" Sam protested. "The man's a killer! There were witnesses!"

"I'm telling you, Sheriff, sometimes witnesses are wrong. I've known Luke Majors for years. He is not a bank robber. Hasn't he lived here in your community for quite a while now? He never gave you any trouble before, did he?"

"Well, no," Sam admitted grudgingly.

"I believe Luke's story about what happened, and I've convinced him to help us. That's why I didn't order you to free him right away."

"Majors is going to be working with us?" Sam was incredulous. "But the man—"

"The man is my friend. He may be a fast gun, but he is no bank robber. He came here to Del Fuego to settle down."

"We don't want his kind in our town."

Jack was growing furious, but he understood the sheriff's reluctance to believe him. "Majors's very presence at the bank saved lives. He interrupted the gang. If he hadn't been there, who knows how many might have been killed? You should be thanking the man, instead of keeping him locked up. Didn't you listen to anything he said?"

"I heard his lies."

"He wasn't lying."

Sam still looked doubtful. "I guess I have to trust your judgment."

"You won't be sorry. We're going to find out who El Diablo is and bring him and his gang down. Did you have any luck recovering the money from the robbery?"

"No. We tracked the one who got away for about five miles, but then lost his trail. He made off with over five hundred dollars."

Jack shook his head in disgust. "All right. I'm going to check in at the hotel and get some rest. You need any more help tonight?"

"No. I'm working the office here, and I got another deputy keeping an eye on things around town."

They both looked up as a young blond woman entered the office. Jack thought her lovely.

"Who is she?" Jack asked, mesmerized by the petite, slender beauty.

"Elizabeth Harris, the wounded banker's wife," Sam told him as he hurried out to speak to her.

"Elizabeth, has there been a change with Jonathan?" the sheriff asked earnestly.

"Oh, Sam, there you are." She sighed in relief at the sight of him. "It's just all so terrible. The doctor says there's nothing more we can do but wait and pray."

"I'm sorry."

"So am I, Sam. That's why I just had to come down here. I couldn't stand seeing my poor husband lying there, so helpless . . . so close to death, while these vermin who pass as men go on as if nothing's happened, locked here in your jail." She wiped a tear from her eye. "I came down here to see the monsters who did this to my Jonathan."

"I understand how you're feeling, but I don't think it's a good idea for you to see them. These men . . . well, they aren't fit to be around a lady like you."

"I want to see them pay for what they've done."

"So do we," Jack put in, and when she looked over at him, he introduced himself. "Mrs. Harris, I'm Jack Logan."

"Ranger Logan has been sent down here to help me."

"You're a Ranger?" she asked, turning to Jack, her dark-eyed gaze widening with respect. "Thank heaven you've come. Poor Sam here has just been overburdened by all that's gone on. I'm Elizabeth Harris. My husband is the banker who was shot in the robbery."

"I'm going to do everything I can to bring the El Diablo gang to justice."

"Bless you. It's been such a terrible time for me since the robbery—not knowing if my husband is going to live or die."

Jack found that she stirred a protectiveness within him. She was such a delicate young woman to have to face such tragedy and hardship alone. He wanted to shield her from pain and hurt. "I'm sorry this had to happen, ma'am."

Sam spoke up, too, as he put a comforting hand on her shoulder. "I promise you, Elizabeth, these men aren't going anywhere as long as I have a breath in my body."

"Thank you . . . both of you. I've felt so alone

this last week. So helpless. There's so little I can do to help right now. I know it was foolish for me to come down here, but I thought if I just saw them, I could somehow understand why." She managed a pained smile at the two lawmen. "I only wish I could turn back the clock to that fateful day . . . but even as wonderful as you Rangers are, I don't think you're capable of that, are you, Ranger Logan?"

Jack shook his head. "No, ma'am. I wish I could."

"So do I," she said in a weary, strained voice. "Good-bye."

Jack watched her go. He said good-bye to Sam, who'd been watching her, too, then headed for the hotel. In that moment, all he wanted to do was bring down El Diablo and erase the sadness from Elizabeth Harris's eyes.

Chapter Four

Somehow, Deputy Davis was managing to stay awake as he prowled the streets of Del Fuego, keeping watch. It wasn't easy staying alert. The night was proving to be exceptionally dark and quiet. Even the saloons were more subdued than usual. Things were so peaceful and so calm that sometime long after midnight, his weariness caught up with him. He sat down to rest at the rear of one of the general stores. He figured it wouldn't hurt if he dozed for a minute. The decision was a fatal one. The member of El Diablo's gang who'd been trailing him for some time struck quickly and silently.

The guard disposed of, the outlaw rejoined four others from the gang, and they closed in on the jail.

Sam Gregory was growing restless. He was very sleepy, but knew he couldn't afford to rest. His relief wasn't due to show up until near six A.M., and he had to stay alert. The judge wasn't due back in town for another two weeks, and Sam was pretty certain that the next 14 days were going to be some of the longest of his life.

Sam got up from his desk and made his way to the little room in the back just to keep moving. It was there that they were waiting for him, having forced the window and climbed in from the back alley.

"What the . . . !" Sam stared at the three men who stood in the shadows of the room with their guns trained on him.

"You look surprised, Sheriff." They were smiling at his look of shock. "You should have been expecting us."

"You know why we're here, so let's go."

"This is crazy. I've got a man out there watching—"

"You *had* a man," the outlaw interrupted. "He won't be helping you anymore." He gave Sam a hard push toward the jail cells. "Unbuckle your gunbelt and leave it on your desk."

"You won't get away with this."

"We already have."

Carson and Jones had heard the sound of their friends' voices and were standing up, ready and waiting to be freed.

"It took you long enough, Sully. Where the hell have you been? Drinking and whoring and having a good time, while we been rotting away in this

53

damned jail?" Carson asked when he saw his friend.

"We were waiting till the time was right. The boss said this was the night to do it. And, as usual, the boss was right."

"Unlock the door, Sheriff, and don't try anything," the man called Sully ordered.

Sam was helpless and knew it. Silently he cursed his vulnerability and wished he'd had more deputies working with him. He hoped they were lying about Deputy Davis, for the man had a wife and kids. With great regret, the sheriff unlocked the door and stood back to let the outlaws go free.

"Let's get out of here," Carson declared, starting for the door.

"I'm ready!" Jones paused to look back at Majors.

"You coming?"

Luke couldn't believe what was happening. If he stayed, even though he was innocent, the town already had him convicted of the robbery and the shooting. If he went with the gang, he'd have the chance to find out about El Diablo and fulfill his deal with Jack, but he'd look guiltier than ever. Luke made a snap decision.

"I'm with you."

The three men raced toward the sheriff's desk, where they knew their guns were locked up. They broke open the drawer that held them and strapped on their gunbelts.

"Who the hell is he?" Sully demanded, angry that Carson and Jones were bringing someone else along.

"He's Luke Majors, the gunfighter."

"I don't know if the boss is going to like us bringing along a stranger or not."

"His reputation speaks for him."

Sully was not happy, but he relented. "All right. Get going. I'll take care of the sheriff." He was ready to shoot Sam in cold blood.

"No, let me!" Luke said in a determined voice. Acting quickly, he drew his own gun and stepped between the two men. "You go on. I'll catch up. It's payback time for me."

Sully and the others looked at him and then shrugged. "Just make it fast. We got horses waiting."

Luke motioned Sam back into the cell, and when he did, he leaned close. "Tell Jack I'll contact him as soon as I can."

He hit the sheriff then with the butt of the gun, knocking him unconscious. He had to make this look good in case any of the gang came back to check on him. Luke locked the cell door and then raced from the jail to join the others. They were already mounted up and ready to ride.

"Let's go," Luke urged as he swung up on the horse they'd just stolen for him.

"Did you take care of the sheriff?" Sully asked as he held his mount tightly in rein. He didn't want the lawman coming after them, and he was ready to go back in and finish the job if he had to.

"Don't worry, he won't be causing us any more trouble." Luke's answer was terse. "Now let's ride before somebody sees us."

"I knew you belonged with us," Jones said with satisfaction.

"Let's get outta here."

More than an hour later, an elusive, dark-clad figure moved furtively through the alley. The intruder quietly entered the jail to see if the break had been successful. In the jail cell, the sheriff was just beginning to stir.

"Damn . . ." The muttered curse reflected the intruder's fury.

"Thank God you're here!" Sam gasped, struggling to rise at the sound of the voice. His head throbbed from the blow he'd received, and he was weak and dizzy. "I need help! They killed Davis and broke the bank robbers out! You have to call the other deputies and Logan! We gotta go after them!" He groaned as pain shot through him with every movement.

The intruder hurried out to the office to pick up the sheriff's gun from where it lay on his desk, then returned. "I'm not calling anybody for help."

"What?" Sam was confused.

"And neither are you—ever again."

El Diablo shot him point-blank and left him lying dead on the floor.

No one heard the shot, and no one saw El Diablo leave the jail. The outlaw disappeared into the streets of Del Fuego.

Jack was roused at dawn by fierce pounding on his door.

"Logan! Get up now! This is Deputy Halloway!"

Jack bolted from bed, pausing only long enough to pull on his pants before he threw wide the door. "What happened?"

Halloway rushed inside and closed the door. "There was a jailbreak last night. The sheriff's dead . . . so's Davis."

"The prisoners are gone? Even Majors?"

"They're gone! All of them! And to think, Majors wanted us to believe he was innocent!" He spat the words with hatred. "If he was so damned innocent, why did he run?"

Jack started throwing on the rest of his clothes as they talked. "I don't know. You got any idea what time it happened?"

"No. The sheriff's been dead a while. Shot down while he was already locked up in the cell. It was probably Majors who killed him!"

"What if he didn't?" Jack challenged.

"If he didn't, and if he wasn't part of the gang like he kept saying, why did he go with them?"

Jack cursed under his breath as he strapped on his gun. He knew exactly why Luke had gone with them—the money.

Jack had never planned for Luke to get this involved. He'd thought it would be simple for him to pick up the information they needed and feed it to him. But suddenly there was nothing simple about the setup. Luke had ridden out with the gang. Jack knew he had to find a way to help Luke, but right now he wasn't sure how.

"There's a crowd gathering over at the office," Halloway told him. "The mayor and all the deputies are there. We gotta hurry."

"Let's go." Jack grabbed his hat and started from the room.

A short time later, the Ranger stood alone in the jail cell staring down at the bloodstained floor. Sheriff Gregory had been a good, decent man, and Jack mourned his passing. He made a silent vow to personally see the sheriff's killer pay.

Sarah Gregory had gotten word of her husband's death. She came running into the jail, her expression desperate, tears streaming down her face. "Where is he? Where's the Ranger?" she demanded.

"He's there, Sarah." Fred Halloway motioned toward the cell.

"You're the Ranger my husband told me was here to help him?" she asked coldly as she confronted Jack.

"Yes, ma'am. I'm Jack Logan."

"Well, you didn't help him very much, did you? My husband is dead!" she accused hysterically.

"I'm sorry, Mrs. Gregory."

"Sorry? You think being sorry matters? That gang has cut a swath of death and destruction through this town. My husband is dead, Jonathan Harris is just as good as dead, and yet these murderers are free to kill and rob again!"

"We're going to get them, ma'am. I promise you that."

"How? When? I want to know how many innocent people are going to die before you do something, Ranger Logan!"

"I say we put a bounty out on Majors!" Halloway spoke up. "Dead or alive!"

"Yeah!" the deputy named Stevens agreed. "It had to be Majors who pulled the trigger."

"We all know he's the one who shot Harris and no doubt my husband, too! I want to see him pay! Pay with his life!" Sarah Gregory said.

A rumble of agreement went through the rest of those gathered there.

"The Rangers will catch them, ma'am. The gang will be brought to justice," Jack replied.

"If you couldn't help keep them in jail, how are you going to see that justice is done? We need the bounty!" she insisted.

"I'll put up the money," Mayor Atkins offered. "A thousand dollars for Majors. Five hundred a head for the other two. We want them dead or alive, but preferably dead for Luke Majors."

"Thank you," Sarah Gregory said softly, then left the office, heartbroken over her loss.

Jack knew a deep and real fear for his friend's safety as he listened to what transpired next. The deputies were rabid in their desire to see Luke dead. Jack alone knew that Luke was innocent, yet he couldn't openly defend him. With Gregory dead, he didn't know who to trust, and he couldn't risk revealing Luke's cover. The responsibility of keeping Luke safe was his and his alone. He had to make sure nothing happened to Luke at the hands of the outlaws or at the hands of these well-meaning lawmen and the bounty hunters they sent out. Jack knew he needed help, and he needed it fast.

"Deputy Halloway, the sheriff's job is yours—if you'll have it," the major was saying. "I need someone to take control, and you worked with Sam the longest."

Halloway was taken aback by the offer. "Well . . . yes . . . but—"

"This isn't a happy time for any of us. The town needs you."

"I'd be honored to follow in Sam's footsteps," he replied humbly.

There was an awkward moment as they quietly mourned Sam's passing. Then Halloway pulled himself together and prepared to lead his men in a posse to see if they could pick up a trail. He knew it would be tough since the gang had such a head start, but they had to do something.

"Logan, are you riding with us?" Halloway asked.

"I'm with you," Jack said.

"We'll ride out in half an hour, men. Meet here."

The men who'd gathered in the jail dispersed to get their horses.

Jack headed for the stable to get his own mount, but on the way he stopped at the telegraph office to send a wire to a bounty hunter he'd heard a lot about. Talk had it that one Cody Jameson out of San Antonio was good at bringing men in alive, and that was just who he wanted looking for Luke.

The wire was simple and straightforward: *Have a job I think will interest you. Concerns the El Diablo gang. Contact me privately in Del Fuego at the Homestead Hotel within seven days if interested. Signed, Jack Logan.*

His mood was grim as he went to the stable and saddled up to join the posse. The trail would be cold, but there might be some clue along the way that would help them. His worst fear was that the posse might accidentally stumble across the gang. If that happened, the posse would either end up dead or Luke would end up on the wrong end of a rope. Jack had to make certain that neither one happened.

The posse returned four days later, frustrated, tired, and dirty. It had been a very long four days. They had lost the trail about 20 miles west of town and had spent the rest of the time combing the countryside in a fruitless search.

Jack was relieved that things had turned out that way. He wanted Luke to come to him with El Diablo's identity. He believed that once the people of Del Fuego found out what he'd been doing, they would be more receptive to him.

Once the posse was disbanded, Jack headed to the hotel to see if there were any messages for him. It frustrated him to learn that there weren't, and, more tense than ever, he went straight to the Garden of Eden Saloon. He got a bottle of whiskey and a glass from the barkeep and settled in at a table in the back of the saloon. He wasn't sure what he was going to do if Cody Jameson didn't show up to take the job. He had a lot of thinking—and drinking—to do.

The stagecoach rumbled into Del Fuego late that same night. After it rolled to a stop before the stage office, the driver jumped down to open the door for the passengers. A wizened, harmless-looking old Indian climbed down, followed by a well-dressed, pretty young woman. The man riding shotgun dropped the lady's trunk down to the waiting stage line employee, who toted the trunk to the hotel for her. No one noticed as the Indian slipped off down the street.

"Good evening. I need to register, please," Cody said as she came to stand at the desk.

"Evening, ma'am," the clerk greeted her as he put the ledger before her on the counter. "Will you be staying with us long, Miss . . . Jameson?"

"For at least a day or two. I'm not quite sure yet."

The clerk handed her the key to her room and quickly told her how to reach it.

"Thank you. By the way, is there a Mr. Logan staying here?"

"Yes, ma'am. Ranger Logan's in room 203, but he's not up there right now."

The news that he was a Ranger surprised her. She wondered why a Ranger wanted to hire a bounty hunter. "When he comes in, would you please give him my room number and tell him that Cody Jameson is waiting to hear from him?"

"I sure will, but it might be late."

"That doesn't matter. I'll be up."

Cody retired to her room to await Jack Logan's arrival.

Jack was feeling little pain when he finally left the saloon and headed back to the hotel. Despite all the liquor he'd consumed, though, he still couldn't stop worrying about Luke. As he crossed the small hotel lobby, the clerk caught sight of him.

"Mr. Logan? I have a message for you."

Jack glanced at him quickly, his senses suddenly sobering.

"Cody Jameson has arrived in town and is waiting for you right now in room 211."

"Jameson's here?"

"Yes, sir. Came in on the late stage."

Jack nodded and made his way toward 211. His worries about Luke did not lessen as he headed to his rendezvous with the bounty hunter. He reached 211 and knocked.

"Can I help you?" Cody asked as she opened the door to find herself face-to-face with a tall, dark-haired, very handsome man.

"I'm sorry to bother you, ma'am. There must be some mistake. My name's Jack Logan, and the clerk at the desk told me that room 211 was Cody Jameson's room."

"It is."

"Oh." Jack suddenly felt awkward, wondering why Jameson had brought his wife along. True, she was one good-looking woman, with her auburn hair and sparkling green eyes, and any man in his right mind would want to have her around, but with the kind of work Jameson did, it seemed dangerous. "Well, I wanted to speak with Cody Jameson, if I could."

"Come in, Mr. Logan. I've been expecting you." Cody was smiling as she held the door open for him.

"You've been expecting me?" He moved into the

room, frowning in confusion.

Cody closed the door behind him. "I'm Cody Jameson, Mr. Logan, and I'm interested in hearing about the job you have for me."

"You're Jameson?" Suddenly he grinned as he stared at her. Now he understood a lot of what he'd heard about Cody Jameson—how few people had actually met him, but how effective he was at his job. No wonder! Jameson was a woman. Doubt shadowed his amusement, though, and his smile faded. "Miss Jameson . . . I know you're supposed to be one of the best bounty hunters, but I don't know if this is going to work."

"You know my reputation, don't you?" she asked icily, weary of always defending herself to men.

"Well, yes."

"Then I don't understand your problem. I take it there's someone you want brought in. That's what I do, and I do it very well."

Jack stared at her, seeing the strength in her regard and the calm way she was dealing with him. He realized she was more than up to the job. "All right, Cody Jameson, here's what I want you to do."

Jack told her only the most essential of information. That Majors had broken out of jail with the El Diablo gang, that the sheriff and deputy had been killed in the attempt, and that he wanted Majors delivered back to him—alive.

Cody went cold at the news that the lawmen had been slain. Her own father had been a sheriff who'd been murdered in a jailbreak. His death had been what had inspired her to take up bounty hunting.

"There's a big bounty on Majors. The town is offering a thousand dollars—dead or alive. But I will pay you an additional five hundred if you bring him to me here, alive."

"Why are you willing to pay me so much more?"

"I have doubts about Majors's guilt in any of this. I want to see justice done." Jack's expression was stony, revealing nothing. "It won't be served if he's hanged first and questions are asked later."

"Why is this man so important to you?" Cody asked suddenly.

Her question surprised Jack, and he realized then just how intelligent and perceptive she really was. He smiled wryly.

"You find something amusing about this, Mr. Logan?"

"Quite the contrary, Miss Jameson. I was just thinking how perfect you are for the job you've chosen. You're a worthy match for any man."

For the first time in ages, Cody found herself liking one of the men she had to deal with. "Thank you. Your attitude is refreshing."

His smile broadened with respect. "I hope you're as good as your reputation says you are. I need Majors brought in alive."

"I'll deliver Majors to you alive. You have my word on it."

Chapter Five

El Trajar was a wild town, full of saloons, demon liquor, loose women, gambling, and a lot of sinners who enjoyed each and every vice to the fullest. The well-known decadence and hostility of the place didn't deter Sister Mary's Salvation Show from coming to town, though. If there were souls the revivalist could claim, she intended to do just that.

Sister Mary's entrance into town stirred talk. The single wagon, the kind traveling salesmen used, had rumbled into El Trajar earlier that afternoon. The messages painted in bold red letters on the sides of the vehicle proclaimed salvation and justice at the hands of the Lord.

REPENT AND BE SAVED! one slogan read.

Another said, VENGEANCE IS MINE SAITH THE LORD!

And on the very rear of the wagon was painted, HALLELUJAH!

The prudish-looking, bespectacled woman of indiscriminate age who was driving, reined in before the busiest saloon in town, which was aptly named the Flames of Hell. Without a thought to her own personal safety, she climbed down from her wagon, grabbed up her Bible, and walked straight inside. She stood for a moment just inside the door, watching and waiting, her piercing green-eyed gaze sweeping over the sinners before her. Those inside were so caught up in enjoying themselves that they paid her no attention. Only when she started to shout at the top of her voice did they look up in amazement and irritation.

"Hear the word of the Lord! Only he can save you from the fate you're so actively courting! Save yourselves! Save your soul from eternal damnation! Repent, sinners! *Repent and be saved!*" Sister Mary marched straight back through the saloon, Bible in hand, exhorting the men and women there to clean up their lives.

"What'll it take to shut you up?" one cowboy asked. "How much do you want to go away? Five dollars? Ten?"

"I don't want your money! I want you!"

Raucous shouts of laughter surrounded them.

"She wants you, Willy!"

"Damn, I'd run if I were you, boy!"

The cowboy flushed hotly and did as the other

man had suggested, fleeing for another, quieter saloon.

"Get out of here, woman!" the barkeep bellowed. He made a threatening move toward the stalwart female, but to everyone's surprise, two of the dance-hall girls came to her defense.

"She's right, Henry. We are sinners," Lucy told him.

"Don't blame her for speaking the truth," the one named Gena offered.

Sister Mary gazed upon her two protectors and smiled at them warmly. "You are true angels of the Lord to come to my aid. Repent of your ways. Turn to God with your lives. Only with him will you find true happiness."

"It's too late for us, Sister." Lucy smiled at her in a kindly way.

"It's never too late. God always forgives—if you are truly sorry for your deeds."

Sister Mary looked both women in the eyes as she spoke. She saw the good-natured sadness in Lucy's expression, but she also saw a glimmer of hope in Gena's.

"Come to my show tonight, my children. I preach God's forgiveness and love." She spoke mainly to Gena, wanting to encourage the dark-haired, green-eyed beauty to forsake this sinful way of living.

"Love!" a drunken Sully bellowed from where he was sitting nearby. In a lurching move, he snared the preacher woman around the waist and pulled her unceremoniously onto his lap. "If it's love you're giving away tonight, then I'll be there, Sister!"

"You need to be!" she declared with dignity.

"If I'm a sinner, I might as well enjoy it!" He tried to fondle her, but Sister Mary reacted quickly. She managed to swing her Bible and thump him heavily on the head. She took him so by surprise that she was rewarded with her freedom for her effort. "The Lord's justice can be painful to those who do not heed his call!"

Those in the saloon had been laughing at her, but at her effective use of the Bible, silence reigned. Everyone knew how mean and ugly Sully could be when crossed. They waited to see what was going to happen.

"Tonight at eight o'clock. All sinners are welcome," she stated. Holding herself ramrod straight, she walked with dignity toward the door, her manner controlled and completely civilized in the midst of decadence.

"That was one ugly woman!" Sully snarled as she disappeared through the swinging doors.

Everyone started laughing again, relieved that he hadn't taken any action against her.

"She don't care if you think she's pretty or not. She just wants you to listen to her preach the word!"

"I'll give her the 'word,'" he went on, furious over being so humiliated in front of the crowd.

"Take it easy, Sully," Lucy said as she came to sit on his lap. "If you want a good time, I'm your girl. You don't need to worry none about Sister Mary. She wants your money to save your soul. I want your money to pleasure you. Which one sounds better?"

"Lucy, honey, you know which one sounds better to me. Let's go."

The fallen angel took the drunk upstairs.

Gena watched her friend lead him off, and she was glad Lucy had helped to distract him from his anger with the preacher woman. Sully could be real mean when he was drunked up, and Gena didn't want anything to happen to the good woman. Strange as it seemed, Gena knew that somehow she would sneak away tonight and be at the tent at eight o'clock—no matter what.

"How did it go?" Stalking Ghost asked when Cody joined him at the site of the revival.

A lifelong friend of her father's, Stalking Ghost was Cody's partner in bounty hunting. He provided her with information she couldn't get through her own sources, and he accompanied her on each trek, always staying quietly in the background. While she was in disguise, he was her eyes and her ears. He protected her, hovering ever near, like a guardian angel. On this trip, Cody had dropped him off at the edge of town before continuing on to the Flames of Hell. He'd taken the time to look around and familiarize himself with El Trajar. What he'd seen, he didn't like.

"It was wild in there. I was wishing I was openly armed with a gun instead of the Bible," Cody told him as she climbed down from the wagon.

His expression revealed some surprise. It wasn't often that she thought about carrying a weapon.

"You have worries about your plan?"

"Tonight could be dangerous," she began, then paused and shrugged. "But then, it's dangerous every time we do this."

He grunted in agreement and went about taking care of the horses. There was still a lot of work to be done. They had to set up the tent and the benches and get the torches ready to light the way. They only had a few hours left.

"I saw no sign of anyone even remotely resembling Luke Majors in the saloon." She drew the wanted poster Jack Logan had given her out of her purse to stare at it. If the artist's likeness was close, and Jack had said that it was, then Majors was a very handsome man. Handsome or not, though, he was a fast gun . . . a killer, and he was running with the El Diablo gang. Everyone knew how terrible they were. They were notorious for their savagery throughout west Texas.

"The hardest part will be getting him alone . . . if he shows up," she murmured thoughtfully. "There's no way to tell for certain that they'll be here. All we've got to go on is what we found out before we left San Antonio."

Cody was a stickler for getting all the information she could on her quarry before she began her hunt for him. She'd questioned her main source of information—her father's friend, Sheriff Nate Thompson—about the El Diablo gang at length. The information he'd supplied had been sketchy at best, and most of it she'd already known. The El Diablo gang were murderers and thieves. They took what they wanted, when they wanted, with

71

no concern about the consequences. They always seemed to know just when the next shipment of arms would be passing through on the way to one of the forts or when was the best time to rob the banks in the towns. They were coldly cruel. They would just as soon shoot someone as not. Wanting to know more, Cody had then sought out some of her father's less than savory acquaintances. While she'd been talking to them, Stalking Ghost had made his own inquiries. Between the two of them, the most reliable thing they'd been able to find out was that the gang regularly visited the town of El Trajar.

Cody knew it wouldn't be easy or pretty bringing Majors in, but for the money Logan was offering, it would be worth the effort. If he showed up in El Trajar, she was sure that somehow everything else would fall into place. She still had to figure out how she would get Majors alone, but the minute she did, Stalking Ghost would be there to help her subdue him. Then with a change of disguises, they'd be on their way—before any of the gang realized he was missing. It would be tricky, but she was confident she could pull it off. After all, she reflected as she adjusted her glasses, she did have the town convinced that her fire-and-brimstone preaching was real.

"So, when will El Diablo be meeting up with us?" Luke asked the man he knew only as Hadley as they sat together at a back table in the Flames of Hell. Since joining the gang in their box canyon hideout after the jailbreak, Luke had been very careful to keep a low profile. He'd known they hadn't trusted him completely, so he'd done nothing to rouse their suspicions. El Diablo had yet to make an appearance in the camp, but from what Luke had been able to figure out, Hadley was the man closest to the outlaw leader.

Hadley stared straight at Luke, his gray-eyed gaze hard and challenging. "All in good time, my friend. El Diablo is busy with many things. Why the rush?"

Luke shrugged; he did not look away from the other man's regard, for he did not want to give him any reason to doubt him. "No rush. I've just heard so much about him, I wanted to meet him."

The outlaw nodded, but said no more.

Frustrated, but not showing it, Luke settled in for some heavy drinking. He hoped the whiskey would take the edge off the disgust he was feeling. He cursed the series of events that had thrust him into this brotherhood of murderers. The only thing he was thankful for as he sat there surrounded by El Diablo's henchmen was that he'd been able to save Sheriff Gregory's life during the breakout.

He stared around at the Flames of Hell and wondered how he'd come to this. The saloon was a hellhole, just like the town it was in. It was lawless and wild, filthy and decadent.

Luke took a stiff drink of his whiskey. In the two weeks he'd been riding with the gang, he'd done everything they'd asked of him. The day before they'd robbed a stage. Luke had hated being a part of it, but there had been no way out. He'd been relieved when no one had been killed. It was one thing to infiltrate the gang for Jack. It was another to watch innocent people shot down.

The robbery had gone so smoothly that Hadley had suggested they come to El Trajar to celebrate. So Luke sat there, watching and listening, waiting for someone to give him some clue to the mysterious El Diablo's identity so he could get out of there. Had it really been only a few weeks before that he'd believed he could live a civilized life, that he could raise cattle and grow crops? If he'd been alone, he would have laughed at his own naivete. Instead, he downed more whiskey.

It was growing late. The members of the gang were still drinking heavily. Most had forgotten about Sully's earlier incident with the preacher woman, until his slurred, drunken voice boomed across the room.

"I think we should run her outta town!" Sully shouted, still angry. The more he'd thought about the way she'd treated him, the more he wanted to teach the arrogant woman a lesson. He wanted to see her on her knees begging for forgiveness from *him*.

"Aw, hush up, Sully. Have another drink," Lucy coaxed. "That Sister Mary ain't hurtin' nobody. She was tryin' to help ya."

Sully was in a mean mood. "She ain't nothing but a little slut, just like you!"

At his insult, Lucy grew angry. She stepped closer so her words would have greater impact on him.

"You listen to me," she said in a low, almost

threatening voice. "That woman is brave and pure. If there are low women like me in this world, it's because of men like you. If no men wanted it, then women wouldn't have to provide it, would they?"

"Barkeep, give me a double whiskey!" He drunkenly shoved Lucy away from him, ignoring her. He didn't need to hear anything good about the preacher woman. She had embarrassed him in front of everyone, and he was going to pay her back. "After I finish this drink off, I think I'm gonna go get saved."

"You want some more Bible thumpin' tonight, Sully? I thought you might have had enough for one night!" a drunken Carson taunted, then guffawed at his own humor.

Sully drew his gun. Had he been of a mind, he might have shot Carson right then and there for his remark, but he had more important things to do.

"I was just jokin', Sully," the other outlaw said quickly, suddenly nervous.

Sully didn't answer; he just checked to see that the revolver was loaded. He downed the rest of his whiskey. "I want me a piece of that bitch, and I'm going to get it."

Luke had witnessed the earlier exchange between Sully and the woman named Sister Mary from where he'd been sitting in the back of the room. When he heard what was going on now and saw the other man draw his gun, he knew he couldn't just sit there and do nothing. He rose from the table and claimed a spot at the end of the bar.

"All right. I think I'm ready for a little revivin'," Sully announced. "You comin' with me, Carson?"

"Sure, Sully." He was relieved that Sully wasn't going to pick a fight with him. "Let's go have us some fun with Sister Mary."

"She might talk like an old prude, but I bet there's one helluva hot woman inside those cold pants of hers. Let's go find out."

Luke saw just how ugly Sully's mood was and knew the revivalist was going to be in for some trouble. He hoped she had a guard with her, someone to protect her from roughs like these two.

"You know, it isn't my place to try to tell you what to do, but—"

"You're right about that, Majors." Sully's expression was hard. He didn't like this fast gun that Carson and Jones had brought into the gang, and he wasn't shy about letting everyone know it.

"But this Sister Mary is a good woman. She's a woman of God."

He snorted in derision. "She's a slut, just like the rest of 'em. It don't matter none that she carries a Bible with her. Women are all the same," he sneered. "Just pieces of ass. That's all they're good for."

Luke stiffened at his crudeness. He had been raised to respect women. Even Clarissa's betrayal had not darkened his feelings for the fairer sex. His mother had been a genteel woman of class and elegance. Women needed and deserved men's protection.

"Sully ain't never met a good woman in his life,"

Jones joked from where he still sat at one of the tables with a saloon girl perched on his lap.

"Good for what?" Sully came back at him, swilling more whiskey as he prepared to raid the salvation show. He glared at Majors. "If you think women are pure and chaste, you're a fool, Majors. Those kind don't exist. Every woman's a whore at heart. Some are honest and sell it for money. Some sell it for a wedding ring. Ain't no difference between them."

Luke took a casual drink as he watched Sully. He tried to ignore what the other man was saying, but with each slur his hatred for Sully grew. Luke knew Sully was a longtime member of the gang. He knew he himself had only just been accepted into the inner fold and that there was still some distrust among the others about him. He knew he should play it easy and keep quiet, but there was no way he could let Sully hurt an innocent woman like Sister Mary. He had seen much ugliness in his lifetime. He could put up with a lot personally if he had to. But he would not stand by and let anything happen to an innocent woman.

"Let's stay here," Luke suggested, trying to distract Sully from his need for revenge. "Let's get drunk and maybe play some poker. That's what we came into town for. If God wants that preacher woman to preach, let her. Maybe no one will show up, and she'll move on."

Sully turned viciously on him. "Maybe I don't want her to move on! I kinda had a hankering to get a taste of her. She was a spirited one. I like taming them kind." His eyes were glowing with a fierce inner need to seek out the woman and punish her in all the ways he knew how—and he knew many.

Luke drank deeply of his whiskey as he realized there would be no distracting Sully. He tried to figure out what to do. He couldn't overpower him, not with all his friends gathered around. He was just going to have to follow along and keep watch.

Chapter Six

The size of the crowd that gathered at Sister Mary's tent on the outskirts of El Trajar was surprising.

"Brothers! Sisters!" Sister Mary shouted above the noise of the crowd. "The Lord is pleased by your presence here."

And Cody was pleased, too. She would never have guessed that nearly a hundred people would show up for her show.

"Your presence here proves that there are God-fearing people living in this pit of Satan—people who believe in the promises of the Bible . . . people who believe in the punishments of the Lord. You are saved, brothers and sisters! Hallelujah! Say Amen!"

"Amen," the crowd repeated.

"We have here with us tonight a lost soul . . . a woman whose heart is filled with love and who seeks God's forgiveness so she can start a new life! Sister Gena, stand so the good folks can see you."

Cody had been shocked when the young woman had come up to her just before she'd begun preaching and introduced herself. She looked nothing like she had when they'd met earlier in the saloon. Gena had washed off all her makeup and had brushed out her hair and tied the dark, thick mass of curls back with a simple bow. She'd donned a demure dress and looked for all the world like someone's pretty young sister. Gone was the woman who made a living selling drinks, among other things, to men at the Flames of Hell saloon. Gena had chosen to forsake that life. She had come to Sister Mary because she'd been impressed by the other woman's courage in coming into the saloon. Cody could not fail her.

Gena blushed hotly at being so singled out, but trusting Sister Mary, she did as she'd been bid.

"Tell everyone your name and why you've come here."

"My name is Gena Mager. I've come because I want to live a better life."

"Do you believe, Sister Gena?"

"I believe," she said tentatively, frightened by the step she was taking, but emboldened by the preacher woman's kindness and support.

"Do you believe?" Cody repeated, wanting to hear her shout it louder.

"I believe!" Gena answered with more force and conviction.

"Will you folks of El Trajar help this young woman to live a godly life?"

"We will!" the crowd shouted, amazed at the change in the girl and, in their hearts, wanting the best for her.

"Say hallelujah!"

"Hallelujah," they echoed her lead.

Gena did believe, and tears filled her eyes. Never again would she have to suffer the ugliness and degradation of working in the saloon. She would go back to the Flames of Hell only long enough to claim her few belongings, and then she would leave and never look back.

"Let us pray," Sister Mary encouraged. Her voice carried far and was filled with power.

As Sully and the others left the bar and started toward the revival, they could hear the sound of her preaching.

"Lord, save us from the fires of Hell. Lord, keep us free of the temptations of this world. Fill our souls with the power to turn away from sin. Fill our hearts with the desire to follow you, to do what is chaste and pure and good. Oh, Lord save us! Say Amen!"

"Amen!" the townsfolk prayed.

Sully listened to her sermonizing and grew even angrier. He didn't need any damned woman telling him he was a sinner. There wasn't a god, and there wasn't any hell. Heaven and hell were right here on earth. He quickened his pace. He wanted to watch her in action. He wanted to see how she reacted to his presence in the crowd. He wanted to humiliate her as she had humiliated him. He was going to enjoy this.

Luke stayed close as they headed for the clearing at the edge of town where the revival was being held. As they neared the site, he was surprised by the size of the crowd. The tent was full and the overflow of people were gathered around as close as they could get to the small stage at the front.

He turned his gaze toward the stage and the woman preaching there. Sister Mary stood at the center of the platform. She wore a plain, almost stark, black, long-sleeved, high-necked dress, its only ornamentation simple white cuffs and a matching collar. Her hair was pinned back in a tight bun at the nape of her neck. But though she did nothing to enhance her womanly features, there was something charismatic about her as she stood before the audience, Bible in hand, exhorting them to forsake their evil ways and live more God-centered lives.

Luke almost allowed himself to get caught up in her preaching, but then he caught sight of Sully moving closer to the stage. Luke forgot all about the power of Sister Mary's words. The only soul he was worried about saving right then was hers from the hell-bent-on-vengeance outlaw.

Luke glanced around and was surprised to see an Indian standing off to the side by her wagon. He was watching the crowd carefully, keeping track of all that transpired, and Luke wondered if he was with her. The Indian wasn't armed, and Luke wasn't sure if that was good or bad. If there was trouble with Sully, he might need help.

Luke kept hoping that Sully would just sit down and be quiet, but he knew that was doubtful. If Sully had something to say, he said it, and most of what came out of his mouth was pure stupidity.

Luke found a place to stand at the back of the tent that gave him a good view of everything that was going on. Pretending interest in Sister Mary's sermon, he leaned one shoulder against an upright pole and folded his arms across his chest as he kept watch. His gaze followed the woman who'd taken Sully on earlier and won as she moved back and forth before the crowd. Her speaking ability was amazing, for she inspired and entranced the crowd. Luke admired her courage; it took a hardy soul to do what she did.

The more Luke watched her, though, the more he realized that there was something else about her that intrigued him. He wasn't quite sure what it was, but he couldn't take his eyes off of her. Sister Mary was tall, but not overly so. With her severe hairstyle and wire-rimmed glasses, she was definitely plain-looking. Her figure beneath the stark gown was not lacking . . . in fact, it was quite womanly, and Luke wondered vaguely what she would look like without the glasses and with her hair brushed out around her shoulders.

At the direction of his thoughts, Luke got angry with himself. Sister Mary was obviously a good woman, untouched by man, and he wanted her to stay that way. He remembered Sully's lustful thoughts toward her, and grimaced. He didn't like to think that he was little better than the man he was trying to protect her from.

"Say Amen!" the preacher woman cried.

Her loud call jerked Luke back to reality.

"Amen, Sister!"

"Say, 'Sister! I want salvation!' "

Sully pushed his way to the front.

"Sister! Can you save my soul?" The hatred in his sneering voice was obvious.

A murmur went through the worshipers. They knew Sully and the gang, and they knew just how savage they could be. Everyone tensed as he approached the stage.

Luke straightened and watched the scene being played out before him. Sister Mary reminded him of a deer transfixed by a predator in the woods.

"Only you can save your soul, brother," Sister Mary said, recognizing the drunk from the saloon. She stood her ground, not giving in to the terror that threatened. She tightened her grip on her Bible. Stalking Ghost was near, and she hoped he was ready to help should she need him.

"But I thought you saved souls," Sully pressed, licking his thick lips in anticipation of carrying her off and teaching her a little humility of her own.

"I can show you the path to righteousness." She held the Bible aloft. "You have to be open to the word of God and choose his path. But only you can make the choice. You must choose to do the right thing. You must choose to live righteously or be condemned to the fires of Hell for all eternity."

"How about condemning me to the Flames of Hell?" He guffawed. "Then I could spend eternity being happy in the saloon drinking! What d'ya think?" He closed in on her.

A gasp went up from around them.

"There is no salvation in demon liquor! There is only degeneration and disgust. There is only sin and sorrow in drunkenness. Let the wine of the Lord's words be your spirits. Let the happiness of the Holy Spirit fill you and lift your heart to a higher joy than you've ever known."

Cody didn't pray often, but she was really praying right then—praying for a way to get Sully out of there without trouble. The townsfolk looked cowed, and she didn't blame them. He looked like the kind of man who killed and maimed for pleasure.

Her gaze swept the tent, seeking a way out, seeking help, and it was then that she saw him—Luke Majors. She went stock-still at the sight of him, standing in the back of the tent watching her, his expression inscrutable.

Luke Majors looked like the devil incarnate, she thought as she stared at him. He was tall, lean, and darkly handsome, and there was a compelling aura of power about him. A shiver of anticipation ran down her spine. Instinctively, Cody knew bringing him in was going to be one of the hardest things she'd ever done. But right now . . .

"C'mon, Sister Mary. What's it going to be? Eternal damnation or eternal salvation?" Sully shouted up at her as he reached the foot of the stage.

Cody wanted to scream in frustration. Majors was there! Yet she had to force her attention back to the drunk. She'd been desperate to find Majors, then to isolate and capture him. Now here he was right before her very eyes, and damned if she wasn't surrounded by a crowd and being attacked by this fool at the same time. She hoped Majors didn't disappear while she handled Sully. She wanted Majors, and she was going to get him.

As frustrating a moment as it was for Cody, the knowledge that her sources of information had once again paid off pleased her. She'd found the gunfighter more quickly than she'd ever thought she would. She would trap him and get him back to Logan just as fast as she could, but first she had to deal with Sully.

"It shall be salvation, brother. Come forward and let me anoint you with the blessing of the Lord." She focused on the troublemaker, wanting to get him out of her way.

"I want more than anointing from you." He leered up at her.

"Behold, a sinner," she announced to the crowd as he started to climb up on the stage. "Come, brethren, lay hands upon this man and ask that the demons who haunt him—the demon desire for liquor and the demon of lust—be driven from him!"

Cody didn't know where the idea had come from to call upon the congregation to help her, but it worked. The crowd stood and came forward en masse to surround the drunken outlaw.

"What the hell?" Sully snarled as they closed in on him just as he was about to reach her. "Get away from me!"

"Pray, friends, for this man's tortured soul. Pray

for his life that he may seek the ways of the Lord. Pray that he sees the light!"

"Get the hell away from me!" he shouted. His expression was full of hatred at being outwitted by her again. He retreated quickly, elbowing his way through the gathering and storming off toward the saloon.

Cody offered up a silent prayer of thanksgiving. She'd been saved. She looked up, wanting to see if Majors was still there, and to her surprise he was. He caught her gaze and reached up to tip the brim of his hat toward her in salute for her quick thinking.

Cody felt herself flush at his action. She quickly turned back to her preaching. When she glanced up again, Majors was gone. She wasn't sure whether to be glad she'd avoided the confrontation with Sully or to be angry because she'd missed a chance to get her man. At least she'd found him. Now it was just a matter of trapping him, getting him back to Jack Logan, and collecting her reward.

Sully had been angry when he'd gone to the salvation show, but now he was downright furious. His sodden mind was racing as he tried to figure out just what he was going to do to pay the little bitch back. The townspeople might have protected her once, but they weren't going to be around forever. He would bide his time until the prayer service was over; then he'd go back and see about being "saved." He followed Carson into the Flames of Hell and went to stand at the bar and order another drink.

"Were you saved?" Lucy asked as she came to him.

He smiled coldly at her. "There ain't no saving this soul of mine."

Lucy laughed, thinking he was teasing. "I could have told you that, Sully."

Sully drank more whiskey. An hour later, he was ready. Though he was unsteady on his feet, it didn't matter because what he had planned to do, he was going to do on horseback.

"Carson, I got an idea. You want to have some fun?"

"Sure," the drunken Carson answered. "But I was already having fun here." He had a girl on each knee and had been enjoying himself immensely.

"I mean real fun."

"Doing what?"

"I want to go back to the preacher woman. I want to rile her up a little bit."

"But why? There's women here who want you. Why do you want to mess with that one?"

"I didn't ask for your damned opinion! I asked if you wanted to have some fun."

Carson knew how hot Sully's temper was, and he didn't want to fight him. He knew Sully wasn't about to rest until he'd taught that woman a lesson, so he might as well go with him and get it over with.

"All right. Girls, will ya wait for me?" he asked the two beauties he was holding.

"You bet, Carson. We'll keep your place here nice and hot for you." The girls laughed, and each kissed him passionately before he stood.

Luke had been playing poker, winning some and losing some. It had been a quiet night since they'd returned from the salvation show, and that had been just fine with him. But when he saw Sully start for the door with Carson following him, he knew they were up to something. Luke threw in his hand and went up to the bar.

"Where are Sully and Carson going?" he asked the barkeep.

"He's still got that Sister Mary on his mind. She never should have given him any trouble earlier. He is one mean son of a bitch."

"You got a sheriff in town?"

"Yeah, but he's useless. I think the little lady's in for a rough time."

Luke swore under his breath. He hurried to follow the two from the bar and saw that they'd already mounted up and were riding toward the tent. They'd drawn their guns.

The tent still held a few people who'd lingered after the service to speak privately with Sister Mary. Their presence didn't deter Sully. He was ready.

As Sister Mary stood talking on the stage with young Gena, Sully put his heels to his horse and urged it to a gallop. He rode straight at the tent, firing his gun wildly as he went. Carson followed his lead. Horses tied nearby whinnied in fright, and people scrambled frantically to get out of his way. Cody saw the two men coming and knew a moment of fear.

"It's Sully!" Gena told her, grabbing her hand in terror.

"Where's the sheriff?" Cody asked Gena.

"The sheriff doesn't do anything but hide when these men are in town. They're the El Diablo gang, you know. When they're here, most folks just stay indoors."

"You go on and get out of here," Cody said.

"Are you sure you'll be all right? You should get in your wagon and stay there till they're gone!"

Cody patted her hand, knowing how brave Gena was to have done what she'd done that day. "Thank you for caring. Go on now. Save yourself."

Gena gave the preacher woman an impulsive hug and then rushed off.

Cody moved to stand near the wagon with Stalking Ghost. She held her Bible tightly as they watched Sully ride through the tent, knocking over chairs, ravaging the place. Carson followed right behind him.

Stalking Ghost started to get a gun out of the wagon, but Cody shook her head, not wanting to risk anybody getting shot. She'd dealt with drunks of Sully's kind before, but usually they slept it off. It looked like the drunker this one got, the meaner he got. The thought that she'd created an enemy didn't please her. Majors was the man she was after, but after watching Sully in action, she knew it would give her great pleasure to put him away for a long time, too.

"Sister Mary! I want to be saved. Come and save

me," Sully shouted at her. "Or am I too far gone for you?"

"I'd better go talk to him," she muttered to Stalking Ghost. She knew this one wasn't going to go away until she came forward.

"Don't," Stalking Ghost warned.

"I have to. There's nowhere to run. I don't think he'll hurt me, but get a gun and keep it on us just in case."

He nodded, then advised, "Take the Bible with you."

Knowing it just might save her life, she clutched the Good Book to her breast as she stepped boldly forward.

"I'm here, Brother Sully," she stated. "Why have you torn apart the house of the Lord? Are you here doing the devil's work?"

"I'm here to teach you a lesson, woman." He rode toward her.

"The Lord works in strange ways, sir. If you venture any closer, you'll find that a gun is trained on you."

He laughed. "If you're talking about your Indian friend, well, I got news for you. I got him covered; he ain't covering me."

Cody glanced back to find Carson standing behind Stalking Ghost, his gun on him.

"Now, missy, I don't like your highfalutin' ways. I think you need to come to the saloon and have a few drinks with us. Maybe I can convert you to my way of thinkin'."

"Your offer is kind, but I have already visited that den of iniquity once and that was more than enough. I want no trouble from you, brother. I want only to preach the Lord's saving word. Your soul is in need of cleansing."

She stood there looking so prim and proper, so pious and righteous, that Sully's fury erupted. With a snarled oath, he rode for her, intending to grab her up and throw her across his horse in front of him.

Suddenly, to his shock, another rider charged past him.

"Let me go!" Cody shrieked as the strong arm of the unknown rider snared her around the waist. She twisted and fought the man's grip as he hauled her up with him. As he fought to control both her and the horse, she twisted around to get a look at the man who'd dared to accost her. "You!" she gasped as she stared into the mesmerizing blue-eyed gaze of Luke Majors, the man she'd vowed to capture and bring to justice.

"Hold it, Majors!" Sully shouted. "The preacher woman's mine!"

"Sorry, Sully. You took too long. She's one feisty little spitfire, and I'm claiming her for my own."

"You bastard! I've waited all day for this!"

Luke wheeled his horse around so he was facing the outlaw. He slipped Sister Mary farther across his lap, so his right hand was free to go for his gun.

"She's mine, unless you feel like fighting over her." Luke paused to look down at her. Her face was smudged with dirt. Her hair was coming loose from the bun. Her glasses were askew, and she was still clutching her Bible to her breast. "But she doesn't look like she'd be that good that she'd be worth dying over. What do you think?"

"You ain't got no right—"

"I got her. What right do I need? You saying she's your woman?"

"I wanted her first."

"But I've got her," Luke repeated.

"I could take her from you!"

"Go right ahead and try," he said in a steely voice as he drew his gun in a lightning move. "But that might not be smart."

Cody gasped at the speed of his draw.

For a minute, Sully had been drunk enough to think he could take him on. But as he stared down the barrel of Luke's gun, he suddenly sobered.

"Well, Sully?" Luke deliberately goaded him, wanting to push him to the limit right now while he was facing him. "What's it going to be?"

"You'll pay for this one of these days, Majors."

"Just let me know when, Sully. For now, Sister Mary's mine. You'll have to look somewhere else for your fun."

Chapter Seven

Sully rode away, leaving the revival site in a shambles. He was quiet now, and those who knew him knew he was most dangerous at times like these.

Carson quickly mounted up, leaving Stalking Ghost sprawled on the ground unconscious near the wagon. When Sully had charged forward to grab the woman, the Indian had started to go to her aid and Carson had been forced to hit him from behind.

Carson had thought about challenging Majors when he was facing down Sully, but after witnessing the speed of the other man's draw, he'd quickly changed his mind. There were few men alive who could beat that draw. The gunfighter's reputation had been well earned. He was one dangerous man. Sully would think of some way to get back at him, Carson was sure. As Carson rode off, he did not look back.

Holding the preacher woman before him on his saddle, Luke waited until both men were out of sight.

"They're gone," Cody breathed, relieved. "You can let me down now, friend. I thank you for your help."

"The name's Majors, Luke Majors, and sorry, Sister Mary, but you're not going anywhere," Luke told her. He turned his mount in the direction opposite the one Sully and Carson had taken and headed out of town.

"Wait a minute!" When Cody realized that he was taking her off somewhere, she started to struggle in earnest against his restraining hold. Until that moment she'd appreciated his help. Things had gotten out of hand, and he'd saved her from Sully. But now she quickly wondered if she'd gone from the frying pan into the fire. It was one thing for her to be taking Luke Majors in. It was another entirely for Luke Majors to be taking her somewhere. She'd heard what kind of man he was. "You can't do this!"

He chuckled as he pinned her tightly against his chest to still her squirming. "Who's going to stop me?"

It was then, as they rode past the wagon, that Cody caught sight of Stalking Ghost lying unmoving in the dirt.

"Stalking Ghost!" There was real horror in her voice as she stared at her friend. "Sir, if you have a drop of Christian kindness in your heart, you must release me! I must see to my friend! He's injured. He may be dying."

Luke's answer was to knee his horse to a quicker pace.

"Let me go!" she demanded, trying to break free.

"No, you're with me now." Luke's grip was an iron restraint around her waist, stifling her struggles.

"Do you want to go to Hell, sir?" Cody realized the fruitlessness of her efforts, and so drew upon her character to try to convince him to free her.

"I'm already there," Luke answered as he reined in to look back toward the revival site. One of the torches had fallen and had fired the tent. The red flames cast a devilish glow over the night.

She went still at the sight, then turned to look up at him over her shoulder. Earlier that night, she had thought him handsome, but now in the strange light his features appeared harsh and unfeeling. Cody feared what she'd gotten herself into. She was glad she had the Bible with her. It might prove to be her saving grace after all.

"It's not too late to save your soul." She hoped to talk her way free.

"It's too late to worry about my soul. I lost it years ago. It's your soul I'm worrying about."

"Mine?" She frowned. "If you're concerned about me, then let me go. Sully's gone. I'll take care of Stalking Ghost, and we'll be fine."

Luke shot her a look of disgust. "Do you want to stay alive to see the sunrise, Sister Mary? Sully may not be here right now, but he's not the type of man to give up on something he wants, and believe me, he wants you."

Cody paled at his blunt statement. "But Stalking Ghost—"

"Can take care of himself," he said grimly. He saw her distress and was glad that she was finally realizing what she was involved in. "Sully likes to take his revenge slow. You humiliated him in the saloon. He didn't take kindly to that. If I let you go right now, he'd be on you before you could get your wagon out of town. And from the looks of things, your Indian friend wouldn't be much help."

Cody shivered, silently praying that Stalking Ghost was all right. She clutched the Bible closer. "I was only trying to bring him to God. Why is he so intent on harming me?"

"Why do evil men do the things they do?" He shrugged. "You're the one in the business of saving souls. If you managed to save his, I bet you'd be guaranteed a place in heaven."

"Can't you just let me down somewhere? I'll hide until he's gone."

"He's not going to give up that easy. He's got the single-mindedness of a . . . never mind." He stopped himself from using too base a term for her gentle spirit. "Let's just put it this way, Sister Mary: you're safest with me."

"But I don't want to be with you!" she protested.

Luke was frustrated. All he was trying to do was a good deed. "Look, lady, you're not exactly my cup of tea, either. I like my women younger and prettier and a helluva lot more fun. Your virtue is definitely safe with me. But if you want to stay alive, then you'd damn well better do everything I tell you to do."

"Please don't use such vile language with me, sir. Using foul language to make one's point is the mark of an inferior intellect."

"Listen to me, preacher woman. If foul language was all you had to worry about right now, you'd be in great shape. I can't believe you thought that one Indian was going to keep you safe in a town like this. There's no way that one old man could protect you from the El Diablo gang."

"And you think you can?" she challenged.

"I'm one of them."

She gasped at his statement and twisted around to look up at him. "If you're one of them, why are you trying to protect me? Won't they turn against you for taking me?"

"I've held my own against worse, but it hasn't been pretty or easy."

"But—"

"If you want to stay alive, sit still," Luke commanded, bringing her firmly back against him. He felt the resistance in her, and smiled to himself. Sister Mary was a fighter.

"I appreciate your gallantry and kindness toward me, Mr. Majors."

"Luke."

"Luke. But where are you taking me?" she asked, deliberately holding herself as stiffly as she could so she wouldn't be leaning against him as they rode. It wasn't comfortable, but comfort was the last thing on her mind. There was no way she could allow herself to relax—not now, and probably not again for a long time.

"Away from El Trajar," he replied evasively. "I want you where I know he won't try anything."

"Where's that?"

"You'll see."

"How long are you going to keep me your prisoner?"

"If you ask me any more questions, I'll dump you right here and leave you for Sully. Do you understand?" Luke had had enough. How he'd gotten stuck being nursemaid to a traveling salvation-show preacher was beyond him. All he wanted to do was identify El Diablo and get the hell . . . er, heck out of there.

At the realization that he'd amended his thoughts because of her, Luke grimaced inwardly. The last thing he needed was this puny little Bible-thumper complicating his plans. He was sure he was a wanted man right now, and he wanted to put an end to that before someone put an end to him. He had to get the information he needed out of the gang and get back to Jack.

Cody was angry, but her anger was directed more at herself than anything. If only she hadn't annoyed Sully that afternoon, everything would have worked out just fine. Luke Majors had been in El Trajar, and she'd have had him by now. It was too late for "if onlys," though. This was the hand she'd been dealt, so this was the one she'd have to play.

Cody had to admit that in a perverse way she'd

gotten what she wanted. She had Luke Majors all to herself. But even if the opportunity arose and she did manage to knock him out and tie him up, without Stalking Ghost's help she wouldn't be able to move him. Plus, except for her Bible, all of her things were in the wagon back in town. She was stuck. She was going to have to play the role of Sister Mary for now. The thought did not appeal, but that reward was a lot of money.

Mentally girding herself for the challenges to come, Cody continued to hold herself rigidly away from Luke. She had to admit that the fact that he even cared what happened to her surprised her, and now as he kept her in the saddle before him, his hold was neither painful nor lecherous. Given their situation, he was being quite mindful of her, and she found it puzzling for a man of his repute.

Cody decided that it was good that he didn't desire her. If he'd tried something, she would have been forced to take action, and she couldn't do that. She had promised Logan that she'd bring him in alive, and she would.

Lost deep in thought, she frowned slightly. Certainly she didn't want him to desire her. He was Luke Majors. He was an outlaw. Still, his statement about liking prettier, younger women had stung. It was one thing to play the role of Sister Mary for a few hours before the crowds as she preached. It was another to live it for days on end without reprieve. She was definitely going to be earning her money this time.

They rode on in silence at a steady, ground-eating pace.

"Don't you want to get rid of the Bible?" Luke finally asked, noting how stiffly she was holding herself and how she was clutching the book to her breast.

"No!" She managed to sound outraged at his suggestion. "The Lord's word is my salvation and my protection. This Bible has saved me from more than your weapon has ever saved you. I can never be parted from it. It was a gift from my dear father, who is now deceased."

"Was he a minister, too?"

"In his own way. He tried to right the wrongs of the world and help people, but sometimes people don't want to be helped."

"You're right about that," Luke remarked, thinking of the bank robbery and how drawing his gun to save the tellers had ended him up in jail.

They fell silent again as they continued on. Luke did not want to rest until they were safely back at the gang's canyon hideaway. Only then would he allow himself to relax.

It happened as Luke had feared it would. About an hour out of town, he heard the sound of horses coming after them at a rapid pace, and he knew instinctively who it was. He rode to the top of a small bluff and reined to wait. Within minutes, Hadley, Sully, Carson, and the others appeared below.

"Evening, gentlemen. Anything I can help you with?" Luke called down.

They stopped abruptly, their weary horses rearing in protest at the rough handling.

"We were just trying to catch up with you," Carson said.

"Fine. You found us. I want to make camp before dawn, so you go on and we'll follow right behind you."

The men grumbled to themselves. Sully had told them that Majors was probably taking Sister Mary just a little ways out of town, where he would use her and then let her go. They had intended to follow him and then take her for themselves. It irritated them that Sully had been wrong. Obviously Majors really did want to keep her. It was going to be a lot more difficult than Sully had thought to get her away from him, and the one thing they didn't want was trouble with Majors. They weren't about to risk a gunfight over her. She just wasn't worth it. They were a tense, angry group as they rode on.

Cody was shocked that Sully had followed so quickly. Everything Majors had told her was true. Again she wondered at his motives. If he was the cold-blooded killer everyone said he was, why was he so worried about her? Did he really fear the Lord? Was there good inside him or did he have an ulterior motive she couldn't fathom?

As she looked ahead at the others, Cody found suddenly that the supportive strength of Luke's arm around her was comforting and not binding. His nearness left her feeling safe, not endangered. The thought amazed her, but still she did not lean back against him. Instead she held herself away from him, reminding herself that while he might be a little better than the others, he was still a killer. It was near dawn when exhaustion claimed her and she finally sagged back against him.

Luke's deep voice chuckled in her ear. "I wondered how long you could hold yourself that way, Sister Mary."

Cody was too weary to take the bait and quarrel with him. She closed her eyes and, still holding the Bible close, prayed for the strength and wits to see herself through this dilemma. She prayed, too, for Stalking Ghost.

They reached the canyon just at dawn. Luke was exhausted, but he wasn't about to let his guard down until he was certain Sully was going to leave them alone. They followed the others past the guards at the narrow entrance to the canyon; then Luke headed for the one-room adobe house that had been given to him when he'd joined the gang. The others went on to their own homes, but Sully paused to look back and glare at Luke.

Luke returned his regard, then said in a low, threatening voice, "She's mine, and what's mine, I keep."

"We'll see about that, Majors." Then he was gone.

Luke swung down from his horse and reached up to take Sister Mary in his arms.

"Don't touch me! I can dismount myself!"

She all but threw herself from the horse's back trying to avoid his touch, but in the end his overwhelming strength won out. She was unceremoniously dumped on her feet on the ground next to him.

"Don't try my patience too much." His words

were hard. "Now get inside, while I take care of the horse."

Cody stared up at him. He was a hard, arrogant, demanding man, and she knew it was going to take all her wits to outsmart him. Playing the role of the prudish preacher, she obeyed his command, but with her head held high.

Once inside the structure, she took a look around. It wasn't pretty. There was a narrow bed shoved against one wall, a table and two chairs, and that was it. Cody was used to roughing it, but there were days like today when she would have liked to have been disguised as the Queen of Sheba so she could enjoy a little luxury for a change. She poked warily at the bed with its unwashed blanket and was pleased when nothing crawled out of it. It looked infinitely softer than the chairs did, so she sat down on it to await Majors's return.

Luke tended his horse, then returned to the house carrying his rifle with him. He stopped in the doorway to stare at her where she sat on the bed. Cody looked up at him, and when she did, she was suddenly painfully aware of where she was sitting. She jumped to her feet. The last thing she wanted him to think about was going to bed.

"You took care of the horse?"

"Yes, and now it's time to take care of you."

"What do you mean?" Her eyes widened as she watched him cross the room toward her. She swallowed nervously. He had said her virtue was safe with him. Had he been lying? Her hands tightened on the Bible, which she refused to put down.

"Just this." He put his hands on her shoulders and gently directed her back to the bed. "Go to sleep. You need some rest."

"But it's sunup. What are you going to do?"

"I'm going to sleep, too."

"And just where are you going to sleep?"

Luke smiled at her. "Right beside you, and right next to me is going to be this rifle."

"You won't need it! I won't try to run away!"

He gave a short, harsh laugh. "I'm not keeping it close to use on you. I'm keeping it close to protect you. Now lie down and be quiet. I'm tired. It's been one long night, and the day promises to be even longer. We need to sleep while we can."

"All right." She acquiesced, scooting as far away from him as she could. She lay against the wall, stiff as a board.

"There is one thing you have to do, though."

"What?" she managed in a voice that was little more than a whisper. She thought he was going to demand that she undress, and she wondered what to do if he did.

Luke gave her a mocking smile. "All I want you to do is to put the Bible down."

"Is that all?" Cody practically beamed at him, for she'd feared the worst.

For a minute as she smiled so brightly at him, Luke was surprised to find that he almost thought her pretty. But then he blinked and she was once again mousy and bespectacled.

"Bless you."

And Bible spouting, he added in his thoughts. He told himself he must have been just tired and in desperate need of rest to have thought her attractive even for a moment. "Go to sleep."

She eagerly put the book between herself and the wall, and then lay perfectly still as he stretched out beside her.

Luke wanted to sleep, needed to sleep, and he would allow himself to doze for a while, but he wouldn't let down his guard too much. Until he'd gotten the information that he needed and delivered it to Jack, he would never let his guard down.

"Here." He handed her the only blanket.

Cody wrapped herself in it, feeling as if she were donning armor.

Luke stared at her as she cocooned herself in the cover. He knew she wasn't going to like it, but there was no helping the situation. Until he could find another blanket, she was going to have to share. "This isn't going to work, Sister Mary."

"What isn't?" she asked.

"There's only one blanket. Isn't there something in the Bible about sharing with those less fortunate than you?"

Cody's eyes widened at his unspoken request. He wanted to get under the covers with her? A mental alarm sounded in her head. Had all of his talk been just that? Talk?

"Yes, there is, and I shall abide by it. You have stolen me from my home and friends. You have dragged me out here into the middle of a nest of sinners, and now you want me to sleep under the same blanket with you. I'm afraid I can't do that, sir. My virtue is all I have left right now, and I dare not risk being in such close contact with you." She untucked the cover and sat up, handing it to him. "You may have it all. I have my faith to warm my soul."

Then, kneeling on her side of the bed, she began to pray out loud: "Oh, Lord, deliver me from the midst of these sinners. Save my soul, O Lord, that I may proclaim your glory. In this I ask you, Lord, Amen."

Luke stared at her. He remembered saying bedtime prayers with his mother when he was little. It had always been a sweet, loving time, but tonight, listening to Sister Mary, he felt miserable. "Keep the damned blanket! I'll sleep over here."

With that, he snatched up his rifle and sacked out on the floor across the room.

Cody had always had a firm faith, but she was beginning to believe there really was something to this religion thing. She found herself almost crowing out loud in hilarity at his reaction to her prayer, but she bit her lip to bring herself back under control. She took off her glasses and placed them on top of the Bible, then snuggled down under the blanket.

She sought sleep, but sleep didn't come. Her mind was racing as she thought of all that had happened. In some ways, things couldn't be any better. Majors was surprising her with his manners. She knew from what she'd learned about him that he was Southern by birth. Perhaps, she mused, somewhere in his distant past he'd been a gentleman.

* * *

Luke managed to doze, but he had too much to do to waste time sleeping. He had gone into El Trajar because he'd thought he might learn something about El Diablo. To his frustration, there had been no contact with the gang's boss. Even in camp, the name was seldom mentioned, and when it was, it was done in such a way that you could tell those speaking feared for their lives if caught saying something derogatory about the mysterious leader. Luke tried to envision the man who led them. He had to be savage by nature, without conscience or morality. Certainly he would be big and powerful, for men the likes of these wouldn't follow anyone less intimidating. He had seen many big, mean-looking men in camp, but none were the leader. Wherever El Diablo was, he wasn't in camp or in El Trajar. Luke's frustration grew.

He supposed since he knew where the camp was, he could sneak away and report that back to Jack, but somehow it seemed less than worthy of him. Luke had told Jack that he would find out who El Diablo was. If he could bring down the whole gang by staying where he was for a little longer, it would be worth it. It had been dangerous from the start, and now with Sister Mary under his protection, his situation was even more complicated. Still, he had to try. If he didn't succeed, he had no life to go back to. All he wanted was to return to the Trinity and raise horses.

Luke roused himself after a few hours and went outside, leaving a sleeping Sister Mary behind. Though he had been in camp for a while, he knew he still was not completely accepted by the others.

Jones was sitting by a campfire, drinking coffee, when he saw Luke emerge. "Want something hot to drink?"

"Sounds good." Luke hunkered down by the campfire to help himself to a mug of the steaming, too-strong brew.

"Rumor has it you brought a preacher woman back with you." There was real humor in his voice.

"Sometimes rumors are right."

Jones shot him a look of disbelief. "I been to El Trajar, Majors. There are a lot of nice women there. Why the hell would you mess with a preacher when you coulda had one of the girls at the saloon?"

Luke shrugged. "She suited me at the time."

"How does she look now that you're sober?" Jones laughed.

Luke's smile was lopsided with self-derision as he stood up and avoided answering the question. It was one thing to drag her here to keep her safe; it was another to ridicule her. "She'll do," was all he answered.

"Well, when you get tired of her, just let the rest of us know. I'm sure there's quite a few who wouldn't mind trying out something new."

"Believe me, Jones, if and when I get ready to share, you'll know."

Jones smiled, believing him.

"Where is everybody today?" Luke asked. The camp seemed quieter than usual. There was no sign of Hadley, Sully, or Carson.

"They went to meet with El Diablo."

Luke was instantly alert. "El Diablo's coming in to camp?"

Jones cast him a look. "No. El Diablo don't come around here too much. The boss just keeps us informed, and we take care of the rest."

"Doesn't he ever ride with us?"

"Not very often."

"Well, if he never leads you, how did the gang come to be known as his?" Luke was puzzled.

"Don't worry. We're El Diablo's gang all right. The boss tells us where to go and what to do, and we do it. The ones who don't follow orders don't last long around here. Hadley sees to that personal."

"I'll just bet he does," Luke muttered under his breath. "What about me? I've been with you for weeks now, and we've only had that one job."

"That's why they're meeting with El Diablo. The boss will tell us where the next job will be. The boss knows everything. When they get back, they'll probably know whether you're really to be accepted or not."

"I didn't know joining up was a popularity vote."

"It's not, but there is a lot we didn't know about you. You did try to stop the robbery at the bank."

"And what did I get for my heroics? Thrown in jail and threatened with a noose."

"You yelled enough about being innocent."

"I thought someone would believe me."

Jones snorted in sarcasm. "It's about time you realized you're better off with us. Here, there ain't nobody got any redeeming qualities. We're all liars and thieves and murderers. There ain't an honest man among us, and, even if there was, we wouldn't believe him. Now take you, for instance; you had no intention of robbing that bank when you went in there, but look how you ended up. The good people of Del Fuego were damned well ready to lynch you. If there had been a run on the jail, Carson and me would have got off easy. You're the one they woulda hanged."

Luke grunted in agreement. It was true.

"So what do you think of the good townspeople now?"

"I'm here. That should tell you what I think of them. At least here I'm accepted for who and what I am. Sully and some of the others may not like me, but I don't want to be their friend."

"There ain't many real friends in this place. We all respect each other because we don't trust each other. We stay 'cause the money's good."

"I've yet to see any of that. It had better be or I'll be on my way. I could earn damned good money hiring out as a gun for some of the ranchers down south."

"Don't worry. Once El Diablo says you're in, you'll be paid right along with the rest of us."

"How the hell am I supposed to find out if El Diablo approves of me if I never get to see or meet the man?"

"El Diablo has ways of finding things out. Wouldn't surprise me none if the boys came back saying you were okay in the next couple days."

Luke nodded, then dumped out the rest of his coffee and started back to check on Sister Mary. It was good to know that Sully was gone for a while. They could relax. Still, it angered and frustrated him that he hadn't gotten to go along to meet the elusive leader of the group. He was going to have to keep biding his time.

Luke returned to the shack to find Sister Mary still sleeping. Her back was to him and she looked small and vulnerable. He knew, though, when she came awake she would have the ferocity of a she-wolf; she was well armed with nothing but her Bible and her unconquerable spirit. He wondered what he was going to do with her.

Some hours later, Cody came awake abruptly. Startled by her unfamiliar surroundings, she sat up, her heart pounding. It took her a moment to remember exactly who she was pretending to be and what she was doing there. As she stared about the filthy hovel, it all came back to her, and she wasn't sure whether to be glad that she was with Luke Majors or not.

Cody took a deep breath and told herself that she was going to be fine. The situation was perfect. She had the man she was after all to herself. All she had to do was figure out how to trap him and get him away from the infamous El Diablo gang and back to Logan.

Cody donned the glasses, even though wearing them annoyed her tremendously. She had perfect vision, but the glasses were an integral part of her disguise. Sister Mary she was, and Sister Mary she would be . . . for as long as it took.

Rising from the bed, she went to the door and looked out. The thought of escape came to her, but she dismissed it. There was nowhere to go.

Her hair was coming loose from the tight bun, so she quickly refastened it. Then, straightening her dress, she smoothed what wrinkles she could from the skirt. After picking up her Bible, she left the hut, determined to scout out the camp.

Chapter Eight

The outlaws' hideout was obviously a permanent one. Water was ample, and there were numerous buildings, along with corrals for the horses and other livestock. Cody saw a number of women and children there, too, but it didn't surprise her. As protected as this canyon was, it was probably the safest place for the outlaws' families.

Cody had been wandering through the area for a while when the heavenly scent of coffee came to her. A surly-looking man was sitting by one of the campfires tending a coffeepot and watching her with open interest. She assumed her best Sister Mary manner and approached him.

"Good morning, friend. Your coffee smells delicious. I was wondering if I might have a cup?"

"Help yourself." He gestured toward the pot and

gave her a toothless smile.

"Thank you. You're most kind. My name is Sister Mary, by the way," Cody told him as she poured the hot, black brew into a tin cup that looked as if it hadn't been washed in months. Ignoring the dirtiness of the cup, she took a sip.

"I'm Gene."

"It's lovely to meet you," she said with a smile that was genuine, for the coffee was good. She kept an eye out for Sully, ready to retreat to the safety of Luke's house should he appear, but there were few men around. "We've been blessed with a fine day, it seems."

He shrugged. "It'll be quiet, if nothing else."

"Why is that?" She looked at him curiously.

"Most of the men rode out a while ago. They won't be back for a few days, maybe even a week."

"Did Majors go with them?" she asked with a mixture of hope and fear that she didn't understand.

"No. He's seeing to the horses." He pointed toward a distant corral at the back of the canyon.

"Thank you for your kindness. Is there any food around?" From the look of things, this was a commune of sorts; whatever was out was for all to share.

"Check with Juana, over there. She may have something left."

"Bless you, Brother Gene."

Gene stared after her as she moved off, wondering what a woman like her was doing in a place like this. He couldn't imagine what Majors had been thinking, bringing her here. He smiled as he watched her cross the campsite to Juana. Sister Mary was certainly different. She walked straight and tall, her head held high, her Bible under her arm. It had been years since he'd been preached salvation. He wondered if she was going to try. It would be interesting to see what happened. This wasn't exactly a holy bunch.

Juana had heard about the woman Majors had brought into camp. She saw the newcomer walking toward her now and studied her with open interest. With just one look, Juana knew she didn't like her. The woman was thin, pale, wore glasses, and carried a Bible. Juana had no idea why Majors would want her in his bed. She certainly didn't look like the kind of woman who could satisfy a man.

Juana scowled at the thought of this witch bedding Luke. She'd wanted him for herself ever since he'd come into camp, and both she and her friend Maria had been vying for the handsome gunfighter's attention. It irked her that he'd taken this woman to be his. It didn't make sense when he could have had a hot-blooded woman like herself. Juana's eyes narrowed dangerously as the newcomer drew near.

"What do you want?" she challenged without waiting for her to speak.

"Are you Juana?" At her nod, Cody went on, "Brother Gene told me that you might have something to eat here."

"No. All the food is gone. We ate at sunup."

Cody could see the open hostility in Juana's expression. She didn't know why this woman hated her when she didn't even know her, but she knew she would never turn her back on Juana.

"Thank you anyway," she replied cordially. "I'm Sister Mary, by the way. It's nice to meet you." She decided to kill her with kindness. "It's always good to meet new people and make new friends. God bless you, Juana."

Juana stared at her as if she were crazy as Cody walked away.

Cody wondered if "kill her with kindness" would really work, as she felt the other woman's hate-filled regard on her. It was not a pleasant sensation.

Ignoring her hunger pangs, she considered what to do next. She needed to get a look at the lay of the land. Obviously she couldn't apprehend Luke by herself, so whatever she did, she was going to need help. It was important that she find out how many guards there were and if there was an escape route out the back of the canyon. Heading toward the corral where Luke was, she was greeted by many unfriendly stares.

"Bless you this fine morning," Sister Mary responded with a smile to each strange look.

Most turned away from her without speaking, and that suited her just fine. The more they ignored her, the more she could get a good look around without anyone guessing what she was up to. Usually she had Stalking Ghost to help her with this. At the thought of her friend, she prayed once more that he hadn't been seriously hurt.

Through all of the four years of her bounty hunting, she had always known that Stalking

Ghost was near, silently watching over and protecting her. Now, for the first time, she was on her own, and it was a bit unnerving. Not that she wasn't confident of her own abilities. Her father had taught her well before he'd died, and Cody knew she was good at her job. She just wasn't used to working completely alone. It was intimidating to realize that she had no one to rely on but herself.

"Good morning, Luke," she said as she found him currying his horse. "It is a beautiful day, isn't it?"

"Morning," Luke growled, surprised that she'd sought him out and surprised that she was in such a good mood. "I thought you'd stay in the house until I got back."

"Oh, no. There's too much of God's work to be done in this place to laze around. Have you ever seen a place more in need of the Lord's help in your life?" she asked, looking around.

"Yes, I have," he said without looking up from his work.

"Really? It truly must have been Hell on earth if it was worse than this. Where was it?"

"The South, Sister Mary. Georgia, to be exact, at the end of the war." His voice was emotionless.

Cody was taken aback by his answer. She'd expected him to say some other hellhole where outlaws hid out. "Are you from there?"

"I was, but now I'm from nowhere."

She fell silent for a moment at the harshness of his response. "I'm sorry."

"For what?"

"For whatever caused you so much pain."

"You have to care to be hurt, and believe me, Sister, there isn't much I care about anymore."

"That's obvious. Why else would you be here, living this life with this gang? Perhaps it was through divine providence that I was sent to El Trajar to deliver you," she remarked with seeming thoughtfulness.

"I don't need anything from you, Sister, least of all 'delivering,' " he growled, wondering if the only time she shut up about saving souls was when she was asleep. If that was true, he was ready to encourage her to go take a nap.

"Surely you do. Look at your life! You're a thief and possibly a murderer, judging from the company you keep. If that doesn't qualify you as needing saving, I don't know what does." She paused, acting as if she'd just had a brilliant insight. "Then, too, perhaps I was sent to deliver not only you, but the whole gang as well." This time she allowed herself to smile broadly at the thought.

"If you value your hide and want to keep it in one piece, you'd better be careful what you do around here. The last thing I need is for you to start stirring up trouble."

"How can preaching the good news be trouble?"

Luke groaned in frustration. "These aren't your normal run-of-the-mill townsfolk eager for redemption. These people probably would just as soon shoot you as listen to you lecture them on the evil of their ways."

"Most sinners are that way. They're convinced their way is right and that it doesn't matter what happens in the next life. That's why we are called to testify to the truth. It's our duty. If we are to see our own souls to the paradise that awaits us, we must show these unfortunates the way. Those who have never heard the word are to be pitied and loved, for they can still turn to the Lord and be saved. It is those like yourself, who have been taught God's ways and know of his undying love and then choose to reject him, who are the most difficult to deal with. You, sir, are going to be a challenge to me."

"Sister Mary." Luke stopped what he was doing and faced her, his expression hard. "You can preach all you like, but you're going to be wasting your breath on me. I gave up asking God for help a long time ago. He didn't help me then, and I see no reason why he might have changed his mind in the passing years. So believe me when I tell you I'm not worth saving."

"You can't mean that! Everyone has good points. Sometimes, like with you, it's just more difficult to find them. But don't worry, I'll find yours. I mean, look what you did for me, bringing me here. I'm sure you thought at the time you were performing a good deed. Your heart was in the right place no matter how much you'd like to deny it," she finished with firm conviction.

"I'm beginning to regret that decision more and more with each passing minute."

"All right, Luke. I shall be like the grain of sand in an oyster. I shall test you and test you until I have changed you into a valuable pearl."

At his thunderous look, she knew she had

pushed him as far as she could right then. It was time to change the subject.

"I'm hungry," she admitted. "I managed to get some coffee, but Juana told me there would be nothing to eat until later."

Luke looked surprised. Whenever he'd wanted anything to eat, Juana had always been more than happy to oblige. "Come on, let's go see what I can find for you."

"Thank you."

He finished up his horse, and they started walking back toward the village.

"It's a rule around here that everyone helps out. You're going to have to do some chores in camp in order to earn your keep."

"Of course, I'll be more than happy to conduct services for those who want to come."

"I'm not sure your rabble-rousing will earn you any friends or any meals. If you're smart, you'll keep quiet and stay out of everyone's way. A woman should be seen and not heard."

"I thought that was children."

"It applies to you, too," he insisted as they reached his abode. "I'll be back in a little while."

So dismissed, Cody turned without another word and went inside. It appeared she was being submissive by doing his bidding, but the truth was, she'd eyed the surrounding terrain and knew the lay of the land perfectly now. There was no back exit. The only way in and out of the camp was through the main entrance. As steep as the canyon walls were, if a lawman tried to raid the place, he and his men would be easy targets for the guards.

Cody wandered around inside for a little while, then went outside and sat down in the shade of the cabin. It was a good vantage point, for she could keep an eye on most of the camp from there. She needed to commit to memory the location of all the houses and the number of people there, too. Every detail was important. It might prove fatal to dismiss something as unimportant.

Luke returned a short time later with a tortilla filled with some unidentified meat. Cody thought about questioning him as to the contents, and then told herself she was better off not knowing. Thanks to Luke she wouldn't starve to death—at least not today.

"Where are Sully and the others?" she asked, knowing from Gene that they'd ridden out, but not knowing where they'd gone.

"They're out of camp for a few days," Luke replied, offering no information.

She smiled. "I'm glad they're gone, but why didn't you go with them?"

"Trying to get rid of me, are you? I stayed behind to take care of you," he lied, frustrated that the others were probably meeting with El Diablo right then, and he wasn't with them.

"Don't stay here on my account. In fact, since Sully's gone, just give me a horse and I'll be on my way. There's no need for you to protect me anymore."

Luke glanced at her, wondering at her naivete. She might be safe from Sully right now, but who knew what other dangers lurked in this camp? He'd already realized he'd made a mistake in bringing her here, but there had been nothing else he could do at the time. Now he wasn't sure how to get rid of her.

Turning her loose sounded like a great idea, but to do that he'd have to take her back into town, and he didn't want to take the chance of missing El Diablo. The leader just might ride back into camp with the others when they returned, and he had to be there. He had to convince them that he was one of them. He hadn't won anyone's complete trust yet, and if he let her go too soon, they might wonder about him.

"I'll let you go, but all in good time."

"When exactly is 'all in good time'?"

"When I get tired of you! I talked to Juana about you, and from now on, you can earn your keep working for her."

Cody ground her teeth in frustration, but said nothing. She hated the drudgery of women's work. It was dull, boring, and the main reason she'd asked her father to teach her how to use a gun when she'd been eight years old. The boys always had more fun than the girls. Who wanted to be cleaning house and cooking meals when they could be out riding or hunting or shooting?

"I'll do whatever you think is necessary, but I cannot in good conscience give up my vocation," she said seriously.

"I won't be responsible for how anyone reacts to you. These are not your ordinary townspeople.

The women are more than likely prostitutes and the men—"

"Mary Magdalene was a prostitute, and she was saved," Cody pronounced, slightly offended by his attitude. "Besides, a woman would not be able to ply her degrading trade were it not for a man willing to pay for it."

"And the men are far worse," he concluded, trying to ignore her.

"Yourself included?"

"Myself included."

"Then I shall consider what time I have here a challenge to be met with faith and good works."

Luke mentally groaned at her ever-present good spirits. He gave up trying to reason with her. As long as Sully was away she'd be safe. He'd just have to keep an eye on her.

"Juana said you can help with the evening meal."

"How kind of her."

"You want to eat, don't you?" He gave her a telling look. "If you don't like cooking, there are other ways you could earn your keep, you know."

"I'll be glad to help her cook," she answered quickly, blushing at his insinuation.

"I thought you might."

Cody left him then, heading for Juana's cabin. The other woman was not overly pleased to see her.

"I see you have come to help."

"I'll be glad to do whatever you want me to do, good sister."

"I am not your sister."

"In the eyes of God, we are all brothers and sisters."

"In the eyes of God we all gotta eat. Here, stir this while I see to other things." She handed Cody a large ladle and pointed toward the kettle of boiling stew over the campfire. "I'll be back."

Juana turned her back and walked away. Cody stared down at that which would ultimately be their dinner. It didn't look too appetizing, but she was coming to realize that in this place one couldn't be choosy. She kept stirring.

Juana was glad to be away from the other woman. She tried to act casual as she crossed the encampment and sought Luke out.

"Thank you for sending the preacher woman to help. I have already put her to work," she said as she stood in the doorway of his cabin watching him as he sat at the table cleaning his gun.

"Good. She was eager to help in any way she could," Luke said, concentrating on his revolver.

"Why did you bring her here?" Juana asked, her dark-eyed gaze upon Luke, visually caressing his broad, powerful shoulders and the hard line of his jaw, darkened now by the shadow of his beard's growth. A hunger grew within her. She watched as he worked on the gun; she could well imagine those same strong hands touching her. The thought excited her. She'd wanted him ever since he'd joined the gang, and now was the time to make her move on him. With Sully and the others gone, she could devote herself completely to pleasing him.

Luke glanced up at her question, surprised for

a moment, until he saw the look in her eyes. He hadn't paid much attention to Juana since he'd been in camp. He knew she satisfied the other men when they wanted a woman, but he was not in the market for that kind of satisfying. Wanting to end her desire for him right away, he answered, "I brought her here because I wanted her."

Juana had started forward, wanting to touch him, wanting to feel him deep within her, but at his words she stopped. "She is your woman then?"

"She is."

"She satisfies you?"

Luke heard the disbelief in her voice and recognized her jealousy. "That is none of your business."

"Ah, but I could make you my business." She refused to be put off. "I can make you happier than she can."

"How do you know? She makes me very happy."

"She does not look like the kind of woman who could please you."

"There is more to Sister Mary than meets the eye. She is all the woman I'll ever need." Even as he said it, though, Luke wondered for a moment what kind of woman could please him. He glanced out the door at Sister Mary. She was a plain woman, totally dedicated to her calling, unconcerned with things of the flesh. Yet he had just told the lusty Juana that the preacher satisfied him.

"I do not believe you, Luke Majors," Juana said in a throaty, seductive voice. "She looks like an old prude. I do not think she knows the first thing about pleasing a man."

Luke smiled enigmatically. He was going to have to do something with his preacher woman to convince Juana that he wasn't lying. He'd been afraid that he'd be challenged on his desire for her, and now he would have to prove it. "There is more to making some men happy than just satisfying their carnal urges, Juana. Sister Mary may not be what most of the men want in the way of a woman, but she's just what I need."

Juana gave a snort of disbelief. "I could show you what you really need," she offered silkily, moving closer.

She wanted to sit on his lap, to kiss him and arouse him until she'd wiped the other woman from his mind. She stood before him, then leaned forward, putting her hands on his shoulders. The scoop neckline of her blouse gapped and offered him a full view of her breasts. They were heavy and lush. It was a ploy that always worked with men, and she eagerly anticipated Luke's reaction. She expected him to grab her and take her right then. The thought excited her.

Luke could feel the heat of her desire for him. She was not an unattractive woman, and he knew she was his for the taking, but he was not about to touch her. If he did, she would never believe that Sister Mary was his woman. "I appreciate the thought, but like I said, I have all the woman I need."

He rose in a leisurely move, evading her grasping hands, and walked away from her. He knew she followed him outside and was watching and he was glad. He wanted to discourage her once and for all.

Cody saw Luke coming toward her and wondered what he wanted. She had seen Juana go into the cabin; now, a few short minutes later, he had come out. The other woman was standing just outside the cabin door watching him. Cody gave him a questioning look as he drew near.

"Is something wrong? Juana doesn't look too happy."

"She's angry all right, but that's good."

"It is?"

"If you want to stay alive, go along with what I'm about to do," he said in a low voice.

"Are you threatening me?"

He didn't answer, but instead took her in his arms and kissed her. His mouth claimed hers in a hot, demanding exchange.

Chapter Nine

Cody was shocked, and she struggled against him. Never in her wildest imaginings had she conceived that Luke would do something like this, and right here in front of everybody! He had told her he wasn't attracted to her, that he wasn't interested in her, that she was safe with him. And now . . . ?

"What are you doing?" she demanded when the kiss ended.

"Juana's watching. She thinks you're my woman. For once in your life, be quiet and don't argue," he ordered as he swept her up in his arms.

To the others in camp, his expression was that of a man in passion's grip, yet Cody could see the warning in his gaze. The ladle she'd been holding fell from her hand as she looped her arms around his neck. This was crazy! It was broad daylight! They were standing in the middle of the camp! Everyone could see them! Luke could see all the questions in the depths of her green eyes, and he muttered under his breath, "Just kiss me."

"But—" she started to argue again.

"Please," he whispered just as his lips sought hers.

His mouth moved over hers in a persuasive assault, and suddenly Cody wasn't thinking about fighting him anymore. She told herself it was because Juana was watching and she had to make the embrace look good. She told herself it was to convince the other woman that she was Luke's. She told herself to act as if she were enjoying his kiss, but, in truth, there was no acting involved. Luke's kiss was the most magnificent one she'd ever had in her life. She'd been kissed by several young men who'd attempted to court her over the last few years, but none of their embraces had made her feel like this.

A small, involuntary sigh that was almost a groan escaped her, and at the sound, she could feel Luke tense. Then suddenly his lips upon hers were hard and demanding, yet there was nothing painful about the exchange. Luke was dominating her, and to her heady amazement, she delighted in it.

Cody clung even more tightly to him as her world spun dizzily out of control. She was vaguely aware that Luke had started carrying her away, but she didn't care. When at last the kiss ended and she looked up, she found he was carrying her right past the stunned Juana, who was scowling at them.

Luke stopped in the doorway of the cabin just long enough to speak a few words to Juana. "Maybe you'd better go watch the cookfire. Sister Mary won't be back to help you for a while. She's got another fire to tend." His voice was deep and husky as he spoke, and then he turned away and disappeared inside, closing the door behind them.

Juana stood in furious silence for a moment. It wasn't often that a man refused her, and jealousy raged within her. She was tempted to put a torch to their cabin just so she could keep that phony pious preacher woman from getting what she wanted. But she didn't. Not wanting to hear the telltale sounds that she was certain would soon be coming from within, she stormed off to tend the stew.

Inside the cabin, Luke set Cody on her feet. She quickly backed away from him, a hand on her lips, her eyes wide in confusion. She looked every inch the put-upon, innocent, virginal preacher woman. Her disguise had never been more effective. Though the truth was, she was breathless and speechless before the power of what had just transpired between them. She had never known she could feel this way, and she stared up at Luke, wondering how a simple kiss could have set her pulse racing and left her heart beating such a frantic rhythm.

"Why did you do that?" she demanded, her own voice sounding oddly breathless to her.

"Shhh," he told her quietly, listening, trying to

hear if Juana was still hovering nearby outside.

Cody was annoyed by his total lack of interest in her. He didn't seem to care that he had just humiliated her in front of everyone, and he certainly didn't seem to have been affected by the embrace at all.

It dawned on her then that he really didn't care about her, that he really didn't want her in the way a man wants a woman. It had all been an act. The realization hurt, although she quickly assured herself that she didn't care. Certainly she didn't desire him. That would be crazy. The only way she wanted him was as a bounty hunter wanted her prey. She wanted nothing else to do with him— except to take him in and collect her reward money. Period.

"I think she's gone," he finally said in a low voice as he faced her. "I'm sorry about having to kiss you, but Juana didn't believe me when I told her you were my woman. We had to put on a show to convince her."

"And did we?"

"I hope so. She offered herself to me, and I turned her down." He gave a rueful shake of his head. "She couldn't believe that I preferred you to her. I had to show her that I did."

"Oh." Cody's ego was definitely taking a battering. "So what do we do now?"

He gave her a rakish grin. "We stay in here long enough to convince her, and anyone else who was watching, that you are indeed my woman—in all ways."

She groaned at the thought. "This is so humiliating. They'll all think I'm a loose woman. Chastity is a biblical imperative. Living a moral life is the only path to Heaven."

"You don't have to worry." He sighed heavily at her censure. "I'm not about to take you. I told you before that your virtue was safe with me. We just can't let anyone else know it."

"I may know, but how will I ever hold my head up when I'm preaching? They'll all be thinking that you and I . . ." Cody found herself blushing in spite of herself. She knew he thought she was blushing because she was embarrassed by the thought of their being lovers, but, in truth, she was blushing because of her own unbridled response to being in his arms. His shoulders had been powerful beneath her touch as she'd clung to him. His body against hers . . . the hardness of him . . . the strength of him as he'd carried her to the cabin had been an erotic caress. Her heart raced at the memory.

"I've always thought that preachers who've never sinned are a boring lot. Maybe this will make your sermons more exciting," he taunted. He was irritated, but he was not sure why. He realized that he'd put her in a difficult position, but there had been no other way to discourage Juana.

"Oh, you!" She turned away.

Luke laughed at her outrage as they bided their time.

Outside by the fire, Juana was straining to hear what they were saying, but all she could make out was his laughter. At the sound of it, her jealousy grew even hotter. She should have been the

133

woman in there with him! She should have been the one pleasing him! Juana kept her gaze trained on the closed door, waiting for him to emerge.

Within the cabin, Cody was still standing with her back to Luke, wondering what was going to happen next.

"Sister Mary . . ."

He sounded more conciliatory, so she looked back at him over her shoulder. To her shock, he had stripped down bare to the waist. Her mouth went dry at the sight of his beautiful, hard-muscled chest.

"What are you doing now?" she demanded, whirling on him. She had never thought of a man as beautiful before, but she did now. She found that she wanted to touch him, and the thought embarrassed her. Cody forced her gaze away from him.

"Playing my role, what do you think? Just closing that door isn't going to convince Juana. She's one shrewd woman."

"So are you going to get completely naked, just to fool Juana?"

He gave her another rakish grin. "Only if you want me to."

Cody went for the only protection she had. She grabbed her Bible and held it to her. "You are no Adam, I am no Eve, and this is definitely not the Garden of Eden. Keep your pants on!"

Luke laughed at her discomfort. "All right. I'll keep my pants on, but what about you? You can't go back to helping Juana looking like I never laid a hand on you."

"What do you mean?" Her eyes widened as he advanced on her.

"Turn around."

"Why?"

"Just do it."

She heard the impatience in his voice and did as he directed. She stood stock-still as she felt his hand in her hair, pulling out the pins that held the heavy mass restrained in the spinsterish bun. "Wait!"

"You have to look like I've made love to you," Luke was saying as he worked at freeing her hair.

"And how is that?" She found herself challenging him.

"Happy . . . sated . . . hungry for more," he said in a deliberately low, seductive voice as he let her hair down.

She shivered at his words as she stood rigidly before him, and behind her, he smiled. Her hair tumbled free then. The silken softness of it surprised him. She was so prickly and so guarded with him that he had somehow expected her hair to be coarse and unkind to the touch. Instead, it was a lush mane of shiny, natural curls.

"Your hair is lovely," he said in a voice that reflected his amazement. Her response to him earlier had surprised him, too. For a moment, while he'd been kissing her, it had almost seemed as if she'd been enjoying it.

"Thank you," she answered tersely, cautiously, not understanding the change in his voice or her own reaction to his hands upon her as he'd freed the pins and now raked his fingers through her hair. An image of him—tall, lean, and naked to the waist—played in her mind, and she found herself closing her eyes as he continued to smooth out her hair.

"Now," he said huskily, "turn around."

His words jarred her back to reality, and Cody gave herself a silent, stern warning. This was Luke Majors! This was the man she was bringing to justice! What was the matter with her? She spun around and glared at him.

"Are you finished messing up my hair?" she demanded with as much outrage as she could arouse.

Luke found himself staring down at her. There was a flush to her cheeks that, coupled with the beauty of her hair framing her face, made her look lovely, even with the glasses on. He frowned and gave himself a mental shake. This was not a desirable woman. This was Sister Mary, and he would do well to remember that. He had brought her here to save her, not to ruin her.

"Just one more thing."

He reached out and unbuttoned the top buttons of her dress, stopping where she held the Bible clutched to her. Then, unable to help himself, he lifted his hand and gently traced a path from her cheek, down the arch of her throat, to the place where the fabric parted over her breasts. He lifted his gaze to her face. "Now you look like a woman well loved."

Despite all her admonishments to herself, Cody had been mesmerized by the gentleness of his touch. At his words, though, she stiffened. "And that pleases you?"

"Very much." He grinned again. "We have to make this look good. You have to go help Juana."

With that, he turned and left her, emerging from the cabin shirtless and smiling.

From her place by the fire, Juana stared at Luke. She visually caressed the broad width of his furred chest as he shrugged into his shirt. His movements were those of a conquering male—satisfied, sure, and confident. As he moved out of sight, Juana watched him go, aching to have him in her bed. She vowed to find a way to bring him to her.

Cody waited another few minutes before emerging from the house.

"Here." Juana shoved the ladle back at her. "You may have put one fire out, but don't douse this one."

"Do not believe that I was a willing participant in such decadence. Sin is everywhere and we must fight against it. Even when it threatens to overwhelm us, even when it forces us to do things against our will, we must try to do the right thing."

"I didn't hear any cries for help coming from your cabin."

"Who would save me? You? I will be rescued from this fate one day, and, God willing, I will be forgiven for my sins. For now, I can only suffer his touch and hope that the end will come soon."

Juana stared at her, hating her, pitying her. "You are a fool, preacher woman."

"You think I'm a fool because I believe in the beauty of marriage vows? Because I believe that a man will respect you more if you do not give him freely that which he wants the most? I did not choose to be brought here and suffer these indignities. But I will do so knowing that God is keeping me safe from further harm."

"If I were you, I'd be praying to be back in his bed again, not rescued from it."

Cody saw the jealousy in Juana's eyes. "Not if you were dragged there against your will. You should save your most precious gift—your love—for marriage with a man who loves you and will care for you forever."

Juana just stared at the preacher woman, thinking her crazy. If Luke Majors had wanted her, she would never have left his bed.

It was late afternoon when Jack sat with Fred Halloway in the sheriff's office. His mood was dark. The only thing he'd accomplished in the two weeks since the breakout was that he'd given Jessy the money to pay the taxes on the Trinity. Other than that, there had been no word about anything. He'd heard nothing from Luke or from Jameson. His frustration was at an all-time high, yet he was forced to stay where he was and wait. It didn't sit well with him.

"Have you heard anything new about Harris?" Jack asked Halloway.

"Nothing good," Fred answered. "I talked to the doc day before yesterday, and he said Jonathan's been running a high fever and has been in and out of consciousness."

"How's his wife holding up?" Images of Elizabeth Harris had been haunting Jack. He couldn't forget how desperate she'd been that night, wanting to face the men who'd shot her husband. She was a beautiful woman, and she didn't deserve what had happened to her.

"According to the doc, she's been at Jonathan's bedside almost constantly."

"She's one special lady."

"You want to go on by the house and check on Jonathan? I don't know how much he'll be able to tell us once he is better, but it would be interesting to hear what he has to say about Majors's part in all this."

"Very. If you need me for anything, I'll be heading back to the hotel after I stop by the Harrises'."

Jack left the office and made his way to the Harris house. It was one of the nicest in town.

Jack removed his hat as he went up the few steps to the front porch and knocked on the door.

"Ranger Logan, how nice to see you," Elizabeth said.

"Evening, Mrs. Harris."

She nervously smoothed her hair back into place as she stepped outside to speak with him. "Has there been some word? Have you found the gang?"

"No, ma'am, not yet, but don't worry. We're going to find them. When this is through, El Diablo will hang."

Elizabeth shivered at the determination in his words. "Thank you."

Their eyes met, and for a moment he was spellbound. She was so vulnerable and lovely. The reason he had come to her jolted him back to reality.

"I came to see how your husband is doing. Has there been any change?"

She nodded, smiling a little this time. "His fever broke late yesterday. He's much improved."

Jack wondered at her mood, for her happiness seemed tempered.

"Do you know when he'll be strong enough to talk to me? It's important that I hear what he has to say about the robbery."

"You can speak with him now, but he does tire easily."

"Thank you."

"There is one thing I have to tell you."

Jack glanced at her expectantly.

"The doctor just left a little over an hour ago. Now that Jonathan has improved a little, he was able to examine him more fully." She paused as emotion choked her. "The bullet damaged his spine. My husband . . . is paralyzed. . . . He's going to be confined to a wheelchair for the rest of his life." Tears filled her eyes as she spoke, and there was untold suffering in her expression.

"I'm sorry." He felt an overwhelming urge to reach out to her, to hold her and tell her that, somehow, he would make everything all right. But he couldn't.

"It's not your fault." She turned away to hide her sorrow. "It's just that Jonathan's so angry. He told me that he'd rather be dead than live as half a man."

Jack touched her shoulder gently. "I'm sure he didn't mean it. He has so much to live for."

At his words, she looked back at him. Her eyes were luminous as they met his. When she finally spoke, her tone was soft. "He's back in our bedroom. You can speak to him there."

She led the way to the master bedroom and pushed the door slowly open.

"Jonathan, the Ranger I told you about is here. Ranger Logan wants to talk to you about the robbery."

Jonathan Harris lay still on the wide bed. At the sound of her voice he turned only his head to look her way. His coloring was ashen, but the look in his dark eyes was hard.

"Mr. Harris, I'm glad you're better."

"You call this better?" he snarled. He was weak, but his hatred gave him the strength he needed to talk to this man. "I'd rather be dead, but not until I see that bastard hang!"

"Who are you talking about?"

"Luke Majors! I knew he was no good from the beginning! Then when he said I'd be sorry . . . He could never have known just how right he was going to be."

Jack followed Elizabeth farther into the room and went to stand by the bedside. "He said you'd be sorry? For what? Exactly what was going on as the robbery started?"

"He had come in looking for a loan to pay the taxes on his ranch. But I turned him down. I told him we didn't loan money to his kind."

"What kind is that?" Jack pressed, angered by his attitude.

"Majors is a killer . . . a gunfighter. Just before I

was shot, I told him he couldn't have the loan. He didn't have any money with us. He wasn't a good prospect. He threatened me then and said I'd be sorry."

"And what happened when the shooting started?"

"He was standing up as the man behind him announced it was a robbery. Majors drew and they fired their guns. That was when I was hit."

"Are you certain it was Majors who shot you?"

"Of course I'm certain! They were all in it together! We don't want his kind in *our town*." He was so fervent that he almost maneuvered himself up on one elbow.

"Did you actually see him shoot you? Could it have been the other man?"

"You didn't see the look on his face when I told him he couldn't have the loan. He shot me down just like he shot Sheriff Gregory. Find him, Logan. Find him and kill him!"

Jonathan collapsed back, and his head lolled weakly as exhaustion overtook him and sweat from the strain beaded his brow.

"Kill him," he repeated dully, all the emotion having poured from him. "Like I wish he'd killed me. Instead of leaving me like this."

"I think you'd better go now," Elizabeth suggested from where she'd been standing behind Jack.

Jack turned without speaking and quit the room. Elizabeth said a few soft words to Jonathan and then followed the Ranger out.

"I'm sorry if I upset him, but I needed to hear

from him what happened."

"I know, and I appreciate everything you're doing for us." She opened the door for him.

"If you ever need anything, Mrs. Harris, just let me know. I'm staying at the Homestead."

"That's very kind of you, Ranger Logan, and please call me Elizabeth."

"I'm Jack."

"Thank you . . . Jack."

He left her then, and when he'd gone from sight, Elizabeth returned to her husband's side.

Jack started for the hotel, then changed his mind. After having listened to Harris's account of what happened in the bank, he needed a drink. Everyone seemed so certain that Luke had been in on the robbery. Jack knew he was going to have one helluva time proving his innocence. His thoughts were in turmoil as he entered the saloon and got himself a bottle of whiskey and a glass. He settled in alone at a back table.

Chapter Ten

Hadley, Sully, and the others had to wait several days for El Diablo at the rendezvous place. When El Diablo finally showed up, the men were glad, for they'd feared something might have happened to their leader.

"It's good to see you!" Hadley called out.

El Diablo reined in before them and dismounted. The outlaw leader's expression was hard. This was the first meeting they'd had face-to-face since the bank robbery in Del Fuego, and El Diablo was still furious over the way things had gone there. "I am not pleased to see you, my brother. What the hell happened at the bank? I know Majors got in the way, but why didn't you fools just shoot him and everyone there, like I told you? And especially Harris! I gave you explicit instructions that he was to be killed."

"Harris is still alive?"

"Damned right he is! You bungled the whole thing. You left witnesses, and now the law's on our trail, not to mention an army of bounty hunters trying to claim the big rewards they put on you after the jailbreak. It's a miracle you managed that without a mishap, but why the hell didn't you kill the sheriff?"

"He wasn't dead?" Hadley looked over at Sully, who'd led the escape.

"I went into the jail about an hour after you broke out to make sure everything had gone as planned. I found the sheriff locked in a cell, just coming around. I finished the job for you."

"Why didn't you shoot him, Sully?" Hadley demanded.

"As we were leaving, Majors said he'd take care of him."

"He must have just knocked him unconscious so there wouldn't be any gunfire," Hadley offered.

The leader glared at Sully. "Next time don't trust anyone else. Take care of it yourself. For now, keep an eye on Majors and see what he's up to."

Sully was humiliated and angry. "Don't worry. I will."

Hadley did not cringe before El Diablo's justified criticism. Their leader had told them not to leave anyone behind who could talk, but as badly as everything had gone, they'd been forced to cut and run. Next time they planned a big job, they'd be ready for all possibilities. "It won't happen again."

"It had better not. You start making mistakes like that too often, and men start dying . . . our men."

"What's happening in Del Fuego? How high are the bounties?"

El Diablo told Hadley all the news from town as the others listened in.

"With the sheriff and deputy dead, and Harris shot, the town is up in arms. It's not safe for you to try anything right now," the outlaw leader advised. "Just stay in camp and keep an eye on Majors. I'm not sure I would trust him completely just yet. The witnesses are all swearing that he's the one who shot Harris, and everyone else is convinced he killed the lawman, too."

"I won't ever trust him," Sully put in.

El Diablo never paid much attention to Sully's opinions. He might be the one of the meanest men in the gang, but he certainly wasn't one of the smartest. He formed judgments based strictly on whether he liked a man or not, not on how the man could help the gang.

Luke Majors held promise. He was a fast gun with a reputation. The mere mention of his name could put some people into panic. El Diablo liked that. The more people were terrified of them, the easier it would be to take what they wanted.

"It's too soon to know for sure about him. That's why I want you to keep track of his movements. Watch who he talks to and what he does. He could be trouble, but then again, he might turn out to be just the man we need."

"We don't need him!" Sully argued. "He almost

got Jones and Carson killed in the robbery!"

"Things happen for a reason sometimes."

"What reason could Luke Majors have for wanting to join up with us? You should just let me shoot him in the back when we get back to camp and be done with it."

El Diablo turned a piercing gaze on Sully. "I said he might be just what we need."

There was a deadliness to El Diablo's tone that warned Sully to back off.

"Aw, it ain't nothing to get excited about. Sully here's just jealous of the man," Carson spoke up. "There was a woman in El Trajar that Sully wanted, but Majors took her for his own."

"You're letting your lust for a woman impair your judgment?" El Diablo again impaled Sully with a deadly look. "A man needs to be in control of himself and his emotions if he's riding with me."

Sully glared at Carson as he responded to the boss. "This one was different. She was one of them salvation preachers. She was too uppity for her own good, and I wanted to show her what life was really all about."

El Diablo found Sully tedious. Someday he was going to cause the gang trouble because of his single-mindedness when he was angry. "Remember this, Sully: that preacher is a woman just like any other. Take your fun with the girls at the saloon, but don't try to take a woman from Luke Majors if you want to stay alive. I'd hate to hear from the others that they'd had to bury you."

Sully was insulted. "I can take Majors any day, anytime!"

"You can think about taking him all you want, but I wouldn't act on it. He's one dangerous man. I'd walk softly around him if I were you."

Sully was angry, but knew better than to cross the boss. He would make his own plans in his own time.

"Now, to business." El Diablo looked at Hadley. "There's a shipment of rifles due at the fort soon. I don't know the exact date yet. I'll send word as soon as I find out."

"Until then?"

"Lay low, let Majors think he's one of us, and then wait to see what happens. I'll be in touch as soon as I have definite information."

With that El Diablo left them. Hadley, Sully, and the others watched until their leader had disappeared back in the direction of Del Fuego. It was late in the day, so they decided to camp where they were and return to the canyon the following day.

"I guess we sit tight for a while, eh, Sully?" Hadley said.

The short-tempered outlaw cast the other men a hate-filled look. "I'll sit tight all right, but not until I've figured out just what Majors is up to. The boss said to keep an eye on him, and I'm going to do just that. And I'm going to get my hands on that little bitch of his. Sister Mary's going to be mine. Wait and see."

"Why do you still want her? He's probably already had her a dozen times by now."

The thought infuriated Sully. "Just because he

put it to her doesn't mean she's been had by a real man. There's a lot I want to teach her. With all her talk about God and salvation, I'll see how she likes being possessed by the devil." He gave a demonic laugh as they bedded down for the night.

Back in the canyon, everyone gathered around the campfire for the evening meal. Cody helped Juana and several of the other women with serving the meal. Staying in her role, she waited until the last ladle of stew had been served up before she called out in a clear voice, "We must say grace before we eat. Let us pray."

Those within earshot stared at her as if she had lost her mind. She did not care.

"Oh, Lord, bless this food you have provided for us."

A guffaw sounded from one of the outlaws. "God didn't provide this slop. Sam went hunting this afternoon. He's the one who got the food."

"Watch over us, O Lord, and keep us safe. Amen," she finished.

Most of those gathered there had ignored her and had gone ahead and started eating. Only a few of the women and several of the children paid attention. Cody couldn't help wondering what kind of lives the children were going to lead, growing up in a place like this. It was a scary thought. She wished there were something she could do to encourage the women and children to change their way of living, but she wasn't sure what it was.

Dishing herself up a plate of the stew, she got a

mug of coffee and went to sit with Luke near their cabin.

"Tomorrow is Sunday, you know," she told him as she began to eat.

"So?"

"I'll need to be up at dawn so I can hold a Sunday service."

"You're not serious?" He shot her a look of complete disbelief.

Cody stiffened in an appropriate move for Sister Mary. "I am more than serious. I am determined. If ever anyone needed to hear God's word, it's these people. Have you looked around? You are living in a den of thieves and murderers. And the children . . ." There was a catch of emotion in her voice.

"You're wrong to think these people want saving. They're here because they want to be. They're free to go whenever they want to. No one's being held against his will."

Cody shot him a telling, condescending look. "Maybe none of them are, but I am. Perhaps some of the other women came to be here in the same way I did, and by the time they would have been allowed to go, it was too late for them to return to their old lives."

Luke felt the bite of her words, but did not weaken in his defense of what he'd done. "If I hadn't taken you when I did, you might have been killed. Certainly you would have been raped by Sully, and maybe by some of the others."

"How can you know that? You could have just

ridden out and taken Sully with you. You could have left me to my life."

Luke felt a sting of guilt, but ignored it. "If you had had a life after I left you. Men like Sully are deadly when they believe they've been insulted or humiliated."

"Humiliated?" she repeated in outrage. "I'll tell you what humiliation is! Humiliation for me is trying to hold my head up when everyone in this camp believes I'm your woman!"

Luke chuckled, then asked in a quieter tone, "Would it really be such a terrible thing? Being my woman?"

His gaze was upon her as he remembered her kiss. He wondered anew how she could have evoked such a response in him.

At his words, Cody glanced at him. The glasses were the only thing that saved her from revealing her confusion about how she felt. She was able to hide her bewilderment behind the thick lenses.

"I have planned a life of chastity and morality for myself. It is difficult to maintain any semblance of dignity when everyone thinks I'm a—"

"I get the picture." He cut her off, not wanting to hear her say the word *whore* or *slut*. It didn't fit her. She didn't deserve it. "I want you to think about one other thing, though. I want you to imagine what would have happened if I hadn't taken you with me, if I'd left you, and Sully had gotten his hands on you. Take that thought to bed with you tonight. Think about how your friend Stalking Ghost was going to manage to protect you from Sully when he'd been knocked unconscious.

Dream about that. I think you'll find your sleep won't be very restful, Sister Mary."

Luke stood up and stalked away. As Cody watched him go, she saw Juana get up and follow him. The other woman called out to him, and he stopped to talk with her. They walked away together.

For some reason Cody couldn't fathom, she resented the fact that Luke went off with Juana. She told herself she should have been glad he'd left her alone. But instead she grew angry. She got up and went inside.

It was near dusk, so she lit the one lamp on the table. Frustrated and furious, she stared around herself. She knew the best remedy for her temper was hard work, and the cabin was dirty. Urged on by her anger, she started to clean, beginning with the blanket. Taking it outside, she shook it out relentlessly. She was sorry that she didn't have lye soap and hot water to use on it.

As she tended to the task, memories of home assailed her. She usually tried not to think about her family while she was working. She didn't want to risk being distracted by thoughts of her little brother and sister and her aunt who cared for them when she was away. But this case was turning out to be so complicated that it was driving her to distraction! She had never been in a situation like this before.

Cody took the blanket back inside and next dragged the mattress out to pound on. She beat the lumpy pad within an inch of its life.

As she grew tired in her labors her anger eased,

and she smiled grimly. The mattress had borne up well under her assault, but it still was far from clean. She dragged it back indoors, vowing to find a way in the next few days to hang it in the sunshine for a while to air it out. She remade the bed and smoothed the blanket over the mattress.

As always when her anger drained from her, Cody felt exhausted, but she still needed a bath. It had been far too long already since she'd last had the chance to wash up. Taking the bucket that stood by the door, she went to get fresh water from the well and lugged it back all by herself. Luke seemed to have disappeared somewhere with Juana, and that was just fine with her, for it gave her the time she needed to bathe. She closed the door behind her.

Cody had found a sliver of soap in the cabin, and she couldn't wait to be clean again, even if she did have to wear the same clothes once she was done. She was cautious how she undressed, though, for she didn't want to leave herself vulnerable to anyone who might force their way in. She unbuttoned her dress and slipped it down from her shoulders, then began to wash. The cool water felt heavenly to her, and though the soap was harsh, the cleanliness it afforded was wonderful. She sighed in ecstasy.

Luke had tolerated Juana's company for as long as he could just to stay away from Sister Mary. The fact that she could make him feel guilty bothered him, and the fact that he hadn't been able to stop thinking about her kiss bothered him even more. Luke knew he wasn't attracted to her physically. He couldn't be. She was a preacher. Yet her kiss had stirred something within him that he didn't understand.

Luke tried to analyze what he was feeling. He knew she wasn't pretty, but when he'd carried her inside and freed her hair from the tight old-maid's bun, she'd looked almost lovely. She was a virgin, no doubt, a woman he should not even consider laying a hand on, yet the memory of holding her near would not be banished.

Despite the aggravation she'd caused him, Luke had to admit that he was glad he'd protected her. She was an innocent in the ways of men, and he wanted to keep her that way until he could get her safely out of camp and back to her real life.

Luke walked with Juana for some distance. He found it almost amusing how she directed them away from his cabin so Sister Mary was out of sight. Luke knew Juana thought she was going to entice him to her house and bed, but he went to her home only to get an extra blanket from her. It was almost dark when he left her without even a kiss, and she was more than a little angry with him.

Luke drew a deep breath as he approached his own cabin. He was tired, and he wasn't looking forward to sleeping on the floor again. Actually, he would much have preferred his own bed back at the Trinity, but he wasn't going to have the luxury of that comfort again until he had identified El Diablo for Jack.

Reaching the cabin, he started to open the door, but stopped when he had it ajar. The vision inside

left him frozen in place. He stood there, undetected, taking in the glorious view.

Luke could not believe that the angel standing
before him was the same woman he'd spent so
much time with, the same woman he'd thought
rather homely. Her back was to him. She had
slipped her dress down to her waist, and though
she was still wearing her chemise, the beauty of
her ivory flesh was bared to his hungry gaze. Her
hair was still pinned up, but undressed as she was,
the swanlike beauty of her neck was revealed and
her skin was gilded by the soft glow of the lamp.
Sister Mary appeared a most practiced seductress.

Luke's body responded to the beauty of her. He
was on the verge of barging in and taking full ad-
vantage of the moment. He was going to take her
in his arms and lay her upon the bed and—

Then he saw it. There on the bed, big as life . . .

Her Bible.

Luke couldn't believe that he'd nearly forgotten
himself. He forced his carnal desire under control
as he turned away from the cabin. He was disgusted with himself. Just one look at her and he'd
been tempted to take that which she was not offering. He walked some distance away and stood
in the darkness, staring out into the night, waiting
for the pounding need to ease from his body.

Luke waited quite a while before going back.
This time as he approached he made enough noise
to make himself heard. He couldn't decide if he
was relieved or disappointed when he found her
in bed under the blanket.

"Bedding down already, Sister?"

"Tomorrow is the Sabbath. I have to get up early."

"Are you really planning to preach in the morning?"

"I must. It's my calling. If I don't preach to them, who will?"

Luke grunted, his dulled ardor cooling even more as he stared at her from across the room.

"You have another blanket?" she noted.

"Juana gave me an extra one of hers."

"I'm glad you won't be suffering any more discomfort because of me."

"You wouldn't believe the discomfort I'm suffering because of you," he growled to himself as he blew out the lamp and sought his night's sleep on the floor.

As he moved to put out the lamp, Cody stared at him. He looked very handsome, and she swallowed nervously, remembering how his lips had felt on hers and how her heart had pounded when he'd held her near.

He's a gunman, she reminded herself. He'd murdered the sheriff, and he'd shot the banker. It was her job to bring him in, not fall under some ridiculous sort of spell he was casting on her. Cody rolled over and pulled the covers all the way up to her chin.

"Good night," she said softly.

He grunted in reply. The night was very long.

Chapter Eleven

"And the Lord said, 'Come ye unto me like little children.' "

Cody was preaching as several of the women and three small children sat at her feet. She held the Bible before her for them to see.

"The Bible contains all the truths of the world. You need search no further for the truth of how to live a happy life. There are ten commandments that govern all civilized men," she told them, and then she began to recite them, pausing with emphasis on "Thou shalt not steal" and "Thou shalt not kill."

"God loves each and every one of us, but we must strive to be worthy of that love. We can never earn His love. It is freely given to us. We must choose to obey God's will because we want to, because it's the right thing to do."

She looked up to find Luke's eyes upon her. His expression was inscrutable. She did not stop preaching, but went on.

"It is only by living by the word of the Lord that true and lasting happiness can be found. All the answers to your problems can be found here." She touched the Bible reverently. "This is where you should put your faith.

"Come forward, brothers and sisters, and confess your sins. God forgives those who repent and change their ways," she urged, her voice a calming influence. Her expression was kindly, not condemning, but loving and understanding. "God sees all, and he forgives all if you truly repent. Come forward and take God's loving forgiveness into your hearts."

Cody bowed her head as she waited. One little boy ran up to tug on her skirt. She knelt down before him, taking one of his hands in hers. She spoke to him in a soft, low voice.

Luke stood back to watch, and when she began to talk to the child, he could just barely hear what they were saying.

"What is your name?" Cody was asking.

"Carlos," he told her.

"Bless you, Carlos." She could tell he felt awkward talking to her, so she encouraged him. "What did you want to tell me? Is it important?"

He nodded earnestly. "I got mad at Esteban, and I stole his toy soldier."

"Did you feel better after you took it?"

"For a while." He was honest.

"Why are you telling me this?"

"Because you said stealing is wrong."

"It is. Do you still have the toy?"

"Yes, Sister Mary," he admitted, dropping his gaze from hers as he felt the first pang of conscience.

"Then take the toy back to Esteban and tell him that you're sorry. Tell him that you will not steal again. Can you do that?"

Carlos swallowed tightly. "It won't be easy."

"Which one? Telling him you're sorry or not stealing again?"

"Both," he said miserably.

"Sometimes it's very difficult to be good," she told him. "But the rewards are greater than you can ever imagine." She touched his cheek. "Go now and do the right thing. You will be proud of yourself, and you will make your mama proud."

She looked up to see one of the women watching closely. "Your Carlos is a good boy. He is fortunate to have a mother who loves him as much as you do."

"Thank you, Sister Mary."

The youngster hurried off to do as she'd bid, and the mother followed after him.

Cody waited. She had never been in quite the same situation before, and she wasn't sure what to expect. The men who had wandered up while she was talking did not venture forward to speak to her, and that didn't surprise her. At least she had convinced the children that her preaching was real. She glanced up toward Luke again and found that he was still there, watching her.

"If there are no more who wish to confess this day, then our service is ended. Enjoy the beauty of the Lord's Sabbath. Keep his word in your heart and avoid evil. Do these things and eternal life shall be yours. So saith the Lord." She held the Bible up for all to see. "God bless you."

Still clutching the book, she left the group and headed back toward the cabin.

"Nice preaching, Sister Mary," Luke complimented her as he casually came to her side and walked with her. There was a peace about her that impressed him, and he liked her gentleness with the children.

Cody shot him a sidelong glance. "If I were really good, I would have convinced you to confess your sins and free your soul."

"You think I need to confess?" he asked, pretending surprise and grinning at her.

"If everything I've heard about this gang is true, then yes, you need to wash clean the laundry of your soul. You need to bare your deepest, darkest secrets and seek forgiveness."

Luke's smile turned devastatingly rakish. "I don't think you're old enough to be my father confessor."

Cody was annoyed to find herself blushing again. "I've heard many sad stories in my time."

"What if I told you I haven't done anything that needs confessing?" he teased.

"Then I would think your conscience needs some work," she retorted. Then she added more seriously, "If you ever feel the need to confess, I'd be more than willing to listen."

"But Sister Mary, I'm as innocent as a newborn babe." There was a twinkle of amusement in his blue-eyed gaze.

She stopped walking to look him straight in the eye. "Then what are you doing here?"

He shrugged. "It's as good a place as any," he replied cryptically, and then he turned the tables on her. "What about you, Sister Mary? Why do you travel from town to town, never putting down roots, never staying in one place long enough to establish a life of your own? Why don't you have a husband and children?"

"Because I have a calling. My father encouraged me to listen to my heart, and I cannot deny that I need to do this job." For once her words to him were the absolute, complete truth, not half-truths artfully disguised.

"What about your own confessions? Do you ever admit your failings to anyone?"

"I confess my faults and sins before God, but I will admit to you that my weakness, my biggest failing is the need to see justice done in this world. I want each to receive his reward according to his deeds. Unfortunately, what I want and what happens in the world are often two very different things." She looked up at him, studying the strong lines of his ruggedly handsome face and wondering how he could have become a killer. He looked so kind.

Supposedly, Luke had shot and killed an unarmed sheriff. That fact alone should have filled her with undying hatred for him. It was said that he had shot the banker during the robbery, too.

Yet there was something about him that made those accusations seem false. He had been nothing but kind and respectful to her. He had saved her from Sully when he could have left her to face the outlaw alone. Why? Those actions just didn't fit with what she'd been told about the gang and him.

Then Cody remembered the moment when Sully had challenged him when Luke had first grabbed her up back at the revival. She remembered the coldness in Luke and the steel in his voice. She remembered his lethal intent and the tension in his body. He had seemed every bit the gunfighter then, but why would he be so concerned about her? It didn't fit, and for the first time since she'd been on his trail, she began to question her belief in his guilt. Luke Majors was a confusing, puzzling man, and Cody didn't like puzzles. She liked answers.

"What is your biggest failing, Luke? Where are you the weakest? Where do you most need the Lord's help?" She was hoping for an honest answer from him. He seemed truly involved in the conversation, and she wanted to learn all she could about him.

Luke glanced down at her, seeing the complete earnestness of her expression. The last thing he needed was her prying. He smiled slowly, appreciatively. The look in his eye was decidedly leering as he answered, "I tell you, little girl, your ears just aren't ready to hear about my weaknesses. Especially the one I have for innocent little preacher women like you."

"Oh." She stared up at him, her eyes rounding, her throat going dry. She met his gaze and saw for a moment a flicker of desire that could sear a woman's very soul. She knew he was taunting her. She knew he was just teasing her to get her to shut up, but the effect of that heated regard upon her set her pulse racing and her heart pounding within her breast.

Cody tightened her grip on the Bible so her hands wouldn't shake. Luke Majors was definitely a force to be dealt with, and in that instant Cody was completely thankful for her disguise. Had she been facing him as herself, she seriously doubted that she would have been able to handle him. The thought both frightened and excited her. Heat rushed through her and she could feel her cheeks start to burn.

"You, sir, are no gentleman," she said, turning away from his mesmerizing gaze.

"You're an astute judge of character, Sister Mary." Luke laughed. He'd enjoyed watching her expression as the realization of what he was implying had sunk in. The truth was, he found her reaction appealing. The women he was used to being around these days never blushed. It was a pleasant reminder of the gentler side of life.

To save herself from further embarrassment, Cody moved quickly ahead of him. The sound of his mocking laughter was still ringing in her ears as she disappeared inside the cabin.

Frustration was the name of the game for Jack as he bided his time in Del Fuego. He was a man of action, and it wasn't easy for him to sit and wait for news either from Luke or from Cody Jameson. Jack knew patience was his most important ally, but with each passing day it became harder and harder to wait. The plan he'd set in motion the night he'd recruited Luke could yield far more than he'd ever dreamed—if things went right. But it was the not knowing what was happening that was driving him crazy.

Jack left the hotel and headed off to meet with Halloway. He had gone only a short distance when he heard two women speaking behind him.

"They've done nothing, Caroline! Nothing. They sent that Ranger down here to help, but he hasn't done anything. Sam would have had them all locked up by now." There was a pause and a sharp intake of breath. "Look, that's him now. That's Ranger Logan. The coward!"

At that Jack stopped and turned to find Sarah Gregory glaring at him.

"It's amazing you're brave enough to face me!" Sarah was deliberately insulting.

"Sarah, you really shouldn't be saying these things." Caroline tried to stop her.

"Afternoon, Mrs. Gregory," Jack said with a tip of his hat as he walked toward her. "Ma'am." He nodded toward the other woman.

"Ranger Logan," Sarah said coldly. "Has there been any news about my husband's killer? Have you found that terrible Luke Majors yet?"

"No, ma'am," he answered respectfully, understanding her frustration and pain. "But we're doing all we can."

"Oh, I can see that." She was deliberately sarcastic. "That's why you and Fred are just hanging around town waiting for Majors to ride in and turn himself over to you."

"Mrs. Gregory, there is no proof that Luke Majors is the man who murdered your husband."

"Of course he's the one! He shot Jonathan, didn't he?" she demanded.

Facing Sarah Gregory reminded Jack of the reason he had to stay in Del Fuego. "We want to see justice done."

"I can tell. That's why you're just sitting here day after day, while those killers are running loose and my husband is lying dead in the graveyard! Why aren't you out there searching for his murderer? What are you afraid of?"

"Sarah, you don't mean what you're saying." A soft voice spoke from behind Jack.

Jack recognized Elizabeth Harris's voice immediately, and he quickly turned to her.

"Elizabeth." Sarah was surprised to see her friend.

"Hello, Sarah . . . Jack," she said, looking up at him and giving him a soft smile. She touched his arm.

"Hello, Elizabeth," he returned, once again struck by her delicate beauty.

"Sarah, I've spoken with Jack on several occasions, and I know he and Fred are doing everything humanly possible to see that the ones responsible for Sam's death pay for their crimes."

"Then why haven't they found them yet?" Sarah's voice broke, her anguish real.

Elizabeth went to her and put an arm around her shoulders. "They will. I'm sure of it."

"That's right," Caroline put in.

"But why is it taking so long?" Sarah was openly weeping now.

Caroline took her friend's arm to guide her away. "Come on, Sarah. I'll take you home."

"I'll be in touch as soon as we hear something," Jack promised, wishing this whole thing was over, yet knowing there was no simple solution.

He stood quietly with Elizabeth by his side, watching the two women walk away.

"You're a very kind man, Jack Logan," Elizabeth said.

Jack glanced down at her and managed a tight smile. "She's got every right to be upset. Her husband was shot down in cold blood. It doesn't get much uglier than that. I don't blame her for being angry."

"But it's not your fault. None of this is," she championed him.

He appreciated her supportive words. "Thanks. How are you?"

Sadness shadowed her eyes for a moment, but she quickly recovered. "I'm fine."

"And your husband?"

"He's much the same," she said quietly.

"Has he improved at all?"

"He is eating, but he's still so angry. . . ." She stopped herself from saying too much. "I really shouldn't trouble you with my problems."

"I don't mind. I just wish I could do something more to help you."

She smiled at him, but there was no happiness in it. "You already have helped me, more than you'll ever know. I'd better go. Jonathan's waiting for me."

Elizabeth started to walk away.

"Elizabeth?"

She stopped to look back at him.

"If you ever need anything, anything at all . . . let me know."

She nodded, her gaze meeting his for one fleeting moment, and then she hurried on.

Chapter Twelve

Cody lay awake long into the night. Things were getting far too complicated. When she was tracking her man, she liked to be in control. That was why she did so much research before setting out on a job. But the checking she'd done on Luke Majors's background after meeting with Jack Logan hadn't yielded much useful information, and now she was trapped in a camp of outlaws with this man who was a mystery to her.

Glancing over to where Luke lay sleeping, she could see that the harsh guardedness that was so evident in his expression when he was awake was gone. He looked devastatingly attractive. She felt an odd tugging at her heart. He had not complained about not sharing the bed, and strangely her female vanity was hurt by his complete lack of interest in her as a woman.

Her feelings were ridiculous, she told herself. She was there to arrest him, not seduce him, but still there lingered the memory of his kiss. She had to admit to herself that she had been greatly affected by it. But judging from his reaction since, it hadn't seemed to affect him at all.

Cody supposed she should be grateful that he hadn't made any demands upon her that way. She glanced down at the Bible that lay on the floor beside the bed. She had it with her for protection, but she had never dreamed it would work this well. She glanced at Luke one last time before she reached down and opened the Bible for just a moment. There was just enough light in the cabin for her to see her father's revolver secured in the cutout space at the center of the book. Yes, the Good Book was offering her protection in more ways than one.

Cody let the lid close again and lay back down. She tossed and turned the rest of the night trying to figure out exactly what she was going to do. Worries about Stalking Ghost troubled her. She couldn't keep playing this role much longer. She had to take some action soon. It was near dawn when she finally fell back asleep.

Luke was growing extremely restless. He needed to keep busy, to do something, but there was nothing to do in camp until Hadley and the others returned from their meeting with El Diablo.

He glanced over to where Sister Mary was working with several of the women and children. Over the last few days there had been times when he'd caught her watching him, and he'd seen how troubled her expression was. A part of him wanted to relieve her worries, to confide in her and tell her the truth. He wanted her to believe that no harm would come to her while he was with her. Certainly he'd kept his word about not touching her. Surely that had counted for something. He didn't know what more he could do to convince her that she was safe, and it troubled him.

Luke knew things might turn ugly when Sully returned. He wasn't sure how long he could keep the other man away from her without a fight. It was a difficult situation. His only real hope was to get Sister Mary out of camp as quickly as he could without raising any suspicions and then close in on El Diablo. He could not effectively hunt for the leader of the gang and worry about her safety at the same time.

A call from the lookout that riders were coming in echoed his way, and Luke felt a renewed sense of purpose. He looked over at Sister Mary again and saw that Juana had come out to join her.

Juana glanced up at him then, saw him watching, and gave him a sultry, inviting smile. Luke smiled blandly in return, not wanting to encourage her. She was one dangerous female, and he wouldn't have bedded her even if Sister Mary hadn't been there.

Luke liked honest women, women who told the truth, women who were soft and gentle without a deceitful bone in their bodies. He'd had all he could take of cunning and lying with Clarissa. If he was going to spend time with a female, he wanted the woman more than anything to be forthright and honest. He supposed that was why, for all the aggravation she was causing him, he liked Sister Mary. She was a completely honest woman, a rarity.

Luke got up from where he'd been sitting and went to stand off to the side where he could see the trail into camp more clearly. He caught sight of the riders coming in and counted them, hoping there would be an extra man, hoping El Diablo was returning with them. But his hope was dashed.

As the outlaws drew near, the women hurried out to greet them. Juana ran to Sully and threw herself at him. He dismounted and gave her a hot, wet kiss before dragging her off into her cabin. The other men quickly dispersed with their own women.

Luke found Sister Mary keeping a low profile as she carefully edged his way. She was carrying a bundle he hadn't seen before, along with a wide-brimmed sombrero.

"What are those?" he asked.

"I desperately need to wash my clothes, and Maria was kind enough to give me these to wear." She held up a pair of trousers and a man's shirt.

"You're going to wear pants?" he asked, amazed that she would even consider it.

"The Lord has provided, and since cleanliness is next to godliness," she said with a grin and a shrug, "I thought I would sleep in them while I let my dress dry overnight."

Luke grinned, trying to imagine her in the boyish garb. "It'll certainly be a change."

"I have to do something. This is the longest I've ever gone in my life without clean clothes."

He realized then just how dirty his own clothes were. "Since you're so inspired, while you're at it, you can wash some of my things, too."

Cody had a difficult time not telling him what he could do with his clothes. She told herself that she had to stay in character. "It's good that you care about cleanliness. A bath for you certainly would not be out of order either," she replied with dignity.

"Do you want to help me wash?" he invited.

"I'm sure you are perfectly capable of washing yourself, but if you need some help, I expect I could get Juana to come to your aid," she countered quickly, drawing a scowl from him.

"That's all right."

"There's soap in the cabin, should you decide to use it."

"I'll keep that in mind."

"Majors!" The call came from Sully as he emerged from Juana's shanty fastening his pants.

"Stay here," Luke commanded Sister Mary as he headed toward Sully.

"But I was supposed to go play with some of the children for a while. . . ." she started to argue, but the look he shot her quelled any further protest.

Luke strode to where the outlaw was standing. Sully looked quite pleased with himself.

"Juana tells me the preacher woman satisfies you," Sully began, his mind still on the same track.

"She does," Luke answered stiffly.

Sully eyed him hatefully and was about to say more when Hadley walked up.

Hadley had seen the two together and thought that trouble might be brewing.

"We met with El Diablo, Majors."

"I know. The others told me that was where you'd gone."

"El Diablo says that we are to trust you, that you are one of us now." Hadley watched Luke closely, wanting to see his reaction.

At his announcement, Luke smiled.

"You're happy about that?"

"Very."

"So is El Diablo. The boss was pleased that you had chosen to join us. A gunfighter with your reputation will make us even more feared and more respected." Hadley thought Luke's reaction seemed honest enough, but, as El Diablo had said, he'd still keep an eye on him.

"When do we ride?"

"There are plans being made, but nothing is set yet. We have to wait until the time is right."

"It seems all I've done since I joined you is wait," he complained.

"Ah, but you have the preacher woman to entertain you," Hadley remarked knowingly. "Our next job is worth waiting for. It will be our biggest ever. As soon as I get word from El Diablo of the exact day the shipment is to go out, we'll ride on it. If all goes well, we'll cross the border right afterward, sell the merchandise there, and wait in Rio Nuevo until things quiet down."

"The job's that big?"

Hadley met his regard. "It's that big."

"Let's hope it doesn't take too long. Sitting around here can drive a man loco."

"Enjoy your woman . . . relax," Sully put in, not distracted from his original thought.

Luke smiled tightly. "I'm looking forward to the job and to meeting El Diablo. Does he ever come into camp?"

Hadley answered guardedly, "When El Diablo is ready to meet you, it will happen. Not before."

Sully was staring hard at Luke, wondering at his eagerness to meet the boss.

Cody stayed where she'd been told, but she'd been straining to hear what was being discussed. From what little she could pick up, there was a big robbery coming up. She had no idea where or when, but she did know that afterward the gang would be hiding out in Rio Nuevo. She'd heard the place mentioned when she'd questioned her father's friends about the gang before she'd taken the job. Had she not located Majors in El Trajar, she would have gone to the border town next. Her informants had cautioned her about Rio Nuevo, and now she understood why. Cody went back to the cabin to wash her things.

Luke remained with Hadley and the others. They started drinking, and as the sun went down, their celebrating continued. The women joined them, and it was a scene of decadence straight out of Sodom and Gomorrah. The flames of the fire burned bright and hot, while Juana and some of the other women boldly propositioned the men. Couples disappeared for a time, then reappeared to continue their revelry.

Cody only looked out occasionally from her refuge in the cabin. Everyone seemed to have forgotten she even existed, and that was just fine with her. She had taken the time to wash out her dress and undergarments, and now she sat on the bed with her hair down, wearing the pants and baggy shirt, trying to smooth some of the tangles from her wayward mane. She was wishing for a good brush, but knew it was pointless. She had to make do with the simple comb Maria had been kind enough to give her.

Cody was intent upon her hair, and she started nervously when she heard the door being opened. Her heart was in her throat as she grabbed her Bible. She feared that Sully might have managed to sneak away from the others and come after her, and she was determined to be ready for him. She opened the Bible partially and slipped her hand inside. Her courage was bolstered as her hand closed over the butt of her father's gun.

"Sister Mary?" The door opened wider and two of the children peered around it, looking for her.

Profound relief swept through Cody, and she quickly withdrew her hand, lest one of them notice that all was not what it seemed. "Chica, Rafael . . . you surprised me. What are you doing here?"

"We missed you, Sister Mary. We wanted to see you. Our mama told us we should stay inside, but when we didn't see you with the others, we hoped you'd be here," Rafael said earnestly.

"Can we stay here with you, Sister Mary?" Chica asked, jumping in fright as wild gunfire exploded outside followed by the drunken guffaws of some of the men.

Cody had no choice. She got up from the bed, set the Bible aside, and opened her arms to them.

"Of course you can," she said sweetly, meaning it. She could understand how frightened they were by all the lewd behavior, and she hugged them to her.

"You look funny in those clothes," Rafael said, seeing what she was wearing.

Cody giggled with them. "I had to wash my dress, so Maria loaned me these to wear until my dress is dry."

"You have pretty hair," Chica remarked in amazement as she stared at the cascade of burnished tresses that fell in long waves past Cody's shoulders.

"Thank you. I don't get the opportunity to let it down much anymore."

Gunfire erupted again, followed by more loud shouts and curses.

"Will you sing to us?" Chica asked, her eyes wide and imploring.

"I'll sing, but only if you sing with me," Cody told them with a smile.

Both children beamed, and they went to sit on the bed with her. The two nestled close on either side of Cody as she began to sing a sweet hymn. The children joined in.

"You sing pretty," Chica said.

"Why, thank you. You sing pretty, too."

"I'm glad you're here," Rafael told her, gazing up at her as if she were an angel.

Cody gave them each a tender hug. "I'm glad I'm here, too. Otherwise I would never have gotten to meet you." In that moment, she meant it.

The two children giggled, relaxing now that they felt safe with her.

"Can you tell us a story? The one about the big boat and all the animals?"

Cody laughed and began telling the tale of Noah and the Ark.

Luke had matched Hadley and Sully drink for drink as they'd stood around the fire, speaking of El Diablo's new plan. Juana and the other women danced their pleasure before them, eager to keep their men happy now that they were back. Liquor was flowing freely, whiskey and tequila both, and drunkenness became the order of the night.

Juana went to Sully and clung to him, whispering all the lurid things she wanted to do to him in his ear. He openly fondled her for a minute, but then his mood suddenly turned foul. He shoved her away from him.

"I want something fresh. . . . I don't want no woman who's already been with every man in camp," he snarled.

"I was good enough for you a couple of hours ago," she snapped.

Sully slapped her across the face for talking back to him. "You ain't good enough for me now.

177

Where is she?" He leered about the campfire. "Where's the preacher woman?" His gaze settled on Luke.

"That's none of your business," he answered tersely.

"It's my business. I found her first. Where're you hidin' her? You've had her to yourself long enough. Now it's my turn."

Luke had always known this moment would come. He only hoped that now that it was here, the others would back him up. He didn't want to kill Sully, but he had to keep him away from Sister Mary. "I wouldn't worry about her, if I were you. She's probably off somewhere praying for our souls."

"I don't want her praying for my soul. I don't give a damn about my soul. I want her to pray for this ache I got right here." He grabbed himself demonstratively. "Maybe if she prays over this . . ."

The other men laughed loudly at his crudeness.

"I'll ease your ache," Juana offered. She was still tasting blood from her cut lip, but she couldn't bear the thought that Sully wanted the preacher woman more than he wanted her.

"Shut up."

"I know I can make you feel good. I know exactly what you like and how you like it."

Sully reached out, snared her arm, and twisted it violently. "I said shut up." He shoved her away from him. "I got a taste for some fresher meat tonight, and I mean to be satisfied."

"I'd take Juana up on her offer, if I were you,"

Luke said slowly. His gaze was cold and deadly as he stared at Sully.

"I'm tired of Juana. I want the preacher woman."

"I told you that she was mine, and what's mine, I keep."

His quietly spoken words sent shock waves through the gang. Silence fell over the crowd. Hadley looked up and at the sight of Sully confronting Luke, he shook his head in disgust.

"You're one of us now. You should share what is yours," Sully argued, concentrating only on his need to put the high and mighty preacher woman in her place. He was just the man to do it, too. He could teach her some things she'd never find in the Bible.

"You didn't hear me, Sully," Luke repeated. "I don't share. Not my gun, not my horse, and not my woman."

"Why you . . ." Sully started to draw. By the time his hand reached leather, Luke already had his gun out and had it trained on the center of Sully's chest.

"I'm feeling generous tonight, or you'd already be dead."

"Gentlemen . . ." Hadley stepped between them. He was smiling, but it was only to cover his fury at the drunken Sully. "Tonight is a night for revelry, not gunfights. Is there a problem?" He glanced from man to man.

"Ask Sully," Luke ground out, gun still in hand.

"Sully?"

Sully blanched as he slowly moved his hand

away from his sidearm. He wanted to gut-shoot Majors. He wanted to see him down and screaming in pain. He wanted him dead. The preacher woman had humiliated him, and now Majors had, too. One day they were both going to pay. He'd make them sorry they'd ever crossed him.

"No, no problem here." He was sullen, glaring at Majors.

"Good," Hadley said.

"I don't want to see you anywhere near Sister Mary," Luke told Sully. "Remember what happened tonight anytime you start thinking about taking her."

The others were impressed by Luke's nerve.

Sully was cussing vilely as he stormed off. Juana was tempted to follow him, but knew better. He had already hurt her twice tonight, and in the mood he was in, there was no telling how vicious he would be. She would bide her time before she approached him again. She valued her life too much to ask for trouble.

Luke shared a few more drinks with Hadley.

"You know you made a deadly enemy in Sully tonight, don't you?" Hadley remarked as he handed Luke a bottle of whiskey.

Luke turned an inscrutable look on him. "The important question is, does Sully know that he made a deadly enemy in me?"

Hadley saw the coldness in Luke's expression. "Just watch your back. Sully has a lot of friends in camp."

"You one of them?"

"I am."

Luke nodded silently. After taking a deep drink from the bottle Hadley had handed him, he gave it back and turned and walked away.

Chapter Thirteen

As Luke approached the cabin, he could see a dim light glowing from the cabin window. He was glad to know that Sister Mary was inside, safely out of harm's way.

Moving past the window, he glanced inside. He expected to see Sister Mary clad in her high-necked, long-sleeved gown sitting quietly reading or doing whatever it was that she did when he wasn't around. Instead, he stopped short at the sight that greeted him. Sister Mary, or at least he thought it was Sister Mary, was sitting on the bed, talking softly with two small children, one on either side of her.

Luke frowned. He knew it was she. Who else could it be? Yet she looked so completely different that he could only stare in amazement. Her hair was down, tumbling around her shoulders in a silken, burnished mass. He had never realized the beauty of the color before. She was wearing loose-fitting men's garb, but there was absolutely nothing masculine about the way she looked in the clothing. The soft cotton shirt hung fully around her, yet hinted at the sweet curves beneath. The pants were short, baring a good length of her slender calves to his gaze. The soft light emphasized the creaminess of her complexion, and, though she still wore the glasses, she looked young and desirable. The memory of her kiss and how she'd felt when he'd held her returned, and he knew a driving urge to take her in his arms again.

He wanted her. Damn, but he wanted her.

Luke started for the door. One thing was on his mind. And then they started singing.

The lighthearted song gave him pause. It was one that he remembered distantly from his childhood. The voices of the children were high, clear, and sweet, and when Sister Mary joined them in singing the refrain, he was mesmerized. The words of the song swelled around him, stirring old memories. He opened the cabin door and stood there, staring at the three of them.

Cody had allowed herself to relax and forget everything, to enjoy this time with the children. When the door opened so abruptly, she looked up fearfully, for she realized too late that she'd let her guard down. At the sight of Luke, she was relieved, but then she saw the look in his eyes. She suddenly realized that her hair was still unbound and she was wearing men's clothes. She struggled to maintain her equilibrium as she smiled at him.

"Children, say hello to Mr. Majors."

They did so in chorus.

"Go on home," Luke directed almost tersely.

Cody sensed that there was something very different about him as he stood there. She could smell the whiskey on him; she knew all about the dangers of drunken men. "We were just singing some songs I remembered from when I was a child," she said, hoping to distract him from whatever was on his mind.

"The singing's over for tonight," he said. He wanted to be alone with her. He wanted to hold her, to touch her, to kiss her, to free the flesh-and-blood woman within her that she kept so tightly under control.

The two children looked at Cody, but she gave them a small, tight smile. "I guess you'd better go. I'll see you first thing in the morning."

"Are you still gonna be dressed like that?" Chica and Rafael giggled.

"No, I'll be wearing my own dress again." She laughed with them. "Good night, now."

They gave her quick hugs and ran from the cabin, leaving her alone to face Luke.

"You should have joined in with us. You might have enjoyed it," she said, feeling suddenly more nervous than she ever had in all the time she'd been with him. As Sister Mary, wearing her high-necked dress and carrying the Bible, she could handle him. As a woman, she had never dealt with a man like Luke before.

"Singing isn't what I do best."

"What do you do best?" she asked, trying to re-direct the conversation.

"It depends on who you ask," he said with a wry smile as he crossed the room to her.

Cody had to tilt her head back to look up at him. She saw the strange light in his eyes and knew she was in a very tricky situation. "If you'd like, I could wash your shirt for you," she offered.

Luke began to unbutton it, revealing the furred width of his powerful chest to her gaze. She tried to look away, but he seemed to fill her entire range of vision. "Thanks. It needs it."

"And there's some clean water in the bowl there, if you'd like to wash."

He shrugged out of the shirt and tossed it on the small table as he went to wash.

"I'll take care of this right now," she told him, intending to run down to the stream and stay there until he fell asleep.

"No, stay right where you are. You can wash it in the morning."

"But what will you wear?"

"It doesn't matter. I don't want you leaving here." His reasoning was sound. Sully was out there.

Cody, however, didn't know why he was forbidding her to leave, and it angered her.

"There's no reason why I can't do it now. That way it will be dry for you by morning."

Luke turned and grabbed her by the wrist as she reached for the shirt. The contact was electric.

"I told you to stay right here." His tone was threatening as his gaze met hers.

Cody instinctively recognized the raw, hungry desire revealed there and knew she was way out of her depth. Luke wanted her. Yet with that realization, something stirred within the feminine heart of her, something that took pride in seeing that look in his eyes, something that responded to him in the same way. Cody knew she should draw away, but she couldn't. The touch of his hand upon her arm was searing. She could only gaze up at him, mesmerized by the strength and sheer male beauty of him.

"I . . ." She tried to speak, to say something that would jerk them both back to reality, but no words would come as Luke slowly drew her to him.

Luke didn't stop until they were but a breath apart. Without another word, he kissed her. He could feel her trembling. He could feel her heart racing as he clasped her to him. It was a soft kiss at first, but then he heard her whimper, softly, sweetly, and he could not control himself. He crushed her in his arms, his mouth plundering hers, seeking the sweetness of her, tasting her, letting her know just how much he wanted her.

Cody was lost in the ferocity of his embrace. She'd known her attraction to him was strong, but she'd never dreamed it could be like this. Without the protection of her long-sleeved, high-necked gown, not to mention the Bible, she was defenseless against the overwhelming male power of him.

And she liked it.

Looping her arms around his neck, she clung to him. Her knees threatened to buckle before his sensual assault.

His lips left hers to explore her throat, and his hand slipped beneath the loose shirt to cup her bare breast. Cody stiffened, frightened by the force of the feelings that surged through her at that contact. It was electrifying. It was exciting, and it frightened her, for no man had ever touched her so intimately before.

"No!" She tried to escape, but his arms were like bands of steel around her.

"Easy, sweet," he murmured. He sought her lips again in a coaxing kiss as his hand remained on her breast, caressing the soft fullness, exploring the taut peak.

Cody had never known the sensations that were vibrating through her. She felt vulnerable. She wanted to flee, to run from him. Yet at the same time, a part of her wanted to stay . . . to know more.

His touch was heaven; then a flash of sanity assailed her. This was an outlaw! God only knew what terrible things he'd done in his life. She should be taking him at gunpoint, not kissing him like a wanton!

Loathing filled Cody at the thought that she'd forgotten the reason she was there. She was Cody Jameson, bounty hunter. She was there to do a job. She might give her all to bring a man in, but she wasn't giving this much *all!* Bedding Luke was not part of the deal. Anger at her own weakness surged through her, and with a herculean effort she tore herself from his arms.

"I know you can force me to your will, but know

this: I will not come to you freely." She backed toward the bed.

Luke's breathing was harsh as he stared at her. She looked the wild-eyed, passionate temptress. Her hair was a glory about her, and her breasts were heaving beneath the shirt. His body ached to be one with hers. He took a step toward her, wanting to be close to her. It was then that he saw why she had backed to the bed and what her hand was resting on . . . the Bible.

He stopped.

The Bible. Her Bible. She was Sister Mary. She preached moral living, not sin and lust. She sang hymns and prayed with the women and children. She was honest, and forthright, and a total innocent in the ways of men.

In that instant, all the passion drained from him. The heat that had been driving him cooled, and he was filled with self-loathing. Had he gone on with what he'd intended, he would have done just what she'd accused him of. He would have seduced her. He would have forced her to go against her every moral standard. He would have bent her to his will, and made love to her.

And when he'd been through despoiling her, he would have hated himself.

The thought was sobering. He wondered if all the time he was spending with these outlaws was affecting him.

Luke told himself he wasn't degenerating. He told himself it was just because she'd looked beautiful tonight. He also told himself that she'd damned well better put her ugly dress back on and tie up her hair real quick.

But he said nothing. He only stared at her, seeing the determination in her eyes not to succumb to him.

"Go to bed. I won't bother you," he said harshly, then turned and strode from the cabin.

Cody couldn't move for a moment. She'd been terrified that he wouldn't stop. She'd been terrified, too, that if he didn't stop, she wouldn't have the willpower to resist him. Her emotions confused her. She had never felt this way about a man before.

She sat down heavily on the bed, and realized then that she'd had her hand resting on her Bible. She opened it now and touched her father's gun. That weapon was her last line of defense, and, right now, she needed a defense of some kind against this attraction she had for Luke. That thought alone was a powerful motivator. It was her job to bring him in, not seduce him. He was a wanted man, and she didn't mean desired.

Cody got up and blew out the lamp. She sat back down in the darkness to think. A long time passed before she made her decision. She knew what she had to do. She could not stay. She had to get away from Luke, far and fast. She would make her escape, and she would do it tonight. Cody twisted her hair up into a tight bun again and started to get ready.

Luke stalked away from the cabin and did not look back. Guilt riddled him. Was he no better than Sully? Had he become such a lowlife that he was reduced to seducing innocents? He had never imagined that Sister Mary was so lovely. He marveled at how good a defense her preacher woman's clothes were. No man would ever have guessed how beautiful she really was, even wearing the glasses.

Again Luke found himself regretting the direction his life had taken. Sister Mary was a good woman, a gentle woman, a God-fearing woman. He was a fast gun, whom most in polite society thought was a cold-blooded killer. Their kind didn't mix. She might be trying to redeem him, but he doubted he could be saved. The situation in Del Fuego was the perfect example. He'd been trying to start a new life, to wipe the slate clean and begin again, and what had it gotten him? He'd been accused of bank robbery and murder and thrown in jail. Luke gave a disbelieving shake of his head as he rejoined the others near the fire.

"You came back," Juana said with a smile as she sat down beside him.

"I felt like doing some more drinking," he answered.

Juana silently handed him a bottle of tequila. The night passed slowly for Luke. He sat there before the flames of the fire, staring into their searing depths. He wondered if his soul was going to end up burning in hell. He took another deep drink.

Cody waited over an hour before she plumped up the cover to make it look like she was in bed, and then crept from the cabin. She donned the sombrero and carried the Bible. She'd thought about carrying the gun openly, but decided against it. The Bible had proven so far to be a far better defense than any bullet could ever have been.

Oh, God, please let me get away without anyone seeing me, she prayed silently as she crept from the house.

In the distance, she could see the group gathered by the fire. She took care to go in the opposite direction, staying in the cover of darkness as she made her way to the corral. To her surprise and joy, there was no one around. Her prayers had been answered. So far, so good.

After quickly saddling a horse, she led it from the corral and headed toward the canyon exit, staying close to the canyon walls. A noise came to her, faint, indecipherable. She froze, fearing the worst, waiting to be found and dragged back to Luke's cabin. But time passed and no one approached her.

Cody moved on as quietly as possible; she waited until she was near the front of the canyon before mounting up. Riding at a creeping pace, she headed toward the place where the guard was posted. Her heart was in her throat as she made her way from the hideout. Her every nerve was stretched taut, for she anticipated being discovered at any moment. She rode slowly, trying not to make noise, trying desperately not to arouse suspicion. The going was rocky and tricky, but taking her time, she managed without incident.

The guard noticed a rider coming. It looked like one of the men, and he didn't care about people leaving. He only worried about those trying to ride in and raid the place.

Cody lifted her arm in greeting as she rode past him. She was grateful for the lack of moonlight this night. She maintained a steady pace until she was completely clear of the canyon. Out of sight of the guard, she put her heels to her mount's side and raced off across the west Texas countryside.

It was near sunup when Luke stumbled back toward the cabin. He had finished off Juana's tequila, and then had started on whiskey. His thoughts had been dark. Memories of all he'd lost during the war and the loneliness he'd suffered since had possessed him, leaving him to wonder if he'd not only lost his family in the war, but his soul as well.

Luke had wondered what his mother would have said to him if she could have seen him sitting there with Juana hanging all over him and the El Diablo gang gathered round. His mother had been a lady through and through, the perfect example of gentility and grace. He had loved her deeply . . . and his father and his brother. But they were all gone now, and he was alone. More alone than he'd ever been before. Turning introspective, he'd examined his soul and had definitely found it wanting. Luke had told himself that he'd done what he'd had to do to survive. That it had been kill or be killed. But somehow, with each successive drink of whiskey, it seemed to matter less and less.

Luke felt as if he were filled with darkness. There was no light in his soul. And the fact that he'd almost forced Sister Mary to his will left him even more disgusted with himself.

Entering the cabin, he could make out the shape of her in bed, and he chose not to disturb her. He wanted to apologize, but it could wait until later. He would let her sleep for now. He wasn't in the best condition for dealing with females right then anyway. Luke lay upon his hard, unwelcoming bed and was asleep almost immediately.

Dawn came far too soon, and with the brightness of the new day came a splitting headache, testimony to the fine job of drinking he'd done the night before. Luke roused slowly, miserably, to look over toward the bed. To his surprise, Sister Mary was still asleep. It was very unusual, for most days she was up at first light. He gave a low, protesting groan as he sat up and then got to his feet.

"Sister Mary, you're being lazy this morning," he growled, expecting her to start moving.

When she didn't respond, he wondered if she was going to give him the silent treatment. The thought didn't appeal, and his mood grew more foul.

"Sister Mary, I just wanted to apologize for what happened last night. I gave you my word when I brought you here that your virtue was safe with me, and I am a man of my word. What happened last night will not happen again."

He waited. He'd humbled himself. He'd spoken from the heart. He'd told her the truth. He expected a response.

He grew irritated when she didn't say

something. Didn't she realize what it had cost him to walk out of here as he had last night? Didn't she realize what it had cost him to say what he'd just said?

"Sister Mary," he began again, taking a step toward the bed as he tried to focus more clearly. Everything was still a bit blurry. "I really am sorry. I never meant to hurt you in any way."

It was then, as he all but stood over the bed, that he realized she was gone. He'd been talking to rolled-up covers the whole time.

Chapter Fourteen

"What the . . ." Luke tore the blankets from the bed.

Sister Mary was gone.

His frustration combined with the humiliation he'd just suffered apologizing to a bedroll sobered him. He'd known she was upset when he'd left her. He'd thought she was just ignoring him when he'd apologized. He'd had no idea she would do anything this crazy. And it was all his fault.

Luke cursed vilely as he tried to anticipate where she might have gone. His first thought was that she was with the children, so he set out to find Rafael and Chica. Twenty minutes later, he'd learned that the children hadn't seen her, and so he'd begun to search the camp. He'd found Sully and Hadley and the others, but found no trace of

Sister Mary. It was then that the cry went up from the outlaw named Barney that his horse and tack were missing.

That news confirmed what Luke had already feared in the pit of his stomach. He'd frightened her so badly that she had fled alone and defenseless into the night. Guilt weighed heavily upon him as he tried to decide what to do. Whatever it was, he had to do it before Sully got wind of what had happened.

"I know where your horse and tack are," Luke told Barney.

The outlaw eyed him suspiciously. "How do you know?"

"It looks like the preacher woman ran off during the night. I figure she was the one who took your mount." Luke dug in his pocket and drew out enough money to pay Barney for his horse. "Here, take this until I go after her and bring her back."

"I thought Sister Mary was your woman," Barney said as he greedily pocketed the money. "It looks like you need to teach her a lesson or two."

"Don't worry. When I get my hands on her again, I'm going to set a few things straight between us."

"Well, get my horse back. I'm right fond of that animal."

"I will. This shouldn't take long." He headed for the corral to get his own mount.

Barney went quickly to Sully to tell him what had happened.

As Luke rode slowly through the camp on his way toward the entrance, he saw everyone staring at him. When Sully stepped forward from the group, he tensed, waiting to see what the man wanted.

"I hear the little preacher woman outsmarted you," he announced sarcastically.

Luke's jaw was set as he stared down at the other man. "She won't get far." He was relieved to discover that Sully knew nothing of her whereabouts.

"You must not be much of a man, if the preacher woman runs away from you," Sully taunted. "I thought she was your woman. I thought she made you happy. I guess you just weren't good enough for her, eh, compadre?"

The group gathered around, laughing with Sully as Luke urged his horse on.

"Need any help bringing her back, Majors?" Sully called out. "My women don't run away. They come back begging for more, eh, Juana?" He drew the sultry camp girl close for a kiss.

Juana responded wildly, hoping to make Luke jealous. Now that the obnoxious preacher woman was gone, she would have Sully's full attention and Luke all to herself. Not bad. She didn't care if the other women and the children were crying because Sister Mary was gone. She was glad.

Juana smiled to herself secretly as she clung to Sully. They would never know that she'd seen Sister Mary making her great escape dressed as a man. She'd thought about alerting the others, but had decided it was in her best interest to let the witch go. That had been long hours ago, and that pleased her, too. Sister Mary had several hours head start. The farther away the preacher woman was, the better, as far as Juana was concerned.

The sounds of the outlaws' mocking laughter followed Luke as he rode out of camp, but he didn't care. They were the least of his concerns right now, though he knew that was crazy. All he could think about was that Sister Mary was out there somewhere, riding the range by herself. Heaven only knew what might happen to her. He had to find her. Luke stopped to talk to the guard.

"No women left, Majors. There was only one rider a few hours before dawn, and that was a man."

"Do you know who it was?"

"It looked like Felix to me, but then I saw Felix a little while ago, so I can't be sure who it was." The guard gave him an indifferent shrug. "It's not my job to worry about who leaves. It's more important that I keep watch over who's trying to come in."

"What was the man who left wearing?"

"It was dark, but I think just plain pants and shirt, and a sombrero."

"Thanks."

Luke now knew exactly what he was looking for. Sister Mary was wearing the men's clothing she'd had on earlier last night. He realized then what an effective disguise it was, for the guard certainly would have noticed had she tried to leave wearing her gown. Luke headed out, following her trail.

Unfamiliar with the terrain, Cody had waited until first light to start riding at a steady, ground-eating pace. She wanted to get as far away as possible. She had no doubt that Luke would come after her, and she did not want to go back with him . . . not after last night.

Cody tried not to think about Luke and what had happened between them. She couldn't deny that she'd wanted him, yet if what was said about him was true, he was just like the man who'd killed her father. He was a murderer.

None of this made sense to her, and she forced her thoughts away from Luke Majors and to the gang itself. She found it strange that El Diablo never rode into camp, that Hadley, Sully, and the others had to ride out to meet with him. She'd heard snatches of conversation during her time in the outlaw camp, and one in particular stood out in her mind. Hadley had told Luke that he was one of them now. Did that mean he hadn't been at the time of the robbery? Had he just joined up with them now? And if he hadn't been a part of the gang to begin with, why had he run during the jail-break? Things were not coming together as they usually did when she was dealing with outlaws. When men murdered without conscience, they didn't deserve to walk this earth. That was why she did this job. She wanted justice.

As she thought about it, she realized that in this case, she wasn't sure just what justice would mean. The Luke Majors she'd just spent time with was a far cry from the likes of Sully and the others. A gentleman who killed in cold blood? Somehow that didn't fit. There was more to this than she knew, and she wasn't quitting yet. She had just found herself outnumbered, and she needed to retreat, to regroup and try again.

Her goal was to make El Trajar and check on Stalking Ghost. She'd been worrying about him constantly since Luke had dragged her out of town, and she had to find out what had happened to him. Once she'd learned his fate, she would make her next move in bringing Majors in.

From what she'd overheard, there was a big robbery being planned, after which they were going to hide out in Mexico. When the El Diablo gang got to Rio Nuevo, they were going to find she was already there waiting for them—but not as Sister Mary. This time she was going to have to be more Delilah than preacher woman. Disguised as a saloon girl, she would feel more in control with Luke than in her Sister Mary character. The preacher woman persona had served its purpose. It had protected her for as long as she'd needed it, but now was the time for her to bring Majors in.

Luke smiled grimly as he followed Sister Mary's trail. As he'd suspected, she was heading for El Trajar. No doubt she was worrying about the old Indian who'd been with her, but he wondered if she realized that the town was the first place Sully would look for her if he came after her. Luke was glad the others hadn't ridden with him. He had a few things to say to her when he found her, and he wanted to say them in private. It would be an interesting reunion.

It was midafternoon when Luke topped a low rise and caught sight of Sister Mary riding less than a mile ahead of him, looking much like one of the outlaws in her sombrero, pants, and shirt. He reined in to watch her. He'd been surprised at how far she'd gotten in her escape, and as his gaze followed her now, he could see why. She was riding smoothly, as if born to the saddle. She certainly was a woman of many talents.

Luke started to go after her, but stopped. His plan had been to take her back to the canyon with him, but he realized now that he couldn't. Thoughts of her embrace could not be erased from his mind, and she had become a dangerous distraction he didn't need. He was in with the gang. He'd been accepted. All he had to do was identify the leader and get the information back to Jack. The last thing he wanted was to have Sister Mary around.

Luke knew what he had to do. He followed her at a distance until she was close to El Trajar. Then carefully backtracking, he erased all signs of her trail. If anyone else tried to track her, he would fail.

Feeling satisfied that she was as safe as he could make her for the time being, Luke camped for the night. That night as he lay under the stars, sweet memories of Sister Mary came to him. He remembered the heaven of holding her and the sweetness of her kiss.

With more regret than Luke had known in years, he told himself that she was not for him.

Alone in his room at the hotel, Jack stared out the window at the dark, deserted streets of the town. His thoughts were on Luke. His friend was in a very difficult situation. The gang had been relatively quiet since the bank robbery, and that bothered Jack. He would have preferred to be out tracking them, instead of holed up in town, wasting days on end waiting to make sure some money-hungry bounty hunter didn't bring Luke in on his own.

A soft knock at the door startled Jack, for he wasn't expecting anyone. He got up quickly and grabbed his gun from the holster, which lay atop the dresser. When he started to open the door, he kept the gun out of sight.

"Yeah?" He thought it would be Halloway or one of the new deputies who had been hired since the jailbreak. He was shocked when he found himself facing the lovely Elizabeth Harris. "Elizabeth?"

"Jack," she said softly, her smile bittersweet. "May I come in? I need to talk with you privately."

Her question sounded more like a plea and touched something deep within him.

"Of course." Jack felt awkward standing there holding his revolver. His gentlemanly upbringing dictated that he step outside, but at her request he moved back and held the door wide for her to enter.

The faint, delicate scent of her perfume came to him as she walked past him, and he found it entrancing. Minutes before, the night had stretched before him, long and lonely. Now there was a beautiful woman standing in his room gazing up at him with the most expressive dark eyes he'd ever seen. A man could lose his soul in those eyes.

"I'm sorry to stop in on you like this. To trouble you this way." She could see that he was caught off guard by her visit, and she hastened to explain.

"It's no trouble. Would you like to sit down?" He gestured toward the only chair in the room, the one he'd been sitting in by the window.

"Yes, please."

She sounded breathless, adding to the quiet desperation Jack sensed about her. He quickly put his gun away, then retrieved the chair for her. Once she was comfortable, he sat down on the side of the bed facing her. He knew it was an intimate scene, but there was no helping it.

He anticipated the worst as he asked, "What is it, Elizabeth? Has your husband worsened?"

Elizabeth lifted her troubled, tear-filled gaze to the handsome Ranger. "Oh, Jack . . . It's all been so terrible."

"What's happened? Has he . . . ?"

"No, Jonathan is still alive, but it's become a living hell for me. He's angry, so completely furious over having been maimed that he's become vicious. I fear that I'm the one he's blaming . . . the one he's directing all his anger at."

Jack saw the pain in her expression, and he instantly felt the need to protect her. "He hasn't hurt you, has he?"

She drew a strangled breath, trying to pull herself together. Then, as if suddenly realizing that coming there to him, a virtual stranger, had been crazy, she stood to go. "I'm so sorry. I should never have come here to you. I'm sorry."

She started to rush toward the door, embarrassed by her impetuous action in seeking him out.

"Elizabeth!" Jack blocked her flight from him.

She looked so frightened and desperate that he couldn't bear to let her go without trying to help her in some way. She was a lovely, fragile woman. He would have been proud to call her his own, and the thought that she might be suffering in any way aroused his gallantry. Women were made to be worshiped and adored, not abused.

"No, Jack. I have to go."

"Are you all right?" he asked as he took her gently by the shoulders and turned her to him. She felt small and delicate beneath his hands. It was then as he gazed down at her that he saw a mark on her arm. "What did he do to you?"

"It's only a small bruise," she whispered, averting her eyes from his probing gaze.

"Jonathan hit you?"

She quickly tried to make excuses for her husband. "He was frustrated. I'm sure he didn't mean for it to happen. It's just . . ." She looked up at him. Her eyes revealed the starkness of her pain as she pushed her sleeve back a bit more so he could see all of the vivid, ugly bruise on her forearm. It marked the imprint of a hand.

"He did this to you?" Jack ground out.

"It's just that he's so upset and . . ." She defended her husband. "Oh, I shouldn't have come here. I should go."

"Elizabeth." He said her name gently this time, wanting to calm her, wanting to assure her that she'd done the right thing. Of their own volition his arms went around her and he drew her to him. His desire was only to comfort her, to ease her pain. "You're a beautiful woman. No one should ever lay a hand on you in anger . . . ever."

A shudder racked her as she gave in to her tears and began to cry openly. She clung to Jack. In him, she sensed she'd found someone who could help her. He felt so strong, so warm . . . so good. The more she thought of all that had transpired, the more she knew she needed him. She was desperate for what he could give her.

"Elizabeth . . ." Jack said her name again, but this time his voice was hoarse as he battled the emotions that were churning within him.

She drew another deep breath as she brought her crying under control. Jack sensed her anguish at being so mistreated and wanted to reassure her that he would protect her. He gently cupped her chin and tilted her face up to him so he could look in her eyes.

It was meant to be the gesture of a friend, of someone who cared about her, but when she whispered his name, it was his undoing.

"Oh, Jack . . . I'm so afraid." Her eyes were luminous with tears.

In that moment, Jack could no more have stopped himself from kissing her than he could have stopped breathing. He bent toward her slowly, mindlessly, caught up in a web of sensual allure from which he didn't want to be freed. Elizabeth needed him, his protection, his comforting. . . .

A distant cautioning voice in his mind warned

him that what he was doing was wrong, but he ignored it. He moved slowly, gently, not wanting to frighten her, his lips seeking hers in a tender caress.

A part of Jack was prepared for her rejection. She was another man's wife. He had no right to touch her.

But another part of Jack believed that Jonathan had forfeited any right to her when he'd abused her. He had betrayed her with violence. Her slender arm bore the mark of his fury. Jack could only think of helping her, of healing her hurt, of caring for her and erasing the sorrow he saw in her eyes.

Jack was thrilled when Elizabeth did not reject him. He could tell she was fearful at first, withdrawing slightly at that first touch of his lips. But when his mouth settled over hers in a possessive yet undemanding kiss, she did not balk, but uttered the slightest of sighs as she gave herself over to him. Her surrender sent his emotions soaring. He wanted her more than he'd ever wanted another woman.

The warning voice echoing in his thoughts cautioned Jack to stop, but as Elizabeth's lips moved under his it faded away. And then when she leaned into him, her breasts brushing his chest as he deepened the kiss, the voice of his conscience disappeared completely.

They were man and woman, and there was no need for words or guilt. They needed each other, wanted each other. Right then, nothing else mattered.

Jack lifted her into his arms and carried her to

the bed. He laid her upon the softness and followed her down. Covering her body with his own, he branded her with the heat of his desire. He had somehow known she would feel this way beneath him, deliciously soft, completely inviting, undeniably perfect.

There was no stopping. His hands were upon her, skimming over her slender curves. When Elizabeth reached out for him, he gloried in her touch as she caressed his chest, sculpted the muscles of his back, and then slipped her hands lower to tug at his shirt. Jack groaned and started to help her. As he took over stripping off his shirt, she began to unbutton the bodice of her gown.

His gaze met hers, and Jack paused. He realized what he was about to do and knew he should stop. He started to speak, to keep them from going any further, but she lifted one soft hand and pressed it to his lips to silence him before he could say anything.

"Don't say it," she whispered. She rose up and kissed him, silencing any argument he might have made. It was as if she feared that to speak of it would ruin the moment—so precious, so special.

When she'd finished with the buttons, he helped her slip the dress from her shoulders. The straps of her chemise followed, and her breasts were bared to him.

"You're beautiful," he said in a passion-husky voice as he reached out reverently to touch her.

The crests of her breasts hardened at his caress, and he drew her to him, crushing her to him. He kissed her passionately, and she responded without reserve. Her answering hunger drove him on, and he pressed hot kisses to her throat. Jack could feel her trembling as he moved lower to explore the silken glory of her bosom. When she arched in pleasure at the touch of his mouth upon her flesh, desire stronger than any he'd ever known surged through him. He knew he had to have her. He had wanted her from the first time he'd seen her, and he could not, would not stop. Not now.

Elizabeth slipped away, but only long enough to take off her dress and her chemise. She returned to the bed and opened her arms to him in invitation. Jack went into her embrace, and they came together in a heated frenzy. Theirs was pure, hot desire as they sought the ultimate pleasure that could be found only in each other.

Jack was surprised that Elizabeth matched him in his ardor. He'd expected her to be shy, but she proved a tigress. She led him to her, urging him on, creating a firestorm within him. As his body sank into the silken depths of hers, Jack groaned in exquisite agony. She began to move beneath him before he had time to think, and he was lost in the power of her embrace. He had never known passion could be so completely overwhelming. They moved together wildly, searching for ecstasy's peak.

When it burst upon them, Jack was shocked by the power of it. He held her close as the lightning storm of their joining passed. She had needed him as much as he had wanted her.

The knowledge excited him, but as his mindless ardor cooled and his sanity returned, the realization of what he'd done left him unsettled. He had always considered himself a moral man, and he couldn't believe he had just taken another man's wife.

It was then that Jack realized Elizabeth was quietly crying. He pulled away from her to try to comfort her, to apologize for what he'd dared, but she wouldn't let him.

"Please don't say a word," she told him in a tearful voice. "I know this should never have happened between us, but you must know"—she rose up on one elbow to look down at him—"I will never regret that it did."

His gaze met hers in wonderment. He had expected recriminations. He had expected her tears to be of regret and sorrow.

"You are a wonderful man, Jack Logan. I hope you don't think less of me because of this."

Jack could find no words to express what he was feeling, so he kissed her as his answer.

"You're a beautiful woman, Elizabeth. I'll do anything I can to help you," he said when they broke apart.

He kissed her once more, and she sighed. When the kiss ended, she rested her head on his shoulder, her hand splayed across his chest. Jack didn't want to think about anything right then, so he lay quietly with her beside him, savoring what little time they had together. He feared he would never have her with him again.

It was Elizabeth who shifted away first. It was Elizabeth who, regretfully, left Jack's bed and began to dress.

His blood heated as he watched her move about the room. Regret that they could never be together again filled him. Making love to her had been one of the most wonderful experiences of his life, and he didn't want to let her go. He hated the thought that he would never hold her again, never kiss her again. He couldn't let her leave this way, so he got up, and, after quickly donning his pants, he went to her and took her in his arms.

"There's no need for you to worry. No one will ever know this happened between us."

She looked up at him. "I'll never be sorry, Jack."

He wanted to kiss her one last time, but Elizabeth moved away. She went to the door and then stopped to look back over her shoulder at him. "The reason I came . . . What I needed to know . . ."

"What is it?" He could see that there was something troubling her deeply.

"Jonathan has been so vicious . . . so cruel. I've been trying to encourage him, to keep his spirits up, but he wants to see that Majors and the rest of the gang are caught. He wants them to pay for what they did to him. I just wanted to know if you'd heard anything yet. If any of the rewards the town offered has done any good?"

Jack understood her need for reassurance, but he could offer little. "I know there are bounty hunters looking for Majors and the others, but there's been no news yet. I promise you, the minute I hear something, I'll send word."

She managed a sad smile. "Thank you. It will mean so much to Jonathan." She started out the door, then paused for a moment to look back. "And to me." A lone tear was tracing a crystalline path down her cheek. "Good-bye."

The door closed soundlessly behind her.

Jack stood there staring at the closed portal, trying to come to grips with all that had happened. He didn't know how it was that she had come to him, but he gloried in the fact that she had. Jack knew he should have felt guilty, but the memory of the bruise on her arm shielded him from any attack of conscience. Any man who abused a woman didn't deserve her.

Jack wanted to help Elizabeth. He needed her. And she had done something that no other woman had done in years. She had touched his heart.

Jack stood unmoving in the middle of the room a few minutes longer, steadying himself, clearing his thoughts. Then, unable to bear the loneliness of his room, he finished dressing and went down to the saloon.

Chapter Fifteen

Cody was tense. El Trajar was just a few miles ahead. She was almost there, yet something within her was warning her to be careful, that someone was watching, that she was not alone. She urged her horse to an even quicker pace. She wouldn't feel safe until she was in town, and even then she wondered how safe she'd be. No one had tried to save her when Luke had carried her off, and she doubted anyone would come to her aid today, if the gang came after her again.

Glancing back, Cody checked to see if she could spot someone following her, but it looked quiet. She knew quiet could be deceptive, though, so she rode even harder.

Miles passed, and then he appeared before her like an apparition, emerging from his hiding place behind some rocks and brush. Startled, Cody reined in quickly and her horse shied nervously. With a practiced hand, she controlled her mount as tears clouded her vision. In an instant, she was on the ground and running to him to throw her arms around him.

"Stalking Ghost! You're alive! Thank God!"

Stalking Ghost accepted her embrace, then held her away from him. He studied her for a moment, his expression, as always, impossible to read. He nodded slightly as if confirming that she was all right, before he spoke. "Where is Majors?"

"Back in camp. I'll tell you about that later. What about you? What happened? I was afraid you were dead!"

"I am fine," he answered, disdaining any more discussion of his situation.

"I'm glad." Her words were heartfelt.

"So am I." It was as close to an emotional exchange as he ever allowed himself to have with her. "Why didn't you bring Majors out with you?"

"I couldn't. There were too many of them. I kept up the Sister Mary ruse as long as I could, but last night I got the chance to get away, so I took it."

"We will go back together."

"No. It won't work. The camp is too well guarded. I've got another idea. Where's the wagon?"

"I left it in town."

"Then let's head there. We don't have a lot of time. They may be coming after me. I'll explain on the way."

They mounted up and rode together into El Trajar to where the wagon and their belongings awaited them. Cody quickly changed back into her Sister Mary role before speaking to anyone. The townspeople were amazed that she'd gotten away from the terrible gang.

Cody did not deviate from being the preacher woman until they were well out of town and headed for the border. Only then did she change clothes again. She'd had enough of high-necked, long-sleeved gowns. She just wanted to be herself for a while. She would worry about transforming herself in another day or two, but for now she just wanted to be comfortable. They had a lot of ground to cover.

His days were passing with an infuriating sameness, and Jonathan Harris was in an uglier mood than ever. He hated all the false happiness being put on around him. The doctor had been in to see him earlier that day. He'd told him that he was recovering nicely. Recovering nicely? He would never walk again! What was so nice about that? As far as Jonathan was concerned, the doctor could go to hell. The long weeks since the shooting had been torturous for him, and it wasn't going to change.

He was sitting in his hated wheelchair by the front parlor window staring out across the street, watching and waiting for Elizabeth to return. She'd gone to the store to pick up a few items and had been away the better part of an hour. He didn't like being alone. He wanted her beside him all the time. She was his wife and she should be there to take care of him. When she finally came into view, his temper was hot. He was waiting for her by the door when she entered.

"Hello, darling," she greeted him.

"Where the hell have you been?" he demanded, confronting her the moment she closed the door.

"I told you. I was at the general store."

"For almost an hour? What took that long?"

"I was visiting with Mr. Wayman. He said to tell you hello and that he hoped you were feeling better."

"Sure he does," he snarled, grabbing her by the wrist and yanking her toward him. "When I tell you to hurry back, I mean it!"

"But I did hurry, Jonathan," she protested, trying to twist free of his painful grip. "I have to get out and see other people sometime. I can't stay locked in this house forever!"

"Why not? I'm going to be locked here from now on!"

"Jonathan, you know that's not true. Just this morning, the doctor said you could go back to work."

The look in his eyes turned glacial at her words and he tightened his grip even more. "Do you think I want to go back to the bank so people can come by and stare at me? So they can tell me how sorry they are that I'm half a man? Think again! I won't play the freak for anyone!"

"Jonathan, let me go. You're hurting me."

"You will do what I say from now on!" His tone was threatening. "If I say be back in ten minutes, then you get back here. Do you understand me?"

"You can't mean this. This is crazy! What about me? What about my life?"

"Your life ended the day I was shot, just like mine did. Now fix me something to eat and be damned quick about it!" he raged as he shoved her from him as if touching her was suddenly a vile thing to do. He turned the wheelchair awkwardly away from her so he could stare out the window again.

Tears burned in Elizabeth's eyes as she spoke to her husband. "I don't know what's happened to you, Jonathan. You're still alive. You're not dead. You need to get out and see your friends. You need to start living again, and not hide here in the house."

"Hide? I'm not hiding. I'm just burying myself prematurely."

"But the doctor said you could live a nearly normal life."

Jonathan gave a harsh, cruel laugh. "Nearly normal? What's that? I'd rather be six feet under."

"I won't be buried with you."

He turned on her, his expression threatening. "Don't tempt me, woman."

"You're not the same man I married."

"You're damned right I'm not. I'm going to be in this chair for the rest of my life."

"But there's no reason why things can't go back to the way they used to be."

"Go back?" His vicious, savage anger showed in his expression. "Go back to walking? Go back to being a man again? Don't you understand that it's never going to happen? Never! And it's all because of that . . . that Luke Majors. I'm living only for the day I get to see him hang for what he's done."

There was so much venom in his voice that Elizabeth ran from the room. She'd been hoping he'd go back to work and resume his old way of life, but it would never be. She wondered what she should do next.

It was evening before Elizabeth managed to slip away from the house. Jonathan had gone to bed after drinking himself into a stupor, and she felt it was safe to leave him alone for a while. As drunk as he was, she was certain he would sleep all night.

She made her way to Sarah Gregory's house. She had not had the opportunity to speak with her in the days since she'd met her on the street with Jack, and she felt the need to see how her old friend was doing.

"Evening, Elizabeth," Sarah said, smiling in welcome as she answered the knock on the door. "Come in. It's so good to see you."

"Is this a good time? I'm not intruding?"

"Never. I need a friend right now."

The two women embraced as Elizabeth entered the house; then they settled in the parlor to talk.

"How are you doing?" Elizabeth asked in earnest.

"Terrible. Sam was my life. I'm lost without him," she admitted painfully.

"I'm so sorry. Sam was my friend, too. This whole ordeal has been a nightmare. Have you heard anything yet?"

"There's been no word, not even with those big

bounties they're offering."

"I don't understand how those murderers can just disappear like this. It doesn't make sense."

"None of this does. Lives ended . . . lives ruined forever. Oh, Elizabeth." Sarah reached out and took her hand. "You are so lucky to still have Jonathan."

Their gazes met as Elizabeth began to answer. "I don't feel lucky and neither does he." She gave a small sob as she continued, "Oh, Sarah, Jonathan wishes he were dead. You know he'll never walk again or—"

"I didn't know. When I'd heard that he was better, I thought he was going to recover fully."

"No. He'll never be the same again. He's changed so much. He's so bitter. All he thinks about is revenge. I try to keep him calm, but I don't know what more I can say to him."

"It must be awful for you."

"It is, but then when I start to feel sorry for myself, I realize how self-centered I'm being."

"You're not self-centered. You're a wonderful woman, who's trying hard to be a good wife in a horrible situation. You're so brave. I don't know how I would have handled it, if our situations had been reversed," Sarah said.

"And I don't know what I would have done had I lost Jonathan."

The two women shared a look of mutual understanding and sorrow.

"I'd better get back. If he wakes up and finds me gone, he'll be angry."

"I'm so glad you came. I've missed our visits."

"If you need anything, let me know."

"You, too. I'll never get over Sam's death, but I will go on. I have to. I have no other choice." She sighed. "One day, justice will be done and Sam's killer will hang. Until then, I just have to live day to day, and keep praying for strength."

Sarah showed her out, and Elizabeth started for home. She was lost in thought as she walked along the darkened street. There still was no news about the gang . . . nothing.

"Elizabeth?"

The sound of her name being called softly jerked her back from her thoughts of the gang and Luke Majors. She looked up to find Jack crossing the street toward her.

"Jack. I hadn't expected to see you."

"What are you doing out so late alone?" He was worried about her safety.

She quickly told him where she'd been. "Sarah said there still hasn't been any news about the gang."

"I know. I'm sorry there isn't any more to tell you. Shall I walk you back home? I don't like the idea of you walking the streets alone after dark."

Elizabeth looked up at the handsome Ranger, thinking of everything Jonathan had said and done to her that day, and knew that home was the last place she wanted to be. "Jack, I don't want to go home. I don't want to go back there."

Jack saw the desperate loneliness in her eyes. "Elizabeth . . ." His voice was hoarse as he stared down at her.

"Please don't make me go to him, not now. I'm so lonely, Jack."

He took her arm and drew her with him into a dark area around the corner of the building. His gaze was an intense, burning flame as he gazed down at her. "Do you know what you're saying?"

She lifted her gaze to his, and he saw her need in the depths of her soul. She was trembling beneath his touch.

"Yes," she whispered breathlessly.

Their gazes locked for what seemed an eternity until finally Jack spoke. "This won't be easy or simple."

"Nothing about us is."

" 'Us,' " he repeated quietly. "Is there an 'us,' Elizabeth?"

"I don't know what I'd do without you. You've become so important in my life, Jack."

Jack pulled her to his heart and kissed her then, a tender kiss of promise and need, showing her that she was important to him, too. When they broke apart, his breathing was ragged. "I don't want to put your reputation at risk. You mean too much to me."

"Is there another way to your room? Some way I can come to you so no one will see me or know?"

Jack frowned, trying to remember. "There's a back staircase by the kitchen."

"I could come to you that way."

They shared a look that spoke of desire and need, and without speaking again, they made their way through the streets to the back entrance to the hotel. It was deserted. Jack tried the door and found it unlocked. Only one low-burning lamp glowed inside, and they could see the narrow steps that led to the second floor.

Neither spoke as Elizabeth crept inside and quickly disappeared up the stairs. Jack watched until he was sure she was safely away, then went around the building and entered from the front. He went straight up to his room and left the door unlocked. A moment later, Elizabeth was there, in his arms, kissing him hungrily.

Much later, they lay together.

"I have to go. If Jonathan wakes up, I have to be there."

The mention of her husband's name jolted him, but the pleasure he'd just experienced in her arms helped him to ignore it.

"I don't want you to leave," he told her, his hand tracing a sensuous path down her spine as she leaned over to kiss him.

"I would stay with you if I could, but there's so much else to consider," she told him honestly.

Jack was filled with regret as they both got up to dress. He went to her as she was about to leave. "When will I see you again?" This time he allowed himself to hope.

"Are you going to be in town long?"

He nodded. "I'll be here until this is resolved."

"Then I will come to you as often as I can. It will have to be late at night . . . much later than this."

"I'll be waiting."

She lifted one hand to touch his cheek, and then she was gone, disappearing into the night. Jack sat alone in his room, savoring the memory of loving her. He could hardly wait to be with her again. Knowing her pain, he became even more determined to find the man responsible for hurting her so badly.

"How do I look?" Cody asked Stalking Ghost as she turned to face him.

He grunted.

She took his response as an enthusiastic reply and turned back to the small mirror she was carrying with her. Squinting into the square, she tried to judge her own looks. This was one of her most ambitious disguises ever, and she had to be sure that she was perfect. Cody studied her reflection. Her naturally auburn hair was now coal black, and thanks to the wild-herb combinations Stalking Ghost knew, her fair skin was now as dark as any Mexican woman's. The dyes would last for quite a while, so she knew she was safe—for now.

All that was left to do was get a job at the cantina in Rio Nuevo. Cody had changed into a flaring skirt and white blouse with a scoop neckline to try to achieve her goal. The times she'd worked as Delilah had prepared her for what she might encounter. It would be tricky. The first thing and the hardest to do was to get hired and convince the cantina owner that she was no whore, but a legitimate entertainer. She would sing, serve drinks, and dance, but she would not do anything else. Then she had to get settled in and established before the El Diablo gang showed up. She hoped her ruse worked.

As they neared the border town, they stopped.

She was glad they had gotten rid of the wagon long miles back. She didn't want to take any chances of Luke recognizing her.

"It's important that you stay out of sight."

"You will be all right?" Stalking Ghost asked, worrying, though his expression betrayed no sign of it.

"As all right as I ever am. I hope this works." She looked a little troubled at the thought of riding into the border town alone. She knew it was going to be rough, and she had to be prepared.

"I will be near. You have your knife and your gun?"

"Yes." The knife was strapped to her thigh, and her gun was in her saddlebag. "I hope the gang shows up soon. If we can work this right, just like we did bringing in Hank Andrews, we'll be in good shape. The big thing will be waiting for them to get here. Once they show up, I'll go to work on him right away."

"Until then, be careful," he warned.

She managed a smile. "Don't worry. The last thing I want is trouble before Majors shows up."

Turning her horse toward the border town, she rode in slowly. Stalking Ghost kept watch for a while, then chose his own route into town.

There were several cantinas in Rio Nuevo, so Cody chose the cleanest-looking one. She dismounted and tied up out in front, ignoring the stares of the few folks who were out and about. Girding herself, she walked brazenly into the saloon and up to the bar.

Cody sized the place up quickly. It was as clean

as border-town bars went. Customers were few, but it was a quiet time of day. The man behind the bar looked at her hungrily. She knew what he was thinking, and she wanted to put that thought out of his mind right away.

"My name is Armita. I want to work for you," she said without preamble.

The bartender leered appreciatively at the thought. She was a pretty little thing, and he wouldn't mind tasting some of that. "I'll try you out myself first to see if you're good enough for my customers."

Cody's hand moved lightning fast and her knife appeared before his eyes. "I am a singer," she announced with dignity. "I will sing for you. I will serve drinks for you. I will wait on your customers for you."

The bartender's eyes widened at the sight of her well-honed blade. He could tell by the way she held it that she knew how to use it. "Pity. You would do good business here."

"I will do better business for you with my singing. The other I do for my own pleasure in my own time, not for money," she replied haughtily. "Now, shall I sing for you?"

He frowned at her. "I don't need a singer."

"No," she replied sarcastically. "You need customers." She gestured around the nearly empty cantina.

He snorted in irritation. "And you think your singing will bring them in here?"

"Do you have any entertainment?"

"Only the few girls who pleasure them. Nothing more."

"Then it's time to offer more. When you hire me, they will come to hear me sing, and they will spend their money with you."

"Sing," he ordered, wanting to hear if her voice was as strong as her nerve and spirit.

Cody moved away from him and went to stand on the far side of the room. She wanted to show him how her voice could carry. She began with a sweet tune, and her voice rang out clearly across the nearly empty cantina.

The few men who were there—who hadn't been paying much attention to her conversation with the bartender—quickly perked up. They turned to watch her, their expressions at first curious, then rapt. Her voice was beautiful. The song was a lilting melody, one good to prove her range, but not really suitable for a bar. The bartender liked her voice, but didn't like the song.

"Is that all you know how to sing? That ain't gonna bring no customers in here. Sounds like a church hymn." He was scowling as he spoke to her.

Cody tossed her hair over her shoulder and glared at him defiantly before she broke into a rowdy song whose lyrics would have turned the ears red on some of the old maids back in San Antonio. She'd learned the words for this one and quite a few more when she'd worked in the saloon in Arizona as Delilah. The minute she stopped the customers broke into thunderous applause. The barkeep finally managed a grudging smile.

"All right, Armita. That innocent look of yours is just that—a look. You know what you're doing. You're hired."

"*Gracias.*" Cody was excited. She was closing in on her goal. She'd gotten the job.

"There's no need to thank me. You're just what this cantina needs to spice it up. When can you start?"

She didn't hesitate. "Tonight. Do you have a room for me?"

"Take any of the ones upstairs that the other girls aren't using." He told her what her pay would be, and then added with a suggestive smile, "You know you could make more. . . ."

Cody lifted her head high. Her eyes were flashing as she turned to him. "I will sing for you."

The bartender shrugged. "Up to you. Go ahead and take a room. The boys usually wander in a little after sundown, although tonight will be quiet. It's not the weekend yet."

She flashed him a triumphant smile as she headed toward the stairs. "I will just have to liven this place up a little bit then, won't I?"

Chapter Sixteen

"El Diablo came through for us again," Hadley was saying with pleasure as he sat drinking at a table in the Cantina del Sol in Rio Nuevo.

For a while there he'd been worried, for there had been no word from El Diablo. But then the message had come detailing all they'd needed to know about the arms shipment. And now they'd pulled off the job and were here relaxing in the border town. The robbery had been bloody. All the guards had been killed and they'd lost two of their own, but the profit they were going to make from the sale of the guns made it worthwhile. The boss was going to be pleased with them . . . very pleased, especially after Del Fuego.

"We got the guns. We're going to make the trade in the morning, and then all we have to do is lay low," Sully put in with a smile. He was feeling quite satisfied with himself, for he had personally killed at least three of the soldiers who'd been riding with the shipment.

"El Diablo has never been wrong," Jones said. "I don't know how the boss does it."

"When news of this gets out, do you realize how feared we're going to be?" Sully remarked.

Luke was standing at the bar, barely able to control his fury as he listened to them. He took another deep drink of his whiskey, trying to drown out the memory of the soldiers who had been slaughtered during the robbery. He'd been helpless to stop the carnage, and it left him feeling impotent and filled with rage over his inability to stop what had happened.

Silently, he cursed his situation. How had he ended up with men like these? They were totally amoral and gave no thought at all to right or wrong. They were men who thought killing just a means to an end, an expedient way to get what they wanted.

True, he'd killed men in his life, but those were times when he'd been fighting for survival. He was not a murderer, no matter what people might say, and it was an abomination to his spirit to be forced to deal with these men. He wanted only to find El Diablo, see him arrested, and get the hell out of there.

"So, when do we meet with El Diablo to tell him the good news?" Luke asked, downing the rest of his liquor as he turned to where they were sitting at the table. He was tired of waiting. He wanted this over with, the sooner, the better. He wanted to get back to the ranch, to start his life over.

Hadley shrugged off his question. "Not for a while. We have to stay quiet and out of sight. I'm sure the army and the Rangers are going to be looking real hard for us. When the time is right, we'll go back. Until then, enjoy." He gestured expansively around the cantina. Liquor was flowing, and the girls who worked there were eagerly luring the outlaws upstairs to show them a good time for the right price.

Luke's jaw tensed in anger at being put off again. He realized he should have expected as much, but it didn't make it any easier to put up with. This hunt for the mysterious El Diablo was growing more complicated every day. The man's contacts and the inside information he was able to get his hands on amazed Luke. The outlaw leader had sent a nondescript messenger with the details of not only how many guns were in the shipment, but how many guards would be riding along as well. He had to have an in at the fort or in town to be privy to such guarded information.

The situation was troubling Luke. It was beginning to appear that Jack might be closer to El Diablo back in town than he was here. Still, Luke knew there had to be a connection somewhere, and he was going to find it and follow it to the end. At the rate things were going, it looked as if it might take months for him to identify the elusive boss, and the prospect galled him. Damn, but he wanted out of there.

The sound of the piano player striking a brash,

single chord to get the attention of the crowd drew his gaze to the small stage at the front of the cantina.

"We are proud to present to our customers, the lovely Armita!" he called out.

All eyes were riveted on the stage as a young woman stepped out before them. She was gorgeous, and the cowboys hooted and hollered their approval of her tight-fitting red dress with its multitude of petticoats.

Luke turned back around to face the bar. He had no desire to be entertained tonight. He just wanted peace and quiet—and plenty of whiskey.

Cody smiled at the customers as the piano player began to play a raucous melody designed to get the cowboys in a drinking mood. This was the beginning of her third week working there, and already word about her had spread. Each night the number of customers had grown. She was pleased, but she didn't really care. Her only reason for being there was to find and trap Luke.

She launched into a chorus of the song that had become her trademark, a raucous ditty that she'd learned in Arizona territory. Flashing her skirts, affording the men glimpses of her high-heeled boots and shapely calves, she moved about the stage, mesmerizing them with the excitement she exuded. When the song ended, cheers erupted from the drunken cowboys. She began another, even more bawdy Mexican song that drew more shouts of laughter from the crowd.

Glancing around the room, Cody almost faltered in her lyrics when she spotted Hadley, Sully, and some of the others gathered at a table in the back of the room. Trying not to be too obvious, she tried to see if Luke was with them, but there was no sign of him at the table.

She thought it odd that he wasn't with them. And it was then that a new worry assaulted her. She'd known they were going off to rob someone else, and she suddenly worried that something might have happened to Luke. He might have been shot or wounded—or caught.

Her worries lasted only a moment, for when she looked toward the bar she saw him standing with his back to her. Excitement shot through her. She told herself she wasn't really glad to see him. She was just excited because he was worth a lot of money to her. Nothing more.

Thrilled that everything had fallen into place for her, Cody began to plot what she was going to do next. All she had to do was get him upstairs to her room. She knew the bartender would be surprised that she was bedding someone. In the time that she'd been here, she'd served drinks, played cards, laughed and drunk with the customers, but she'd never allowed any of them into her bed. Tonight was going to be different. Cody would do whatever it took to get Luke Majors to her room, and if it meant pretending to seduce him, she'd do it. Luke Majors was hers! She was taking him in. She would not fail this time.

Luke ignored the woman onstage and all the hollering from the men around him. He was in no mood. Draining his whiskey glass, he headed for the door. Surely one of the other saloons in town would be quieter than this. It was then that Armita's loud song ended, and she began to sing a sad ballad.

It surprised Luke that Armita's voice sounded so much like Sister Mary's when she'd sung to the children. He stopped when he would have gone. The pure, sweet tones touched something deep within him, and he had to turn back to look at her.

The raven-haired beauty was one of the loveliest women he'd ever seen. Earlier he'd wondered why the barkeep had kept bragging about the nightly entertainment, and now he understood. He found himself mesmerized by the raven-haired singer.

Luke moved back inside, his gaze fixed on the stage. This Armita, who was the darling of those gathered here, was no ordinary bar girl. Her dress was provocative without being revealing. Bright red, it was form-fitting, emphasizing her soft curves without giving too much away. The skirt of the dress was full, and her petticoats were ruffled and colorful. There seemed a certain innocence about her, too, that Luke didn't quite understand, but it held him spellbound.

"She's damned good, ain't she?" Hal, the barkeep, said to him as he moved back to the bar.

"Very," he answered, not looking away from the stage. He was sorely disappointed when the song ended and she disappeared from sight.

"Don't worry. She'll be back. She sings again in about an hour, and sometimes she even comes out and flirts with the crowd."

Just as he finished speaking, Cody emerged from the back and began to make the rounds of the tables, greeting the cowboys who'd come to hear her sing. They were all respectful to her, un-like the way they treated the other girls. They thought nothing of pawing them as they walked by, but they held Armita in a bit of awe.

Cody made her way slowly through the crowd, heading toward her prey. At last she had him where she wanted him. She was ready. Disguised this way, she felt in control. She would lure him upstairs and give Stalking Ghost the signal. Then it would be simply a matter of hauling him away without getting caught. She was pretty sure they could make it as long as the hour was late enough and the patrons had had enough to drink.

She reached the bar and leaned on it with one elbow as she smiled at Hal.

"Good singing," Hal complimented her.

"*Gracias*. It is fun to make the men laugh . . . especially so many of them."

"That's all thanks to you, Armita."

Cody gave a soft laugh as her gaze settled on Luke. "I told you I could bring the men in." As she spoke, she made certain that her accent was soft, yet evident enough to enhance her character. Having grown up in San Antonio, she was very good at it.

She smiled at Luke when he looked over at her.

"You do sing beautifully, Armita," Luke complimented her. "You're a rare treat in a town like this."

233

"Why, thank you," she purred in accented English. She saw pure male appreciation in his gaze and her pulse quickened. Cody had to warn herself to remember who she was and what she was doing. She couldn't allow him to touch her or kiss her. She remembered all too clearly how she'd reacted to his embrace, and she didn't want that to happen again. She was here with him, and he was interested in her, so she was halfway home. All she had to do was get him alone upstairs. The rest would be easy. "You are from around here?"

"No, I just rode in."

"You are with the others?" she asked, glancing toward where Hadley and Sully sat.

"You could say that. Can I buy you a drink?" Luke offered.

"I try not to drink when I'm working, but tonight, with you . . ." She paused to look him in the eye. "Yes. I would love to have a whiskey with you."

Cody smiled serenely as she accepted the glass from the bartender. She sipped the empowering liquor, relishing the burning taste that steadied her. Luke Majors would soon be hers.

"Would you like to sit at a table?" he invited.

"Of course, Señor . . . ? What shall I call you?"

"Just call me Luke."

"All right, Luke," she answered in a throaty voice. "Let us find a table where we can be alone."

With his hand at the small of her back, he directed her to a secluded table as far away from the rest of the gang as he could get her.

"So tell me about yourself," Cody encouraged as

she sat facing him in the quiet corner.

"There's not much to tell."

"Why have you come to Rio Nuevo?"

"I came to hear you sing," he answered, his gaze upon her.

"So the news that I am singing here has already spread so far throughout Texas that it even draws the infamous El Diablo gang to hear me?" She smiled wickedly, knowing he was lying and enjoying matching wits with him.

"As good as you are, one day you will be world-famous."

She nodded. "I would like to be the best at what I do."

"You aren't already?"

"We shall see," she replied, casually sipping her liquor. "So why are you really here, Luke?"

"Business. What about you? How did you end up in a place like this?"

"Sometimes life has a way of taking you to places you never dreamed you'd go," she remarked, looking around the room and taking great care to hide the disgust she was feeling about the place.

"I know," he agreed.

He took a deep drink, then looked up at her. Their gazes met.

Cody stared into the fathomless depths of his blue eyes and felt as if she were losing herself. She took another healthy drink of whiskey to bolster her nerve. She had to tread very cautiously with him, for she knew what could happen if she allowed him to kiss her. She had to be careful, very careful. Remembering the last embrace they'd shared, she suddenly downed the rest of her drink.

"I have to go get ready to sing again," she told him, wondering why she sounded so breathless. "Will you be here when I finish?"

"I'm not going anywhere," he answered with a smile. "Come back when you're done, and I'll buy you another whiskey."

"I will do that." She stood up and touched his cheek. "This is my last performance for the night. Perhaps after we have our drink . . ."

She left him with that titillating thought.

Her next performance went smoothly, and she could hardly wait to be done with it. She left the stage and headed straight to Luke's table to join him for the drink he'd promised. She'd only just taken a seat when Sully's voice sounded from behind her. Shivers of revulsion shot up her spine when the outlaw touched her, lifting a lock of her hair from her shoulder and rubbing it between his fingers.

"Well, well, Majors, looks like you already found somebody to replace the preacher woman," Sully slurred drunkenly. "This one's real pretty, too."

Cody tried to act casual, but he was making her skin crawl. She picked up the glass of liquor Luke had ordered for her and took a healthy swig. She hated Sully and couldn't wait to be done with her job so she'd never have to see him again. Had Logan hired her to bring him in, she would have had trouble bringing him back alive. She turned and looked up at the outlaw, trying not to appear the least bit affected by his presence.

"You and Luke are *amigos?*" she asked politely.

"We're old friends," Sully sneered. "If you get bored with him, come and see me. I'll show you a good time."

"I will remember your offer, señor."

Relief and triumph swept through her as he walked away. Luke hadn't recognized her up close and neither had Sully. She had fooled them both! Her disguise was working! Now if she could just get Luke upstairs alone . . .

"It is crowded in here. Would you like to leave? My room is just upstairs."

Luke smiled, but didn't make any move to get up right away.

"Why are you smiling so at me?" She had expected him to jump right up and head for the stairs. If he refused to go to her room, she was going to have to come up with an alternate plan to get him alone.

"I am smiling because I am pleased with your invitation. Your friend the bartender told me not to get my hopes up, because you didn't take men upstairs."

She smiled, again relieved. "I have not . . . until you. You are the man I want to be with tonight." She took another sip of whiskey.

He lifted his glass and drained it. "Let's go." He picked up the bottle of liquor he'd brought to the table and stood to follow her.

Cody led the way, threading a path through the tables, pausing now and then to exchange greetings with the cowboys. Then she reached the bottom of the steps and waited for Luke to come to her side before starting up the stairs with him.

Many of those gathered in the saloon below watched them go, and each wished he was the man with Armita. She'd proven elusive to all the other men there. Regular customers who returned night after night had never seen her take any man upstairs to her private room before. They wondered enviously what Luke had that they didn't.

Cody opened the door to her room and waited until Luke had entered before closing and locking it behind her.

"You locking me in or locking others out?"

"I want you to myself," she said huskily.

"You have me already," he said with a hungry smile as he set the bottle aside.

Cody knew she should evade his advances, but there was no way to do it without rousing suspicion in him. She had lured him up here, now she had to act the part. With Andrews it had been easy. He had been repulsive, but with Luke . . .

He took her in his arms and without another word, he kissed her.

At the touch of his lips, she went weak inside. She'd hoped she'd be immune to his sensual assault, but she wasn't. Freed by the mind-numbing whiskey she'd imbibed, all the feelings she'd denied surged forth again. Cody found herself leaning into Luke and linking her arms around his neck to get even closer. She told herself she would see about signaling Stalking Ghost and trapping Luke in a minute, but for right now, she just wanted to kiss him.

He tightened his arms around her, and the

woman inside her smiled in feminine triumph. Luke wanted her.

The room seemed to spin as he held her in his embrace. There was no tentativeness in his passion with her as there had been when she was Sister Mary. He was a man who desired her, and he was not holding back.

His lips moved persuasively over hers, coaxing her to deepen the kiss, and she met him fully in that passionate exchange. When they finally broke apart, Cody was breathless and stared at him in bewilderment, not quite sure what to do next. She spied the whiskey bottle where he'd set it on the nearby table and she picked it up and took a swig. The heat of it seeped through her veins, relaxing her strength of will even more and easing the stern control she maintained over herself.

"What did that man mean when he was talking about you and a preacher woman?" Cody asked, trying to get a grip on what was going on.

"He was just talking to hear himself talk." Luke tried to dismiss Sully's comment, wanting to avoid thinking about Sister Mary right now. For just that short time when he'd been kissing Armita, all thoughts of Sister Mary had been banished, and that was good. Somehow it just didn't seem right to be dwelling on the revivalist when he was in the middle of kissing Armita.

"No, I can see that she meant something to you. Why don't you tell me about her?"

Luke picked up his bottle and took a drink. He started to set it aside, but Cody took it from him and drank herself. She didn't usually like liquor, but tonight it was tasting good to her. There were no chairs in the room, so they settled in on the side of the bed to talk.

"What do you want to know?" Luke asked.

He stared at Armita, and though he knew it was crazy, something about her reminded him of Sister Mary. Certainly they looked nothing alike except for the fact that they both had green eyes. Other than that, they were as different as night and day. Sister Mary had been pure and innocent. Armita knew her way around men. Sister Mary had been kind, gentle, and chaste. Armita was no doubt a hellion. She had to be to work here. He'd watched her work the crowd in the cantina. Sister Mary was fair. Armita was dark. Sister Mary had dressed as a woman of God unconcerned about worldly things. Armita dressed to enhance her own beauty and draw admiring glances from men.

"Who was she?" Her question interrupted his thoughts of the preacher woman. "Where did you two meet?"

"In a little town called El Trajar. She was a traveling revivalist whose main goal in life was to save souls."

"And did she save yours?"

Luke gave a derisive laugh. "I'm past saving, Armita. My soul is blacker than pitch. Especially now." Memories of the soldiers who'd been murdered in the robbery came to him, and he took another swallow of the fiery liquor. He handed the bottle to her. "Sister Mary was honest, pure, and sweet. A truly gentle soul. She was all the wonderful things a woman should be. I didn't deserve her, and I'm glad she's safely away from me. I've got a job to do."

Cody listened to his description of her and had to take a deep drink of the whiskey to steady herself. She realized distantly that she'd lost count of the number of drinks she'd had, but she told herself she was still in control. Something he'd said puzzled her and she had to ask, "You said you have a job to do. Do you call running with El Diablo a job?"

Luke's expression turned black as he said tersely, "Actually, I call it hell."

She saw all the dark emotion in his regard and wondered at it. If Luke was really as bad as they said, would he care? Had he really done all those terrible things?

Her confusion reigned, and seeing his pain, she felt a deep, abiding need to ease the torment within him. Thoughts of Stalking Ghost waiting patiently for her signal faded to insignificance. All that was important was holding Luke and kissing him again. She went into his arms. When she ended the kiss and drew back to say something, he stopped her.

"We've talked enough, Armita."

"I know. You've said your life is hell." Her gaze met and held his. "Let me show you a glimpse of heaven tonight."

And emboldened by the liquor, Cody meant it.

Chapter Seventeen

Cody lifted her hands to frame Luke's face and kissed him. His arms came around her, enfolding her in his embrace. In that moment, all the logic and common sense she prided herself on were burned away like a morning mist before the heat of the rising sun. She wanted this. She wanted him.

They came together, the fire of their loving stoked by each caress, each kiss. Desire seared them as they worked to shed the garments that kept them apart.

When Luke stripped off his shirt, Cody hungrily reached for him. She had never forgotten the sight of his bare chest before her that night at the outlaw's camp, and she hadn't realized until now just how much she'd wanted to touch him, to sculpt the muscles of his back and shoulders. He was male beauty personified, so lean, hard, and strong. Cody ran her hands over him, and he shuddered beneath her touch. The knowledge that she could cause such a reaction in him thrilled and excited her.

She did not resist when Luke slipped her dress from her shoulders to bare her breasts to his caress.

"You're beautiful," Luke murmured as he pressed heated kisses to that tender flesh.

Cody arched back at the touch of his mouth upon her. Feelings she had never known existed were awakened deep within the womanly heart of her. She was mindless before the onslaught of his expert caresses, and when he moved to help her shed the rest of her clothing she was pliant and eager before him. She lay unclad on the bed, waiting while he quickly finished undressing. Luke joined her there, and Cody gloried in that heated contact with him. He moved over her, branding her body with his desire, and she opened to him like a flower to the sun.

Ecstasy seared her as his touch traced paths of fire upon her willing flesh. She was an innocent to the ways of men, but the need within her urged her to move against him, to claim what only he could give her. When at last Luke positioned himself to take her, she went still, surprised by the intimacy of that male touch.

Luke didn't realize that she was untouched, and so he took no extra caution with her. He thought she was a woman fully versed in the ways of loving. Only when he took the gift of her love and pressed deep within her, breaching the proof of her innocence, did he realize what a treasure he'd just claimed. Sheathed tightly within her, he stopped. He was stunned by the discovery and pushed himself up on his elbows to gaze down at her. Her eyes were closed and tears were tracing crystalline paths down her cheeks.

"Armita?" Luke said her name softly. He felt terrible because she was crying. He must have hurt her, and that was the last thing he'd wanted to do. He'd wanted to bring her pleasure, not pain.

"It's all right." She looked up at him, smiling tremulously as she lifted her arms to draw him down to her for a kiss. "It's all right."

"But—"

"I want you, Luke."

His mouth sought hers in a passionate domination then, and they were caught up in the wildfire of their need. He did not know how it was that a singer in a border-town cantina could be a virgin, but at that moment he wasn't about to question it. She wanted him as he wanted her. That was all that was important.

Luke tried to pace himself, to go slow, to show her the fullness of love, but soon his desire swept them both away. Caught up in the power of their need for one another, they came together in exquisite union. The starburst of fulfillment swept over them, taking them to the heavens and beyond. And then there was only the silken ecstasy of their bodies entwined in love's afterembrace, and the joy of having known perfect loving.

"I'm sorry if I hurt you. I didn't know," Luke whispered as he held her close.

Cody smiled serenely at him as she pressed a soft kiss to his lips. She had wanted this . . . needed this . . . to be one with him. It had been as beautiful as she'd known it would be. She sighed. "Luke . . ."

Then she closed her eyes as she nestled against him, the liquor having muted her senses and his loving having cooled the fever that had raged within her.

Luke gazed down at her for a moment longer, holding her close, relishing this moment of closeness. It had been so long since he'd known innocence of any kind. Only his dealings with Sister Mary had helped to convince him that goodness and gentleness still existed. Now, for some reason, he'd been given the gift of Armita's loving. He lay quietly, savoring the peace of the moment.

Not too much later, Luke slipped from the bed. Armita did not stir, but slept on. He hated leaving her this way, but the gang was riding out before dawn to meet up with the Mexicans who were going to buy the stolen guns.

Luke dressed quickly and quietly, then turned to watch her sleeping for a moment. He thought about leaving her a note, but decided against it. He would be back just as soon as they made the exchange. He pressed one last soft kiss to her lips, then let himself out of her room.

Cody awoke to sunshine streaming through the window. She closed her eyes quickly against the glare of morning brightness and lay still, wondering why she had such a pounding headache. She moved a little then, stretching out, and it was in that instant, when she realized she was naked, that the whiskey-blurred memories of the night before came flooding back.

"Luke!"

Cody sat upright in bed at the thought of all that had transpired, and immediately moaned in regret at her hasty action. She clutched the blanket to her breasts to cover herself as she fought to ignore the throbbing in her temples. Where was he? Where had he gone? She had to find him!

She got up and searched the room, but there was no trace that he'd ever been there. He was gone, vanished into thin air, and she was alone with the realization of what she'd done.

Cody stared at the nearly empty whiskey bottle on the dresser. She shook her head ruefully and knew it would be a cold day in hell before she ever touched another drop. Staring about the room in disgust, she berated herself for her weakness. She'd known it was dangerous to be alone with Luke. She'd known the effect the man had on her, yet she'd kissed him, and once she had, she'd forgotten everything except that she wanted him.

Glancing over at the bed, she noticed the sheets and felt a pang of remorse at the testimony to her lost innocence. She sat down on the bed and sighed as images of Luke and his lovemaking haunted her—his touch and kiss, his caring and gentleness.

And now he was gone.

By her own weakness she'd lost him. Cody vowed then and there that it would not happen again. She would seek him out tonight. She would get him back up to her room and haul him back to Del Fuego for justice. Even as she made the vow to herself, though, she remembered the glory of his kiss and the fiery brand of his passion. It would not be easy to forget Luke, or to resist him when they were alone together, but she would. She had a job to do.

The day passed slowly for Cody. There were times as she paced her room when she thought evening would never come. But finally it was dark and time for her first show. She was ready. She was going to find Luke, drag him upstairs. She was going to signal Stalking Ghost and they were going to get him out of town—tonight. Too much time had passed already.

Even as she plotted her next move, though, she was thinking about her conversation with Logan. She understood now what the Ranger had meant about having doubts about Luke's guilt. She had her own. But she told herself sternly that she would deal with that when the time came.

The music began and she went out onstage ready to do whatever was necessary to get Luke all to herself again. To her shock, there was no sign of Luke or the rest of the gang. Only her regular customers were there.

Cody did not let their absence affect her singing. She put on a show that left the men panting after her, and even went out and mingled with them afterward. Expecting Luke to show up for the second show, she waited again for the music to start, and then she went out onstage. Again, he was not there.

Luke was gone.

She'd had her chance to bring him in, and she'd lost him.

After the last show, Cody visited with the cowboys for a few minutes and then made her way to the bar to get a drink from Hal.

"Whiskey tonight?" he asked.

"Water," she said seriously.

He laughed. "They were something, weren't they?"

"Who?"

"The El Diablo gang. They scare the hell out of me every time they show up."

"Where have they gone?" she asked casually.

"From what I overheard, they had to meet somebody a couple of days' ride out of town. I don't know when or even if they're coming back."

Cody disappeared up to her room a short time later. She was not happy.

Jack was in the sheriff's office with Fred when he heard the shouts coming from the street.

"They got one of 'em! I think it's Majors!" a man was calling.

Jack and Fred rushed to the window to see a bounty hunter riding in, leading another horse with a man tied on the back. As they watched, the townspeople came rushing out of their houses and businesses. The crowd swelled behind the riders, and it almost looked like a mob scene.

"Hang the bastard right now!" another man yelled. "To hell with a trial!"

"Yeah! We know he's guilty! Let's string him up!"

"If we make this one pay, they'll think twice about robbing our bank again!"

A roar of agreement went through the throng of people. They pressed in close as the bounty hunter reined in before the office and dismounted. He was a tall, dark-haired man, whose long days on the trail had left him bearded and covered with trail dirt. He went to the second horse to yank his captive down.

Fred moved to try to get a good look at the man who was tied up.

"Who've you got there, friend?" he asked.

"I've got Luke Majors here, and I want that thousand dollars," the man declared, shoving his prisoner toward Fred and Jack.

"It's Majors!" someone yelled.

The shout went up, and the mood of the townspeople grew ugly. They started to crush forward, wanting to get their hands on the man they believed was a cold-blooded killer.

Jack realized what was about to happen. He drew his gun and went to cover the prisoner. As he faced him, he saw immediately that it wasn't Luke.

"This isn't Majors, folks!" he called, but they were too angry to listen. He turned to Fred. "Get them inside. I'll handle this."

He confronted the crowd, gun in hand, and they stopped moving forward. Though anger was still plain in their expressions, they knew Texas Rangers meant business when they drew their weapons.

"I'll use this gun if I have to, to break this up. Now do what Fred said and go back home."

"He's a killer!"

"I just got a look at the man the bounty hunter brought in, and it isn't Luke Majors."

"You're lying!" someone yelled.

Jack turned a deadly glare in the man's direction. When he spoke, his tone was fierce. "There's no one in this town who wants Majors back more than I do. But this isn't him. Now get out of here, unless you want to be holding a funeral for one of your own tomorrow."

They could tell he was serious. For the moment they backed down. Grumbling, they moved off.

Once Jack was sure they were going, he hurried inside to find out what the bounty hunter thought he was doing.

"This isn't the outlaw," Fred was saying.

"I'm telling you this is Luke Majors!" Gary Reid, the bounty hunter, was arguing. "Look at him; he matches the description perfectly!"

"I know Majors, and this isn't him." Jack confirmed what Fred had said as he joined them.

"But he looks like him! And he tried to run from the saloon in San Angelo when I went after him!" Gary Reid was furious at the thought that he'd wasted his time.

"I been trying to tell him for days that I ain't Majors, but he wouldn't listen!" The man spoke up in his own defense. "My name's Walt Kinsel."

"Well, Walt Kinsel, you wanted for anything, anywhere?" Jack asked, closing on him, wondering why he'd run from Reid.

Kinsel looked shamefaced. "I'm wanted, but not by the law."

"What the hell does that mean?" Reid demanded.

"I thought you might be after me 'cause I left a girl in a family way back in Austin. Her daddy threatened to come after me for what I did, so I thought you were sent by him."

Fred was disgusted. "Maybe I'll just send him a wire and tell him I got you here. Then I'll just keep you locked up nice and safe until they can come down here with a minister."

"You ain't got no right to do that to me!"

"He's right," Jack said tensely. "Let him go. Mr. Reid, I'm sorry, but you brought in the wrong man."

"I'm not quitting yet. I'll be back." He stormed out of the office and rode off.

Kinsel disappeared as soon as they untied him.

"That was close," Fred said wearily, thinking of how quickly the crowd had gathered and how hostile the townspeople were.

"Too close," Jack said. "I don't like this at all. Luke is innocent until proven guilty. No one saw him shoot Sam Gregory or the deputy."

"Yeah, but we got witnesses who say that he was the one who shot Harris."

"Witnesses can be wrong."

"Why are you so convinced he didn't do it? The

251

whole town believes he's guilty, and frankly, so do I."

Jack glanced over at him, seeing the sternness in his expression and realizing that the new sheriff did believe what he was saying. "You're wrong, Fred."

"How can you be so sure?" Fred frowned, and then looked up at him suspiciously. "Wait a minute. . . . When you were talking to Reid you said you knew Majors. Just how well do you know him?"

Jack had debated for many days whether to confide in Fred or not. He knew now that he had to tell him the truth. It was too dangerous here in town. If a bounty hunter brought Luke in when Jack wasn't nearby, they could have him strung up before he could stop it. He didn't like the mood here at all, and he was going to do something about it. But first he needed an ally to help him keep Luke safe if he was brought in.

"I've got to tell you something that nobody but me knows. I have to have your word that you will not tell anyone else. Lives depend on it."

Fred stared at him, puzzled. "You have my word. What is it?"

Jack quickly told him all that had happened before the jailbreak.

"But he shot Harris!" Fred argued in disbelief.

"You're wrong. The robber drew his gun, Luke drew his gun, shots were exchanged. The outlaw shot Harris, not Luke. He was there to get a loan from the bank, not rob it."

Fred shook his head in confusion. "All this time

you've been waiting to hear from him."

"If he can get back to me with El Diablo's identity, he'll do it. Then we can shut the gang down permanently. But I have to protect him in any way that I can."

Fred was silent for a long moment.

"Sam didn't believe me at first either."

"You honestly trust Majors."

"I would trust him with my life, and right now, he's trusting me with his."

"I'll keep your secret, and if Majors is brought in and you're not around, I'll make damned sure he's safe until you get here."

"I'm going to send word to my captain, too, just to let him know what's going on. I don't want any deadly mistake made with Luke's life. He's working for us, not against us."

Fred nodded and they shook hands on it.

Much later that night, Elizabeth lay in the curve of Jack's body, savoring his nearness. He was a wonderful lover and she had never regretted coming to his bed. He looked like he was asleep. Not wanting to waste a minute of their precious time together, she splayed her hand across his chest and then let it drift lower until she had his attention.

"Were you sleeping?" she asked throatily as she became the aggressor and mounted him.

"No, I was resting. You wear me out, woman," he said with a smile as she ground herself against him.

"Well, if you're too tired . . ."

She pretended to begin to leave him, but he grasped her hips and pinned her to him.

"I never said I was too tired." He grinned. "I'm never too tired for you."

He started to roll with her, to take her beneath him, but she resisted. Leaning down, she offered him her breasts as she rode him. She controlled their joining. She set the pace. She brought him close time and time again, then stopped just long enough to draw out his excitement and make him furious with desire for her. She wanted to enslave him with her passion. Only then could he give her what she needed . . . what she wanted. They reached the peak together, and Elizabeth collapsed in his arms. They lay sated and exhausted.

Later, she finally spoke of what was troubling her. "Have you heard any news at all about the gang?"

"There was some excitement down at the jail earlier. A bounty hunter rode in and said he had Majors."

She looked up at him quickly, hopefully. "And . . . ?"

"And he didn't. Wrong man, but we almost had a riot when the word got out."

"So there's nothing new you can tell me?"

"No, but I've been doing some serious thinking about El Diablo and this gang of his. I'm beginning to wonder if maybe he has an informer who's well connected either at the fort or here in town. How else would they have known the exact date of the gun shipment?"

"Maybe they didn't know," she offered. "Maybe

they'd just been watching and got lucky."

"That could be, but I don't think so. This gang's too smart to leave that much to chance."

"How are you ever going to catch them? The town wants to see justice done. That's why people are so angry."

He tightened his arms around her. "I know, and I'm sorry things aren't moving faster. I'm doing everything I can. We just have to be patient. There are things going on that you don't know about."

"There are?" She looked at him with a questioning gaze.

Jack was quiet for a moment, wondering whether to tell her just to lift her spirits a little. He finally answered. "The reason I've been staying here in town is that I've got a man on the inside. As soon as he can identify El Diablo, he's going to contact me, and then we're going to take the whole gang down. Until I hear from him, I just have to sit tight."

She looked at him with renewed respect. "That's so smart of you! I didn't know you'd done something like that. It must be difficult for you waiting here like this."

"It isn't easy, and it isn't over yet. I just hope everything comes together so I can help you, and bring El Diablo down. I want to stop him and his gang before they can hurt anybody else."

"If anyone can do it, Jack, you can." She leaned over him and kissed him.

He needed no further invitation. They loved long into the night until, driven by the need to maintain their secrecy, Elizabeth crept from the hotel and returned to her loveless home.

With Hadley in the lead, the gang rode straight into the Mexicans' hideout. Luke was riding near the front, wanting to learn all he could about names, locations, and the negotiations that were about to take place.

"Carlos! *Hola!*" Hadley called out as he reined in before the heavily armed bandidos who were waiting for them in front of their leader's shack. These men had a well-earned reputation for being as deadly as the El Diablo gang, and Hadley treated them with respect. "It has been a long time, my friend."

"Indeed it has, amigo," the outlaw replied, his gaze sweeping quickly over the riders who'd accompanied Hadley. "But my heart is breaking. Where is that devilishly beautiful sister of yours? I was looking forward to seeing her again. Has the infamous El Diablo stopped riding with her own gang? This is the second time you have come to me and she has not been with you."

Hadley smiled, but he wasn't pleased that Carlos had said so much in front of Luke. "El Diablo is busy planning what we will do next."

"Ah, Hadley, are you finally admitting she is the brains of your gang?"

"Finally?" He laughed coldly at the insult. "Have we not admitted it all along? Why else would we call ourselves the El Diablo gang? Come, let us have a drink and talk of old times before we get to business."

Hadley clapped Carlos on the back, and the two men led the way farther into the campsite to where they could sit and talk.

Luke dismounted and followed along with Carson and Jones. His mind was racing with the power of what he'd just learned. El Diablo was a female! But who? Tension filled him. He knew he was as close as he was going to get to the outlaw's identity, and he had to get back to Del Fuego and let Jack know.

A woman! The idea was outrageous, but also incredibly brilliant. Who better to listen in on conversations and deliver important information to Hadley? It was perfect. No one would suspect. Luke couldn't imagine how a woman could have come to be such a cold-blooded killer, but that didn't matter. What mattered was that he could help Jack catch her now, and he was going to get back to his friend as quickly as he could.

Getting away from the gang was going to be a trick, Luke realized. When he did it, he was going to have to make sure he had a head start or he'd end up dead real quick. And he wouldn't be of much help to Jack dead.

Luke kept a low profile. He said little, watched all that transpired carefully, and waited impatiently for the deal to be concluded. Several times during the day and a half they were there, the lovely Armita crept into his thoughts, and he had trouble putting her out of his mind. Her innocence had surprised and pleased him. He'd hated leaving her as he had in the middle of the night, but he'd needed to ride out at sunup with Hadley and the others. Luke would be glad to see Armita again. She had been the one bright spot in this whole sordid affair.

Cody met Stalking Ghost in a secluded area on the outskirts of town. Nobody paid much attention to her comings and goings during the day, and, with the gang gone, she wasn't overly concerned about being seen with him.

"There has been no word of them?"

"No, and Hal doesn't even know if they're coming back—not that I could come right out and ask. He actually said he was glad they were gone, but the girls want them to come back because they're big spenders."

"And you?" he asked intuitively, knowing something was different this time in her hunt for her man.

Cody had not told Stalking Ghost what had happened the other night. She had only told him that she hadn't been able to get Luke in a position where they could take him out. He had never had any reason to doubt her judgment before, and he had not questioned her this time.

"What do you mean?"

"This one is important to you."

"No, I—"

"It is in your eyes," he stated, having known her long enough to read her moods.

She sighed in frustration. "When Logan hired me, he told me the reason he wanted Luke back alive was because he had doubts about his guilt."

She lifted her troubled gaze to Stalking Ghost. "I do, too. There's something about him that doesn't fit with this gang. Look at how he's acted since we caught up with him. He rescued me from Sully in El Trajar when he could have minded his own business. If he had minded his own business, we might both be dead right now. Then there was the other night, when we were talking. He said that he was there with the gang because he had a job to do. When I pressed him about that, asking him if he thought riding with the gang was a job, he said that riding with the gang was hell." Cody looked away from her friend, out toward the wilds of the Mexican countryside. "He doesn't belong with these men. For all that we know he was a gunfighter, in my heart I'm sure he's not a cold-blooded killer."

"You will take Majors in?"

It was the point that had been troubling her for days now. She had given the Ranger her word that she would bring Majors to him alive. If she didn't, some other bounty hunter might just shoot him on sight for the money and ask questions later. For his own sake, as well as hers, she knew what she had to do.

"I don't have a choice. I gave Logan my word. I'm bringing Luke Majors in."

Chapter Eighteen

Cody was in the middle of her last show when Luke and the others returned to the cantina. She couldn't believe the thrill that shot through her when she saw him coming through the doorway. He looked dirty and tired, but his gaze was only on her, and she felt the heat of it even across the saloon. She finished off the performance to the rousing cheers of the gathered men, and then went straight to join Luke at the bar.

"I missed you," she said simply.

"We had some business to take care of, but we're back now."

Cody felt a desperate need to touch him, and she rested her hand on his chest over his heart. She felt the powerful, heavy beat beneath her palm, and she lifted her hungry gaze to his. "Would you like to go upstairs?"

"Very much."

"I could arrange for you to have a hot bath."

"I want more than a bath." His voice was a low growl.

Cody smiled as she let her hand trail lower. She remembered seeing Candy, the bar girl, do that to cowboys when she'd been working in the saloon as Delilah, and as Cody recalled, it was a teasing action that always got the man's full attention. And it did.

"Bring your bottle. We'll have a welcome-back celebration in my room."

Luke picked up his belongings and moved off with her. Things were working perfectly. He would play along with Armita as if everything were normal, but as soon as he could slip away, he'd be gone. Her suggestion of a bath was appreciated after all the time in the saddle, and the thought of what would come afterward was exciting and welcome, too.

Cody hated what she had to do, but there was no way around it. She had a vial of a drug she and Stalking Ghost had used to subdue certain prisoners, and while she was helping Luke with his bath, she was going to put a large dose of it in his whiskey. In a few minutes, he would be out, and, with Stalking Ghost's help, they would be on their way.

* * *

It didn't take them long to move the tub into her room and fill it with water. It wasn't the hottest bath Luke had ever had, but right then it didn't matter. All he wanted to do was get clean as quickly as possible, and bed Armita.

It seemed Armita had other plans, though. He found her watching him as he undressed, and he smiled when she turned down the lamp to a soft glow. He stepped into the tub and sat down, ready to start washing right away. But she stopped him.

"Lean back. Relax." Cody cooed as she set a small table beside him and put a fresh glass of whiskey on it within reach.

Luke leaned back with a contented groan. She'd shown him a little heaven the other night, and it looked like he was going to have another taste of it tonight. The thought appealed. Armita was a passionate woman who knew exactly how to please a man. This time with her was just what he needed, and when they were through, he would do what he had to do. For now, though, he was going to bide his time and enjoy it, for if he was seen leaving her room too quickly, there would be questions asked.

"Would you like me to wash your back?" she asked softly, moving behind him.

"You can wash whatever you want," he replied with a rakish grin as he looked up at her over his shoulder.

"Why don't I start here, while you take it easy. Have a drink," she urged, eying the doctored whiskey.

"In a while." He sighed, leaning forward to give

access to his back. "Right now I only want to enjoy myself." There was no way he was doing any heavy drinking tonight. He had to stay sharp. There were too many risks involved.

Cody was momentarily stymied. There was nothing she could do but go along with the scenario she'd set up. At least she had him alone. Now all she had to do was get him to drink the damned whiskey.

Dipping the washcloth in the water, she rubbed the soap to a lather and began to scrub his back. His shoulders were powerful, and the muscles flexed beneath her touch whenever he moved. It was a fascinating display, and she took her time, enjoying the moment.

"That feels good," Luke said. "You aren't stopping now, are you?"

"What did you have in mind?"

His arm snaked out and snared her, drawing her near. "There's a lot more of me that could use your attention."

Cody gave a throaty laugh as she knelt beside the tub and rinsed the cloth in the water. She tried not to look at his more intimate parts, concentrating on lathering the soap again. Keeping her gaze on his chest, she took care to stay above the waterline, yet teasingly went lower and lower as she washed that hair-roughened, muscular width.

"You really should take a drink. It might ease some of the tension I feel in you," she said.

"There's only one thing that's going to ease the tension in me."

She looked up at Luke and was suddenly caught

263

by the heat of his gaze. She stopped her ministrations, mesmerized by the desire she saw there. She remembered his kiss and his touch and the glory of being his in all ways.

Luke leaned toward her, and slipping a hand around the nape of her neck, he coaxed her to him. His mouth settled over hers in a passionate claim, letting her know that he'd had enough of his bath. He drew her to her feet as he stood, and then lifted her in his arms. Stepping clear of the tub, he moved straight to the bed and laid her upon the softness of it.

Hadley sat at the table in the cantina with the other gang members. His expression turned serious as he began to read the note a messenger had just handed him. When he lifted his gaze to the man who'd brought him the letter, the look in his eyes was savage and deadly.

"You can go," he said.

The man quickly disappeared. He could tell the news he'd just delivered was not good. He knew all about this gang, and he didn't want to be around to see what happened next.

"What is it, Hadley?" Jones asked, seeing the barely controlled fury on Hadley's face.

"Seems we've got a little trouble to take care of," he said, tossing the note on the table for the others to read.

Sully grabbed it up first and quickly scanned it. When he looked up at Hadley, he was wearing a feral smile. "The bastard's mine."

"Who's yours? What's this all about?" Jones

snatched the note from Sully as the other man rose from the table and pushed his chair back in a single motion. "I've been waiting a long time for this moment, and I'm going to enjoy myself."

"I'll help you!" Jones offered.

"No." Sully cut him off. "I'm going to be the one to kill Majors. He's been asking for it for weeks now, and the time has come."

"Don't you want somebody with you, just in case?" Jones said.

The look Sully shot his way was terrifying. "I don't need no help—not from you or anybody else. You stay the hell down here and make sure nobody goes up those steps after me. I just might take my time. It could be interesting."

"All right," he said, quickly moving out of Sully's way. Jones saw no reason to incur Sully's wrath over this. If he wanted to be the one to kill Majors, he was welcome to him.

"Majors is mine." With that, the gunman looked at Hall where he stood behind the bar. "Which room is the singer's?"

"End of the hall at the back," Hal answered, knowing better than to hesitate or try to lie. He was only interested in self-preservation and wanted to live to see tomorrow.

Sully started up the stairs.

"Sully," Hadley called out.

"Yeah?" He stopped and looked back.

"Make sure this is done right. I want him dead. There can be no mistakes this time." Hadley remembered all too well what had been revealed by Carlos. Majors now knew El Diablo was female.

He couldn't be allowed to leave the gang with that information.

Sully nodded and continued on.

It was late, and there was no one out in the second-floor hall. He made his way quietly down its length, not wanting to alert them that he was coming. This was going to be a surprise . . . a big surprise.

Cody knew she should resist Luke. Though his every kiss and caress took her closer and closer to mindlessness, the warning voice in her head cautioned her that she shouldn't do this again. But even with the knowledge that she should stop him, she couldn't summon the willpower to deny him. She knew she should try to distract him, to get him drinking and talking, but with each breathtaking kiss, she lost more and more of her common sense. A slow-burning heat grew within her, leaving her craving more of him, wanting him to go on . . . and not to stop.

Luke rolled over then, taking her with him and leaving her on top of him. It was then that Cody saw the chance to escape his embrace for at least a moment. She kissed him wildly and then slipped from his arms.

"Where are you going?" he asked, his eyes aglow with his need for her.

"I thought you might want a drink while I undress for you," she said in a sultry voice as she moved toward the table to get his glass.

Luke started to come off the bed, intent on only one thing. "The only thing I want right now is—"

It was then that it happened. The locked door burst open, the jamb splintering from the force of Sully's attack, and the outlaw charged into the room, gun in hand.

"You're mine, you son of a bitch!" Sully swore, ready to kill Luke.

Luke reacted instantly, diving for cover, cursing the fact that he was stark naked and that his gun was out of reach.

It was Cody who reacted coolly and with lethal intent. Snatching her father's gun from where she kept it hidden on the dresser, she fired a single shot that took Sully squarely in the chest. He was thrown backward, crashing against the door and slamming it shut again.

"Armita?" Luke had seen the quickness of her move and the accuracy of her shooting and was shocked. "Are you all right?"

"I'm fine," Cody said through gritted teeth. She hated killing, but knew sometimes it was a matter of survival. No wonder her father had drilled her so thoroughly on keeping her wits about her and on reacting quickly and surely in unexpected situations.

"Sully?"

"He's dead."

"I've got to get out of here," Luke said as he got up and hurriedly began to throw on his clothes. "They'll be coming up here after him."

"I'm going with you."

Luke paused as he pulled on his boots to look at her. He thought of leaving her, but realized she was the one who had pulled the trigger. They'd kill in her a heartbeat if they found out. "Can you ride in that dress?"

"Looks like we'll find out," she said tersely, trying to steady herself. "Give me a hand here."

Luke went to her side and they dragged Sully's body away from the door, then pushed the full tub against the broken portal to slow anyone coming to check on the shooting.

"Let's get out of here."

Luke buckled on his gunbelt, donned his shirt, and grabbed up his hat. He'd been intent on leaving, but he hadn't planned to do it this way. He went to the window and threw it wide. After climbing out onto the back porch roof, he turned back to give Armita a hand.

Cody had paused only long enough to tear off her multitude of petticoats and pull on a blouse to cover her bare shoulders. She grabbed up the small purse she carried and jammed her father's pistol in it. She took Luke's hand and climbed awkwardly through the window, the skirt impeding her even without the petticoats. When she had safely made it out, they closed the window behind them, then moved slowly and silently toward the darkest side of the building. Luke jumped down, landing lightly on his feet, then caught her as she tried to lower herself.

"Do you have a horse?"

"In the stables," she whispered in answer to his hushed question.

He nodded. "I don't know how long we've got. We have to move and move fast. Get over to the stable. I'll get my horse and meet you there."

Cody hurried off, staying in the shadows, moving undetected through the streets. She hoped that Stalking Ghost had been watching and had seen all that had happened, for there was no time for her to find him or to get a message to him.

By the time Luke reached her at the dark, deserted stable, she'd already claimed her own horse and was saddling him. They rode from town as soon as she was mounted.

The rest of that night passed in a blur as Luke and Cody rode like the wind. The sky was cloudless, and the half-moon gave them just enough light to travel fast. They stopped only long enough to rest the horses, then moved on, never allowing themselves the luxury of stopping to think, only knowing they had to run as far and fast as they could if they wanted to stay alive.

It was near dawn before Cody finally broached the subject of where they were heading; Luke had been riding east. She was having a heck of a time riding with her skirt and longed for more practical riding clothes. "If the Rangers are looking for you, wouldn't it make more sense to head deeper into Mexico instead of east? Where are we going?"

"Del Fuego. It's the only safe place for us. I have a friend there."

Cody couldn't believe her luck. Things couldn't have turned out any better if she'd wanted them to. Luke was riding right into her arms. All she had to do was grab him once they were closer to town. "Is your friend going to be able to save you from not only the gang but the law as well?"

269

His expression was grim and he didn't answer. He just kept riding. He had to get to Jack as quickly as possible.

Hadley and the rest of the gang were shocked when they discovered that Sully was dead and Luke and the singer had run.

"Let's go after them!" Jones said feverishly, wanting to see Majors dead for trying to betray them.

"Let's ride." Hadley was furious, not only because Majors had gotten away, but because Sully had been stupid enough to get himself killed after El Diablo had warned him how dangerous Majors was.

Hadley led the gang in their pursuit, but the darkness hindered them. Had it been daylight, they might have been able to track Majors and the singer, but after several hours of attempting to trail them, they gave up. It wouldn't do for the gang itself to be discovered, not with the way things were right then. They were wanted men, and the deeper into Texas they rode, the more likely it was they'd be caught.

Reining in, Hadley gathered the men around him. He was relieved that Majors had been found out before he could do any damage to them, but he still wanted to see the bastard dead.

"What do you want us to do?" Jones asked, ready to keep searching.

"I want you and Carson to ride for the canyon. Tell them there what's happened and tell them to watch out. The rest of you, go back to Rio Nuevo and wait."

"Where are you going?"

"I'm going to let El Diablo know what's happened. Stay in Rio Nuevo until you hear from me."

Jack sat across from General Larson in his office at Fort Thompson, the fort from which the guns had been shipped. Larson's men had been killed in the robbery, and he wanted the gang that had done it caught.

"I think there's more to this than meets the eye," Jack was saying after filling the general in on what he knew so far. "I'm convinced El Diablo has an informer, someone who knows what's going on here or who is close to someone who does."

"Their attack was perfect," Larson agreed solemnly. "Our men were caught completely unaware."

"That's why I want to know the names of all those who had prior knowledge of the shipment."

The general quickly listed those at the fort who were aware of the day of delivery.

"And in town? Did you speak to anyone there about it?"

The general fell silent as he tried to recall any and all conversations he'd had with those not connected to the military. "I mentioned it to several of my closest friends in town, but that was weeks ago."

"They are . . . ?" Jack was ready to make note of their names.

Larson's expression saddened. "I told Sam Gregory and Jonathan Harris on a night we had dinner together. I might have mentioned it to Fred Halloway, too."

Jack nodded and wrote down the names. "Thanks. Can you think of anyone else who might have overheard your discussions or had access to any of your information on the shipment?"

He shook his head. "Other than my wife, no."

Standing, Jack shook hands with the commander. "I thank you for your help."

Jack was troubled as he rode from the fort. He was convinced that El Diablo did have access to inside information. Talking to Larson had helped. At least now he knew those who'd had prior knowledge of the shipment. He wasn't sure what connection he would find between the robbery and the names he'd been given, but he would keep looking. There was more going on with this gang than just having good luck in choosing targets, as Elizabeth had suggested. Somewhere there was a clue, and once he found it, Jack was certain he would have a direct link to the gang and maybe even to El Diablo himself.

Chapter Nineteen

It was nearly dark, and Cody was exhausted as she tended her mount. It wasn't often that she admitted to herself that she'd reached her limit, but she did now. It would have been a rugged ride in her regular clothes, but dressed as Armita, it had been a trial. Her horse cared for, she groaned slightly as she sat down at the secluded campsite.

Luke heard her and looked over at her from where he was working with his own horse.

"Are you all right?" he asked, concerned. She was one very special woman. He didn't know many men who could have kept pace with him these last 24 hours, let alone a female.

"I'm not sure," she replied wearily. The accented voice speaking was Armita's, but the sentiments were her own. So much had happened, and so quickly. She hoped Stalking Ghost had seen their escape, but there was no way to know for sure that he was following until he made an appearance.

Luke left his horse and went to kneel beside her. Unable to help himself, he cupped her cheek with his hand. "You were wonderful, Armita. You saved my life."

Cody tried to smile at him, but there was a cloud of darkness in her gaze.

"What's wrong?"

She drew a ragged breath. Exhaustion, emotional and physical, racked her. "I've never had to kill anyone before."

Luke saw the stark pain in her expression and gathered her close, trying to shield her from the hurt he knew she was feeling. "It's a horrible thing, killing a man. You never get over the ugliness of it, no matter if it was to save your own life. It changes you forever."

"You're speaking from experience," she said, hearing the raw emotion in his voice.

"I've killed men, but it's always been a matter of survival. I take no pride or joy in it, and I'm sorry you got caught up in my trouble with Sully. I don't know what set him off, but I'm not sorry he's dead. If I hadn't been so distracted by the gorgeous woman I was about to make love to, I would have been ready for him."

"So is that what your life is always like?" she asked, lifting luminous eyes to his. "Do you always live in constant fear, never knowing who is going to come after you next?"

"It's been this way for over ten years now."

"How can you stand it? Don't you ever want to live a quiet life?"

He glanced at her. "It's dangerous to want what you can never have."

"You could quit the gang and settle down somewhere," she said hopefully, seeing so much good in him and hating that he was involved with men like Sully and the others.

"But then I would never have met you," he said, wanting to distract her. He didn't want to think about the Trinity. Not now. "If it hadn't been for you, I'd be dead right now." He held her back away from him a little and tilted her chin up so he was looking in her eyes. "Thank you."

She lifted trembling lips to his.

"I'm glad I saved you," she whispered against his mouth.

Luke held her close when the kiss ended, and they stayed like that for quite a while before finally moving apart to set up camp. There would be no fire for them tonight, nor would he hunt for food. There was no telling if the gang was on their trail and, if so, how close they were. Luke didn't want to risk giving away their location, either by firelight or gunshot.

After washing up in the small watering hole, they shared some hardtack that he'd had left in his saddlebags from the trip into Mexico to sell the guns. Then it was time to bed down. They would have to be ready to ride at first light and needed all the rest they could get.

Cody watched Luke spread out his bedroll. He

seemed to feel her gaze upon him and glanced over at her.

"Are you as ready to bed down as I am?" he asked. "We'll have to share. There's only the one."

There was no thought of refusing. She went to him and lay down in his arms.

"There have been times in my life when I would have given anything to be camped out under the stars in the middle of the wilderness with a beautiful woman . . . and now here I am," he said as he levered himself up on one elbow to gaze down at her. "I guess every situation, no matter how bad it may seem, can have a good side to it."

He gathered her to him and kissed her, sweetly at first. As she responded, his ardor grew. He deepened the exchange and pulled her fully against him so she could feel how much he wanted her.

Cody was pliant in his arms. Thoughts of being tired and wanting to rest faded before his seductive onslaught. Moments before, she would never have dreamed that she could forget about sleep and respond with such excitement, but she did. As she returned his kiss with abandon, linking her arms around his neck to hold him close, she realized how close he'd come to being killed the day before. The realization fueled her passion. She had nearly lost him. . . .

Had she been more logical, she would have wondered at the terror that seized her at the thought, but as he began to caress her, all logic fled. There was only Luke and the hot Texas night.

They came together out of need and want. Tonight, there were no lies between them. They were only man and woman, coming together in a blaze of passion, each seeking to give to the other the utmost of love's pleasure.

When at last Luke claimed her for his own, sinking deep within the heat of her body, they were one. They moved together, sharing the bliss of their union, giving and taking in love's age-old rhythm. The beauty of their loving burst upon them. They held tightly to each other, savoring this moment of peace in the torment of their lives.

Cody lay awake long into the night. Her thoughts were bewildered and chaotic. She had given herself to Luke freely. She had wanted to make love to him. There had been no liquor involved this time. She hadn't been trying to seduce him in order to drug him and take him in. She had wanted this.

Shame colored her emotions. Luke Majors was a wanted man. How could she feel these things for him?

Yet, even as she questioned herself and her feelings, she knew in her heart that Luke hadn't done the things they claimed he had. While he'd admitted to her that he had killed before, it had been in self-defense. He was not a murderer.

Cody tried to justify her own actions in her mind. The bounty hunter within her knew that, as high as the bounty was, if she didn't take him in, some other hunter would. And they might not care if Luke was dead or alive. She was determined to take him safely in to Logan and see him proven innocent.

Cody closed her eyes. She offered up a silent prayer for heavenly help, for she feared she was falling in love with Luke Majors.

They arose before the sun and were on their way as it cleared the horizon. Their need to reach Del Fuego deadened their hunger pangs and helped them to forget their weariness.

"There's a small town we can stop at on the way. At the speed we're riding, we should reach it tomorrow morning."

"Good. Maybe there I can get some different clothes."

Luke smiled at her. "You mean you don't like what you're wearing?"

"It was fine for dancing, but I do not think it was made for riding across the country on horseback," Cody said. "Men are very lucky to wear pants. I would be a happy woman right now if I could don some men's clothing."

Luke's expression softened a bit as thoughts of Sister Mary stirred within him. He remembered that night in the cabin when she'd been wearing the pants and loose shirt. "I knew another woman who liked to wear pants."

"She must certainly have been brave to dare to do such."

"She was." He paused. "Very brave."

They continued on. The trek was long and arduous. Luke was relieved that he could see no sign of anyone following them, but he still did not let his guard down. They rode at a steady, ground-eating pace, stopping only for the horses. As evening drew near, they found a sheltered spot near a good-sized watering hole to bed down in. Again they would build no fire and they would not hunt for food. There would be time to get a hot meal tomorrow when they reached the town just a little north of them.

After helping Luke take care of the horses, Cody gazed at the water. She was sweaty and hot and had a great desire to jump right in the water and take a cold bath.

"Do you want to wash up now?" Luke was watching her.

"Actually, I was wanting to take a bath. Do you suppose . . . ?"

"Go ahead," he encouraged with a smile, thinking how much he'd enjoy the view, but then realizing he had to keep watch. "Take your bath. I'll keep watch."

Cody couldn't help herself. She went straight to him and kissed him on his cheek. *"Gracias."*

"Just don't take too long."

"I won't. I promise."

Luke moved to a spot where he could keep a lookout for anyone coming. They had not seen another soul since riding out of Rio Nuevo, but that didn't mean there weren't people around. There was no telling when somebody might show up in a land like this. Luke positioned himself at a good vantage point where he could keep an eye on the countryside and try not to keep an eye on the lovely Armita.

Cody sat down on a rock and began to undress. She glanced up at Luke to find that he was staring off in the opposite direction. She smiled. He was a gentleman, whether he wanted to admit it or not.

Pulling off her boots, she tossed them aside and stripped off her stockings. Cody put one hand out to brace herself as she started to stand up to take off her dress, and it was then that she heard it—the telltale sound of a rattler. She froze, knowing the deadly danger of a snakebite. She slid her gaze in the direction of the sound and saw the monstrous snake coiled within striking distance of her hand. The snake looked mean and ugly and ready to strike.

"Luke . . ." She called to him in a hoarse whisper as she remained unmoving.

He glanced back, frowning, wondering why she sounded so strange; then he saw the snake. All color drained from his face. His mind raced as he tried to decide what to do. A bite from a rattlesnake that size would kill Armita. "Stay perfectly still."

She didn't answer, but her terrified gaze locked with his as he drew his sidearm and maneuvered closer. He needed a clear shot. He didn't want to risk hitting Armita.

"Don't move."

Luke took careful aim at the snake and fired once. Cody shrieked and jumped back as bits of rock sprayed around her. But even as she screamed, relief washed through her. The snake lay dead, its head blown off by the accuracy of Luke's shot.

"Oh, Luke, thank you." She ran to him and threw her arms around him.

"You all right?" He clasped her to him and kissed her. He'd been scared when he'd fired. He was glad that, for once, his shooting ability had saved a life rather than taking one.

"I'm fine." She was trembling as she realized how things might have turned out if he hadn't saved her. "You were wonderful."

He looked down at her, smiling gently. "I couldn't let anything happen to you."

They kissed, softly, sweetly, and then she turned and went on down to take her bath. Luke returned to standing guard. His expression was grim now, though. The sound of the gunshot could travel for miles, and it would draw anyone looking for them. He girded himself to stay alert and watchful.

Gary Reid was angry as he combed the area south of Del Fuego. It wasn't often that he made mistakes, and he was still mad over the time he'd wasted bringing in Kinsel.

Since leaving town, he'd begun a systematic search of all the towns to the south and west. Majors had to be there somewhere, and if Reid's instincts served him right, the gunfighter and the gang would position themselves close to the border for added protection should things get dangerous. He'd stopped in the small town of Mason Wells and asked questions, but they'd seen nothing of the outlaws and were glad they hadn't.

After a night's rest in town, Reid had started out again. He was tenacious, if nothing else. He wanted that bounty. He was going to find Luke Majors, and in the mood he was in, he didn't

281

rightly care if he brought the gunfighter in alive.

Swinging to the south, then circling back north, he had been patient and methodical in his sweep of the area, with no luck. He was heading south again, instinctively feeling that he would meet with success there, when he heard the gunshot.

He reined in, waiting and listening for another, but none came. It was still, deathly still. Urging his mount on, he traveled in the direction of the shot. There was something going on up ahead, and it was almost dark. He had to make sure he found whoever it was who'd just fired his gun before sundown; otherwise, unless they built a fire, he'd be forced to wait for dawn.

Cody stripped off all her clothes and darted into the water. It wasn't the cleanest bathwater she'd ever gotten into, but it was cool and refreshing. She sank down up to her chin just to soak for a few minutes. She knew she couldn't linger long, but it felt so good to be cool that she wasn't in any hurry to rush back into her dirty dress again.

Luke couldn't help himself. He'd been trying to be a gentleman, but at the sound of her running into the water, he'd had to look. He caught a glimpse of lovely, lush curves and long slender legs before she sank into the depths. He smiled to himself at the memory of how it felt to caress those silken curves. He would have to be careful tonight, though. There was too much at stake.

Gary Reid prided himself on his manhunting abilities. He moved cautiously in the direction of the gunshot, knowing someone was near . . . very near. The low sound of a horse's whicker came to him, and he dismounted. He slid his rifle out of the scabbard and, leaving his own horse behind, he continued on foot.

He heard the sound of water splashing, and he tried to figure out what was going on at the water hole. He crept forward, staying low, moving from brush to rock, trying to blend into the shadows of nightfall. He emerged on the far side of the watering hole, and immediately spotted the beautiful woman bathing. He stayed hunkered down where he was, his gaze scanning the area, looking for the companions he knew had to be near.

Had he been a man easily distracted, Reid might have forgotten his purpose, but he was after only one thing—the bounty for Majors. He wanted that thousand-dollar reward. It was as simple as that. Once he had the money, he could buy all the women he wanted. Right now, he only wanted Majors.

He shifted a little closer, trying to get a look at who else was with her. The woman saved him the trouble when she called out.

"Luke? Would you throw me my dress?"

Luke took one last quick look around and climbed down. He went to pick up the travel-worn garment where she'd left it on the bank.

"Hold it right there, Majors!" Reid's voice rang out, cutting through the silence of the night. He had almost shouted for joy when he'd heard her call him Luke. He had the right man this time!

Cody shrieked, and Luke spun toward the sound

of his voice, gun in one hand, dress in the other.

"Don't even think about it, gunman," Reid dictated. "I got a rifle trained right on you. You're a dead man if you move. The wanted poster says dead or alive, so it won't trouble me none to put an end to you here and just take your carcass back."

"Luke?" Cody was furious. She was stark naked in a watering hole and her gun was nowhere near. She knew now the terror Luke had felt when Sully had burst into their room at the cantina. But this situation was infinitely more dangerous.

"Who are you?"

"I'm the man who just caught your ass." Reid laughed. "Now toss your gun aside real easy like. No funny business. There's no telling just who might get hurt."

"What are you going to do with him?" Cody asked, playing dumb.

"He's a wanted man, señorita. I'm taking him in for murder."

"But he didn't do anything!"

"I don't care. They're offering money, I'm earning it. Now shut up. I'm already tired of listening to you. Stay right where you are and don't move. If you do what I tell you, you'll be fine."

Luke wanted to get a shot off at the bounty hunter, but there was no way. He was trapped, and with Armita between them, it was too dangerous. He bent carefully and laid his gun down on the ground.

"I'm glad you're a smart man, Majors. Now kick

it away from both you and the woman. I want it far out of reach."

Luke did as he was told, cursing to himself the whole time. It had been the gunshot that had given them away. But he could have done nothing else. There was no way he could have let Armita get hurt.

"Now turn around and put your hands up."

Luke did as he was instructed, and Reid finally emerged from his hiding place. He hurried over to where the outlaw stood and quickly handcuffed his hands behind his back.

"What are you going to do about the woman?" Luke asked.

"Woman," Reid called out to Cody, who was still neck-deep in the water. "Stay right where you are. I'll leave you something to cover yourself with, and then I'll drop the rest of your clothes about a mile or so ahead, along with your horse. You're free to go. I don't want you. I only need Majors."

"You're going to just leave me here?"

She was furious. There was nothing she could do to help Luke. She was totally useless to him, and she cursed her own stupidity in deciding to take a bath. Cody watched as the man gathered up her things and took most of them with him as he directed Luke toward the horses.

Luke was not about to make it easy for this man. The bounty hunter didn't care if he took him in dead or alive, and Luke had no intention of returning to Del Fuego dead. He knew Armita was good with a gun; if he could somehow distract the bounty hunter long enough to give her the chance to get to either his gun or hers, they might be able to get away from this man. There was a rocky spot on the way to where the horses were tied, and he was going to try something once they reached it. There, at least, the hunter's footing wouldn't be as sure. If Luke could knock him down, he might drop the gun and then . . .

Reid was no fool. He thought Majors was going along too easily, and when Luke made his move, he'd been anticipating it. Luke kicked out at him, and Reid tried to avoid tripping, dodging to the side. Luke thought he was falling and started to run, bending over, crouching low. But the bounty hunter was prepared. He did not waste time yelling. He fired twice at the wanted man and watched in satisfaction as Luke fell and lay still.

Cody screamed at the sight of him collapsing. "Luke!"

"Shut up, woman, or you'll be next."

Cody stayed where she was, watching in horror as the bounty hunter dragged Luke to the horses. As dark as it had become, she couldn't tell where he'd been shot or even if he was dead or alive. Her heart was lurching painfully in her breast. Tears were streaming down her cheeks, yet she stayed where she was. If he was alive and she tried to go to him, the bounty hunter would kill her. She had doubted him before, but she didn't any longer.

Luke made no sound as Reid saddled his mount and then threw him unceremoniously over the back of the horse and securely tied him there.

"We'll be leaving now, señorita," Reid said. "You'll be able to find the rest of your things in the morning. Until then, I'd advise you to stay put. You never can tell what might happen out in the wilds to a woman all alone."

Cody wanted to add "or a man" to his threatening statement, but she held her tongue. The time would come when she would face this bounty hunter down, and when she did he was never going to forget the name Cody Jameson.

Cody stayed silent as she listened to the sound of the horses' hoofbeats as they rode away. If he thought she was going to just sit here in the dark and wait until morning to go after her man, he had sadly misjudged her. She was no simpering cantina singer. She was Cody Jameson.

She was going to follow that man to hell and back to get to Luke. Luke Majors was hers . . . in more ways than one!

Chapter Twenty

Cody was a driven woman as, wearing only her corset, stockings, and high-heeled boots, she headed in the direction the bounty hunter had ridden with Luke. She had to get to Luke. She had to make sure he was still alive.

Anger consumed her, and fear, and guilt. Cody realized it was because of the snake that they'd been found out. If Luke hadn't fired his gun to save her life, he would still be with her. And now he was shot and possibly dying. . . .

Tears threatened, but she controlled them. There was no time for emotion now. She had to think clearly and logically. If she was going to save Luke from the other bounty hunter, she had to do something and fast. The trouble was, traveling on foot, dressed like this, there was no "fast" to it.

Trudging on, Cody concentrated only on trying to find her clothes and horse. The moon was a sliver, providing little in the way of light, but she kept going. Nothing was going to stop her. She had to get to Luke.

At the sound of hoofbeats coming up behind her, Cody knew a moment of panic. She looked around frantically, trying to find a place to hide, until the sound of Stalking Ghost's call calmed her terror.

"Cody!"

"Stalking Ghost! I'm over here!"

He appeared behind her on his horse, looking in the darkness like a fierce Indian warrior. His expression was stern as he stared down at her. "I heard the sounds of gunfire."

"Another bounty hunter showed up. He shot Luke!"

"Is he dead?"

"I don't know. I have to find him!"

Stalking Ghost reached behind himself and freed a bundle he had tied there. He tossed it down to her. "Clothe yourself, and we will ride."

She caught the clothes he'd brought along for her and went behind a bush to dress. It took her only a few minutes, and she felt wonderful to be back in her split riding skirt, comfortable blouse, and boots.

"Here is your hat," he said, handing it to her as she emerged looking more like herself.

He reached down, and when she grasped his forearm, he swung her up behind him in a single, smooth move.

"The man said he was going to leave the rest of my clothes and my horse about a mile up ahead."

He nodded, but didn't speak.

"Mason Wells is due north of here; it's on the way to Del Fuego. If Luke isn't dead, the bounty hunter probably headed there with him," Cody said.

"We will check."

Stalking Ghost walked his horse, listening to the night sounds. They found her horse and the pile of her clothes less than half an hour later. Cody jumped down and quickly ran to the clothing, digging through until she found her purse.

"No." The despairing word was torn from her.

"What is it?"

"He took my father's gun."

"Let us ride for this town. We will find this bounty hunter who has stolen your gun and your man."

The going was slow. They cautiously approached a deserted ranch house on the way. Thinking the bounty hunter might have holed up there for the night, they dismounted and quietly checked it out. Stalking Ghost was armed in case of trouble, but they found no trace of the bounty hunter, only decaying outbuildings and a broken-down wagon. They continued on.

It was about an hour later that they reached the outskirts of Mason Wells. The town looked shut down for the night. Even the saloon was closed. They skirted the area, looking for some sign of Luke, and Cody was thrilled and relieved when she spotted his horse and the bounty hunter's tied up to a rail before a small building at the end of one block. Out front there was a small sign that said DENTIST, and a light was on in the front room.

"He's alive! He must be or the bounty hunter wouldn't have stopped!" Cody breathed, looking over at Stalking Ghost, who was watching the house intently. "I'm going to sneak up there and try to listen at the window."

"No. You stay here. I'll go." With that, he dismounted, handed her his reins, and moved off into the night.

"Be careful."

Cody rode back out of sight with both horses and waited for Stalking Ghost's return. Each minute seemed an hour as she sat in the darkness, anticipating the news he would be bringing her. Was Luke dying? Had he been grievously wounded? Her imagination threatened to run away with her, and she had to force herself to concentrate on trying to come up with a plan to rescue him.

From where she was hiding, Cody tried to get a look at Mason Wells. The town was far from prosperous. It boasted only one saloon, a general store, and a small hotel. The rest of the buildings were nondescript. She was glad things were quiet tonight. She didn't want the bounty hunter to have any idea that she had already caught up with him. She was certain that she was the last person the man ever expected to see again. He was going to be in for one big surprise, once she found out how Luke was. Staying as calm as she could, she waited.

* * *

Reid was tense as he stood in the room watching the man—who was as close to a doctor as he could find in Mason Wells—working on Majors.

"How long is this going to take?" he demanded impatiently.

"I don't know," Abner Fox answered as he continued to probe Luke's shoulder for the bullet. "I can't get a grip on it."

Luke muttered a curse at the man's heavy-handed touch.

"Easy there, mister. Just lie still and be quiet. If you hadn't been running from the law, you wouldn't be in this fix." Abner had little use for men like Majors. He dug deeper, not even trying to be careful.

Luke set his jaw, but did not utter another sound. He would not give the sadist the satisfaction of knowing he'd hurt him.

"There! I got it!" With great pride, Fox extracted the bullet and dropped it into the bowl on the nightstand next to the bed. "Now let me take a look at his head."

He bent over Luke and examined the bloodied crease at his temple. His touch was not gentle. "You're one lucky fella. If Reid here had been a better shot, you'd damned well be dead right now."

Abner thought himself hysterically funny, and he was chuckling at his own humor when his gaze accidentally met Luke's. The cold hatred that shone in those dark eyes sent a chill to the depths of his soul. He almost took a step back to distance himself from this man. He knew now why the gun-fighter was wanted by the law. He'd never seen such a look in a man's eyes before.

"His head will be all right. It's just a scratch. I'll bandage up his shoulder, and you can be on your way in the morning."

"He can't ride tonight?" Reid asked, wanting to leave as quickly as possible.

Abner shrugged. "You could try it, but he's lost blood, and if he passes out on you while you're riding, it'd slow you down."

Reid's expression was black. He'd have been better off if he'd killed Majors. Then the wanted man wouldn't have given him any trouble on the way back.

"All right."

"I'll keep him here. You can get a room over at the hotel."

"There is no way I'm leaving his side. I worked too damned hard to trap him. I'm not letting him out of my sight."

"Suit yourself." He shrugged again, then finished doctoring Luke's shoulder. He bandaged it tightly. "I'll check it again one more time in the morning."

"Fine."

"My fee's ten dollars." He wiped the blood from his hands and waited.

Reid paid up.

"Good night, Mr. Reid."

Reid was glad when he was gone. "Well, Majors, you'd better get all the rest you can tonight, because at dawn tomorrow, we're riding for Del

Fuego as fast as we can travel." Reid settled in a chair in front of the door, his gun in hand. "Don't try anything. I'd hate to have to kill you now that I've spent ten dollars to get that bullet taken out of you, but I'll do it in a minute if you give me any trouble. You hear me?"

Luke glanced down at the bounty hunter. "I hear you."

Luke closed his eyes and tried to think straight. It wasn't easy. His head was pounding. He knew he'd been lucky. Half an inch over on the shot to his head, and he'd have been dead. The thought was not comforting. He considered escape, but as he shifted his shoulder, trying to judge his own condition, the agony that tore through him was testimony enough. As weak as he was right now, he doubted he'd be able to pull it off.

And Reid was good. The bounty hunter watched him like a hawk. It was another three days to Del Fuego. Luke told himself to bide his time and watch for an opportunity to get away. For now, he was just going to rest and get as much of his strength back as he could. He hoped that Jack was waiting for him in Del Fuego.

Cody was about to go crazy, waiting and not knowing how Luke was, and then finally Stalking Ghost returned.

"How is he?" she asked quickly, trying to read something in his expression and failing.

"Your man is alive."

She sighed audibly and closed her eyes for a moment.

"Let us ride out of town a ways to talk. I have much to tell you."

"But shouldn't we keep watch?"

"No. They are not leaving until morning."

They mounted and rode quietly away. They reined in at a deserted spot well out of earshot of anyone to discuss their next strategy.

"What happened? What did you overhear?"

"Majors was shot twice. Once in the right shoulder, and here, his head was grazed." Stalking Ghost pointed to his temple. "The man at the house took the bullet out."

"So Luke's going to be all right?"

"That is what the man said. The bounty hunter is Gary Reid."

Recognition shone in Cody's eyes. "I've heard of him before. Talk has it that he's tough."

"He is guarding Majors now. They will ride out at dawn."

"So we've got just a few hours to figure out what we're going to do." Cody started to pace, her mind racing as she tried to figure out a way to outsmart Reid and reclaim Luke. "I have to get him back, Stalking Ghost."

He remained silent as he always did when she was thinking.

"We have to come up with a disguise that will work on Reid." She stopped pacing and looked at Stalking Ghost. "We're out in the middle of the countryside. I could dress as a boy, and we could just try to outgun him, but that's dangerous. I don't want any more killing. There's been too much of that already."

"What would cause Reid to stop?"

"Dressing like Delilah or Armita again won't work. He didn't pay the least bit of attention to me when I was sitting stark naked in the middle of that pond." She began to pace again, and then looked up at him quickly as she remembered the deserted ranch house. "Do you think you can get that buckboard we saw at that ranch to work?"

He nodded.

"I think I've got it then. But we're going to have to go back into town one more time. I've got to make a few purchases at the general store."

Stalking Ghost mounted his horse and waited for her to do the same. They returned to Mason Wells quietly, keeping to the back streets, avoiding detection.

With Stalking Ghost's help, Cody forced the back door at the general store and crept inside. She took the things she needed, first surprising her companion by her selections, then almost winning a smile of approval from him. She left a note on the counter near the cash box along with enough money to pay for all that she'd taken plus extra to cover the cost of having the door fixed. Silently, they disappeared into the Texas night.

When they reached the abandoned ranch, Cody hurriedly set to work. She built a small fire in the fireplace for light and began her transformation while Stalking Ghost saw to the wagon. They were both concerned about their horses pulling a buckboard, but could only hope that it would turn out all right. One way or the other, they had to get ahead of Reid and Luke and set the trap.

Cody called Stalking Ghost to her when she had completed her disguise. The firelight hadn't been easy to work by, and the small hand mirror she'd taken from the store hadn't afforded much of a reflection to perfect her makeup and hair, but she'd done her best. Now it would be up to Stalking Ghost to tell her whether the disguise was believable or not.

"Well, what do you think?" Cody asked as he came into the dilapidated house.

He stood in the doorway staring at her in silence for a long moment. "Put on the bonnet," he instructed.

Cody did so, tying a bow beneath her chin.

He nodded. "We can be ready to go in just a few minutes. It will take a firm hand to control and steady your horse. He does not like the harness."

"Well, pray that he manages to get us to the other side of town before he acts up. Once we stage the breakdown, I don't care if he never pulls another buckboard again for as long as he lives."

Stalking Ghost went to hitch up the wagon. Very shortly, they would be on their way.

Luke did not sleep. The pain in his shoulder and the ache in his head had combined to keep him awake and miserable all night. When Reid roused him before dawn, he was as ready as he would ever be to begin the trek back. The only positive thought he could hang on to was that Jack would be waiting for him in Del Fuego. Reid cuffed his hands in front of him and prodded him along with his rifle as they headed out to the horses. He painfully pulled himself up on his horse and prepared to ride out. As they started from town with Reid leading his horse, Luke thought of Armita. He hoped she was safe and would find her clothes and horse without any problem once it was daylight.

The sun was up, and they were a good five miles out of town when they came upon an old woman, standing beside her buckboard, desperately needing help.

"Thank heaven you came by," the old lady said effusively. "Young man, you are truly the answer to my prayers." That was no lie, Cody thought. "Could you help me?"

"Ma'am," Reid said, tipping his hat to the grayhaired, elderly lady. She was wearing a sunbonnet that shielded her face from the hot sun, a rather plain calico dress, and a drawstring purse at her wrist. She reminded him a bit of his own grandmother back in Missouri. "You got trouble?"

"I started out for town from my place over the hill there a ways, and this wheel started to go on me." She gestured toward the broken wheel on the decrepit wagon.

"Let me see what I can do for you." Reid had no intention of spending a lot of time with her. But if he could rig it so she could make it the last few miles into town, he'd do it.

"You have a prisoner?" she asked innocently as she saw the handcuffs on Luke.

"He's wanted in Del Fuego."

"What did he do?"

"He's a killer, ma'am, and I'm taking him in." He tied Luke's horse to the side of the buckboard so he could keep an eye on him.

"Law-abiding citizens are lucky to have good, upstanding men like you around to save them."

"Thank you, ma'am." Reid hunkered down to take a look at the axle.

Cody almost shouted "Hallelujah" when he fell for her ruse. She quietly took a step back as he set to work. In a single smooth motion, she drew her gun out of her purse and pointed it at Reid's back.

"Don't move, Mr. Reid."

"What the hell?" He froze. Suddenly her voice didn't sound like a pitiful little old lady's anymore. He took a quick glance over his shoulder to see her holding a gun on him. "Lady, I only got a little money on me; there's no point in trying to rob me. Hey . . . Wait a minute. How'd you know my name?"

"I know more than your name, and I'm not robbing you. You're the one who robbed me."

"What?" He was shocked.

So was Luke. He was staring at the old lady. When she tore off the bonnet and shook out her hair, he was unable to believe his eyes.

"Armita?"

In spite of the flour she'd used to powder her hair and the heavy makeup she'd used on her face, Luke recognized her.

"How did you get here? Are you all right? What are you doing?"

"Not now, Luke." She glanced up at him, then turned her full attention back to the bounty hunter. She knew Reid was tricky and dangerous, a more than worthy opponent, and she had no intention of losing in this confrontation. "Mr. Reid, let me introduce myself. The name's Cody Jameson, and you made a big mistake stealing my man from me last night."

"You're Cody Jameson?" Reid said, shocked. "But . . ."

"Cody Jameson?" Luke repeated, his gaze fixed on her in complete confusion.

Chapter Twenty-one

Luke frowned at the woman who seemed to be transforming right before his very eyes. It was Armita, yet there was something else vaguely familiar. . . .

And then Stalking Ghost appeared over the nearby hill.

"What the . . . ? Sister Mary?" Luke looked from the old Indian to the old lady, and he suddenly saw the connection. The old lady was Armita—was Sister Mary, too. And he was the fool. She was Cody Jameson!

He felt betrayed. He was furious.

"All right if I get up, Jameson?" Reid was asking.

"Just move real slow," Cody answered. "I don't like to use force, but I will if I have to."

"Heard you were one of the best bounty hunters

around," Reid remarked, slowly rising and turning to face her. "Now I know why."

"There's no need for compliments, just unbuckle your gunbelt real careful and drop it on the ground."

He did as he was told. "So Majors here didn't know he was caught?"

"No. And he still wouldn't if you hadn't interfered."

"Sorry if I spoiled things for you," Reid drawled. Even as mad as he was about losing Majors, he had to smile. Jameson was damned good. She'd even fooled him.

Cody shrugged. "It was tricky there for a while, but things will turn out now." She motioned toward his gunbelt where he'd dropped it. "Kick that over here."

He did.

"Now I want you to start walking up that hill toward my friend. Don't make any sudden moves."

Reid headed up the incline, wondering what she had in mind.

"Stalking Ghost, come down here and guard Luke while I take care of Mr. Reid."

He nodded and moved in closer to Luke as Reid and Cody disappeared over the top of the hill.

Cody walked behind the other bounty hunter, keeping the gun on him until they were a good half mile from the road. "You can stop here."

"Yes, ma'am. Now what?"

"Strip." She'd been planning this fate for him ever since last night at the watering hole, and she was going to enjoy every minute of his discomfort.

"Strip?"

"You understand English real good, Mr. Reid. You left me out in the middle of nowhere in my unmentionables last night, and I'm just returning the favor."

"Mighty thoughtful of you."

"Glad you think so." She grinned. "Let's go. Take off your clothes. I don't have a lot of time."

Reid's good humor held, but not by much as he took off his hat, shirt, then his long underwear top. He stood staring at her as his hand rested on the button on his pants. "You sure you want me to do this?"

"Positive."

"You gonna watch?"

"Damn straight." She gestured with her gun for him to get a move on.

"I'm gonna have to sit down and take my boots off so I can get my pants off."

"Go right ahead."

He sat down hard and tugged at his boots. When they were off, he stood and dropped his pants. Reid then stood before Cody in only his long johns.

"Well?" she prodded, enjoying his discomfort.

"Surely you ain't serious about me taking these off? I did leave you your shoes and underwear."

"That you did, Mr. Reid. And I appreciated your kindness. Trouble is, I'm not as nice as you."

His look turned steely as he anticipated the worst—walking naked back into Mason Wells. It wouldn't be pretty, and it certainly wasn't funny. He wasn't a man to beg, but he wasn't above trying to reason with this woman.

"You know, when I came upon your camp last night, I didn't know you were Jameson, and I surely didn't know you had Majors and were taking him in."

She nodded. "I work different. I try to outwit the men I'm after, not outshoot them."

"It worked on me."

"I'm going to leave your boots and the rest of your clothes another mile out of town on the way to Del Fuego."

"And my horse?"

Cody stared at him, trying to judge his character. He might be a rough, tough man, but he had taken Luke into Mason Wells to see to his wounds when he could have let him suffer all the way into Del Fuego. "I'll make you a deal."

"What kind of deal?" He was cautious.

"You forget all about Majors. He's mine and I'm taking him in. I don't want any more trouble with you."

"And?"

"And I'll tell you where the El Diablo gang is in hiding and the exact location of their hideout. You can go after them right now and bring in as many as you want. The bounty on them is five hundred dollars a head. Is it a deal?"

"What if I say no?"

"Then I'll take the rest of your long johns, there." She looked deliberately at his lower body. "Along with your horse and any money I can find in your things, and I'll leave them for you with the law in Del Fuego. However, if you agree, I'll leave you your long johns, I'll put your boots in the buck-board, and I'll leave your horse where I leave your clothes." She waited for his decision.

Reid didn't have to think long or hard about it. He was in his long johns, barefoot in the middle of the wilds with no money. "It's a deal."

"I wish you good luck, Reid." She quickly told him of the cantina in Rio Nuevo and of the canyon and its dangers. "Now, walk back a goodly distance and sit yourself on down. I want you to wait about half an hour before you even think about getting up."

"You're one helluva bounty hunter, Jameson."

"I'll take that as a compliment, coming from you." She moved forward to gather his clothes and boots and then smiled at him. "See you around, Reid."

She disappeared over the hill to find that Stalking Ghost had already saddled her horse for her. Luke was sitting on his mount, his expression stony.

"Did you find my gun?" she asked Stalking Ghost.

He gave it to her, along with the gunbelt that he'd brought along for her. She handed him back his own revolver, which he'd loaned her, then strapped on the belt and slid her father's gun into the holster. She left Reid's boots in the buckboard as she'd promised and tied the rest of his clothes on the back of his horse.

"I'm going to change; then I'll be ready to ride."

Stalking Ghost nodded, but Luke could no longer remain silent.

"And just who are you going to change into this time, Sister Mary?" His voice was hard-edged and cruel.

"There's no more need for disguises," she answered, meeting his eyes. She saw only coldness in his regard and flinched inwardly.

"There isn't, is there? You have 'your man' now, don't you?" There was hatred in his tone.

Cody got her riding clothes and walked away. There was nothing she could say that would change the way Luke was thinking right then.

She had been dreading this moment, and she hadn't expected to have to face it so soon. She hadn't planned on revealing her hand until they were within a day's ride of Del Fuego. She'd thought she was going to have two more days with him as Armita, but Reid's showing up had changed all of that. With the truth revealed before its time, Cody was now forced to play the game with the cards she'd been dealt.

She hadn't wanted Luke to hate her, although, as she thought about it, she realized that there would have been no way around it. The moment he'd discovered her true identity, any warm emotion he'd felt for her had died.

Cody finished changing and went to mount up. Luke didn't speak to her again.

"I'm ready to ride," she told Stalking Ghost. "I'll bring Reid's horse. You take Luke's. I'll follow you."

Stalking Ghost did as she said, and they continued on their way toward Del Fuego.

* * *

Luke had time to think as they rode, and he wasn't happy about it. Memories of the time he'd spent with Sister Mary taunted him. He'd been protecting her, for God's sake, and all the while she'd been trying to take him in for the reward they were offering on him for the bank robbery! He silently laughed at how completely he'd been fooled by her act. There she'd been, spouting the joys of knowing the Lord and talking about saving his soul, and all the while she'd been nothing more than a deceitful little liar herself. She'd gone into El Trajar trying to catch him, and she'd ended up stirring up a hornets' nest with Sully that had gotten her involved more deeply with the gang than she could ever have imagined.

Luke recalled how he'd thought Sister Mary was everything a woman should be—honest and forthright, gentle and caring. He'd thought he wasn't good enough for her. He'd thought that she was a complete innocent. He'd thought wrong. She'd used every trick in the book to try to bring him in, and as Armita, she'd even used her body!

He immediately stopped himself at that thought. There had been no mistaking her untouched state. If there was one thing that Sister Mary/Armita/Cody Jameson wasn't, it was easy.

Memories of their lovemaking spun through his thoughts, making him wonder anew just what kind of woman this Cody Jameson really was. Was she a saint or sinner? A deceitful bitch or clever bounty hunter?

Luke tried to imagine that her response to him when they'd made love had all been an act, but he knew instinctively that that wasn't true. She'd wanted him as much as he had wanted her.

But not anymore.

Cody Jameson had caught him. She was taking him in to collect her reward, and then she was going to go on to her next conquest. He'd been a job to her. Nothing more.

His mood was black. The only good thing he had to cling to was his knowledge that all the time he'd spent with the gang hadn't been for nothing. He had learned that El Diablo was a woman. At least he could help Jack that much.

With Stalking Ghost taking the lead, all Cody had to do was follow, and she was glad. It had been a long day, and she was exhausted. She couldn't give in to her exhaustion, though. She could rest once she had Luke safely delivered to Ranger Logan, not before. If Reid had managed to find them, so could other bounty hunters. They would travel fast and light and quiet. A mile from the wagon, they stopped long enough for her to tie up Reid's horse for him. Then they headed on, and again, as when she and Luke had been riding from Rio Nuevo, they stopped only long enough to rest the horses.

Cody kept an eye on Luke. She knew he had to be in some pain from his wounds, but he did not complain. When at last it was dusk, they sought out a campsite near a small creek. Cody noticed how stiffly Luke dismounted, and she could see the signs of strain and pain etched in his face. She started to go to him to help him, but he caught sight of her and stopped her with a stony glare.

"Are you all right? How's your shoulder?" she asked.

"I'm worth the same to you dead or alive, so it really doesn't matter, does it? You'll get your money."

"I wasn't worried about the money," she protested, but he turned his back on her.

Cody's heart ached. She wished there was something she could do to change the way things had turned out, but there was nothing. Ultimately she had always known that she had to take him in. It was her job. She had given Logan her word.

As she'd seen with Reid the night before, there were bounty hunters who were all too willing to shoot. Luke might not realize it right now, but she was keeping him safe. And she would deliver him alive.

Cody took care of the horses, then got out what food they had. They ate the dry fare without comment. Luke lay down, while Stalking Ghost kept watch. Cody wasn't ready to sleep just yet, so she got out the strong soap she'd taken at the general store and headed down to the water's edge. She'd had about all she could stand of the powder and dye in her hair.

Cody washed her thick mane as best she could, scrubbing hard, trying to erase all traces of the flour from the old lady's disguise and all of Armita's dark color. She deliberately took her time, for she had nothing else to do. It was hard to tell in the darkness when she was done just how true the color was, but she didn't care. At least now she felt a little cleaner and more like herself. She braided the heavy mass into a single plait, and lay down for the night.

As Cody lay staring up at the night sky, she remembered loving Luke, and she knew she would never forget him. He had been protective and tender with her when she was Sister Mary. He had been passionate with her when she was Armita.

The truth came to her slowly, and she faced it, painful as it was. For all that she'd been falling in love with Luke, he had never cared for her. He didn't even know her. He had cared for Sister Mary. He had made love to Armita, but he had never known Cody Jameson. With the realization came blinding pain, for a part of Cody Jameson was Sister Mary, a part of Cody Jameson was the passionate Armita. But Luke would never know.

When she finally fell asleep, her cheeks were wet from her tears.

Texas Ranger Capt. Steve Laughlin's expression was serious as he faced Jack across the secluded table in the back of the saloon the following afternoon.

"All right, tell me what's going on. Your telegram was vague."

"I know. That was deliberate."

"Then something's happening with El Diablo?"

Jack glanced around to make certain no one else was within earshot. "Let me tell you what I've done since I came down here."

As his captain listened, he told him of his connection to Luke and how he'd asked him to go undercover.

"What have you heard back from him?"

"Nothing yet, and once those bounties were set so high, I started worrying that some fast draw would shoot Luke first and ask questions later. So I hired a bounty hunter myself to go after him."

"You what?"

"You've heard of Cody Jameson, haven't you?"

Steve looked thoughtful for a minute, then nodded. "Isn't Jameson the one who's known for bringing in wanted men alive?"

"Yes, that's why I sent Jameson a wire. When Jameson showed up here in town to take the job, I hired her."

Steve gave him a startled look. "Her?"

"Jameson's a woman."

"Are you serious?" His disbelief was obvious.

"Very, and she's damned good at what she does. I did not reveal Luke's cover to her. I didn't want to put him at any greater risk. She's operating blind. I hired her as I would hire any hunter to track him down. She went after Luke weeks ago, and I haven't heard from either of them since."

"So where does that leave the investigation?"

"That's what I wanted to tell you. With all that I'd been able to find out about those who had prior knowledge of the gun shipment, there were two I could not completely clear of any involvement— Fred Halloway, the new sheriff here in Del Fuego, and the banker who was wounded in the bank robbery, Jonathan Harris."

Steve frowned. "If Harris were El Diablo, why

the hell would he set himself up to get shot?"

"That's troubled me, too. I don't know if there's anyone close to Harris he might inadvertently have given information to that led to the robbery of his own bank. No other names have surfaced."

"I'll do some more checking on Halloway. You center in on the banker. Maybe we can tie this up here in town and help out your friend Majors at the same time."

"There has to be a connection here. The sooner we find it, the sooner we bring down El Diablo. Then this whole part of the state can breathe easier."

"Who else knows about Majors other than the two of us?"

"I didn't want to, but I told Halloway about Luke."

Steve shot him a surprised look.

"We had a case of mistaken identity a week or so ago, and things got tense. A bounty hunter showed up with a man he claimed was Luke, and the townspeople were nearly ready to riot to get their hands on him. It was after that, that I confided in Fred. I don't want Luke's life to be in danger when he finally gets back here."

"I don't blame you, not after what he's been through."

Jack thought about mentioning to Steve that he'd said something to Elizabeth, too, but he didn't. What he shared with Elizabeth was private. He didn't want to drag her into the middle of this. She had already been hurt enough.

"Anything else?"

"No, that's everything I know for now."

"Well, let's go over to the sheriff's office, and you can introduce me to Halloway so I can try to read him. This El Diablo is one cold bastard, and I want him."

"So do I," Jack agreed.

Chapter Twenty-two

It was much later that night that Jack sat alone in the dark in his room trying to figure out Jonathan's connection in all this. He could not think of the banker without Elizabeth slipping into his thoughts.

Jack did not know if Elizabeth would come to him tonight. They had not been together in a while, and he missed her. He'd caught a glimpse of her today as she'd gone into a store, but there had been no opportunity to speak. He longed to have her in his arms again. She was exciting and passionate, and he wished things were different so they could be together always. It wasn't to be, though, for he knew she would never leave Jonathan while he needed her.

Jack forced himself to put all emotion aside and

think logically. He rose and began to pace the room, rubbing the back of his neck wearily. Jonathan had known every detail about the bank and he'd known about the guns, too.

A knock at the door drew him from his thoughts, and he opened it to find Elizabeth standing in the shadowy hall. She quickly slipped into the room and as soon as the door was closed, she was in his arms kissing him.

"I've missed you," she whispered against his lips. "When I didn't see a light on, I feared you weren't here."

"I had almost given up hope that you would come to me tonight," he told her hungrily, reveling in holding her near.

Just the scent of her aroused him. Already the fire was burning within him to take her, hard and fast. His mouth sought hers as he moved against her, letting her know exactly what he wanted, needed from her.

Elizabeth was more than ready. She'd been thinking about him all day, and had counted the hours until she could slip away and they could be together. Her hands moved boldly upon him.

They fell together on the bed, their clothing shed in a heated frenzy as they strained against each other. When at last they were naked, Jack moved over her and thrust deep within her. She was ready for him and, wrapping her legs about his waist, she met him in that feverish mating. Clawing at his back, she sought her own pleasure in his pain. He responded by quickening his pace, driving into her powerfully, dominating her as she

315

dominated him, for he was giving her exactly what she wanted.

Elizabeth reached her peak and shuddered as waves of ecstasy throbbed through her. Jack felt her response and sought his own release, collapsing on top of her, exhausted. He had never had a lover as wild as Elizabeth. She was completely unpredictable, one moment sweet and soft, the next clawing and hungry, and he thought that was what aroused him most about her. He never knew what to expect from her. He was mesmerized by her.

"You're magnificent," she said softly as he shifted to the side, and they lay together, their limbs still entwined.

He kissed her, caressing her still. He couldn't bear to be this close to her and not touch her. "I've been too long without you."

He sculpted the firm beauty of her breasts, then moved lower to explore all of her lush body. She lay quietly beneath his caresses, moving just a little to entice him to do more. When her own fire was burning again, she took over, reaching for him, arousing him, bringing him fully to heat before taking him deep within her body. He shuddered as she set the pace, hungrily draining his passion from him with each exciting thrust of her hips.

Elizabeth was in control and she loved it. To control a man like Jack was more exciting to her than any fantasy. He was strong and powerful, yet she could control and manipulate him with her body. She smiled at him and stopped moving. He responded immediately, urging her to continue, but she refused.

"Do you want me, Jack? Really want me?"

"You know I do," he growled, pulling her to him for a kiss.

"How do I know you want me?"

"Can't you feel it?"

"No. I want more of you, Jack. More . . ."

He rolled with her, pinning her beneath him, grinding his hips against hers until she found the bliss she'd sought. He joined her there.

It was much later that Jack lay looking up at the ceiling, his brow furrowed as he thought of Jonathan and his possible connection to the gang and how it might affect Elizabeth. He didn't want her to get caught up in any of this.

"What is it?" she asked, her heavy-lidded gaze upon him, trying to gauge his mood, to read his thoughts. "You look so somber . . . almost worried."

He glanced over at her and gave her a half-hearted smile. "I'm not worried. It's just so many things are happening, and I'm afraid you might get hurt in the process." He lifted one hand to caress her cheek.

"What are you talking about?"

Jack drew a heavy breath. He'd been trying to decide how much to tell her, and suddenly decided that he should be totally honest. In fact, confiding in her might be the smartest thing he could do. She might have inadvertently heard something over the past few months that could help him—

either in convicting her husband or in proving that he wasn't guilty.

"Your husband . . ."

"What about Jonathan?" She couldn't imagine what Jonathan had to do with anything. She kept him in his wheelchair, he complained and made her life generally miserable, but other than that, he was as useless to her as he'd always been except for . . .

Jack levered himself up on an elbow to look down at her as he spoke. "I've been delving into the background of the gang's activities and I'm convinced El Diablo has a contact here in town. I've narrowed down the suspects to two."

"Who are they? Did you hear something from your contact?"

"Not yet. I've figured this out on my own."

Elizabeth looked puzzled as she tried to imagine who he could have come up with. "What did you learn?"

"There were two people in Del Fuego who had advance knowledge of the gun shipment. Fred Halloway and—"

"It couldn't be Fred," she insisted, quickly defending the lawman.

"And . . ." He paused, hating what he had to say next. "Your husband."

"Jonathan?" She stared at him wide-eyed, her color paling, shocked by the suggestion. "You think my Jonathan is somehow connected to El Diablo?"

"If he's not El Diablo himself," he stated firmly.

"I'm sorry, but he and Fred are the two most likely suspects."

"But Jonathan's paralyzed! He couldn't have had anything to do with the robberies. Dear Lord, why would he allow himself to be shot at the bank if he were El Diablo?"

Luke shrugged. "Maybe it was a plan that went awry. Maybe Jonathan was only supposed to be wounded, and the shot went wide. I don't know. And as far as his being paralyzed goes, he could still relay messages to the right people if he were the contact. According to the general at the fort—"

"You mean . . ."

"You're familiar with General Larson?"

"Yes, he and his wife are our close friends."

"Well, according to him, Jonathan was one of very few who knew the details of the gun shipment, and whoever informed El Diablo knew all the details."

"There is no way it could have been Jonathan," she defended her husband.

"Are you certain?"

"Positive. Jonathan may be many things, but he's not an outlaw."

"Then can you think of anyone he's been in contact with who he might innocently have told about the gun shipment or the money at the bank? Someone who could immediately send word to El Diablo and set the gang up for their next job?"

"He's had so many visitors since the shooting." She looked bewildered as she tried to remember all those who'd come to visit. "I don't know if I could pick out even one who might be the one you're looking for. They're all our friends."

"Think. Did anyone want to speak with him alone and uninterrupted? Was there anyone who seemed secretive in any way?"

"No. I was with him most of the time. It can't be Jonathan. It just can't. As his wife, don't you think I'd know it if he were El Diablo? Don't you think I'd be aware of strange comings and goings, of cryptic messages and the like? There's been nothing like that with Jonathan that I've ever seen. Nothing."

Jack fell silent, going over Fred's connections in his mind, trying to fit the new sheriff into the role of informant, wondering if Steve was having any success with him.

"You believe me, don't you?" she asked worriedly.

"Of course," he assured her, drawing her to him for a kiss and then cradling her to his shoulder.

Elizabeth breathed easier. The last thing Jonathan needed was to find out that he was suspected of being involved with El Diablo.

"I just wish I could find that one missing link."

"Maybe there's more than one person involved," she offered.

"There could be, but I doubt it. When there's more than one person involved, people talk, and El Diablo's gang is known for their secretiveness."

"Enough about El Diablo," she said softly, kissing him to distract him from thoughts of the bloody gang.

"You're right."

And they spoke of the gang no more.

It was over an hour later that she dressed and prepared to leave him. Jack took her in his arms to kiss her once more.

"I don't want you to go. . . . ever."

"I wish I could stay, but there's no way. Coming here as I do is so dangerous as it is."

"I know, and I'm sorry to put you in this situation."

"You didn't put me here. I come to you because I need you, Jack. You'll never know how much our time together means to me."

He held her close for a moment longer, then let her go. She slipped from the room.

"What are you doing here?" El Diablo demanded, coming face-to-face with Hadley, standing in the shadows of the front porch.

"Where were you?" Hadley demanded. "I've been waiting for hours."

"That's none of your business. We had no rendezvous set. My life is my own."

"Not for much longer," he said tightly.

"What are you talking about?"

"Majors killed Sully and escaped."

"I always knew Sully was an idiot!"

"He's a dead idiot now, but that doesn't change anything. You've got to get out of here. When Majors gets back here and tells Logan what he knows, they'll know who you are."

"How much time do I have?"

"Who knows? I'm surprised I beat him back here, but then he had the cantina singer with him and that probably slowed him down a bit."

"I may have something else that will slow him down," El Diablo said thoughtfully. "As far as I know, no one else in town has been told that Majors is working for Logan. If Logan is no longer around to save him when he returns, Luke Majors is as good as dead."

"How do you figure?"

"We almost had a riot a few weeks ago when a bounty hunter brought in a man he thought was Majors. You wouldn't have believed the excitement in town. Logan and Halloway had to chase the people off. If Logan's dead and Majors shows up in town, he's gonna hang for sure."

"I like the way you think."

"You always have." El Diablo smiled.

"Shall I take care of Logan?"

"No. You stay here out of sight."

"What about Jonathan?"

"Don't worry about him. He's in bed, and he's not going anywhere unless I move him."

"Poor bastard," Hadley remarked.

"You got the bastard part right. As soon as I finish with Logan, we'll ride. The farther we get away from this town and the people in it, the better. I'm sick of the whole place. You got money?"

"I've got our shares from the sale of the guns."

"Good. That should take us far and fast."

El Diablo disappeared inside. Ten minutes later, the outlaw leader reappeared dressed in black.

Hadley nodded approvingly. "If you stay in the shadows, no one will ever see you."

"That's exactly how I want it. This is how I managed to get inside the jail and find out about Sheriff Gregory that night."

"Be careful. I'll be waiting."

"I'll be back."

El Diablo moved off into the night.

Jack had lain awake for a while thinking about all that had happened, and wondering how Luke was. He hoped his friend was safe. He finally drifted off. He had been sleeping heavily, facedown on the bed, when a sound in the room roused him. He opened his eyes and smiled.

"You came back," he said warmly.

"I had to," came her answer.

And then Elizabeth, moving toward him, kneeling over him, drew out a savage-looking knife and in one smooth vicious move, plunged it into Jack's back.

He rose up with a roar, his eyes wide in agony and confusion. She jumped back and fled toward the window she'd just climbed in.

"You?" he managed in a strangled voice, trying to give chase. He tried to catch her, but the pain was too great and his legs wouldn't work. "It was you?"

Elizabeth smiled coldly down at him as he collapsed beside the bed and lay still. "Yes, Jack, dear, it was me. All the time."

Without a backward glance, she escaped from the room and disappeared.

Her brother was waiting for her when she returned to the house. He met her outside.

"Is he dead?" Hadley asked.

She shot him a disgusted look, irritated that he would question her. "I stabbed him in the back while he was still in bed half-asleep. Let's ride."

"Do you have everything you need? Is there anything you want in the house?"

Elizabeth glanced at the house where she'd lived with Jonathan for the last three years. Had she been a sentimental woman, she might have known a moment of regret leaving it. After all, the only reason she'd married the banker in the first place was to have this kind of a life. She'd been sick of always being on the run and had seen marriage to the lonely banker as the perfect way to settle down in one place and still get the information they'd needed for the gang. Jonathan had never caught on to her, either. He'd accepted at face value her stories that she was going to see her brother whenever she went to meet Hadley, and he'd never questioned her or wanted to accompany her. Had Jonathan ever wanted to go, they would have arranged some kind of miserable meeting so he would never ask to accompany her again. But her husband had never been an adventurous sort, so they'd been safe there.

Now it was over. Elizabeth was going to walk away without a backward glance. Jonathan had meant nothing to her when she'd married him, and he meant less than nothing to her now. He had been a means to an end. She had used him while it had benefited her, but she valued her own life too much to stay around when it got dangerous.

"No," Elizabeth finally answered him, and her

tone was completely devoid of emotion. "There's nothing I want inside. We can leave now."

She walked away with Hadley to where he'd tied up his horse and one for her. They mounted up and rode quietly away.

"Where do you want to go?" Hadley asked.

"Far away from here," she answered.

Once they reached the edge of town, they spurred their horses to a gallop and never looked back.

Jonathan lay in his bed, staring unblinkingly at the ceiling. Elizabeth and Hadley were part of the El Diablo gang. Terror filled him.

It was obvious they hadn't known he could hear them. But he had heard them, every word. Their conversation played over and over in his mind. He'd been helpless to stop them. Had he yelled or called out for help, no one would have heard him but them. He probably would have ended up dead, just like that Texas Ranger was right now.

Jonathan trembled. Elizabeth and Hadley might have said they were leaving, but he didn't trust them. He had no intention of making a sound until morning. Only then would he try to figure out a way to get word to the sheriff about what he knew.

Images of Elizabeth tormented him the rest of the night. Elizabeth as his beautiful bride, as his loving wife. It had all been a terrible lie. She had never loved him. She had only used him. She had even plotted to rob his own bank! She was the one who was really responsible for his injury.

Hatred welled up powerfully within him. He might have been a little cruel to her since he'd been injured, but if he ever saw her again, she would learn the true meaning of the word.

Chapter Twenty-three

"We'll make Del Fuego today," Cody announced as she saddled her horse the second morning out.

Stalking Ghost nodded. "We should reach the town by early afternoon."

Luke didn't respond as he sat waiting for them to get ready to ride out. He'd been mostly quiet since Cody had stolen him back from Reid, speaking only when asked a direct question. There was no point. When he met with Jack, he would tell his friend all he knew; until then he would go along with Cody and Stalking Ghost and pray that they reached town as quickly as possible.

Once he'd told Jack what he'd learned, he was going to collect the money his friend owed him and head for the Trinity. Luke planned to sit out on the ranch with Jessy until they ran out of supplies. The last thing he wanted was to be around anyone. He'd had enough of "civilization" to last him a lifetime. He was looking forward to some peace and quiet.

Cody glanced over at Luke as she finished with her horse. In a few hours she would be turning him over to Logan and would probably never see him again. Somehow she wanted him to know that everything that had happened between them hadn't been an act. She wanted him to know that she had appreciated his kindness and his protection when she'd been Sister Mary. Cody wanted to tell him, too, that she was glad she'd saved him from Sully, but she was certain he would accuse her of having done that only for the money.

When Stalking Ghost moved away, Cody saw her chance to talk to Luke privately, and she went to him.

"There are a few things I have to say to you before we reach Del Fuego."

He glanced up at her from where he sat. His regard was glacial.

Cody almost shivered at the coldness and contempt she saw in it. She was tempted to turn and walk away, to give up, but she didn't. "First I wanted to say thank you."

He gave her a mocking smile. "Thank you? For what?"

"For the way you treated me when you thought I was Sister Mary. You were very kind and very protective, and—"

"And knowing what I know now, I realize you

328

would have been just fine without me. I was a fool."

"No, you were a gentleman. That's rare in—"

"Go ahead and finish what you were about to say, Jameson. 'That's rare in a killer.' Well, your thanks aren't needed or wanted. If I'd had my way, we would never have met."

"I would have found you."

"Because it was your job," he shot back at her.

"I'm bringing you in alive. That's more than some of the others would have done," she countered.

"So I can be hanged by a mob," he finished bluntly.

"There won't be any lynching. The law will see to that. Things were pretty stirred up when I was there, but then, the townspeople were still angry over Sheriff Gregory being killed that way."

"Killed what way?" Luke was instantly alert, fearing he'd hit the sheriff too hard when he'd left to follow the gang.

"He was shot down in cold blood while he was locked in the jail cell." Cody looked at him, trying to read his thoughts. "You might say executed. One of the deputies who'd been keeping watch around town that night was killed, too. Most of the talk said you were the one who killed the sheriff."

"Gregory was alive when I left that jail! I made sure of it! I was the last one out!"

"Well, he was murdered that night!"

"El Diablo . . . It had to be El Diablo," Luke said

softly. Hadley's sister. Was the outlaw leader in Del Fuego?

"Who is El Diablo?" Cody asked him.

"I never met him. I don't know." It wasn't a lie.

"You were a member of the gang and you never met him?"

"He never rode into camp while I was there."

"Why did you run after you shot Sully? If you were one of the gang, they wouldn't have blamed you for killing him in self-defense."

"I wasn't taking any chances." He fell silent, fearing he'd said too much already. What he knew about El Diablo he was saving for Jack.

Steve Laughlin had been working with Fred all night. There had been a disturbance at one of the saloons, and they'd spent most of the long night hours sobering up drunken cowboys. They were tired as they waited in the office for Jack to show up the following morning to relieve them.

"What time have you got, Fred?" Steve asked, wondering what was keeping him. Logan was usually on time.

"After nine. You think Jack had something else to do this morning?"

"Not that he mentioned to me. I think I'll go check on him, though. You want to come with me or wait here in case he shows up?"

"I'll wait here. You go on ahead."

Steve reached the hotel and went up to Jack's room. He knocked, but got no answer.

"Jack . . . are you in there?" he called loudly, knocking again.

It was then that he heard it: a low, barely distinguishable moan coming from inside.

"Jack?" Steve put his ear to the door and heard it once more.

He ran back down to the front desk.

"I need to get into Ranger Logan's room," he demanded of the clerk.

"I'm afraid I can't do that without his permission."

"Look, I'm his boss, and I think something's wrong. I heard a strange noise that sounded like a groan coming from inside. I need the door unlocked now, so I can check."

The clerk looked doubtful, but agreed. He planned on staying with this man the whole time just to make sure everything was left untouched.

"Mr. Logan?" the clerk called out to Jack when he knocked on the door before opening it.

When there was no immediate answer, he unlocked the room for the Ranger captain. As they stepped inside, to the clerk's horror, they found Jack Logan unconscious on the floor.

"Send for a doctor, quick! And get word to Sheriff Halloway!" Steve began issuing orders to the stunned and unmoving clerk.

The man turned and fled, and Steve hoped he remembered to do as he'd been told.

Steve stared down at his friend, at the savage wound in his back and the blood that stained the floor around him where he'd fallen. He felt for a pulse and breathed easier when he found one.

"Jack? Can you hear me?" He bent low just in

case Jack tried to speak. "Who did this to you? Was it El Diablo?"

But Jack did not respond. He lay unmoving, his breathing shallow and labored.

The wait for the doctor seemed an eternity to Steve, and when the physician finally came through the door, he had never been so glad to see anyone.

"I didn't move him. I was afraid to until you had a chance to look at him."

"We can do it together, right now. I want him on the bed," Dr. Michaels directed.

They carefully lifted Jack onto the bed, and then the physician began his examination. Steve went to close the door to the room while he worked.

"Will he live?" Steve asked, unable to stand the waiting any more.

"From the looks of things, the blade was deflected by a rib; otherwise he'd have been dead already."

"Is he going to make it?"

"I think so, but he's lost a lot of blood."

"Do everything you can for him," Steve insisted. "I want this man alive."

"So do I." He continued to work on Jack.

A knock at the door drew Steve from the bedside. He answered it to find Fred Halloway there.

"What happened?" He looked past Steve toward the bed, where Jack lay facedown while the doctor treated him.

The Ranger captain stepped outside and pulled the door almost shut behind him. "Someone tried to murder Jack last night."

Fred was shocked. "But who? Why?"

Steve's expression was determined as he answered, "El Diablo. Who else? Jack must have been getting too close to the truth."

He was glad that he'd spent the night working with Fred. He knew for certain now that the new sheriff was not the outlaw leader.

"Then you know who El Diablo is?"

"I've got a pretty damned good idea. Once I'm sure Jack's going to be fine, you and I are going to pay a call on one of the town's most upstanding citizens."

"Who? How did you figure it out?"

"Jack had been tracking down leads. He knew the names of all those who had advance information about the gun shipment. Larson had told him that two people in town knew about it—you and Jonathan Harris."

"You mean I was a suspect, too?"

"Everyone was for a while, but now we know the truth."

"Harris couldn't have done this! He's paralyzed! There's no way he could have gotten up here undetected, let alone overpowered Jack," Fred pointed out.

"True, but as El Diablo he has an entire gang working for him. He could order it done. He probably thought that no one else knew what Jack had learned, and that if he eliminated Jack, he'd be free. He figured wrong."

Fred shook his head in disgust. "How bad is Jack?"

"The doctor says he should make it. Come on

333

inside; we'll wait until he's through."

The two lawmen went back into the bedroom, to find the doctor washing his hands in the basin.

"Is one of you going to stay with him?" the doctor asked Steve. "There should be someone here constantly until he regains consciousness."

"I understand," Steve said. "I'll stay."

The doctor nodded. "Good. I have to get back to my office. I'll send one of the women who works for me over to sit with you and watch him. Let me know immediately if there's any change in his condition."

"Would it be better for us to take him to your office?"

"I don't like moving him now. Let me know if he starts to show signs of coming around."

"I will," Steve promised.

He was torn by the need to go after El Diablo, but he could not leave Jack. Not now.

"I'll go back to the jail and tell the deputy what happened; then I'll come back and sit with you. Do you want or need anything?" Fred asked.

"The only thing I want or need right now is El Diablo," Steve ground out, not taking his gaze from Jack, lying pale and deathly still on the bed.

Jack felt as if he were trapped by the excruciating pain he felt. He wanted to scream, to cry out to any and all who would listen the name of his betrayer, but he couldn't summon the strength. As if at a great distance, he could hear voices, but he couldn't reach them. It seemed hopeless. He fell back, down into the cold darkness, away from the warmth and light—and pain. Nothingness. Peace overcame him, and he drifted back into unconsciousness again.

It was several hours later when Jack finally battled his way to awareness. He opened his eyes to see Steve seated near the window, staring out. Jack tried to call his name, but managed only a groan.

"Captain Laughlin. He's starting to come around," the nurse called over to where he sat with Fred near the window.

Steve hurried to Jack's side.

"Jack! It's Steve. I'm here." He bent over him, leaning close to hear what Jack was trying to say.

"Steve . . ." His voice was barely audible.

"Who did this to you? Who stabbed you?" he demanded, wanting justice.

Memories of the night before spun wildly through Jack's fevered mind. He closed his eyes as the pain of Elizabeth's betrayal stabbed at him. He had never suspected her. He would never have believed her capable of such treachery. But it had been Elizabeth. He had seen her. Elizabeth Harris had tried to kill him.

"Harris . . ." was all he could say. The word was just above a moan and so softly spoken that Steve could barely understand.

"You were right. All along, you were right," Steve told him. "I'll take care of it from here."

Jack wanted to stop him, to tell him that it was Elizabeth, not Jonathan, but he couldn't muster the strength to call out to him again. He wanted to stop Steve from walking into her lair unprepared, but he was too weak to call him back and tell him which Harris was really El Diablo. The pain overwhelmed him again, and he drifted away once more into forgetfulness.

"It was Harris," Steve said to Fred, who'd been sitting with him.

"Let's go find out how the bastard did it. He must have had a henchman."

"You'll stay with him?" Steve asked the nurse.

"Yes, but you need to let Dr. Michaels know that he did regain consciousness for a few minutes."

"We'll tell him as we go."

The two lawmen started from the hotel room, but Steve paused by the door to take one last look at Jack. As he did, he pulled out his gun and checked to make sure it was loaded. Sliding it back into his holster, he was ready to face the man who'd been identified as El Diablo, the leader of the notorious gang of killers.

They stopped only briefly at the doctor's office to relay the news of Jack's condition before continuing on.

"Do you think we need more deputies with us? Harris may be dangerous."

"If he gives me any trouble at all, he's a dead man," Steve said quietly.

Fred nodded and said no more as they strode the length of town toward the banker's house. They reached it in short order and moved up onto the front porch to knock on the door.

"Do you think he left town?" Fred asked when no one answered.

"I doubt it. If he thinks Jack is dead, why would he run?" Steve pounded on the door again, harder this time. When he heard shouting inside the house, he instructed Fred, "Check around the side of the house and see if you can get a look in any of the windows."

Fred disappeared around the house. "Steve! Break in the door!"

Steve put his shoulder to it and forced it open. Fred was behind him in an instant.

"What did you see?"

"It's Harris. He's in bed and yelling for help."

Steve drew his gun. Charging into the master bedroom, they found the abandoned Harris.

"Thank God you came!" Jonathan cried as they appeared in the doorway. Then he saw the gun and flinched. "So you know . . ."

"Know what?"

"About Elizabeth and that brother of hers!"

"What are you talking about?" Fred asked.

"I don't know how I could have been so stupid. It was her the whole time! Elizabeth was involved with that gang!"

"Your wife?" Steve was shocked.

"Yes! She's the one who was giving them all the information. She knew everything about the workings of the bank, and she was at dinner with us when the general and I discussed the details of the gun shipment."

"That's no proof," Steve said, doubting his story, thinking he was trying to head them off in a false direction. "Where is she, Harris? I want to talk to her."

"That's what I'm trying to tell you. She's gone! Her brother showed up last night. They were outside on the porch, but I heard every word they said. They didn't know I could hear them or I'd be dead right now." He turned red in the face with fury as he relayed all that he'd heard. "Have you checked on Logan yet? She was going to the hotel to kill him, and she must have done it, for she returned in a short time and they rode out."

"You're saying you believe your own wife is part of the El Diablo gang?"

"That's exactly what I'm telling you! In fact, I'll tell you more than that! Elizabeth is not only a part of the gang. She is El Diablo!"

"El Diablo's a woman?" Fred was aghast as he remembered all the conversations he'd had with her since the bank robbery. She had fooled everyone.

"Who better to get the information? Who would ever suspect her? I should have realized sooner, but I kept believing that . . ." His voice became choked with emotion and he couldn't say any more for a moment.

"Kept believing what, Jonathan?" They hoped he was going to give them another clue.

"I kept believing that she loved me."

Steve and Fred glanced at each other, wondering at his story.

"Ranger Logan was attacked last night, but he wasn't killed," Steve informed him.

"Thank God. He can tell you that I'm right! He can tell you that Elizabeth did it!"

"Jack did speak to us briefly, but all he could say was 'Harris.' "

"And you think it was me? You think I'm involved in this? That's why you came in here with your gun drawn!" The sickly banker stared at them in outrage and confusion.

"That's right."

"You think I planned a robbery of my own bank and then told them to shoot me to make it look good? I'm too much of a coward to do anything like that. And if you think it was me, how could I have attacked Logan? There's no way I could have gotten to him, and even if I had, what could a man in a wheelchair do to a strong man like Logan?"

"You could have had someone from the gang do it."

"And that's why I left myself lying here all alone in this bed for more than twelve hours! I'm telling you, it was Elizabeth. She's the one. We've only been married a few years. She was using me."

They knew he was right. They realized, too, that they had missed their chance to arrest the leader of the gang. Still, now that El Diablo's identity was known, they could find her and bring her to justice.

"What are you going to do to me?" Jonathan demanded as the two conferred in low voices.

"Nothing, Jonathan. We're going to send someone over to take care of you."

"Are you going after her? They rode out late last night, but I don't know where they were going."

"We'll be riding out as fast as we can arrange it."

"I hope you catch her. I hope you hang her."

There was vengeance on his mind. The woman he'd thought loved him had been responsible for his injuries. She was a thief, a liar, and a murderer. He hoped they caught her soon.

Chapter Twenty-four

Luke was almost glad when he saw Del Fuego in the distance. He wouldn't exactly call it home, but at least he'd reached Jack again and he could finally put things straight. He hoped Jack was in the sheriff's office when they arrived, for with Gregory dead, he didn't know who else was aware of his undercover work.

"Look! This time someone really is bringing in Majors!"

The shout went up and people rushed out of the buildings to get a look at him as he rode by with Cody and Stalking Ghost. A crowd was soon following them through town.

"I knew it was bad from what Logan had told me, but I didn't know it was this bad," Cody said quietly to Stalking Ghost as she drew her revolver.

She kept the weapon close to her leg as they rode up to the sheriff's office.

Stalking Ghost dismounted, went to help Luke down, and then the three of them entered the office together. Cody glanced around at the deputies who were there, but she did not recognize anyone.

"I'm looking for Ranger Logan. Can you tell me where I can find him?"

One of the deputies looked at her skeptically. "Why do you want Logan?"

"I'm bringing in Luke Majors. I need to talk to him."

Excitement stirred within the deputies as they recognized the captured man. "Let's get him locked up, and then I'll tell you about Logan."

"What's to tell? The man owes me money. I want my reward," she stated firmly.

"There's been trouble, ma'am."

"The name's Jameson, Cody Jameson. What kind of trouble are you talking about?"

"It's Ranger Logan. He's been injured."

"How bad is he?" she asked immediately, sensing Luke tense beside her.

"We don't know yet. They just found him this morning. You can leave Majors here and we'll lock him up while you go check with Sheriff Halloway and Ranger Capt. Laughlin. They're both over at the hotel, waiting to see how Logan is."

"I'll do that. You just make sure nothing happens to my prisoner, or there'll be hell to pay."

"Yes, ma'am."

The deputy had heard of Cody Jameson and knew better than to try to cross the bounty hunter.

"We'll keep a close watch on him. He won't get away from us."

"Good. I'll be back."

Cody stayed until Luke was locked up safely in the back; then she started from the office. She paused once at the door to glance back toward Luke and saw him standing in the cell, watching her. There was no love for her in his expression. If anything, the look in his eyes revealed the contempt and hate he felt for her. Regret stung Cody, but she could waste no time. She headed off with Stalking Ghost to locate Logan.

Worry consumed her as she considered what had happened. This didn't look good. How could the Ranger have gotten injured right there in town? Something strange was going on.

Luke stood alone in the cell, trying to figure out what to do and knowing there was nothing he could do but wait. With Gregory dead and Jack injured, he was in an impossible situation. Tension filled him. If none of the lawmen but Jack knew of his cover, and Jack wasn't able to tell the truth, Luke didn't know if he would survive until morning. He'd heard the excitement in the streets, and he feared a mob would come for him before everything could be straightened out.

Pacing nervously, he realized he was helpless. That didn't sit well with him, but the truth was he couldn't do anything until Jack showed up. Only then would he be free again. Luke sat down on the edge of the hard, narrow cot to await word of his friend.

* * *

Jack swam up from the depths of darkness again, and though pain enveloped him, he knew he could hide from it no longer. He was weak and exhausted, but he had to pull himself back to consciousness; he had to.

With an effort, Jack opened his eyes to stare about the room. The curtains were drawn and the room was dark. He felt disoriented, not sure whether it was day or night. He didn't know why he was there or who was with him. He glanced around and caught sight of a woman sitting in a chair nearby, reading.

"Water," he croaked, his throat parched.

The woman practically jumped at his speaking and she rushed to tend to his needs, bringing him a drink of cool water. "You're awake! The doctor is going to be very pleased."

Jack sipped from the glass she held to his lips. "Who . . . who are you?"

"I'm Matilda Knowles. I work for Dr. Michaels. I'm sitting with you to keep track of your condition."

"And just what is my condition?" he managed to ask, though each word was painful to utter.

"You were stabbed in the back." She watched him closely as she spoke and saw the flash of pain that shone in his eyes at her words. "Dr. Michaels wasn't sure if you were going to make it. I'll have to let him know right away that you've improved."

Jack nodded and closed his eyes. *She would have killed me. She wanted to kill me.* An image of Elizabeth played in his mind: innocent, abused, needing protection. It had all been an act designed to deceive him, and he had fallen for it. He cursed his own stupidity, wondering how he could have been so blind. But he knew how. She had mesmerized him, hypnotized him. She had used him for information.

A stark, horrible thought seared through him: He had confided in her about Luke! He hoped to God that his friend had survived, that Jameson had captured him and gotten him out of the outlaw camp.

The torment of knowing he might have been responsible for Luke's death haunted him and made rest impossible. Jack lay in misery, wishing he had the strength to get up off the bed and go after Elizabeth himself. He did not know where she'd gone, but he would search to the ends of the earth to find her, and he would not rest until he did.

"Are you all right, Mr. Logan?" the nurse asked, seeing the fierce look on his face and wondering if his pain had worsened.

"No, and I won't be until I'm out of this bed," he said.

"You must rest. As severe as your injuries are, I'm sure you'll be restricted to bed rest for some time."

Jack knew she was right. He couldn't have gotten up if he'd tried, and he didn't even have the strength to try. Not yet, anyway, but he would.

A knock at the door drew the nurse to answer it.

"Yes?"

"My name's Cody Jameson, and I need to speak with Ranger Logan."

"I'm sorry, but—"

"Let her in," Jack managed to call out to her.

The nurse glanced back at him, saw his look of determination, and opened the door to admit Cody.

"Jameson. You're back." Jack's voice wasn't strong, but his will was.

"Here," the nurse said, pulling up a chair next to the bed for Cody.

Cody sat down, shocked by the Ranger's appearance. His back was heavily bandaged and his coloring was pale. "What happened to you?"

"Later. Did you bring in Majors?" Jack waited tensely for her answer.

"Yes, he's locked in the jail right now. That's why I came here. I wanted to let you know."

Jack couldn't believe that things had turned out so well. "Good . . . good. It had been so long that I was afraid something had happened to you."

"It was tricky, but I managed to pull it off. I definitely earned my money this time." She thought of Luke's accusation that she was only doing this for the money. It saddened her, for she needed that money to support her family. Why else would she take such risks?

"I'll see that you get paid. Will you be staying here in the hotel?"

"Yes."

"Good." Jack lay back down, closing his eyes for a moment.

"What happened to you?" Cody asked.

"I had a run-in with El Diablo."

"El Diablo was here?" She was shocked. "Who is he?"

Jack opened his eyes and glanced at Cody. A thought formed in his mind. If she could bring in Luke Majors, she was the best. Maybe, just maybe . . .

As Steve and Fred returned to the sheriff's office from the Harris house, they were surprised to see strange horses tied up out front and a crowd gathering at the entrance.

"What the hell is going on?" Steve asked.

"You think somebody brought in one of the gang?"

They hurried on.

"They got him this time!" one voice shouted at them as they elbowed their way toward the door.

Steve was the first one inside, with Fred on his heels. He saw the man in the cell and realized he must be Majors.

"Who brought him in?"

"Cody Jameson, the bounty hunter," the deputy supplied. "She wanted to talk to Logan, so we locked Majors up."

Steve nodded and strode to the back of the room. Fred and the deputies tensed as they waited to see what he was going to do.

"You Luke Majors?"

"I am," he answered, facing the Ranger captain unflinchingly. "I need to see Jack Logan, but they said he'd been injured."

"He was. We've got him bedded down over at

the hotel. What do you say we go see him to-gether?"

Luke had expected trouble. Luke had expected the man to tell him he was going to rot in the cell until Jack recovered. His startled look brought a low chuckle from Steve.

"Jack told me about you working for him. Let's get you out of here. I think you've probably had enough of this jail to last you a lifetime."

Luke couldn't describe the feeling of joy and relief that swept through him at the discovery that this man knew the truth. "You're right. I have."

Steve smiled at him and went into the outer of-fice, where Fred was getting the keys. He returned to unlock the door.

"Thanks," Luke said with heartfelt emotion as he stepped clear of the jail cell.

The deputies looked shocked by this action.

"What are you doing? That's Luke Majors! You can't let him out! He's one of them!"

Fred turned to his men. "Luke Majors was work-ing undercover for us the whole time. He was never involved with the gang and had no part in any of their criminal activities. He was hired by Logan to find out the identity of El Diablo and the location of the gang's hideout."

The deputies were even more surprised by this news. They watched as Luke strapped on his gun, which Cody had left with the lawmen. They looked on in amazement as the gunfighter got ready to walk from the jail with the Ranger captain, a free man.

"I don't believe it!"

"Believe it," Fred insisted. "He's been working for us the entire time."

"What are you going to do about the people outside?" one of the deputies asked, seeing the men milling around in the street before the office.

Fred looked at Steve. "You want to handle this one?"

"My pleasure." Steve strode through the door to face the townspeople. "You can all go on about your own business now. Luke Majors has been brought in, and he is being released as a free man."

"What are you talking about?" one of the men yelled in outrage. "He killed Sam and Davis, and wounded Harris."

"No, he didn't. Majors has been working undercover with the gang for the Rangers. He's one of us, and I won't tolerate anyone saying otherwise. He is not guilty of any crime."

"But he did it! Harris said so!"

"Harris was wrong. Majors is on our side. Now go on home. I don't want any trouble, and that's exactly what you'll get if you don't do as I say."

The men gathered there turned away. Their mood was disgruntled, but no longer openly hostile. One paused to look back.

"He really was working for the Rangers?"

"He was. You tell everybody so they know."

The man nodded and went on.

Steve hoped the word would spread around town quickly so Luke wouldn't be in any danger of some hothead coming after him. He'd wire neighboring towns later with the news that the bounty had been withdrawn.

"You ready to go see Jack?" Steve asked Luke.

"More than ready!"

"Fred, you want to come with us?"

"No, I'll stay here with the boys just in case there might be some trouble. Let me know how Jack is doing."

Steve and Luke headed for the hotel.

"Jack will be glad to know you're back. He's been worrying about you. How was it with the gang?"

"Not pretty. I can give you and Jack the location of their hideout, and the towns where they go after each job."

"And El Diablo? What did you find out?"

"I'll tell you when we get to Jack. He's the one who hired me."

They didn't say any more until they reached the hotel room and were admitted by the nurse. Luke stared in shock at the sight of Cody sitting next to the bed talking to Jack.

She looked up and was surprised by the sight of him. "What are you doing here?"

"I'd ask you the same thing, but I know why you're here. It's all about money with you, isn't it, Jameson?" Luke's tone was sneering and derogatory.

"Luke . . ." Jack managed from where he lay, growing more and more tired with each passing minute.

Luke looked down at his friend and realized how seriously he'd been wounded. "What happened to you?"

"El Diablo."

"It's a woman, Jack. I don't know her name, but her brother Hadley runs the gang for her and she sends him the information."

Jack smiled thinly. "You did good work for me, Luke. But I found out El Diablo's identity the hard way."

"Who is it?"

"Elizabeth Harris, the banker's wife."

Luke was as shocked as Cody.

"Where is she now?"

"No one knows," Steve put in. "We were just checking with her husband. He heard her talking to her brother last night, and then they rode out of town this morning. I'm getting two more Rangers to ride with me, and I'm going after them. Luke says he knows exactly where the hideout is and which towns they lay low in."

"I do," Luke said, and then told them what he knew.

"Incredible," Steve said. "I'll be leaving as soon as I wire two Rangers and arrange to meet them on the way."

"I want to ride with you," Luke stated with determination. This woman was vicious. She'd savagely killed Sam Gregory and had tried to kill Jack. He wanted revenge.

"No. This is Rangers' business now." He dismissed Luke's offer, then turned to Jack. "Jack, I'll check in with you when I get back; until then you take care." He left the room.

Jack stared at the door his boss had just walked through. He was furious. He wanted to be the one going after Elizabeth. He wanted to be the one to bring her in. He had made a fool out of himself, and he was lucky to be alive. He was not a man to forgive or forget.

Cody finally spoke up when Steve had gone. She was baffled by what had just transpired. "Wait a minute. There's something I don't understand."

Logan looked at her innocently. "What?"

"You just said Luke did good work for you. What are you talking about?" she demanded.

"Luke was working undercover for me. Then when things got bad and the town put the big bounty out on him, I got worried. That's why I hired you to bring him in to me alive."

"And you didn't tell me the truth about him." She was outraged.

"I couldn't put him at risk. You needed to believe he was a bad man; otherwise you might have treated him differently and aroused suspicion."

"So you sent me off to find him, deliberately letting me think he was a murderer and a thief." She was furious, and then she turned on Luke. "Why didn't you tell me the truth?"

"Don't talk to me about telling the truth, Sister Mary," Luke retorted. "You wouldn't know it if it introduced itself to you."

"It's my job to deceive."

"And it was my job to be undercover. Before you act so outraged, why didn't you tell me that Jack had hired you?"

"You were the enemy."

"I was alone in the middle of the El Diablo gang. I had to watch everything I said and did. I couldn't trust anybody."

"Luke, we need to talk," Jack interrupted.

Luke looked at Cody as if to dismiss her, but Jack spoke again.

"She stays."

Cody had been ready to leave these two alone and was surprised by his pronouncement.

"Luke, I want you to go after El Diablo. I want you to bring her in."

"But the Rangers . . ."

"You can do it. You and Cody know the gang. You know how they think, where they go, what they do." There was a fever in Jack's eyes as he looked between the two of them. "I want you two to track her down"—he swung his gaze to Cody—and "I want her brought back in alive."

"I work alone," Luke declared. The last thing he wanted was any further involvement with the bounty hunter who'd betrayed him at every turn.

"Luke, you owe me."

It seemed to Luke that it was the other way around, but he wasn't going to argue the point. He wanted El Diablo stopped as much as Jack did. He would see his friend avenged.

"Jameson is damned good. She brought you in, didn't she?" Jack pointed out. "I want Elizabeth alive, and Jameson, here, is the one who can do it."

Luke was trapped and he knew it. He wanted El Diablo. He wanted to avenge what had been done to Jack. "What about the Rangers?"

"They're good, but together, the two of you are better. If anyone can find El Diablo, it's you two.

Get her for me. Bring her in." A fire burned in his eyes as he spoke.

"What's the reward?" Luke deliberately looked at Cody as he asked.

"We've upped it to two thousand dollars."

"Well, Jameson?" Luke asked, wanting to see if the money was enough to tempt her to travel and work with him. "Is the money enough to make you go back out after the gang again?"

Cody stared at him, her gaze cold upon him. "I'll go after El Diablo, but it won't be for the money."

"Then you'll do it?" Jack pressed.

"We'll do it," they answered, but suspicion haunted them both.

Chapter Twenty-five

Cody left Jack's room first. She had a lot to do before she could even think about taking off after El Diablo with Luke. She registered downstairs at the front desk for a room of her own, then sought out Stalking Ghost to tell him what was happening. She found him near the stables tending to their horses.

"As soon as I get the bounty for bringing in Majors, I want you to take it home for me."

"What are you going to be doing?"

Cody quickly explained to him all that she'd learned about Luke and his connection to Logan. Stalking Ghost was surprised to find that Luke was no longer a wanted man.

"Now Ranger Logan wants me to ride with Majors to find El Diablo."

"Aren't the Rangers already searching?"

"Yes, but Logan believes Majors and I will find her more quickly."

"And you do not want me to ride with you?" He was skeptical of her plan.

"It will be better if you take the reward money home. I know it's needed there as soon as possible."

"I'll do it, but I wonder if you'll be safe working with this man."

"I'll be fine. First I have to do my homework, though. I need to find out everything I can about Elizabeth Harris and her brother."

"I will check, too, and see what I can learn before I leave."

"Thanks. You are a dear friend. I don't know what I'd do without you."

"I hope you do not find out soon."

And with that remark, she left him to start making her inquiries. Her first stop was at Elizabeth's home. A woman Fred had found to take care of Jonathan let Cody in, and Cody was allowed to speak with the banker as he sat in his wheelchair in the front parlor.

"My name is Cody Jameson, and Ranger Logan has asked me to look into your wife's background to see if there are any clues there to where she might have gone."

Jonathan eyed her skeptically for a moment, then decided to answer. He'd tell anybody anything, if it would get Elizabeth back in his hands faster. "What do you want to know?"

"First, where did she grow up? What's her background?"

"Elizabeth and her brother were born and raised in New Orleans. They only came to Texas after the war."

"Do they still have any family there?"

"No. None to speak of."

"Does your wife have any close friends?"

"Sarah Gregory was her best friend. They spent a lot of time together. We had a lot of acquaintances." He quickly listed all the women he knew she'd occasionally socialized with.

"Thank you. And knowing your wife as you do—"

Jonathan interrupted her with a sarcastic laugh. "Know her? I never knew her."

"I understand," Cody sympathized. "But can you think of one place where she'd go if she were trying to hide?"

He gave a weary shake of his head. "I wish I could say I did, but other than New Orleans, she never talked much about traveling and such."

"I appreciate your taking the time to see me," Cody thanked him. "If you think of anything else that might be of help, anything at all, let me know."

"If you want to take a look through her personal items before you leave, go right ahead. I was going to have them taken out and burned, but feel free to rummage through her things there in our bedroom. Take whatever you want."

"That's very generous of you."

"Not generous," he said savagely, no longer able to contain the hatred he felt for his deceitful, murderous wife. "I want you to catch her. I want you to bring her back here, so I can look in her eyes when they take her to the hangman. I want to spit on her and tell her what a slut she is."

Cody nodded, understanding what he was feeling. "Do you want to come with me to go through these things? Maybe you can offer me some insight."

Jonathan wheeled his way toward the bedroom with Cody following. Over an hour passed before they finished.

"I'll let you know what happens, Mr. Harris."

"You do that, Miss Jameson. I'll be waiting to hear. Revenge is what's keeping me going right now."

Cody heard the threat in his tone and knew he wouldn't rest until Elizabeth was locked up. She left him then, taking with her several pictures of Elizabeth, including one from her wedding day. Jonathan had no longer wanted it in the house.

The next person Cody needed to talk to was Sarah Gregory, Elizabeth's best friend.

"What can I do for you?" Sarah asked as she answered the door.

"Mrs. Gregory, I'm Cody Jameson. I'm working with Ranger Logan and we're following up on clues to El Diablo's whereabouts."

"El Diablo? They know something new?" A fire lighted her eyes as she looked at Cody.

"You haven't heard what's happened?"

"No. You mean they've discovered something?" At Cody's answering nod, Sarah held the door wide for her. "Please come in. I want to know everything about this man who killed my Sam."

Once Cody was seated in the parlor with her, she folded her hands in her lap, wondering how she was going to tell Sarah that her best friend had cold-bloodedly murdered her husband. She decided straight out was the best way.

"Mrs. Gregory, there have been quite a few developments in the last twenty-four hours," Cody began. Seeing that she had Sarah's complete and undivided attention, she went on to tell her about the attack on Jack, about bringing in Luke and how he'd been working for the Rangers the whole time. "Majors learned that the outlaw leader did not run with the gang. In fact, the entire time he was riding with them, trying to learn El Diablo's identity, El Diablo never came into camp. Then while Ranger Logan was doing his investigating here in town, he discovered a link between Harris and the robberies. He thought it was Jonathan. He was wrong."

"Are you saying . . . ?" Sarah's hand went to her throat and she paled.

"There was a connection to Harris, through his wife. It was Elizabeth. Elizabeth Harris is El Diablo."

"No . . ."

"I'm afraid it's true. The night she disappeared, Jonathan overheard her plotting the attack on Ranger Logan, and then when Majors came into town today, he corroborated his finding, for he had learned that El Diablo was a female."

"It was Elizabeth? Elizabeth killed Sam?"

"It appears that way. Luke Majors has sworn

that Sam was alive when the gang was broken out of jail. Sam knew about Luke being undercover, and they were working together. There was no reason for Luke to harm him."

"So Elizabeth went in there after the jailbreak and shot him . . . just like that?"

Cody was silent.

Sarah lifted tear-filled eyes to Cody. "I thought Elizabeth was my friend. We met and talked just a short time ago, commiserating about what had happened to our husbands." She shook her head in disbelief. "I was telling her how lucky she was that Jonathan was still alive, but now I realize she probably had planned his death, too, and somehow her plan went wrong."

"I think you're probably right. From what I've learned of the woman in the last few hours, she's vicious and completely without conscience."

"How can I help you? What can I do to help you find her? I want to face her again. I want to look Elizabeth in the eye and tell her what I think of her." She was earnest in her desire to help.

"I need you to tell me everything she's ever said to you about her past."

"Well, let me see. I know her family was from Louisiana, and she often talked of how much she missed living there. She used to say it was much more 'civilized' in New Orleans." Sarah paused and looked up at Cody, the look in her eyes almost dead as she was facing the truth about a woman she'd considered to be a close friend. "For all her talk, though, what does she know about civilization? Civilized people don't hurt one another. Civilized people don't rob and steal from one another. Civilized people don't kill."

"I'm going to do everything in my power to bring her in, Mrs. Gregory. I promise you that. This woman has wreaked untold pain and suffering on a lot of good people, and I want to see her pay for her crimes."

"Think of poor Jonathan." Sarah sighed. "If I'm feeling betrayed, imagine what he must be feeling."

Cody remained silent in sympathy.

"Is there anything else I can tell you? Anything else I can help you with?"

"Just one last question. Did she ever mention any place where she'd like to go to get away? Was there any town in particular that she favored?"

"New Orleans, of course. She spoke of it often. She used to tell me that she couldn't wait to travel there again. Why? Do you think she's headed there?"

"I'm not sure where she's headed. That's why I like to check on people's background. The Rangers are already covering the area to the south. I'm just wondering if Elizabeth, as smart as she is, wouldn't head in the opposite direction to what was expected of her."

"She's conniving, all right. It's not going to be easy for you to catch her, but I want you to get her, Miss Jameson. Bring her in. Please don't let her get away with killing my Sam and then lying to me all those times we were together." Sarah's spirit was back.

"I'm going to try. If you think of anything else

she might have said that could help me, I'll be staying at the hotel for another day yet."

"Don't worry. I'll probably be awake all night trying to remember every word of every conversation we ever had. If I think of anything, anything at all, I'll let you know right away."

Cody started for the door.

"Miss Jameson?"

She looked back at Sarah.

"Thank you. If anybody can find Elizabeth, I'm sure it's you."

Cody managed a small smile, knowing there was nothing she could say to ease the pain of betrayal and heartbreak for Sarah Gregory. She was going to do all she could to catch El Diablo as fast as possible.

There were two more names on the list she'd garnered from Jonathan, and after short interviews with those women, Cody figured she had all she was going to get on the subject of Elizabeth Hadley Harris.

Now she had to meet with Luke. She wasn't looking forward to it.

Luke stayed with Jack another hour, filling him in on everything he could remember about the gang.

"So tell me about Jameson and how she caught you," Jack finally ventured, wanting to hear firsthand how one young, pretty woman had gotten the upper hand with a man as smart as Luke.

Luke grimaced. "What do you want to know?"

"Everything. I'd only heard of her reputation before I hired her and found out she was a woman. How did she do it? What tricks does she use? Obviously any man who wanted to could overpower her. But she's so damned smart and quick and good, she must catch you before you realize what hit you."

"Something like that."

Jack shot him an impatient look, so Luke elaborated.

"When I first met her, she was disguised as a revivalist preacher."

"You're kidding." He grinned widely at the thought.

"I'm dead serious. Then she got one of the gang members mad at her, and I had to keep her out of trouble with him."

"So you ended up saving her?"

"Looking back now, I'm sure she could have saved herself if she'd wanted to. As good as she is with a gun, she could have shot him and been done with it. But then I had to go and rescue her."

"You really thought she was a preacher?"

"Yes."

"And what happened?"

Luke quickly told him about the general things that had happened while she'd been in camp and how he'd let her escape when he'd gotten the chance. "That's when she transformed herself into Armita."

"Armita?" Jack was enjoying himself tremendously at Luke's expense. "Who was Armita?"

"A singer in the cantina in Rio Nuevo."

"And?"

"And that's when she shot Sully when he came after me."

"Jameson saved your life?" Jack was impressed.

"Yes," he admitted. "And then we had to run together because I didn't know if the gang had found out about me, and I was worried that if they discovered she'd shot Sully, they'd hurt her. So we stayed together until we were found by the other bounty hunter."

"Who was it?"

"A man named Reid, but Cody outsmarted him. He thought she was just a cantina girl so he left her behind when he took me. I tried to get away, but I was wounded."

"I saw your forehead."

"My shoulder, too," Luke told him, testing it and finding it still sore.

"You'll be all right?"

"I've had worse. I'm definitely better off than you are. At least I'm up and moving."

Jack grunted. "Go on."

"Somehow Cody managed to get ahead of us the next day. She was posing as a little old lady with a broken-down buckboard when we came across her. Reid stopped to help, and she got the drop on him. He was not a happy man."

"And neither were you right then, I imagine."

Luke shook his head as he remembered his shock at discovering Cody's many faces. "It was quite a revelation, learning all this time I'd been played for a fool—that Sister Mary was Armita, was the little old lady, and was now the bounty hunter Cody Jameson. You're right. She is damned good. She can change her looks like a chameleon. Who knows who she's going to be when she comes through the door next?"

"But she brought you in alive, and that's what I was paying her for," Jack concluded with satisfaction.

"I'm real happy she got her bounty. I wouldn't have wanted her to lose any money because of me."

"If you're going to work with her, you'd better start realizing her strengths can help you. With her ability to disguise herself, she can get into places you can't."

Luke grudgingly conceded that he was right, but that didn't make him like Cody any better.

"You're going to need her. Bringing Elizabeth and her brother back is not going to be easy. But the two of you together can't fail. I know you can do it."

"I'm glad you think so."

"Let me know what your plans are."

"I'll be in touch before we leave."

"Good." He watched as Luke stood to go. "And Luke?"

Luke glanced back.

"Thanks."

He nodded and left the room. He was not pleased with what he had to face, but he would do it. They were going to bring El Diablo to justice, and that part he was going to enjoy.

Luke was on his way from the hotel, intent on heading out to the Trinity to meet with Jessy, when he came face-to-face with Cody on her way back from her interviews.

"How soon can you be ready to leave?" she demanded immediately upon seeing him.

"Why? Where are we headed? Rio Nuevo?"

"No. There are a few things I want to show you. Come on up to my room, and I'll go over these with you."

Luke went along with her. When they were in her room, she spread the pictures and diary out on the bed for him to look over.

"These are things that Jonathan said I could take. I haven't had the chance to read all the diary yet, but I've got a gut feeling that I know where she went."

"Gut feelings are great, but they're not going to catch you many criminals."

Cody shot him a disgusted look. "Call it insight or instinct, whatever. It works for me. I'm telling you right now that Elizabeth Hadley Harris did not head for the border."

"How can you be so sure?"

"Number one, this woman needs to disappear. She knows she's going to be a suspect, and she needs to get somewhere quickly where no one will connect her with El Diablo. Two, having just sold the guns to the Mexicans, she's got money. She can go wherever she wants. Funds are not going to be a problem. Three, over and over to her friends and in her diary, she talks about how much she misses living in 'civilization' and how much she wants to go back to New Orleans. I'm almost a hundred percent certain that she's headed east, and not south or west."

"How do you intend to prove that?"

"By riding for San Antonio at sunup. I've already wired my father's friend Nate Thompson, the sheriff in San Antonio. With any luck, he can do some checking for us before we get there. The railroad comes into San Antonio now. If Elizabeth is heading to New Orleans, that's where she would have gone to catch the first train east. Are you with me on this or not?"

"And if we discover that she and Hadley were in San Antonio, then what?"

"Then we follow them as far and as long as it takes. We are bringing her back."

"That two thousand dollars means a lot to you, doesn't it?"

Cody glared at him. "Get out of my room. I'll meet you at the stable half an hour before sunup. Be ready to ride." Her words were a challenge.

"Don't worry. I'll be there." He accepted.

Chapter Twenty-six

Luke took a room in the hotel, too, rather than try to make the trek out to the Trinity and back. There was no time for a visit with Jessy. It would to have to wait until they'd returned with El Diablo and Hadley.

Once he'd settled in, Luke lay awake for hours going over in his mind all of the new information Cody had gotten talking to Elizabeth's friends and husband. He had to admit Jack was right. She was good at her job. He'd had his doubts about her plan to begin with, but after talking with her, he'd understood what was pointing her toward New Orleans. He only hoped they were able to track Elizabeth and her brother down before they reached the city. He had been there a few times, but was by no means familiar with it. It was a big town, and finding Elizabeth and Hadley there would be a challenge.

When Luke roused himself long before dawn, he thought he was going to be early meeting her at the stable. He headed there an hour before sunrise, but discovered he was wrong. As he neared the place, he could see that Cody was already there with Stalking Ghost. Her horse was saddled, and she was ready to ride.

He didn't speak right away, but watched them from a distance for a moment. They were talking in earnest, and then Cody pressed an envelope into his hand that Luke could see was filled with money.

Luke had been thinking about how good she was at her job, but seeing the exchange of money just now reaffirmed his first opinion of her. This was all a job to her. She was in it for the profit, and cared nothing whether justice was served.

"Are you ready to ride?" Luke asked as he strode forward to make his presence known.

"Do you want to have breakfast first? It's a day and a half ride to San Antonio, and this will be our only chance for a good meal between here and there."

"No. I'm fine. We need to ride. El Diablo's already got too much of a head start on us."

"Then let's go. Stalking Ghost will be riding with us as far as San Antonio."

They mounted up and headed out of Del Fuego.

Cody was aware of Luke's disapproval of her, but she forced herself not to think about it as they covered the miles to San Antonio. She had a job to do. Jack wanted her to bring in El Diablo, and she would. No one should be allowed to get away with what that woman had done. No one.

Memories of the time when her father had been killed in a jailbreak returned, and she remembered how outraged she'd been at the law's inability to find the one responsible. She'd gone looking for the man who'd killed her father, and she'd found him, too. It had been her first case, and her most painful. As miserable as her father's killer had been, he had been more stupid than anything. El Diablo, on the other hand, was as cunning and savage and vicious as they came. Cody had never run into anyone who killed with such cold deliberation before—and with such obvious enjoyment.

"When we get to San Antonio, the first thing we need to do is check all the hotels to see if she's been there. We'll use pictures of her rather than her name, because she's probably using an alias."

"What if no one recognizes her?" Luke played devil's advocate.

"I'm betting they will." Cody was confident.

They rode until dark, having stopped only to rest and water the horses during the day. They ate a cold meal and bedded down early. They needed to be riding out again at dawn.

The following morning they arose and started off again. When they were a few miles out of town, Cody reined in.

"You're not coming to the house with me?" Stalking Ghost asked.

"No. There's no time. But tell them I'll be back as soon as I can."

"They will not be happy."

"Just explain that it was something I had to do, that I'm working."

The old man nodded, glanced toward Luke, and then rode off. She watched him go, a part of her longing to be with him, to go home to her aunt, brother, and sister, but she couldn't. She had to hunt down El Diablo. Urging her horse on toward town, she told herself she had a job to do.

San Antonio was bustling and busy as they rode in. Cody was eager to check with Nate Thompson to see if he'd found out anything for her. They stopped at the sheriff's office first, but to her disappointment, the deputy told her that Nate had been out of town for several days. Her telegram was there waiting for him, unopened on his desk.

As they left the office, Cody was frustrated, but ready to start from scratch. "Do you have the picture of Elizabeth I gave you the other night?"

"Yes."

"Good. I've got mine, too. I'll check the train station on Austin Street and then take the hotels on the north side to see if anyone recognizes her."

"Then I'll do the rest."

"Let's meet at the Menger Hotel and register there for the night."

"Fine."

They started off in two different directions, and it was more than an hour later when they finally met in the lobby of the Menger Hotel.

"Any luck?" Luke asked. He had had no success at all in his endeavor to find her.

"No. But I'm not ready to give up yet." Cody marched up to the desk and smiled at the clerk. "Good afternoon. We need two rooms for the night."

"Yes, ma'am."

As he began to take down their names, Cody drew the picture of Elizabeth out of her pocket.

"I was wondering if you could help me with something?"

"Of course."

"I'm trying to locate my sister. She was supposed to meet me here two days ago, and I was delayed and just arrived in town. Have you seen her? Do you recognize her?" She slid the picture across the counter toward the clerk.

He picked it up and studied it for only a moment before recognition dawned. "This is Miss Hadley. She was here last night."

"Is she still in town? I desperately needed to see her before she left."

"I'm afraid not. She checked out this morning."

"Did you happen to hear her say where she was going? I really need to catch up with her."

"No, I'm afraid not. She wasn't as friendly as you are. She rather kept to herself."

"Thank you for your help. I'll just have to keep looking for her. She might have gone on home."

"Come to think of it, I did hear her say that she would be glad to be home as she was walking away from the desk, but I have no idea where 'home' is."

Cody flashed him her most brilliant smile. "You've been most helpful. Thank you."

"Your rooms are on the second floor, two-ten and two-eleven. If there's anything else you need, just let us know."

Cody's expression was triumphant as she turned to Luke and handed him one of the keys.

"They're a day ahead of us, and they're 'heading home,'" she said, relieved that she'd been right. She didn't usually doubt herself, but Luke's skepticism and lack of trust in her had undermined her confidence a little.

"New Orleans . . ."

"But no one at the train station recognized her picture."

"That doesn't mean anything. The people you questioned could have been working on a different shift when the two of them boarded. When's the next train to Galveston?"

"Tomorrow morning, early. I already checked when I was there."

"Then let's get the tickets now, and be ready to go."

They went together to the station to purchase the tickets, but on the way back, Cody realized she should stop and buy some clothes for the trip. She had few things with her and desperately needed a few different outfits if she were going to successfully mingle in Galveston. If there was one thing Cody was, it was prepared when she went to work on a case.

"If you don't mind, Luke, I'd better do some shopping while I'm here. Do you want to meet for dinner a little later?" Cody prepared herself for his refusal.

"All right. When?"

"Let's meet at seven. That should give me the time I need to get everything put together. I'll see you then."

She stood outside the dress shop watching Luke walk on. He moved with a male grace that held her gaze even when she wanted to look away. He was mesmerizing, tall and handsome as he was, and she wondered how she was ever going to forget that they'd been lovers.

Cody stopped to amend that thought. They had never been lovers. He had made love to Armita. He had never made love to her. In fact, he'd made it plain that he had little use for her, and she had to keep reminding herself of that. She'd managed to maintain a businesslike attitude around him so far, but it hadn't been easy. The most important thing was bringing in El Diablo, and she would concentrate on doing that. If nothing else, when they were through working together, he would know that she was very good at what she did.

Turning away from the sight of his broad-shouldered, narrow-hipped form retreating in the distance, Cody entered the dress shop. It was time to plan for what might happen next in Galveston, and she needed to be prepared. It was over an hour later that she emerged from the shop with two new dresses to wear.

She returned to her hotel room and ordered a bath. After a long, luxurious soak, she scrubbed her hair until she was sure it was clean and then dried herself with the thick, soft towels the hotel provided. It felt wonderful just to be herself again as she settled in at the dressing table in the room. With gentle strokes, she worked the tangles from her hair and was pleased when she finished to find that it was completely back to its normal auburn color. She studied her own reflection, trying to see if her adventures had changed her at all, but the only difference she could see in herself was a shadow of sadness around her eyes. She lay down across the bed to rest for about an hour before she had to meet Luke for dinner. Cody wanted to be at her best tonight.

Luke had stopped on the way back to the hotel to buy himself some more clothes, too. He knew Cody was right. Once they got to Galveston, they had to be prepared for anything and everything. At seven o'clock, shaved, cleaned up, and wearing the new suit he'd bought, Luke was ready for a good, hot meal. He knocked on Cody's door and waited.

"I'm ready," she was saying as she opened the door to find him standing there, looking more devastatingly handsome than he'd ever looked before. In his suit he was transformed. No longer was he the gunfighter; now he was the gentleman. She couldn't stop herself. She smiled up at him.

Luke was staring at her in amazement. He hadn't known what to expect, but it wasn't this delicate beauty who stood before him. Cody Jameson was tough, quick-witted, and good with a gun. This woman was lovely and feminine, and his reaction to her was so strong that he grew angry with himself.

"And just who do I have the pleasure of dining with tonight?" he asked sarcastically. "Surely not Sister Mary, and the hair is all wrong for Armita or the old lady."

Any pleasure Cody had been feeling at seeing him was dashed. She kept her smile in place as she moved out of the room and closed the door behind her. "You're dining with the same person I've always been. You didn't know me before, and you still don't know me now."

As she moved past him, the faint scent of her perfume teased him, and his iron control over himself weakened a little. Luke was scowling as he followed her downstairs to the dining room.

It was not crowded, and they were seated at a secluded table toward the back of the room. They ordered quickly and then settled in to await their food.

"We have to be on that train that leaves for Galveston at six in the morning. If they're heading for New Orleans, I'm sure they'll be sailing from there," Cody told him, keeping strictly to business. His earlier sarcasm had reminded her all too clearly of just what he thought of her. He might have changed his looks and appear the gentleman tonight, but that didn't mean anything had changed within him or between them.

"I'll be ready," he answered, trying not to look at the modestly cut bodice of her gown. It revealed just enough creamy flesh to let a man know she was all woman, without being flagrant or obvious.

Her hair was styled up away from her face and fell in a cascade of curls down her back. He remembered how beautiful he'd thought her hair was that night he'd come upon her in the cabin when she'd been playing Sister Mary. As the heat flared deep within him again, he forced his thoughts to El Diablo. "What if we miss them in Galveston? We are over a day behind them."

Cody had been thinking the same thing. "We'll just keep searching. We'll follow the Hadley connection all the way to New Orleans if we have to, and see where it leads. We can't let them get away with what they've done. They've hurt too many innocent people . . . ruined too many lives." She looked at Luke across the table, and her expression was filled with sorrow. "When I think of how she connived and lied around Sarah Gregory . . . I don't think I've ever met anyone that completely heartless before. She let this woman believe she was her close friend, when all the while she'd murdered her husband—it's inconceivable to me."

"And what she did to Jack . . ." Luke added. "We're going to find them," he vowed solemnly, his thoughts on Hadley and the gang, and all the ugliness he'd witnessed while he'd been with them.

Cody saw the change in him and almost shivered. "I understand how you got a reputation for being so deadly. You look positively dangerous right now."

Luke glanced up at her quickly, forcing away his dark thoughts. He smiled at her, but it wasn't an easy smile. "Looks can be deceiving, can't they, Sister Mary? Tell me, Cody, how did you get involved in all this? A woman like you should be home raising babies."

" 'A woman like me?' What is a woman like me, Luke?" she demanded, anger flashing in her eyes.

Luke frowned, seeing her reaction to his words and wondering how he'd offended her. "I meant, you're a pretty woman. Surely there are men around who wanted to marry you. There's no need for you to be out there taking such risks and putting yourself in such danger."

"There may very well be men out there who want to marry me, but I haven't had time to find out. I've been working as a bounty hunter since I was seventeen."

He was surprised and it showed. "Why?"

She told him how her father had been killed in the jailbreak and how the townspeople had been too afraid to go after the one responsible.

"Any dreams I had were shattered by his death. Someone had to bring his murderer in, so I did it. I hadn't thought about the money at first. I just did it because I couldn't go on, knowing that killer was free and my father was dead. But then when they paid me for turning him over to the law, I realized this was something I could do to support my family."

"You have a family?"

"A little brother, Charlie, and my sister, Susie. My mother died when Susie was born, so my aunt Clara lives with us and takes care of them when I'm away. What about you? Do you have any family?"

"No. Everyone died or was killed during the war.

Jack's the closest to family I have. We just met up again recently. We grew up together, but got separated during the war."

"No wonder he was so adamant about making sure I brought you in alive. When he hired me all he would say was that he had doubts about your guilt. I guess that was as close as he could come to telling me you were innocent, but feeling the way I do about outlaws who kill lawmen, I wasn't too willing to listen to what he wasn't saying."

"So did you think I was a killer?"

Cody looked up at him, studying the hard lines and angles of his face. "When you backed Sully down that night at the tent in El Trajar, I thought you were capable of anything. But I didn't understand why a cold-blooded killer would worry about a preacher woman's safety. You were a puzzle to me. Then when we got up to the camp and I had to try to figure a way out of there, either with you or without you, it got even more complicated."

"It was very complicated," Luke agreed, his gaze meeting hers across the table.

In that instant, it seemed that time stood still as they were lost in their memories of that last night in the outlaw's camp. Cody couldn't forget the heat of his kiss or touch, and Luke remembered all too clearly how wonderful it had felt to hold her close.

"And it still is," Cody said.

Their meal was served then, and the enchantment of the moment was lost.

Cody concentrated on her food. The rest of the night she spoke only about El Diablo and their plans for the next day. She told herself that Luke had never really cared for her, that he didn't even know her. Tonight had been the first time he'd even bothered to ask her about herself.

Their working together was strictly business. Together they would find El Diablo and take her in to Jack, and then they would each go their separate ways.

Chapter Twenty-seven

Cody was frustrated. She'd hoped to find Elizabeth and Hadley before they reached New Orleans, but things were not looking good. She'd just spent four hours combing Galveston, trying to get a lead on them, and she'd come up with nothing. All she could hope for was that Luke was having better luck than she was. She started back toward the hotel where they'd taken rooms for the night. She'd already checked all but two ticket offices for the shipping lines, and she was heading to those two next. When she'd finished with them, she would have exhausted every angle and would be at a dead end for her part of the search.

The one thing that had made Cody successful over the years was her doggedness, and it was that fervent desire to capture the two she was after that kept her going, even in the face of so many rejections. She had almost reached the shipping office when it happened. The door to the office opened, and Hadley stepped out onto the sidewalk right in front of her.

Cody had to do a double take. Hadley no longer looked the outlaw. He was dressed for polite society and appeared quite the gentleman. Had she not known what was in his heart, she might have been fooled. Luckily he gave only a cursory glance in her direction before starting off the opposite way.

It was only as he walked away that Cody realized she'd been holding her breath. She wanted desperately to go into the office and ask the clerk what tickets he'd bought so she'd know when they planned to sail, but she knew it was far more important to follow him.

Assuming a casual manner, Cody dogged his footsteps through town, keeping a safe distance so no one, not even Hadley, suspected that she was watching his every move. When he reached the best hotel in town and turned in there, Cody was not surprised. From what she'd learned about Elizabeth, the woman enjoyed life's finest amenities.

Her manner ever at ease, she followed him into the lobby and watched as he started up the steps. She trailed him without being obvious as he made his way to the second floor and entered a room midway down the hall.

A shout of victory welled up within Cody, but she managed to control it. Comporting herself in a ladylike manner, she went back downstairs and straight up to the front desk.

"I need two rooms for tonight, please."

"Yes, ma'am. Just sign here." The clerk pushed the registration book toward her.

"I was wondering if it would be possible to have them on the second floor?"

"Of course, we have several vacancies there."

In minutes Cody had paid for the rooms and had the keys in hand. She exited the hotel, fighting to contain her excitement. The only outward sign of her eagerness she allowed was a quickening of her pace. Control was important in her business. It was dangerous to let emotion affect judgment and actions.

Luke wasn't due to meet her back in their other hotel rooms for another hour, but Cody hoped he had finished early. They didn't have a minute to lose. She'd located Elizabeth and Hadley and wanted to take them into custody as quickly as possible. She smiled as her hand tightened around the two keys she held. It was only a matter of time now.

Cody reached the hotel where they'd originally registered and went straight up to their rooms to find, to her disappointment, that Luke still had not returned. She took the time to throw her things in her bag and get ready to move to the other location. Once they did, their prey would be only a few doors away. When she had finished packing, she had nothing left to do, and so she began to pace and plot.

It would not be easy taking the Hadleys, no matter where they tried to do it, so Cody figured they might as well make their move in the hotel rooms. That way they knew their confines, all the entrances and exits, and would have some control.

Nervously awaiting Luke's return, she thought she heard him in the hall and opened the door to check. She saw only the maid coming out of one of the neighboring rooms after having cleaned it.

It was then that an idea struck. Cody knew Elizabeth did not know her, and with any luck, as had happened this morning, Hadley would not immediately recognize her either. If she could just get her hands on a maid's uniform, she could gain access to their rooms. For the second time that day, Cody smiled. She closed the door and went to sit on her bed. She was ready. All she needed was for Luke to return.

Luke felt as if he'd searched Galveston from one end to the other. For hours now, he'd been walking the streets, showing Elizabeth's picture to hotel clerks in the hope that someone would recognize her, but no one had. He hated to go back to Cody empty-handed, but he didn't want to be late for their meeting. He was unprepared for the burst of enthusiasm that greeted him when he knocked on her hotel room door.

"Thank God you finally got here!" she exclaimed, grabbing him by the arm and practically dragging him into her room. She shut the door tightly behind him and then faced him.

"You found them?" he asked. He could think of no other reason for her to be this excited.

"Hadley walked right out in front of me from one of the shipping offices. I followed him to his hotel. I know his room number and everything. So quick! You have to pack your things! I've already booked us two rooms at their hotel on the same floor. We have to get over there so we can keep an eye on them."

"What about Elizabeth? Did you see her? Was she with him?"

Cody frowned. "No, as a matter of fact, she wasn't. But that doesn't mean she isn't close."

"Give me five minutes, and I'll be ready."

"I've got one other thing to do. I'll come and get you when I'm finished."

He started for the door, and as he opened it, he looked back at Cody. Her eyes were bright with the knowledge that she'd been right, and her cheeks were flushed with excitement.

"Cody?" When she looked up at him, he said, "Good work. Jack was right about you."

She smiled at him, but tempered their enthusiasm. "We haven't brought them in yet."

"No. But we will. We can't miss, working together."

With that, he left to go pack his things. Cody went to the door and peeked out. There was no one about, so she walked quickly and quietly to the servants' stairs. She was hoping that the servants' workroom at the rear of the building on the main floor would be deserted at this time of day, and she was relieved to find that it was. Soundlessly Cody took what she needed and then hurriedly retreated back upstairs, hoping no one would miss the borrowed items right away.

Luke knocked on her door minutes later, and they were off to close in on Elizabeth and Hadley.

An hour and a half later, Cody stood in the middle of her room surveying her image in the mirror over the dressing table.

"Not bad," she murmured approvingly to herself. "Perhaps if this bounty-hunting job ever fails . . ."

A knock at the door drew her from her pondering, and she went to answer it.

"Who is it?"

"Luke."

She let him in and grinned at the expression on his face when he saw her for the first time.

"Well, what do you think?" She spun in a circle for him.

"What are you planning to do?" he finally asked, having shaken off the surprise of finding her dressed as a hotel maid in a dark blue dress, white apron, and small hat.

"I'm planning on doing a little investigating."

"What kind?"

"I'm going to sneak into Hadley's room and see if there's any sign there of Elizabeth. Since they're brother and sister, they might be sharing a room. I don't know. If her things are there, then we know we can take them together. If not, we've got some more work cut out for us."

"I don't like it. If Hadley comes back and catches you in there, there's no telling what he'd do to you." Luke found himself worrying about her putting herself in danger.

Cody shot him an exasperated look. "I don't care if you like it or not. I'm going."

"But it's too dangerous," he argued.

"This is my job, Luke. It's always been dangerous. That's why it pays so well."

At her mention of the money, something inside Luke hardened. "Then for God's sake be careful, and if anything goes wrong just yell and I'll be there. Are you taking your gun with you?"

"No. The pockets aren't big enough, but I do have my knife." She patted her thigh to let him know where she'd hidden it.

He smiled at her. "I should have known that you wouldn't go into battle unarmed."

Cody found herself smiling back at him as she left the room. It almost felt good to know that someone was actually right there, concerned about her. She'd always had Stalking Ghost, but he made it a point to stay in the background, keeping watch over her in his silent but effective way. It was different somehow with Luke, and strangely, she found she liked it.

Drawing a deep, steadying breath, Cody turned her thoughts to her job, concentrating on what she was about to do. She made her way down the hall to the room Hadley had entered earlier and knocked lightly on the door. When there was no answer to her second knock, she drew the special key she carried for just such occasions out of her apron pocket and worked the lock until the door opened. With all the manner of a maid ready to start cleaning, she entered ready to start her search.

Luke waited a minute and then left her room. He walked down the hall like a man on his way out of the hotel, but all the while he was keeping an eye on Cody. When she slipped inside Hadley's room undetected, he breathed a sigh of relief. He didn't like letting someone else take the risks. He didn't like this feeling of not being in control. He was used to working alone and not being responsible for anyone. Not that Cody wanted him to be responsible for her. Far from it. She made it plain that she was on her own, and she liked it that way. Still, he was going to linger in the hallway as long as he could without drawing attention to himself.

Cody saw it the minute she was inside Hadley's room; there was a connecting room and the door was open. She'd found Elizabeth!

"Maid service . . ." she called out, just wanting to make sure she was alone.

When no one answered, she started her methodical search. Digging through Hadley's things, she found the tickets he'd purchased earlier. She checked their sailing date and time. They weren't scheduled to leave until late the following day, so she and Luke had one full night to trap them. Moving silently into Elizabeth's room, she was just about to dig through her valise when the door opened and Elizabeth walked in.

"What are you doing in here?" Elizabeth demanded, outraged at finding someone in her room.

"I'm with housekeeping, ma'am. I'm here to clean your room," Cody lied coolly.

"It doesn't look very clean to me," Elizabeth charged, always suspicious.

"I was just going to start, but if you'd like, I can come back when you're gone."

"Empty your pockets for me. I don't trust people going through my things."

"I didn't take anything!" Cody said quickly, wanting to sound as intimidated as a maid would be.

"I didn't say that you did. I just want to make certain. Now do as I say or I'll notify your employer." Elizabeth glared at her.

"Yes, ma'am. Please don't report me. I don't want to get in any trouble. I was only doing my job." Cody quickly emptied her pockets for her. There was only a handkerchief and the key she'd used.

"All right. You can go. Come back in about half an hour. I'll be gone by then, and you can work undisturbed."

"Yes, ma'am." Cody left through Elizabeth's door. Just in case the other woman was watching, she went on to Luke's room and knocked, announcing herself, "Maid . . ."

Luke opened the door immediately and all but dragged her inside. "Come in. I was wondering when you were going to show up," he said in a voice loud enough that any observers could hear him. Then he shut the door. "That was crazy!" he told her. His anger was obvious. "Are you trying to get yourself killed?"

"What are you talking about?"

"I'm talking about El Diablo catching you in her room like that! I'd been keeping watch for you and saw her coming, but I didn't have time to warn you without letting her know something was going on."

"Look, Luke, that's what my disguises are for," she said impatiently. "Have you known them to fail?"

"No, but there's always a first time!" he retorted. "And I don't want it on my conscience that it happened while you were with me."

"Listen, Majors, the only reason you're here is because of Jack. I didn't need you along or want you with me. I suggest you either cooperate with me and the way I work, or stay out of my way." Her tone brooked no argument.

"And I suggest you stop taking so damned many chances. There's no reason to put yourself so squarely in harm's way."

"If I don't do it, who will?"

"Me!"

"You'd look mighty funny in this maid's dress!" she retorted.

Suddenly they were both grinning at the thought.

"What did you find out?" He was suddenly serious, recognizing as much as it pained him that she was right—her ways did work, and he would look funny in the maid's dress.

"Elizabeth's room is connected to Hadley's. I

found their tickets, and they're not due to sail for New Orleans until late tomorrow. Whatever we do, we've got to do tonight."

At that moment, they heard someone in the hall, knocking on another door. They put their ears to their door and listened. They were rewarded when they heard Hadley speak.

"I made our dinner reservations for seven-thirty downstairs in the dining room."

"Good," Elizabeth answered him. "I'd like to do some more shopping this afternoon. Do you want to come with me?"

"All right."

Cody and Luke heard her door shut, and then their voices faded away as they moved down the hallway.

Cody and Luke exchanged looks.

"We'll take them tonight."

"What are we going to do until then?" Luke asked, impatient, wanting it to be over.

"I think," Cody said thoughtfully, studying Luke, "we're going to have dinner downstairs in the dining room."

"But Hadley knows me. He'll recognize me right away."

Her smile was quixotic. "Not if I have anything to do with it."

"What have you got in mind?"

"I have to do some shopping myself. You can come with me if you want or you can stay here."

"I think I'd better come with you, but we have to take care. I don't want to come face-to-face with Hadley on the streets of Galveston. It wouldn't be pretty." Luke rested his hand on his sidearm.

"I know. Give me a minute to change; then I'll be ready to go."

Luke waited for her in the hall and as soon as she came out they were on their way. An hour later they were back, and Luke wasn't looking particularly happy.

"We have to do this, don't we?" he said.

"We could sit in their rooms and wait for them. But if we go downstairs and eat dinner when they do, we can see how much they drink and be able to judge how quick their reaction time will be. It's a shame I can't drug them. It would be so much easier."

"Drug them?" Luke glanced at her in surprise.

"What do you think I had in your whiskey that night I shot Sully?" she asked.

His eyes widened. "No wonder you kept wanting me to 'take a drink and relax.'"

Cody smiled innocently. "I had Stalking Ghost all ready to help me get you out the window once you were knocked out. Only trouble was, things didn't go the way I'd planned."

Luke just shook his head. "I'm glad I wasn't in the mood for heavy drinking."

"Looking back, so am I. If you'd been unconscious when Sully broke into the room, they might have discovered my disguise and you might have been killed."

"Perhaps I should give up drinking altogether."

"I never knew a man who died from abstinence."

"Yeah, but sometimes life can be much more fun when you're not abstaining." He gave her a knowing look, remembering.

Cody felt the heat of his look to the very depths of her soul, but she fought against it.

"We've got work to do," she said brusquely, forcing them back to business.

Chapter Twenty-eight

Gray-haired and wearing a mustache, Luke Majors had aged 25 years when Cody got through with his makeup and disguise. She sat back to study her handiwork and nodded in satisfaction.

"I don't think Hadley's going to recognize you now," she said with pride in her accomplishment.

"Let me take a look." Luke spun around in the chair where he'd been sitting while she worked on him, to gaze at his reflection in the dressing-table mirror.

"Well? What do you think?" Cody asked.

Luke was so intent on staring at his strange reflection that he didn't answer right away. Finally all he could mutter was, "Damn."

"Is that good or bad?"

He glanced at her, and she saw that he had the

strangest look on his face. It was sad, and pain filled his eyes.

"What's wrong?"

"Nothing." He paused.

"Nothing?"

Luke looked up at her again. "I look the way I remember my father."

She could hear the emotion in his voice. "That's good, isn't it? What was his name?"

"His name was Charles."

"What happened to him?"

"We were separated during the war. I got word about six months later that both he and my brother, Dan, had been killed. I think they died at Gettysburg, but I was never sure."

"I'm sorry."

"So am I. He was a good man; so was Dan. There isn't a day that goes by that I don't think of them. My father and I tried to keep Dan from enlisting, but he insisted on it, and there was nothing we could do to stop him."

"I've noticed that that is a family trait."

Luke's mood lightened at her observation. "I can't imagine why you'd think that. Shall we change and go to dinner, Miss Jameson? I believe I am too old to have anything less than honorable intentions toward you tonight."

"You can have all the intentions you want, Mr. Majors, but we've got a job to do, and we're going to do it."

Luke started back to his own room, but as he opened the door he saw Elizabeth and Hadley leaving their rooms. He turned back inside pretending to have forgotten something and waited until the sounds of their voices had faded away. He and Cody shared a knowing look before he once more attempted to go. This time he was successful.

When he called for Cody a short time later, Luke was once again taken by her beauty. This night, she was wearing a short-sleeved, low-cut, emerald green gown that was fitted at the waist, emphasizing her slender figure, and flared to a slight bustle in the back trimmed in matching rosettes. She was stunning.

"I don't feel quite so old anymore," Luke said, his gaze warm upon her.

"Then I'll carry a mirror with me to remind you," she told him, smiling up at him as they made their way down the stairs.

The hotel dining room was well known for its gourmet fare, and it was reasonably crowded. Cody caught sight of Elizabeth and Hadley already at a table, and though Hadley did glance their way, there was no flicker of recognition in his regard. His had been merely a male's leering appraisal of a pretty woman; there was no flicker of recognition as his gaze swept over Luke at all. Luke was pleased.

Luke and Cody were seated close to their table, but not too close. They could hear snatches of the conversation, but it was mostly general; their quarry said nothing that would help them with their plans. Cody and Luke enjoyed their meal and watched with interest as Elizabeth and Hadley finished dining and left the restaurant to retire upstairs.

"How much time do you want to give them?" Luke asked, ready to follow them right then.

"An hour. Then we make our move. They'll be relaxed by then and probably ready to go to bed. If we can catch them unawares, things will go smoothly."

They retired to their own rooms shortly thereafter to get ready for the action to come.

Luke had donned his regular clothes and had strapped on his gunbelt when he went to meet Cody. She was wearing her riding clothes, too, for freedom of movement, and had buckled on her own gunbelt.

"You ready?"

"As I'll ever be. Let's get El Diablo."

Luke led the way, but Cody was the one who knocked on the door.

"Yes, who is it?" came Elizabeth's call.

"The maid, ma'am."

"What do you want at this time of night?"

She sounded irritated, but Cody could hear her unlocking the door. When it started to swing open, Luke made his move. With brute force, he shouldered the door open. Elizabeth uttered only one small cry before Luke clamped a hand over her mouth and jerked her back against him. He held her pinned there, his gun pressed to her side.

"Don't make a sound or you're dead," he told her in a low voice.

Elizabeth's eyes had narrowed to slits as she glared at Cody, but Cody was unmoved by the malice she saw there. All she wanted to do was arrest these two and head for Del Fuego. She quickly gagged Elizabeth, and Luke dragged the outlaw to the bed so he could cuff her by one hand to the bedstead.

"That should hold her while we get Hadley," Luke said as he started for the connecting door, leaving Cody to keep an eye on Elizabeth.

He turned the knob cautiously and was relieved to find it unlocked. No light shone from under the door, so he hoped it would be a simple matter to catch Hadley already asleep. His gun at the ready, Luke threw the door wide and charged into the room.

Cody stood with her gun on Elizabeth, not trusting her one bit. "Don't try anything, Elizabeth. I shot Sully, and I can shoot you."

She saw the woman's eyes widen as she spoke and thought it was in reaction to her statement. Only when Hadley's strong arm closed around her neck and his gun was pressed against her back did she realize what had happened. The outlaw must have heard them entering Elizabeth's room, and he'd exited his own to come back around through her doorway. He'd closed it behind him, too, so no passersby would know what was going on.

"Drop your gun," he ordered quietly, not wanting to alert Luke to his presence.

There was no forgetting Hadley's voice. It was as cold and deadly as ever, and, trapped, Cody did as she was told. Elizabeth quickly stripped off her gag and smiled victoriously at her. At that moment, Luke had completed his search of Hadley's room and had come up empty-handed. He turned, ready to tell Cody they'd have to wait for Hadley to get back, when he saw what had happened.

"Well, well, well," Hadley sneered, greeting his adversary. "So we meet again, Luke Majors."

"Just as I was hoping we would," Luke taunted deliberately.

"Oh, really? You were looking forward to this reunion?" He chuckled. "I have to tell you, now that's it's happened, I am enjoying myself. I do give you credit, though. You were very good, but it looks like I'm better."

"I wouldn't count on that. I can still outgun you." Luke was standing in the doorway, his gun out and aimed straight at Hadley. "Just let her go."

"I don't think so. You put your gun down and take those cuffs off my sister."

"No." Luke slowly and deliberately cocked his gun. "You two are wanted dead or alive, and we're taking you in one way or the other."

"Like hell you are!" Elizabeth erupted, seeing her brother's indecisiveness. "Enough of this, Hadley! Shoot him!"

In an abrupt move, she lunged toward her night-stand and knocked the burning lamp to the floor. Flames erupted as the oil spread across the floor toward Luke. Hadley started to fire at Luke just as Luke lunged into the room, but Cody jabbed her elbow back into his stomach and the shot went wide. Hadley's grip on her loosened enough for her to tear herself from his grasp and throw herself from him just as Luke fired the fatal round that took Hadley square in the chest. He was thrown back against the wall and fell heavily to the floor.

"You murderers!" Elizabeth screamed as the fire grew. "You killed him! You shot my brother!"

Cody didn't waste time with her, but grabbed the bedspread and threw it on top of the flames. It took her a minute, but she finally managed to smother the fire.

They could hear loud voices in the hall and then someone pounded on the door.

"Open up!"

Luke walked to the door and opened it. "Go get the sheriff. There's been trouble here."

The man who stood there looked shocked at the sight of Luke and the gun he still held in his hand. He could see the carnage and destruction in the room, and he quickly ran for help.

Elizabeth was still screaming at Cody and Luke. "I'll get you two for this! I'm going to see you two rot in hell for what you've done!"

Luke turned on her. His expression was stony as he spoke. "You may very well see me in hell, but the good news is, you'll have gotten there first. Now shut up or I'll be tempted to take you in just like your brother."

Elizabeth's glare was venomous, but she knew Luke Majors was a killer. As long as she was alive, there was hope she could find a way out of her situation. She didn't cry often, but as she stared at her dead brother, emotion welled up within her. Hadley had always been there for her, and now he was dead. She would seek revenge for him if it was the last thing she did!

The hotel manager appeared then and Luke went out into the hall to explain what had happened.

"What's going on here?" the sheriff asked as he came running down the hall a few minutes later.

"These two are the leaders of the infamous El Diablo gang operating out west near Del Fuego. They're wanted for murder and bank robbery, and we're taking them in," Luke explained as he handed over the wanted posters for the sheriff to see.

"A woman? Are you sure?"

"We're positive," Cody said as she came out to join the discussion. She knew Elizabeth wasn't going anywhere until she let her go. "I'm Cody Jameson, and this is my partner, Luke. We're planning to take them both back to Del Fuego. We'll be leaving first thing in the morning."

The sheriff read the posters carefully and saw that they were legitimate. "Is there anything I can do to help you?"

"Could we borrow a cell for the night for the woman? All he needs is an undertaker."

"I can help you with both."

"We'd appreciate it," Cody told him.

"I'll get Elizabeth," Luke said.

"And I'll help."

She went with him, not trusting the other woman one bit. Together they released her from the bedstead, then handcuffed her hands together. They led her from the room. Elizabeth remained strangely silent. They'd expected her to keep screaming curses at them, but she went along quietly.

A short time later, Hadley had been taken to the undertaker to be prepared for the trek back to Del Fuego, and Elizabeth was safely locked away in a jail cell.

"We'll be leaving for Del Fuego in the morning," Cody informed the sheriff.

"She'll be right here waiting for you."

"We appreciate your help."

As Luke and Cody started from the jail they glanced back at Elizabeth to find her standing at the door to her cell, watching them. She did not look cowed. If anything she appeared conniving and sly. When she saw them looking at her, she smiled sweetly at them.

Cody felt a chill run down her spine as she left the sheriff's office. "I've been around a lot of killers in my time, but I've never met anyone like her before. She's positively vicious."

"I've seen men who were like her, but never a woman before. She's the consummate actress, convincing everyone that she's an innocent victim, when really she's the victimizer."

"She's incredible. We'll have to watch her every minute on the trip back."

"Don't worry about that. I have no intention of taking my eyes off of her. In fact . . ." Luke paused. "I think I may go back to the jail tonight and just keep watch with the deputy on duty. Knowing Elizabeth as we do, there's no telling what she might try tonight."

"If you want, I'll stay with you," Cody offered.

"One of us has got to get some sleep. You rest tonight; I'll sleep on the train tomorrow."

"Do you want to go back now?" They hadn't quite reached the hotel yet.

"No. I want to see you safely to your room," he insisted.

"There's no need."

"There's every need."

He said no more until they were outside her door and she was unlocking it. The excitement on the floor was over, and Elizabeth's and Hadley's rooms had been closed up for the night.

"I was worried about you tonight," he said as he followed Cody inside.

She'd left a lamp burning low, and the room was bathed in a soft golden glow. He stared down at her now, seeing her for herself and knowing that he had met his match in a woman. He'd never known anyone like Cody before. She was smart and beautiful and challenged him in all ways. Painfully, he admitted that he'd fallen in love with her.

He hadn't meant to. He'd despised her for the trickery she'd played on him, but now that he'd come to know her, to work with her, he recognized just how special she was. His throat tightened. When he'd seen Hadley holding the gun on her and realized she could have been killed, it had been the most terrible moment of his life. He would have done anything to save her from Hadley.

Luke gazed down at her. He wanted to tell her that he loved her, but he couldn't. The truth of his life stopped him cold. He had nothing to offer her. Look what had happened to him in Del Fuego when he'd tried to start up the Trinity. It was pointless for him to think that he could start over again, that he could have a life. When they got back to town, he would sell the Trinity, take whatever he could get for it, and move on. The people of Del Fuego didn't want him there. It would be best if he just kept on living the way he'd been living.

"You were?" Cody looked up at him and smiled. "There was no need. Everything turned out fine. I told you we'd do it."

Luke couldn't stop himself. He reached out to her and drew her into his arms. "When I saw Hadley holding that gun on you . . ."

"It's over."

"I know." He hid the anguish of his words by kissing her, hard and passionately.

When they broke apart, her cheeks were high with color and she was breathing hard. "Luke . . . Luke, I—"

He interrupted her. "I have to go."

Luke left her standing there. He walked from her room and the hotel, a solitary man.

Chapter Twenty-nine

The two men entered the saloon in Del Fuego and went to stand at the bar. It was late at night and business was slow. The barkeep waited on them quickly, and as they downed their first drinks, the younger of the two men spoke up.

"I was wondering if you could give us some information."

The barkeep eyed the man skeptically. He wasn't sure just what kind of information the stranger was after.

"What do you want to know?"

"We're looking for a man."

"A lot of people are," he replied, rubbing the bar top. "Which man?"

"A man named Luke Majors."

The barkeep shot them a quick glance. "The

bounty on him has been dropped. There ain't no point in you looking for him. He ain't worth nothing to you."

"Maybe he's not worth anything to you, but he's worth plenty to us. We've been looking for him for a long time," the old man said curtly.

"Sorry. I can't help you. I ain't seen him since all that trouble with the bank and all."

"What trouble?"

He quickly explained about the robbery and the El Diablo gang. "Last I heard, he wasn't a part of the gang, but I ain't seen him since. You can check over at the sheriff's office. Maybe Sheriff Halloway can help you."

"Obliged for the information." The younger man tipped his hat as they finished their drinks and left the saloon.

"It sounds like we might be closing in on him," the older man said.

"Don't get your hopes up. We thought we were close before, and we weren't. It's late. Let's take a room at the hotel and see the sheriff in the morning."

"But he might be—"

"Tomorrow. One more night isn't going to change anything."

The older man acquiesced and they headed for the hotel.

Cody lay in bed in her room in Galveston, unable to sleep. She couldn't believe the way she and Luke had parted, and she'd been lying there for hours trying to figure out what had happened.

He'd kissed her. . . . It wasn't Sister Mary or Armita or anybody else this time. He had kissed *her*.

She sighed as she remembered the passion of it. But just as quickly as he'd embraced her, he'd left her, and he hadn't looked back. It had seemed almost as if he had been pushing her away from him, and she didn't understand it.

Cody had thought that they'd come to like and admire each other over these last days that they'd been working so closely together. But now she supposed she'd been wrong. When he'd left her to return to the jail, he had been cold. It had seemed, in an unspoken way, some kind of final parting.

Cody had known she was falling in love with Luke. She'd known that since the beginning, but now there could be no denying it any longer. She did love him, and she had no idea what she was going to do about it.

Tears burned in her eyes, and deny them though she might, the pain in her heart was too overwhelming. It was near dawn when she finally fell asleep. Even then, it wasn't restful, but was filled with dreams of Luke.

"I appreciate all your help, Sheriff," Luke told him as he shook hands with him early the next morning.

"Glad to be of service. Good luck getting back with her, but truth be told, it's hard to believe she's the one you been talking about."

"That's why she's so dangerous," Luke explained, knowing it was a good thing he'd spent the night there. When he'd left Cody and come back, the sheriff had already been lured back near to the jail cell and was talking with Elizabeth. God only knew what she might have tried with him, if Luke hadn't shown up. "But she's not going to be doing much anymore except standing trial back in Del Fuego for murder and bank robbery."

"Take care going back."

"We will."

Cody arrived at the office ready to travel. She'd already wired Nate Thompson in San Antonio that they would need his help that night, and she'd had their bags delivered to the train station and checked to make certain that Hadley's coffin was ready to be loaded. She'd come to the office to help Luke with Elizabeth.

"Good morning," she greeted them as she came through the door.

Luke was hungry for the sight of her, and it was all he could do not to cross the room and take her in his arms. "Ready to go?"

"Everything's set. The train pulls out in less than an hour."

She thanked the sheriff for his help, too, and then they cuffed Elizabeth again and led her from the jail.

The trip to San Antonio seemed to take forever. Luke napped, while Cody kept a close eye on Elizabeth, never letting her out of her sight. Elizabeth did everything she could to make the trip more difficult, but Cody did not relax her vigilance, and she was thrilled when they reached San Antonio. The dangerous journey was almost over.

Cody found things between herself and Luke to

be oddly strained. She wanted to try to breach the wall that had suddenly been erected between them, but with Elizabeth there, there was no time for personal conversation. She hoped that evening when they were alone again, she could find out what was wrong.

Sheriff Nate Thompson was ready and waiting for them when they came to the office.

"Evening, Cody," he said, smiling when he saw her. "Looks like you're bringing in another one."

"My father taught me well," she answered. "We appreciate your help."

"Did you have any trouble?"

She told him what had happened and how Hadley had been killed.

"I'm just glad you're all right. Your aunt and the kids were in town a couple of days ago. I know they'll be glad to have you back home."

"I'll be glad to be back home, too," she answered. "All we have to do is deliver her to Sheriff Halloway in Del Fuego and we're done. I'll be able to wash my hands of this one in about two more days. Then I can go home for real."

"Sounds good. You two get some rest. We'll keep a real good watch on her tonight. She's not going anywhere."

Cody knew he was a man of his word, so she had no qualms about leaving her with him and told Luke so after they'd left the office to go to the Menger. "We won't have to stay with Nate tonight. He'll be fine. He's one helluva lawman."

"As good as your father?"

Cody smiled at him. "Almost."

They took their rooms and agreed to meet for dinner later. Cody bathed, and as she soaked in the hot water she wondered what she could do to get through to Luke. She had never considered herself a temptress or seductive in any way except when she was playing at it as Delilah or Armita. Right then, though, Cody Jameson was wishing she knew more about basic feminine wiles. All her life she'd been honest and forthright. It was all she could do not to blurt out to Luke that she loved him. She considered that maybe she should, but then she also ran the risk of driving him even farther from her. Trapped in her dilemma, she decided she would have a drink with dinner that night, and then decide what to do.

Luke took his time getting ready for their dinner, too. He could feel the confusion in Cody, but did not want to talk about it with her. It was better if he just left her once they got to Del Fuego. In fact, he'd thought about disappearing that night back in Galveston, but he needed to make sure she made it back safely.

As he dressed, he realized this would be the last time they would be having any private time together. He did not plan to tell her that he was leaving. He was just going to go once he saw her to Halloway's office.

"You look lovely again tonight," he complimented her as she met him in the hall.

"Why, thank you. It feels nice to be able to relax a little." She had worn the emerald gown again, and her hair was down and brushed out, held back

410

from her face by only a matching ribbon.

Luke thought she looked innocent and sweet and completely irresistible, and the desire he felt for her heated within him. Cody thought he looked more handsome than ever in his suit.

Her heart beat a little faster as Luke took her elbow to guide her through the restaurant when the waiter led them to their table. They were given a candlelit table for two in a secluded corner.

"Would you care for any drinks tonight?" the waiter asked.

"Do you have champagne?" Cody blurted out. She had never had any before, but she'd heard it was meant for celebrating. Tonight she wanted to celebrate their success.

"Yes, ma'am."

"Bring us a bottle, please," she directed.

"Do you like champagne?" Luke asked, surprised by her request.

She giggled nervously. "I don't know. I've never had it before, but I wanted us to celebrate tonight."

He thought she was charming in her innocence. It was her innocence and purity that drew him to her, that had wrapped its spell around him and held him by his heart. Yet it was also that innocence and goodness that convinced him he could have no place in her life. He would not drag her down. As much as he loved her, he would not ruin her life by asking her to marry him. It was better this way. He was sure of it.

When the waiter returned with a chilled bottle of the sparkling wine and two beautiful crystal glasses, Cody was excited. She forgot that it had been long hours since she'd eaten anything. She was just fascinated by the bubbling wine in the delicate crystal. The waiter did the honors on the first drink and Cody took her glass, holding it as if it were the most precious thing she'd ever held. Then she lifted her gaze to Luke's as she raised the glass in toast.

"To you, Luke Majors. You are a kind, gentle, intelligent man, and I . . ." She stopped, unable to say the words she really wanted to say—that she loved him and didn't want to live without him. "I hope our association on this job is only the first of many."

Luke touched the rim of his glass to hers. "And to you, Cody. May you always be happy."

As they sipped from their glasses, their gazes met and held. It was a moment Cody had longed for, and she wished she could just reach across the table and kiss him. She didn't. Instead, she concentrated on drinking her champagne, marveling at how it tasted better and better with each additional sip.

Cody was on her third glass by the time their dinner arrived, and she continued to partake of the champagne until the bottle was empty. She didn't notice right away that her lips had gone numb or that suddenly the night seemed brighter and the world seemed nicer. She felt good, and happy, and as if she didn't have a care in the world. She liked the feeling. Luke ordered dessert for them, a decadent chocolate concoction that was creamy and bittersweet and that Cody loved.

"That was delicious." She sighed as she sat back, contented. She felt all warm inside.

"Are you ready to call it a night?" Luke recognized that she'd had too much to drink, but then so had he. She was having such a wonderful time that he hated to say anything to her. They were enjoying themselves. That was all that was important. It had been a long, long time since he'd last been able to relax and just be himself this way.

"I think I'd better. We've got a long couple of days coming up, but it's going to feel very good when we deliver Elizabeth to the sheriff's office."

"It's going to feel wonderful."

Luke helped her from her chair and kept his hand at her waist as they left the dining room and went back upstairs. They paused before her room and Luke took the key from her to unlock her door. She stepped inside and lifted her starry-eyed gaze to him.

"Good night, Luke." Her voice was breathless with promise. Her eyes were luminous. Her lips were slightly parted as if begging him to kiss her.

He told himself no. "Good night, Cody."

He started to leave, needing to get away from the enchantment of her.

"Luke?"

He turned back.

"Thank you."

"For what?"

"For everything. For protecting me as Sister Mary. For taking me with you as Armita. For saving me from the snake. For helping me find El Diablo . . ."

She'd taken two steps toward him, and it was his undoing. Luke returned to her and took her in his arms. He crushed her to him, his mouth swooping down to claim hers in a devouring kiss that spoke of passion unleashed.

Everything seemed to swirl around him as he held her to his heart. Somehow the door was closed and locked, and, finally, they were alone. Clothes were strewn about the room in their haste to touch one another and to be close. When at last they fell together on the bed, the rest of the world did not exist. There was only feeling and need. Distantly, as if in a dream, Luke heard her softly call to him, "I love you, Luke."

But then it was gone, and all that was left was their joining. Tender yet fierce. Fiery yet gentle. Consuming yet giving. They loved.

It was long into the night before exhaustion claimed them and they fell asleep in each other's arms. Their limbs entwined, they clung to the joy that had been theirs for just that little while.

Cody awoke an hour before sunrise. Luke slumbered peacefully beside her. She carefully extricated herself from the bed and went to stare out the hotel window.

Tears traced a path down her cheeks, yet Cody did not bother to wipe them away. She loved Luke with all her heart, and he did not love her. She had hoped last night would break down the barrier he'd put between them. She'd hoped by telling him she loved him, she would touch his heart. But it hadn't happened.

The pain was fierce. She had known he was a dangerous man, but she'd never known how dangerous. She had never known that he could break her heart this way.

Silently she dressed and gathered her things. She sat down at the dressing table and wrote two short notes. Propping Luke's note up so he'd be sure to see it, she took one last look at him as he slept. She would never forget him. She would love him forever.

Fighting the pain deep within her, Cody left the room, locking the door behind her. She got her horse from the stable, stopped by the jail to leave the other note for Nate, and then headed home. It was time.

Luke awoke just after dawn and immediately reached for Cody. When he encountered an empty bed and cold sheets, his eyes flew open and he sat up looking around the room for her. It took him a minute to realize that she was gone. And then he saw the note.

Getting up, he grabbed the missive and read it quickly.

Dear Luke,
I realize now that things will not work out between us. We're too different. Please take Elizabeth, and Hadley's body, on in to Del Fuego and claim the reward. Keep it all. I wish you much happiness.

Cody

* * *

He crushed the note in his hand, his knuckles whitening with the power of his grip. She was gone. Just like that and in the middle of the night. She must have realized that he couldn't give her the kind of life she wanted.

Pain knifed at Luke, but he refused it. It was better this way. He had planned to leave her in Del Fuego, so this was just ending it early. He should be relieved. It was over.

He threw the note in the trash can and began to dress. A few minutes later he was heading for the jail.

Chapter Thirty

Fred looked up as the two men came through the office door. "Can I help you?"

"The bartender at the saloon down the street told us you might be able to," the young man began.

"What is it?" Fred studied the two. They looked respectable enough, though a little travel-weary.

"We were trying to locate someone, and from the reaction we got from the barkeep, we figured we might be getting close."

"Who is it?"

The two exchanged looks and then the older one said, "Luke Majors."

Fred's expression grew serious as he regarded the pair. "The bounty is off Majors. So you can just go on your way. He's not a wanted man anymore."

"Not by the law."

"Not by anyone."

"He is by us."

"Why?"

"He's my son," Charles Majors said.

Luke retrieved Elizabeth and, after getting her settled next to him on the seat in the buckboard, they headed for Del Fuego. He didn't relish the trip. He was going to have to keep track of her every minute, and she was a challenge. He could never let his guard down or underestimate her. If he did, he'd end up dead. He had no doubt of that.

Elizabeth was strangely quiet as they left San Antonio. Luke had expected the worst from her, and wasn't quite sure what this mood of hers meant. They were several hours' ride out of town when she finally spoke up.

"Where's your partner?"

"Cody wasn't my partner."

"Your lady friend?"

"No."

"Really? Then why were you two together?"

"We were doing a favor for Jack."

"Jack?" She glanced at him quickly.

"You're not as good as you think you are. You didn't kill Jack, you didn't kill your husband, and you missed your chance with me."

"We aren't in Del Fuego yet, Luke Majors. Are you certain you're man enough to bring me in alone?"

Her words were meant to be taunting, but Luke didn't respond to them.

"I've dealt with your kind before," he answered flatly. "They just never wore skirts."

"I'll take that as a compliment," she cooed.

"You can take it any way you like. You're a killer, and I don't like killers."

"What a disappointment," Elizabeth said, her tone petulant. "And all this time I thought you were someone special."

Luke shrugged. "You thought wrong."

"Obviously."

She fell silent again, and Luke was glad. They had a long way to go, and he didn't want to listen to her.

They traveled on, not stopping for the night until it was almost dark. Luke roused her again before sunup, and they once more headed out. It was midafternoon when Del Fuego first came into view.

Luke didn't want anything to do with the town, but he had to admit he was glad to see it today. He couldn't wait to get rid of Elizabeth and be on his way. Luke planned a trip out to the ranch to visit Jessy, and then he would head west, maybe to Arizona territory. He'd heard a man could lose himself there.

As they entered town, word that he'd returned with Elizabeth traveled fast. By the time he'd tied the buckboard up in front of the sheriff's office, a crowd was gathering. Luke helped her down and turned to find Fred waiting for them in the office doorway.

"I sent a deputy to find Jack. Bring her on in," Fred told him. "Where's Cody?"

"She stayed behind in San Antonio."

They ushered Elizabeth quickly into a cell and locked the door securely.

"Hello, Fred," she said sweetly.

He turned an icy glare on her and walked away. "Hadley in the pine box?"

Luke nodded. "There was no other way."

"Poster said 'dead or alive.'" He shrugged off the outlaw's death. Hadley was not a man to be mourned.

Jack came through the door right then. He'd seen the coffin outside and spotted Elizabeth in the jail cell, and went straight to Luke to shake his hand.

"You did it! Where's Cody?"

"I just asked him the same thing," Fred put in.

"She decided to stay on in San Antonio. I brought Elizabeth in alone from there."

Jack glanced toward the jail cell again. "Wait here. I have a few things to say to her."

He walked toward the cell area, while the other men discreetly moved away.

"Hello, Elizabeth."

"Why, Jack," she said coolly, "I can't say that I'm happy to see you up and about."

"You really had me fooled."

"That wasn't difficult. And you weren't the only one."

"Obviously, but all good things do come to an end."

"Was I good for you, Jack?" she asked in a sultry voice as she stepped nearer to the bars of the cell.

For one fleeting moment his expression was

haunted; then he turned and walked away. "Good-bye, Elizabeth."

He returned to talk to Luke again.

"Where did you catch up with them?"

"We had to follow them all the way to Galveston, but luckily we got there before they sailed. It wouldn't have been pretty if we'd had to go after them in New Orleans."

"Good job! I'll see you get the bounty right away. That'll be two thousand for El Diablo and another five hundred for Hadley."

Luke shrugged. Somehow the money didn't seem important anymore. "Just give me the hundred you owe me and send the rest to Cody."

"You don't want a share?"

"No."

"Do you want to take it to her and let her know you got here all right?"

"No. I doubt I'll be seeing her again. You were right about her, though, Jack. She was good. Damned good."

"So were you. You did it! You brought down the El Diablo gang."

"Have you heard any more from Steve?"

"Got a wire yesterday. They met up with the bounty hunter Reid near Rio Nuevo. He had two of the gang already in custody and was bringing them in."

"Cody would be glad to hear that."

"I'll let her know when I wire her. Are you planning on heading out to the Trinity now?" Jack asked.

"Might as well."

"Give me a few minutes. I'll get your money and I'll ride with you."

Luke was surprised that Jack wanted to go to the ranch with him, but now that the ordeal with El Diablo was over, he guessed they could relax and visit for a while, catch up on old times.

"Fine. I'll wait here for you."

Jack was starting from the office when Sarah Gregory came rushing through the door.

"Is it true?" she demanded of them, breathless from having run all the way from her house. "Did you bring her back? Is Elizabeth here?"

"Yes, she is, Sarah," Fred answered sympathetically.

"I have to talk to her. I have to see her."

"She's in the back," the sheriff told her. "You want me to come with you?"

"Why? I'm in no danger. She can't hurt me any more than she already has. I just want to look in her face and tell her what I think of her."

"Go ahead."

Sarah walked sedately past the three men and into the cell area.

Elizabeth had heard Sarah's voice and was sitting on the bunk waiting for her. Her expression was casual, almost nonchalant.

"So they caught you," Sarah sneered.

"Obviously," Elizabeth answered, bored with what she knew was coming.

"I'm glad. It's almost too bad they didn't shoot you like they did your brother."

Elizabeth continued to ignore her.

"How could you do it, Elizabeth? What kind of

woman are you that you could shoot and kill my husband in cold blood and then come to my house and sympathize with me? What kind of woman are you that you could have arranged that bank robbery and had your own husband shot?"

"Are you through?" Elizabeth's tone was indifferent.

Her attitude infuriated Sarah even more. "I don't know why I never saw through you."

"Because you're stupid like the rest of the simpletons in this pitiful excuse for a town."

Sarah gasped. "We weren't so stupid that you got away with it!"

"Ah, but I did get away with it, and for a long time, too!" Elizabeth stood up and strode to the bars to look Sarah straight in the eye. "You make me sick. All of you! You didn't know it, but Sam only stayed with you because he had me."

"What!" Sarah went pale at the vindictive words. "What are you saying?"

"Do I have to say it more clearly for you? Spell it out? I was bedding Sam, Sarah. I got a lot of information out of him. He always knew what was going on, and I fed everything I learned directly to Hadley and the gang."

"You little—"

"And he enjoyed bedding me, too. I kept him satisfied. I suppose if you had been as good a wife as you say you were, he wouldn't have come to my bed. But he did."

Sarah was holding herself rigidly as she turned and quietly walked away.

"Bye, Sarah, honey. Do come back again." Elizabeth went to sit down on the cot again.

"Sarah, are you all right?" Fred asked, seeing the look on her face as she emerged from the cell area. They had all heard Elizabeth's devastating comments, and they knew Sarah had to be heartsick. Fred went to her, thinking she might need an arm of support.

The only support Sarah needed right then was in his gunbelt. As he started to put an arm around her, she grabbed his revolver and ran back toward the jail cell.

"This is for Sam!" she screamed as she began firing repeatedly at Elizabeth.

Fred, Luke, and Jack gave chase. Luke reached Sarah first and snatched the gun from her hand, but it was too late. Elizabeth lay sprawled on the jail cell floor.

Sarah collapsed into Fred's arms as all her strength finally failed her. "She deserved it! She killed Sam."

"I know, Sarah," Fred said, supporting her as he led her into the outer room. "I know."

He handed Jack the keys as he passed him, and Jack quickly entered the cell to check on Elizabeth.

The door to the office burst open, and the crowd started to push inside.

"What happened? We heard shots!"

"El Diablo's been wounded," Fred announced.

A rousing cheer went up from those gathered, who were avidly trying to get a look in back.

"Someone go for the doctor."

Suddenly a path was cleared through the crowd,

and Jonathan Harris was wheeled forward by the woman who'd been caring for him. He had a blanket over his legs.

"What's this about a shooting? Where is she? I want to see Elizabeth! I want to see my wife!"

Luke managed to get the rest of the townspeople to back up, so they could close the door again.

"Come on back here, Jonathan," Fred said, after helping Sarah to a chair. "She's been shot."

"What?"

"I shot her, Jonathan! She lied to me! She's the one who killed Sam and had you shot," Sarah told him in a monotone voice. "I hope she's dead."

Jonathan was wheeled back toward the cell just as Jack stood up and came out.

"I'm sorry. There's nothing anyone can do. She'd dead," he announced.

Jonathan sat in his wheelchair staring at his dead wife's body. "Good," he said with conviction. He pulled his hand out from under the blanket and gently patted the gun he'd been holding, hidden there. "Looks like I won't be needing this now. Sarah already took care of things."

The woman who'd been caring for him gasped, shocked that he'd had the weapon. She hadn't known he was armed when they'd left the house.

"Get him out of here," Fred ordered, angry. "And, Jonathan, be careful with that damned thing!"

Jonathan was smiling as he was wheeled from the office. The doctor passed him.

"No need to rush, Doc. She'd dead."

The crowd outside heard the news and cheered

even more. The El Diablo gang had been broken. They would no longer be terrorizing the countryside.

The doctor quickly reaffirmed what they already knew. It was over. El Diablo was dead—killed as she had killed. Her body was taken away to the undertaker.

When the crowd had dispersed and the excitement had died down, Jack looked at Fred.

"What are you going to do about Sarah?"

She was still sitting quietly in the chair, her expression vacant, her manner unthreatening.

"I don't know. She'll probably have to go before the judge for a hearing, but he won't be back for another two weeks. For now, I say we just take her on home. She's not a threat to anyone else."

Jack and Luke both knew he was right. Fred helped her up and they started from the office.

Sarah looked back at Luke. "Thank you for finding her and bringing her back."

Luke nodded; then Fred led her out the door.

Jack gave a rueful shake of his head as he watched them go. "You want to stay here now or you want to come with me to my room to get your money?"

"I'll come with you and then we'll head out to the Trinity. It looks like everything's finished here." Luke was thinking of Hadley, El Diablo, and Cody as he spoke.

"That it is."

A short time later they were on the road to the Trinity.

"So how was it to work with the famous Cody Jameson?"

"It was a challenge. She's sharp, real sharp. Did you know her father was a lawman before he was killed?"

"No, but that's probably why she's so good at what she does."

Luke told him all that had happened—almost all of it.

"Why didn't she come with you back to town? I was hoping to see her again."

"She didn't say. She just wanted to go home, I guess."

"Well, that's where you're going now—home. It's been a while since you thought of doing that, hasn't it?"

"It's going to be a longer while."

"Why? What are you talking about? Your taxes were paid. You've got a hundred dollars to tide you over until the ranch starts bringing in some money. You're in good shape."

"I'm going to sell it."

"You're what?" Jack was so surprised, he reined in. He stared at his friend as if he'd gone crazy.

"I'm selling the Trinity to whoever will buy it, and I'm moving on." He smiled regretfully. "I've finally accepted that I can't go back to when we were young. Those days are gone, and they'll never exist again."

"You're wrong." Jack spurred his mount forward, knowing the only thing that would change Luke's mood was waiting for him at the Trinity even as they spoke.

"No, I'm not. I'm leaving Texas. I thought maybe I'd head for Arizona."

"Don't pack your bags yet."

"Why? Nothing's going to change the way I feel."

"Don't be too sure."

"What are you talking about? I had a lot of hours in the saddle to think this over."

They were topping the low rise as he finished speaking.

"Yes, but you never had anybody else to consider when you were making your decision."

"Anybody else?" Luke glanced at him, wondering if Jack somehow knew of his feelings for Cody. But Jack was staring down at the ranch house, pointing at the extra horses in the corral.

"You've got company—at home, Luke."

"What are you talking about?"

Luke followed the direction of Jack's gaze and saw the horses. He frowned. "Who's there besides Jessy?"

"Ride on down and find out." Jack was smiling in an enigmatic way that confused Luke.

He spurred his mount to a gallop and raced forward, leaving Jack to follow. Luke didn't know what awaited him, but he knew it was something special . . . very special.

As he neared the house, Jessy came out on the front porch with two other men he couldn't recognize from a distance. Luke reined in at the hitching rail and stared up at the three on the porch, unable to believe his eyes.

"Welcome home, son," Charles said.

Chapter Thirty-one

Luke all but threw himself from his horse and ran to his father. They embraced, weeping openly.

"You're alive!" was all Luke could mutter.

"And so are you!" Charles added in a tear-choked voice. "I was afraid I'd never find you . . . never see you again."

He kept a grip on Luke as he held his son away from him to get a look at him. They stared at each other in loving awe.

Luke's gaze went over his father. His father's hair and mustache were white now, but otherwise he seemed much the same.

"Hello, Luke," Dan said as he came down to join them.

Luke looked over at his brother. When they'd last seen each other, Dan had been little more than a boy. Now he was a man, hardened by the years. Luke saw a lot of himself in Dan: tall, dark-haired, the same blue eyes. The family resemblance could not be denied.

Charles released Luke so he could hug his brother. When they broke apart, they went inside to catch up on all that had happened. Jack got something out of his saddlebags and followed them into the house. Jessy went off to tend Jack's and Luke's horses.

"I brought this along just for this moment," Jack announced as he held up the bottle of fine bourbon, the same brand they used to drink before the war.

Luke clapped him on the back, grinning from ear to ear. "You knew they were here?"

"That's why I had to come with you. They showed up in town asking questions about you while you were gone, and at first Fred thought they were bounty hunters."

Charles chuckled at the memory. "Once we told him why we wanted you, he was a great help. He took us to Jack and Jack brought us out here to wait for your return."

Luke went to put his arms around his father again. "I can't believe any of this. What happened to you? Where were you after the war?" He explained how he'd heard they'd been killed.

They settled in around the table to drink and talk.

"We weren't killed in the battle. We were caught and sent to prison camp. We didn't get out until the end of the war, and then we had to walk home."

"And you know what we found when we got there," Dan said disparagingly.

"I know. That was what broke my final tie. I headed west after that, and I've been roaming ever since. How did you trace me here?"

"It's been a long, hard search," Charles said wearily. "But it was worth every minute and every mile to be here with you right now."

"We heard someone talking about you in Galveston, and started trying to track you from there. We had no idea where you were, and thought it was a godsend that your name had even come up at the moment when we were there. If it hadn't been for that conversation, we'd still be looking for you."

"And we probably would never have found you," Dan added.

"And now you're here and you have this ranch . . . a home. This place is wonderful, son," Charles said enthusiastically. "Jessy was telling us how hard you were working on it before all the trouble started. You've just been through hell these last couple of months, haven't you?"

"It hasn't been easy, but the important thing was that we shut the gang down."

"We? You and Jack?"

"And the bounty hunter I was working with, Cody Jameson."

"He was good?"

"Yes, she was," Jack said with emphasis. "Cody's a woman, and one helluva bounty hunter. Luke and Cody just brought in El Diablo and her brother, the two main leaders of the outlaws."

"I'm proud of you, son," Charles said. "Maybe now there won't be so much trouble for you in town."

"Well, actually, I was thinking about selling the ranch and moving on," Luke said.

"But why?" Dan asked quickly. "This place is beautiful. If you want the help, we'll stay and work side by side with you to make a go of it."

"You'd want to stay with me knowing what happened in town? That's the way my life's been for many years now."

"We're family, Luke," Charles said fiercely. "You're my son. Jack told us about the mistaken identity, but you've been proven innocent. This is not the time to cut and run. Stay and fight for what you love, for what you believe in."

"If you want to make this ranch work, we're with you," Dan offered.

Luke had hardened himself to his love for the Trinity. He'd prepared himself to sell it for whatever price he could get, then ride away and never look back. He had tried to cut any emotional ties he had to the place. But now, offered the chance to stay on and have a real family again, all the feelings he'd denied for so long surfaced. He smiled.

"Welcome home," he said to his father and brother. "The Trinity is now the Majors family's ranch, not just Luke Majors's spread."

The four men drank a toast to the future of the Trinity and talked long into the night of how Luke planned to improve his stables. By the time they all went to bed, the future of the ranch was already set. They would not fail. They had each other.

The following morning after sharing breakfast with the family, Jack got ready to leave.

"I've got to get back to town. With the El Diablo gang destroyed, I'll be meeting up with Steve as soon as he rides in with Reid and the outlaws he caught. Once he's finished there, we'll be moving on to another assignment," Jack told them as he saddled his horse.

"You just remember the Trinity is your home now, too," Luke told him. "You're one of us, Jack. Come back whenever you can."

They shook hands all around, and then Jack mounted.

"You take care," Jack told them, glad that everything had turned out so well for Luke and his family.

"We will."

Jack urged his horse on, and the three Majors men watched him go until he had ridden out of sight.

They turned back to the ranch that was their future and their dream. They were together. It was a miracle they had thought would never happen.

Luke threw himself into working on the ranch. He was up every day by dawn and worked long past dark. He had a dream now, a future with his father and brother. He would make things grow again. He would raise horses and cattle and see the good side of life once more. There was even a change in the attitude of people in town when Luke went in for supplies. Fred had made sure that everyone knew he was innocent, and slowly the merchants and townspeople began to make friends with him. Life became worth living again.

Days turned into weeks and then months, and life took on a wonderful sameness.

But as much as Luke worked himself tirelessly from dawn to dusk, his nights were still restless. Many were the predawn hours when he'd awake breathless and aching from dreams of Cody. The nighttime visions were always jumbled images of Sister Mary, Armita, and Cody. In his dreams, she chased him, trapped him, loved him until he would wake up wondering how he could ever have let her go. Often Dan would get up only to find Luke already dressed and sitting on the porch watching the sunrise.

Luke thought back to Galveston and the night when Hadley had held the gun on Cody. If anything had happened to her, he wouldn't have stopped until Hadley was dead or he'd been killed trying to avenge her. He loved her.

Thinking back over the years, he realized what he'd thought was love for Clarissa had been but a faint imitation. This emotion he felt for Cody was deep and abiding. It had not faded while they'd been apart, but had intensified. He wanted her still. He missed her always, and he didn't know what to do.

Luke had let her go because he'd had no life to offer her. But now, with his father and brother by his side, he didn't have to move on, he didn't have to keep running. They could settle down here. They could have a life.

Still he hesitated. Cody had left him that night in San Antonio. Luke was convinced that she hadn't meant the words of love she'd whispered in the heat of the darkness.

Luke was hard at work mending a fence late one afternoon when he caught sight of a rider coming. He'd paused in his work, walking out to meet the visitor, only to find that it was Fred.

"Good to see you, Luke," Fred greeted him.

"What brings you all the way out here?"

"Got something for you. Thought you might want it right away," he said, handing him a thick envelope.

Luke opened it to find that it was stuffed with money. "What's this for?"

"There's a letter in there from Cody Jameson. She sent it to me, asking me to deliver this to you. Evidently it's half the reward money for bringing in Hadley and Elizabeth."

Luke opened the missive and read:

Dear Sheriff Halloway,
Please see that Luke Majors gets his fair share of our reward money. He is more than deserving of it.

Sincerely,
Cody Jameson

"There's over a thousand dollars in there. That's why I thought I'd better bring it out personal like."

Luke looked up at him in amazement. He'd had

the entire reward sent to Cody because he'd wanted her to have it. Now she was sharing it.

"Thanks, Fred. I appreciate it."

"Hope it helps you."

"You want to stay for some dinner?"

"Don't mind if I do."

Over the meal that night, Fred started regaling Charles and Dan with stories of Cody's prowess that Jack had told him.

"How come you never mentioned any of this to us?" Charles asked, studying his son's expression carefully.

"There wasn't much to say."

"You don't think Jameson's ability to disguise herself is worth talking about?"

"And she fooled you how many times?" Dan asked with a laugh.

"Three," he answered, grinning wryly at himself.

"I think I'd like to meet this woman someday."

"I would, too," Charles added.

Without a word, Luke got up and walked outside to stare across the countryside. The sun was setting and the western sky was a pink- and gold-streaked panorama. It was beautiful, yet for all the glory of his ranch and his reunion with his family, Luke felt as if a part of him was missing. There was only one way to remedy it.

"Do you love her, son?" Charles's voice came softly from behind him.

"Yes, I do, but I never told her." He sighed.

"Don't you think it's time you did?"

Luke stared out across the heavens for a long moment before answering. "Yes, I think it is time.

Can you and Dan run the place with Jessy?"

Charles smiled. "If you love her, Luke, then go get her. Bring her home."

Luke left later that night with Fred for town, and he rode for San Antonio the next day.

"I need to get in contact with Cody Jameson," Luke told Nate Thompson when he found him in the sheriff's office in San Antonio.

"Sorry, Majors, but I can't help you there."

Luke stared at him in disbelief. "Why not? You know I worked with her to bring in El Diablo. Why won't you tell me where she lives?"

Nate studied Luke for a moment, then answered slowly with the truth. "I'm not going to tell you, because that morning you left for Del Fuego she left me a note asking me not to tell you anything about her if you were to ask. I'm honoring her wishes."

"Thanks," Luke muttered as he left the jail.

He was stymied, but he remembered very well how Cody had tracked people down. He'd learned a lot working with her, and he turned her lessons to his own uses right then. One by one, he visited all the stores in town until a clerk at the general store answered his questions.

"Sure, the Jameson family lives just a short way out of town. It's about half an hour due north." He went on to show him which road to take.

Luke thanked him, and went off to find the woman he loved.

Chapter Thirty-two

Luke faced down Stalking Ghost. The old man had stopped him as he had ridden in to the Jameson homestead. Stalking Ghost's expression was impossible to read, and Luke didn't even try. He knew what he wanted now. He wanted Cody, and he was going to find her if it was the last thing he ever did.

"I need to talk to her," he told Stalking Ghost. "It's important."

Stalking Ghost regarded him quietly, betraying nothing.

"Look, I'm going to find her, with or without your help. It'll be a lot easier if you tell me where she is, but one way or another I'm going to talk to her."

"Why do you want to speak with her? Why must

you come back into her life now?" he finally asked, his black-eyed gaze fixed intently on Luke.

Luke was silent for a long time as he gathered his thoughts. He gathered his courage to speak of his feelings, knowing the old man would not help him unless he was completely honest.

"Because I love her. I want to marry her—if she'll have me."

For the first time ever, Luke saw a spark of emotion in Stalking Ghost's expression. He nodded. "What day is this?" the old Indian asked him.

Luke was completely baffled and frustrated by his question. *What day is this?* Who cared? And what did that have to do with him seeing Cody again? "It's Wednesday. Why?" He tried not to sound impatient.

The Indian nodded again, peering up at Luke, studying him, searching for the truth behind his words. "You will find Cody on the stage to Waco. You will have to ride hard to catch her."

"I'd cross hell to find her."

Stalking Ghost almost allowed himself to smile. He would like to be riding with this one when he caught up with the stage.

"Thanks." Luke hurried to his horse, mounted, and rode off. He thought about going on to meet her aunt and brother and sister, but that could come later. Right now there was no time to waste. He'd been apart from her for too long already. He wanted Cody. He had to find her.

Stalking Ghost watched him ride away, and this time he did smile.

* * *

The stagecoach was crowded as it rumbled along the rough road heading for Waco. Cody sat wedged tightly between an elderly man who was sleeping and a heavyset, kindly looking lady. Across from them sat two armed cowboys and a bespectacled man, who looked like a salesman of some sort.

Cody didn't know why she was doing this. It was crazy, but she'd needed to get away. She couldn't stay home anymore thinking about Luke. He was never going to come after her. He didn't love her. He never had. She had to accept that.

Sighing, Cody rested a hand on the rounded mound of her stomach. It was awkward being this big.

"Is this your first child?" the heavyset, nosy woman next to her asked.

"Yes," Cody answered with an almost bittersweet smile. "My husband and I are very excited."

"Is your husband meeting you in Waco?"

"No, I'm continuing on to Abilene."

"Well, you take care of yourself. Too much of this bouncing isn't good for you."

"It is an adventure, isn't it?" Cody said, grabbing on to the seat to keep her balance as they hit a particularly rough stretch.

"I don't like you traveling all by yourself this way."

"My family was worried, too, but everything will be fine once I get there."

"Well, I'm Mary Bradshaw, and if you need anything, you just let me know." She patted Cody's hand supportively. She was the mothering type, and this young woman looked so forlorn and lonely that her protective instincts came to the fore.

"I will."

They rode on. Though Cody knew the area, for some reason, this time, the miles seemed endless. She was lulled by the monotony of the trip, and then suddenly, she heard the driver shout something that sounded like a warning and the stage began to slow, then stop.

The old man tried to get a look out his window, but couldn't see anything. Across from her the two cowboys looked annoyed, and the salesman awoke from a nap.

"I wonder what's going on," Mrs. Bradshaw said as she strained to see what was happening. "Oh, my!"

"What?" Cody asked.

"The driver just jumped down, and he's coming this way with another man who's leading his horse."

"Maybe his horse went lame, and he needs a ride," one of the men offered.

"Well, he's not going to fit in here." Mrs. Bradshaw sniffed indignantly. "We're crowded already. He'll have to ride up top."

The driver opened the door, and the man stepped from behind him to look inside.

Cody gasped, her heart leaping to her throat. Luke! It was Luke. . . . She almost launched herself into his arms, but stopped herself cold. Not now. She couldn't.

Luke looked inside and went still. Cody was

there all right . . . and she was pregnant! Very pregnant!

Luke couldn't speak. He couldn't think. He could only stare at her in wonder. She was pregnant. And with his child.

Immediately, he mentally berated himself for having stayed away from her for so long. But how could he have known? She'd never sent word. She'd never let him know. Had she planned to have his baby and raise the child alone? Without him ever finding out? His heart ached that she hated him that much, and he was desperate to know the answers to his questions.

Luke lifted his gaze to Cody's after the long silence.

"We have to talk," was all he could say. His declaration of love was important to him, and he didn't want to do it in front of all these people.

"Are you her husband?" Mrs. Bradshaw demanded protectively, wondering what this scruffy-looking cowboy wanted with the sweet young thing next to her.

"I plan to be," he answered. "If she'll have me."

Cody could have groaned in frustration.

"She's already married," Mrs. Bradshaw insisted.

"Cody?" Luke snared her gaze quickly, fearing that she had married someone else just to give his child a name. The possibility nearly made him physically sick.

"We need to talk, Luke." She struggled to rise in the cramped quarters.

Mrs. Bradshaw gave her a helping hand, her expression bewildered by this turn of events. The young girl was married, wasn't she? It would be terrible to think that she was in a family way with no husband.

Luke took Cody's hand in his as he helped her descend from the stage. His gaze went from her face to her stomach and back up again.

"Don't take too long. I gotta stay on schedule," the driver told them as Luke led her a short distance away from the stagecoach.

"Thanks for stopping," Luke said; then, thinking they were out of earshot, he turned to her. "Cody . . . I'm sorry. I never knew."

"Luke, I really don't want to hear this right now."

"If not now, then when? Is what that lady said true? Did you marry someone else to give my child a name? Stalking Ghost didn't tell me any of this. If only he had . . ."

"But you came," she pointed out, feeling the love she felt for him blossom and grow even stronger. "You came."

"How could I not? I love you, Cody. If I had only known about your condition, I would have been here sooner. It's taken me a while to realize what we had, and I don't want to lose it. I don't want to lose you. I want to spend the rest of my life with you. Will you marry me?" The words he'd thought would be so difficult to speak actually came from him freely. He did love her, and he wanted her to know it. He needed her to know it.

"Luke, I can't," she said hesitantly, glancing back toward the stage.

"Did you marry someone else?"

"No, it's not that. It's just that this isn't the time or the place for us to discuss these things."

"If you're not married, then this is the perfect time to discuss these things. In fact, it looks to me like it's already several months too late to be discussing these things. Marry me, Cody."

He reached out to take her in his arms, but she pulled away.

"Luke, no."

"I don't understand."

"Wait right here a minute," she said, turning in frustration back to the stage. "Hold that thought."

"What?"

Cody walked to the other side of the stage from where she'd gotten out and opened the door.

"What is it, my dear? What's that young man want?" Mrs. Bradshaw asked, her expression avid with interest. What she'd thought would be a dull trip had turned into something quite different. Was the girl married or not? Who was the tall, handsome stranger?

"I'll tell you in a minute, Mrs. Bradshaw, but there's something I have to do first."

"What's that?"

"This," Cody announced as she opened the purse she was carrying at her wrist and took out her gun and a wanted poster. "Michael Denton, you're under arrest."

Cody pointed her gun at the shy-looking salesman, who blanched at her announcement.

"*No!* You can't take me back!" he shouted, clutching his small valise to him as he tried to escape out the other door, but suddenly Luke was there, grabbing him by the arm as he tried to get away.

"Cody?" Luke looked at her across the stage.

"Keep a hold on him, Luke. He's wanted for embezzlement. I've got the poster right here to prove it." She circled the stage to confront the man she'd been trailing for days now. She'd meant to make the arrest in Waco, but this was as good a place as any. Especially with Luke here to help her.

The stage driver was shocked by what had transpired, but quickly cooperated, tossing an extra rope down to Luke so he could tie Denton up.

"He was a wanted man?" Mrs. Bradshaw was nearly shouting in her excitement.

"Yes, ma'am," Cody told her. She watched as Luke bound him tightly and shoved him toward the stage driver, who hauled him up on top for the rest of the ride.

Luke turned to Cody. He was furious at the thought that she might have been hurt in some way. "Are you crazy? Trying a stunt like that in your condition? You might have hurt yourself and our child."

Cody smiled sweetly. She knew all eyes were upon them, and she needed a moment of privacy. "Luke, we have a lot to say to each other, but this may not be the best time to do it."

"This is the perfect time to do it." He had no idea what she was smiling so brightly about. They'd been apart for months. He'd just discovered she was having his baby, and she wouldn't give him a straight answer to his proposal.

445

"I love you, Luke."

"You do?" He stared at her in surprise. He wanted to hold her, but something in her manner held him at bay.

"But you don't have to marry me," Cody concluded.

Mrs. Bradshaw had been hanging out the window, trying to hear what they were saying. She collapsed weakly back in her seat and started fanning herself at this last statement. "Goodness gracious! She's having his child, but she won't marry him? And he's offered? Oh, my . . ."

The others in the stage were watching avidly now, too. The young pregnant woman had seemed so sweet and nice. And now she'd just arrested one man and was turning down a marriage proposal from another. What was going on here? This trip to Waco certainly wasn't boring anymore.

"But I want to marry you," Luke said, taking a step nearer to her, wanting to protect her, to shield her from all the ugliness of life, to keep her safe forever. "Marry me, Cody."

She held up a hand to keep him at bay. "Stay there."

She quickly disappeared behind the stage, out of sight of everyone.

"What are you doing?"

When she appeared before him a few minutes later, Luke could only stare at her. Gone was the pregnant woman he'd been proposing to. Before him stood the slender, beautiful woman he knew so well.

"You were in disguise," he said in amazement, and then frowned.

"Oh, my," Mrs. Bradshaw said from inside the stagecoach. "Do you see that?" She looked at the others in shock and they all turned to look out at the couple again, wanting to know what would happen next.

"I was after Denton. The disguise worked." She grinned at him, then seeing his scowl, her smile faded.

"You could have trapped more than just the outlaw," Luke remarked.

"I told you, you didn't have to marry me, and I meant it."

Luke looked up at her, and she saw sadness in his gaze.

"I liked the idea that you were having my baby."

She went to him then, lifting her arms around his neck and drawing him to her. "I like the idea, too. We could work on it."

"It wouldn't be work," he growled just before his mouth claimed hers.

"That's true." She sighed.

"But only if you marry me."

Luke kissed her again. She had won his heart as Sister Mary; she had seduced him as Armita; she'd charmed him as an old lady and completely knocked him for a loop as a pregnant woman. Cody was beautiful, generous, kind, and loving. It didn't matter which person she was. He loved them all. Luke held her to his heart, knowing he would never let her go again.

"I'd love to be your wife."

Cody kissed him to seal her pledge.

"Oh, my," Mrs. Bradshaw said, looking away to give them some privacy and fanning herself even more quickly. But now she was smiling.